JASMINE

Jasmine

THAMES RIVER PRESS
An imprint of Wimbledon Publishing Company Limited (WPC)
Another imprint of WPC is Anthem Press (www.anthempress.com)

First published in the United Kingdom in 2012 by
THAMES RIVER PRESS
75-76 Blackfriars Road
London SE1 8HA

www.thamesriverpress.com

Original title: Jasumin
Copyright © Noboru Tsujihara 2004
Originally published in Japan by Bungei Shunju, Tokyo
English translation copyright © Juliet Carpenter 2012

All rights reserved. No part of this publication may be reproduced
in any form or by any means without written permission of the publisher.

The moral rights of the author have been asserted in accordance
with the Copyright, Designs and Patents Act 1988.

All the characters and events described in this novel are imaginary
and any similarity with real people or events is purely coincidental.

A CIP record for this book is available from the British Library.

ISBN 978-0-85728-250-7

Cover design by Laura Carless.

This title is also available as an eBook.

This book has been selected by the Japanese Literature Publishing Project (JLPP),
an initiative of the Agency for Cultural Affairs of Japan.

JASMINE

Noboru Tsujihara

Translated by Juliet W. Carpenter

THAMES RIVER PRESS

1

On this late-June evening, the rain had ended, leaving a low bank of clouds and a damp wind blowing down off the mountains. The restaurant Teite had just opened its doors for dinner, and already a couple was ensconced at a window table. Through the blinds, they could see the leaves of the vine outside rustling at the window ledge, as if trying to peer in.

The man was in his late thirties and the woman in her mid-twenties, seated not across from one another but obliquely at the small table. The woman, who was wearing an orange dress, had the window seat, and now and again she rested her elbow on the table and looked out absently at the trembling leaves. The man wore a light beige linen jacket, a blue-striped shirt, and a casually knotted cotton necktie, his taste in clothes discerning. As they spoke, their eyes were bright, their expressions animated.

The restaurant had always gone by the name Teite. The current owner and chef, Shi Yang, represented the third generation of the family owners. His grandfather had come to Japan from Shanghai as cook for the manager of the Fisher Company and later went into business for himself, setting up a little Cantonese restaurant midway down Kobe's Tor Road.

Teite now served French food. Orthodox in menu and service alike, it had won acclaim for a style of cuisine that used no butter.

The restaurant's name – unusual even in China – was written with a character meaning "a three-legged kettle" by itself, "great vigour" when doubled. In Mandarin the compound was pronounced *dingding*, in Cantonese, *teitei*. Shi Ying had adjusted the latter reading to make it easier for his Japanese clientele.

The couple was eating striped mullet, their knives and forks making light clinking sounds. Shi Ying had come by earlier to say hello and to provide a rapid-fire explanation of the dish: it was the first of the season, from Akashi, on the Inland Sea. It had been split open, stuffed with prawn mousse, and wrapped in a magnolia leaf. After a light steaming to impart fragrance, the mullet was sprinkled generously with sea salt and grilled.

After the host had left, the man turned to his sister and said, "The food's great, so I have no regrets. This tastes incredible. You know, I'm not the first to say it, but it's funny to think the corpse of a fish could be so succulent."

"For heaven's sake, Aki!" Mitsuru laid down her knife and fork in mock indignation, her bracelet brushing against her wineglass with a faint tinkling. The bracelet was inlaid with lapis lazuli, the deep, dark blue flecked with golden pyrite – a reminder of the legend that the gemstone was formed from the starry sky over Arabian deserts. Azerbaijan, a country caught between the Black Sea and the Caspian, was a leading source of lapis, and the ancient Silk Road owed its origin not to silk, but to this precious stone, routes having opened from China to the east and Egypt to the west in the course of the struggle for its possession.

"Nice bracelet."

"It's from Urumqi."

"So it's from Shuichi. He's back now?"

Mitsuru nodded, lifting the braceleted arm and placing her fingers on her throat where her Adam's apple would have been if she were a man. Her hand was long and tapered, and slightly bony. His own hand, wrapped around his wineglass, looked very much like it.

"I haven't heard from him," he added.

Shuichi, an old college friend, was a Beijing correspondent. Three months ago, public security authorities in Beijing had arrested him for "reporting Chinese national secrets extorted by unlawful means." Just two weeks ago he'd been deported, but his current whereabouts were unknown. He had a wife and child living in Kawasaki, but he hadn't been to see them.

"You know what? I'm a horrible person."

"Mitsuru, how you can say that about yourself?"

"I can, because I *am* horrible. I have wicked thoughts…"

"To do with Shuichi, you mean?"

"I'm not saying, even if you are my brother."

JASMINE

Because you are my brother is more like it, he reflected. He looked over at her, noting her even features, then said in a soothing tone, "They'll go away, these thoughts. I don't know what's on your mind, but believe me, they will."

"Oh? How?"

His eyes took on a mischievous glint. "Easy. You give in to 'em."

She smiled with sudden cheerfulness and took up her knife and fork, handling them as lightly as a pair of feathers. "The corpse... of a fish," she muttered.

"You've seen him, haven't you?"

Mitsuru bent over her plate, feigning interest in the mullet's mortal remains. Ten days ago Shuichi had slipped down to Osaka, and the two of them had spent a few days at a hotel on the southern tip of Awaji Island in a room overlooking Naruto Bridge and the famous whirlpool.

"Where is he now?"

"He's not in Japan anymore."

"So where'd he go?"

"Yugoslavia. He says civil war is brewing."

"Wicked thoughts? Mitsuru, don't tell me—"

She kept her eyes downcast, and twisted the bracelet around her wrist.

She means to follow him, he thought. Which would mean prying him away from his wife and child once and for all. Calling this "wicked" was perhaps a bit strong, but their mother had given her a strict upbringing and that was the way she saw it.

Mother will take it hard, he started to say, and then was brought up short – he himself was leaving in two days for a China still under martial law.

"A minute ago, Aki, you said I should give in to them." She picked up her wineglass and sighed, just enough to cloud the crystal rim. She had on a bright dress, but as her eyes darkened, her whole being seemed to drain of colour.

Aki merely smiled lopsidedly and looked idly around the room. Rather to his surprise, every table was now filled.

Their entrée arrived: roasted young rabbit.

"I'm going to see Mother tomorrow," he said. "What should I expect? Is her memory really slipping?"

"Yes. The other day she asked me where she was. I told her, 'We're in Mikage, Mom, your old neighbourhood in Kobe. Down that way is Fukada Pond, where the ducks are. Beyond it is Henri Charpentier, and just up the hill is the Garden Oriental Soshuen.' She cocked her head like this and said, 'Mikage?' like it didn't ring a bell. Then she looked straight at me and said, 'I'm sorry, my dear, but I don't know your name.' The doctor told me later that when people bring her fresh flowers, she tears them apart and eats the petals."

"That's going beyond forgetfulness," said Aki, pulling white petals from the little arrangement of orchids on the table. He was going to toss them into his own mouth, but stopped when he saw the sheen of tears in his sister's eyes. He took up his knife and fork, cut the rabbit on his plate into petal-thin slices, and ate three of those instead, one after the other.

"That's still not all. You know what else she said? 'I wonder how Dad is.'"

"Hmm. Which one do you suppose she meant – yours or mine?"

Mitsuru lowered her eyes, fringed with long lashes, and shook her head. Aki was the child of their mother's first marriage, Mitsuru of her second. Both of their fathers had died young.

"I told her he was fine, and she glared at me and called me a liar. I wonder if she knew all along and was playing some kind of a game." Opening her cloth handbag, she took out a handkerchief and pressed it to the corners of her eyes. She never carried a leather purse.

Waki Akihiko hadn't learnt of the existence of a mysterious creature known as a "little sister" until he was grown up. When he was three, his father suddenly disappeared, and when he was nine his mother remarried. He then went to live with his paternal grandparents in the city of Tanabe, in Wakayama Prefecture, until he finished high school. During that interval, communication with his mother stopped. One morning, while a university student in Kyoto, he'd found a girl with braided hair outside his lodgings, standing in the soft sun of early spring. That had been no ordinary day: following his first-ever experience with a woman, he had returned home early to encounter for the first time his half-sister.

Mitsuru picked up her glass, which still contained a good deal of white wine, and emptied it in one gulp, exposing her slender throat.

JASMINE

She might have a nice-looking throat, but he felt compelled as her elder brother to tell her off. When had she started to guzzle her wine like that? Yet, nothing could be harder than drawing such lapses in behaviour to the attention of the offender. Considerable courage was required to look a woman of character in the eye and point out her failings – even if she was your little sister. More courage than he could muster, as it happened. Mitsuru was obviously vulnerable at the moment; it wouldn't take much to topple her over. He decided that as her elder brother his only recourse was to reach over and fill her glass with more wine.

"Thanks," she said, leaning an elbow on the table and making lines in the tablecloth with her nails. She made no move to pick up the glass.

"So tell me," she went on, "have you found out anything more about your dad?"

Aki nodded, poured some wine into his own glass, and let a moment pass before speaking. "When he was young he worked for a Shanghai movie company called Huaying. I told you that much, right?"

"Yes, and even though all the other Japanese employees were repatriated after the war, he didn't come back for five years. Then when you were still little he took off for China again, leaving Mom and you behind, and never came home. Which should I say, 'came back' or 'came home'?"

"Same thing."

"I guess so. Anyway, what happened after that?"

"Ah. After that it gets interesting."

Huaying – an elegant name meaning, literally, "flower shadow" – was actually an abbreviation of *Zhonghua dianying lianhe gufen youxian gongsi*, or Chinese Film United, Ltd. This wartime movie company grew out of the cooperation between the Japanese Army, which occupied the city after the 1937 Battle of Shanghai, and the Nationalist government of Wang Jingwei, who had parted company with Chiang Kai-shek. Huaying used to control the production and distribution of all Shanghai films. It was supported by the Japanese film pioneer Kawakita Nagamasa, founder of the Towa Company, and by Zhang Shankun, the big-time Shanghai producer. Huaying distributed over 140 motion pictures throughout China, but these were later dubbed "slave movies" and excluded from the official history of Chinese cinema.

A large number of film-minded young Japanese had found employment at Huaying – among them Aki's father, Waki Tanehiko, who joined the company on graduating from the prestigious East Asia Common Culture Academy, a Japanese institution in Shanghai specializing in Sino-Japanese relations. After returning to Tokyo in 1946, Kawakita had set about importing and distributing Western films, thereby contributing to the revitalization of the postwar movie industry. Former Huaying employees had aided him in this work. For one reason or another, Waki Tanehiko's repatriation was delayed, which kept him from participating in the rebuilding of Towa. An almost 500-page company history, published in 1978, called *Half a Century at Towa*, devoted considerable space to Kawakita's prewar accomplishments on the Chinese mainland; there were a good twenty pages on Huaying, including detailed accounts of the doings of its Japanese employees – but not a word about Waki Tanehiko. Just as Huaying movies were expunged from the history of Chinese cinema, so Tanehiko's existence had apparently been consigned to oblivion.

The assumption that he was dead, however, was open to question. After leaving Shanghai in 1950, he ran a small trading company in Kobe, eventually marrying and fathering a child, Akihiko. Five years after his return in October 1955 he suddenly went back to Shanghai. Some two months later came word of his arrest in Beijing on suspicion of spying. Nothing further was known of his fate. In May 1958, the so-called Nagasaki flag incident brought Sino-Japanese trade relations to a halt. Then in summer 1961 the family learnt through the Japan-China Friendship Association that Tanehiko was dead. Yasuko, Aki's mother, tried more than once to go to Beijing herself, only to be stymied by opposition from those around her – or by obstruction by invisible sources.

Feeling slightly guilty, Aki picked up his wineglass and drained its contents, just as Mitsuru had done, then quickly polished off the remainder of the young rabbit. He couldn't suppress a small belch. "Sorry. That's what comes of eating too well. Anyway, here's the interesting part: I heard he may be alive."

Mitsuru held her napkin to her mouth, unnecessarily, and said in a muffled voice, "Then Mom's question wasn't so far off. I wonder if she knew by some kind of telepathy. Where'd this information come from?"

"Shanghai. That's why I'm going back."

"Isn't there a ban on travel to China now?"

"Not an out-and-out ban anymore. It's left to the traveller's discretion – you can go if you want. This time the day after tomorrow, look for me on the East China Sea."

"You're going by boat?"

"Yes. I bet not many people take a slow boat to China anymore, but it appeals to my sense of fun. Even more so at a time like this. In the old days everybody went by sea – my dad, too. Luckily, I'm on sabbatical and have all the time in the world. And a multiple-entry visa. It'll be a kind of fact-finding mission. What do you say, Mitsuru – want to come along?"

Aki peered into his sister's face. He had issued the invitation on the spur of the moment and half in jest, but now it struck him that this wasn't a bad idea at all – far better than her chasing after Shuichi all the way to Yugoslavia, God forbid.

He went on, "Check out 'Shanghai' in an English dictionary sometime and you'll see something interesting. S-H-A-N-G-H-A-I. The first meaning they give is 'Chinese harbour city,' naturally. Next is a kind of long-legged fowl. But there's more: there's actually an English verb, 'to shanghai.' Nautical slang. Means 'to force someone aboard a ship by plying him with drugs or liquor; to procure sailors for a sea voyage by kidnapping.' How about that? For a city to be turned into a verb, and especially a verb reeking of danger like that – makes you realize the place lived up to its old nickname, 'demon city.' What do you think the next entry is, after 'shanghai'? 'Shangri-la.'"

"Ooh, we can go shangri-la-ing in Shanghai. What would 'to kobe' mean?"

"Unfortunately kobe didn't make it in, not even as a place name. We think of it as our gateway to the sea – one we opened up to foreign countries – but we've got it backwards. It was England that determined the world's ports of call, back when it ruled the seven seas. English domination of the Orient meant they had to secure shipping routes, starting from London and then on to Port Said, Aden, Bombay, Madras, Singapore, Hong Kong, and Shanghai – with Kobe at the very end. We're the back of beyond, the tail end of the world. So what do you say, Mitsuru, want to shanghai? Or be shanghaied? Could be another way for you to carry out your wicked thoughts."

"Okay, okay. What are you going to do in Shanghai – try to find your dad?"

"Yes, but do me a favour – don't blow it out of proportion, all right? After all this time, I won't find out anything to get excited about. I've got no obligation and no responsibility to track him down in the first place. And all this about him being alive is probably nothing. Still, there are worse ways to spend a sabbatical than playing detective for a little while."

"But isn't the city still under martial law? Sounds pretty dangerous to me – ten thousand people killed, they're saying."

"Your Shuichi's Yugoslavia could turn out to be worse. Ten thousand dead may be overdoing it anyway. I'd put the number of deaths at Tiananmen Square more in the range of a few hundred."

Mention of the crackdown that had occurred in Beijing earlier that month, at dawn on 4th June 1989 made Aki feel uncomfortable. He couldn't help recognizing the phoniness that always attaches to any bystander presuming to speak about other people's misfortunes. China was a foreign land, which made the Chinese people strangers – strangers among whom his father's own secrets lay buried. Why had Tanehiko left his wife and child to head back there? What lay behind the charge of espionage? He'd been presumed dead, and almost thirty years had to pass before this rumour surfaced out of nowhere that he might still be alive.

And yet, there was the case of Ito Ritsu to consider. A former member of the Japanese Politburo held in a Beijing prison for twenty-seven years on a spying charge, Ito had been freed in September 1980 and sent back to Japan. With that in mind, Aki couldn't bring himself to dismiss out of hand the idea of his father surviving.

Although Teite was a French restaurant, towards the end of the meal Shi Ying always served jasmine tea. Tonight his wife brought it out in a small white porcelain teapot.

"Mmm, smells heavenly," said Mitsuru.

In their second cups they added a dab of fresh milk from Rokko Ranch, a variation devised by Shi Ying.

Dessert was a chilled mango. Mitsuru weighed hers in her palm as though it were a ripe, heavy sigh, then started to peel it skilfully. Although she couldn't go with him to Shanghai, she was looking forward to hearing about his trip. "But do be careful," she urged. "Remember, Shuichi got arrested in China, and your own father was thrown in prison there."

Aki nodded, his eyes on her hands as she wielded the paring knife. "Mango says that on the third and fourth of June there were no injuries or fatalities at Tiananmen Square whatsoever."

"Mango? Sorry? What about the mango?"

"Shuichi never told you? I learnt it from him. That's what anti-establishment Chinese secretly call the Communist Party. With a mixture of sarcasm and contempt."

And so Aki passed on to his sister, Shuichi's girlfriend, the meaning and origin of the term "Mango," just as he'd learnt it from Shuichi more than twenty years before. In May 1966, when the proletarian Cultural Revolution was heating up, Mao Zedong had rewarded the Red Guard at Tsinghua University in Beijing, who had taken over the university, with a crate of mangoes. Overwhelmed with gratitude, the members of the Red Guard, after distributing the mangoes among themselves, each saved the fruit reverently without eating it. From then on mangoes came to symbolize the cult of Mao, and after he died the word became a code name for the Party.

"How long will you stay in Shanghai?"

"I'll be back by the beginning of August. The 7th of August is the sixth anniversary of Sato's death."

"That long already?"

That long already, he echoed back silently.

Illness had snatched her away at the age of thirty-one. Aki and Sato had met at Tanabe High School in Wakayama and married after he graduated from college. He still loved his wife – even more now, in a way, than when she was alive. For a time he had remained locked within the sadness of knowing that in dying, she took with her all their pleasures and dreams, all the lovely things they might have done together – such as going to Awaji Island to see the puppet theatre. They'd always meant to do it; now they never would. After her death, rather than turn his back on the comforts that money can buy, he had, if anything, increased his devotion to them, polished his savoir-faire. It helped him to forget. These days he seldom mourned his wife. He was glad to be released from his memories – but when they did return, he was hit all the harder by a sadness sharpened by surprise.

Mitsuru was saying something, but whatever it was went by him.

"Aki, it's Mr Xu! Xu Liping," she repeated, standing up. An old man was escorting an even older woman into the restaurant; together they were slowly making their way to a table in the back of the restaurant.

Mitsuru called out in a low voice, which carried across the room, and this made Xu halt and turn around. Removing his monocle, he immediately recognized the brother and sister and waved to them. He saw the elderly woman to her table, then returned to speak to Mitsuru and Aki.

"My dear children, hello, how are you?" His back hunched over even farther as he spoke. He'd known them ever since they were little, and although they were now grown up, his impression of them remained unchanged from the old days. He came up directly behind Aki, who twisted around as he got up.

"How nice to see you again," said Mitsuru warmly. "Thank you again for all you did for our mother."

"It was nothing. Such a big present you sent me – no need to go to all that trouble, my dear."

"It was the very least we could do."

"That reminds me – we were over at the Garden Oriental Soshuen for a get-together, and on the way back we stopped at the nursing home to say hello to her. She was in excellent spirits. It's good you don't have to worry about her anymore, isn't it?"

"How kind of you to do that. Thank you so much," Mitsuru said with a pretty little bow: back straight, palms pressed together lightly at her breast, head dipped slightly. Xu Liping had once praised her for it; it was something she'd learnt from her mother. Still, she couldn't help being a bit shocked to hear that her mother – after having forgotten who her own daughter was – had apparently been able to talk normally with Xu, like old times.

About a year and a half ago, when they were trying to put their mother in the special care nursing home in Mikage, Xu Liping had gone out of his way to be helpful. The home in question was one of the best around, with a long waiting list. Faced with a wait of three or four years, Mitsuru and Aki had been at their wits' end – until Xu stepped in and pulled a few strings. The land on which the nursing home was built had been an outright gift from him to the city, so no one could complain if he was done a favour in return.

"My mother is back in Kobe for the first time in three years," said Xu, turning to look at a big round table in the rear of the restaurant. The elderly woman he'd come in with was now seated, chatting amiably with five or six others, all members of the Xu clan.

Xu Liping was fond of saying that the Xus and the Wakis had been friends since the days of Sun Yat-sen, and would remain friends forevermore. Some ten years ago, his mother had gone to Boston to live in with a daughter there. Xu's business having failed, the family had all taken refuge with his elder sister in Boston, but even after things got back to normal in Japan, his mother had stayed on in the United States. Although down on his luck, Xu had responded to a request from Kobe authorities for land in the upscale residential district of Mikage by offering a plot for free – an act of generosity that was something of a family tradition.

His grandfather, Xu Ruowang, was from the tiny island of Quemoy, off Fujian Province. On coming to Nagasaki, he led a troupe of *budaixi*, performers of a puppet theatre popular in Taiwan and Fujian, before moving to Kobe around 1885 and getting into the import-export business. By exporting matches and other items, he quickly made a pile of money, and his heir Xu Xinglin further expanded the business until he became the most prominent of all Kobe's *huaqiao*, or overseas Chinese merchants. Xinglin also served as comprador for the Yokohama Specie Bank and Bangkok Bank. When the Revolution of 1911 broke out, he formed the Overseas Chinese Merchants Squadron, and when the "Second Revolution" in 1913 failed and Sun Yat-sen fled to Japan, Xinglin provided him with shelter and aid. It was Aki's great-grandfather, Waki Atsuhiko, who had secretly invited Sun Yat-sen to his home in Tanabe for a bit of rest and recuperation.

Aki and Mitsuru asked if they might greet Xu's mother. Xu replaced his monocle and led the way to the back of the restaurant.

"If I may ask, how old is your mother?" Aki asked him quietly.

"She turned ninety-two in April."

As they drew closer, members of the Xu clan stood up amid a general scraping of chairs.

"Mother," Xu said in a loud voice, close to his mother's ear, "this is Waki Akihiko, Tanehiko's boy, and his little sister."

"My goodness, you're all grown up!" The old woman remained seated and inclined her head slightly, wearing a smile as she held out both hands to Aki. He took them in his. The dry, papery skin conveyed a faint trembling, and something suggesting the chill of bones.

"And you, my dear," she added, turning her soft gaze on Mitsuru, "are extremely pretty. How old have you gotten to be, now?" Peeping out from under the table was a pair of dainty cloth slippers like black butterfly wings.

"I'm twenty-eight."

"Are you, really?" She turned to her son. "When our Xiaolan left for the mainland, she was five years younger than this young lady." She pressed a small white handkerchief, Shantou embroidery, to the corner of her eye.

"Xiaolan?" inquired Mitsuru, bending down a little.

Xu Liping explained: "My second daughter."

"Tell me," said the old woman, her voice overlapping with her son's, "how is your good father?"

Xu whispered a mild remonstrance in her ear. She seemed not to understand.

"Be sure to give him my best regards."

"Thank you very much, *lao nainai*," replied Aki. "May you stay well always."

They went back to their table by the window, where they ordered a fresh pot of jasmine tea, and when they had slowly drunk it all, this time without milk, they left the restaurant.

Jasmine

Aki had arrived from Tokyo the night before, and was staying at the Shin-Kobe Oriental Hotel. He'd sent his large travel suitcase ahead by courier. Mitsuru, meanwhile, lived in an apartment along the Ashiya River and worked at an industrial design office downtown in Yodoyabashi. She started down Tor Road in the direction of Motomachi Station.

"I haven't been in Kobe for a while, and it would be nice to go for a drive, so why don't I take you home?" Midway down the slope Aki hailed a taxi. He climbed in first and instructed the driver to head for Ashiya. After the car had pulled out, he said, "Take the Sanroku Bypass."

"Okay, mister, but it only goes as far as Takahane."

"I know. So take a right at Takahane and get on the Yamate main road."

"That ends at Motoyama."

"Yes," Aki replied with mild irritation, "so before you get to Motoyama you'll need to take another right, then go straight, and get on Route 2 somewhere around Morikita."

Mitsuru pressed the button and lowered her window one-third of the way to let in some air. "Wasn't old Mrs Xu a dear?"

"Yeah, but she spooked me when she asked how my father was. Didn't you say Mother said the same thing to you? What's wrong with these old people? Also, I'd never heard of Xiaolan before. That means they had five kids. The other four I know. We never got around to asking what became of her, did we?"

The taxi was heading down the tree-lined Sanroku Bypass.

"What kind of trees are these? They're huge."

"Camphor," said Aki. "These go on for a bit more, till around Gomo Tenjin crossing, and then they're gradually replaced by plane trees. Those go on till Takahane, and from there on it's maples."

At Takahane the taxi turned right, went under the Hanshin Railway line, and entered the Yamate main road.

"Look, we're in Mikage already," said Mitsuru. "Think Mom's asleep?"

"No doubt."

"I hope she's having a nice dream."

"One where you and I ride quietly past as she sleeps, so as not to wake her up?"

"Very nice."

"How old is she now, exactly?"

"You don't know?"

"I know her date of birth all right. I just asked because it's easier for you to do the counting."

"Sixty-seven."

"Too young to be going senile. Look at Xu's mother, she's ninety-two. If my dad's still alive, he must be… seventy-two. Anyway, I'll go check on her tomorrow. We'll see if she still knows her son, or asks, 'And what might you be selling, young man?'"

Near the mouth of the Ashiya River, the taxi stopped in front of a condominium building. Still settled back in her seat, Mitsuru sat quietly for a moment and then said without stirring, "Aki, don't be angry with me, will you? Don't ever give up on me. Be my friend."

Be my friend. The phrase struck him as odd at first, but the next moment he decided no, it was a frank and quite reasonable way of putting things. Instead of resting comfortably within the confines of the obvious relationship of brother and sister, how much better, more meaningful it was to tear them down and renew their relationship day by day. And they did get on amazingly well, he thought, considering that more often than not siblings experienced friction, just like parents and children. The two of them got on so well because the element of friendship was so strong.

"When will I see you again?" she asked, before instructing the driver to open the taxi door. The automatic door swung open, and a gust of warm, moist wind blew in.

"I really don't know." And then, for no reason, the words "Let's stay alive" slipped out of his mouth.

Startled, Mitsuru turned back with a look of perplexity, suddenly close to tears. Let's stay well, he'd meant to say. What the hell had gotten into him? In a city of such beauty and prosperity, in a country free of war for over forty years, what had made him come out with a line that corny and sentimental? He nearly swore in annoyance. With an embarrassed smile, he waved a hand lightly at this friend of long years' standing. He watched her hurry inside the brightly lit entrance of her building and then brusquely told the driver to get going.

Jasmine

The clouds had parted. Looming straight ahead was the dark silhouette of the Rokko mountains, and hanging over them was the night sky, resplendent with a myriad stars. The shallow Ashiya River came tumbling down in a straight line from the mountains. Reflected light from streetlights, headlights, and moonlight played over the surface of the water like a school of tiny leaping fish. For no reason, he felt a mounting irritation.

2

Nowadays, with Shanghai only a three-hour hop by plane from Narita or Osaka, anyone opting for the three-day voyage by ferry had to have a good reason: old folks on tours steeped in nostalgia, vacationing college students with more time than money, high school kids on class trips. For a man in the prime of life with a fairly prosperous look about him to be travelling alone by sea was bound to strike the average person as eccentric, or vaguely suspicious. Stowaways, mused Aki, always go by boat.

Yet he was hard pressed to account for this specific choice. He might have said he was on a journey to follow in the footsteps of the father who disappeared when he was a little boy, but that wasn't it; he had no such sentimental leanings. All he could say was that like his father – and innumerable other stowaways before him – he had an uncontrollable yearning to travel by sea.

The morning of departure, he got up at five o'clock. A call from the front desk woke him as scheduled at four, but he laid his head back on the pillow for another five minutes' sleep. Five minutes stretched to an hour, so he rushed through the checkout procedure and made a dash for the port terminal by cab. At seven o'clock the *Xin Jian Zhen* slowly pulled away from Pier 4. The deck trembled slightly beneath his feet. For a split second he had the illusion that the boat was stationary, that Kobe and the Rokko mountains were in motion and steaming off into the distance.

He remembered the night before last when he saw his sister, telling her about the English verb "to shanghai." In the old days, everyone who went to China had gone by boat – including his father, who'd set off for Shanghai at the age of nineteen to attend university. Shanghaied, every last one of them.

Yesterday he'd been to see his mother in the nursing home; when he told her where he was going, her response had been a negligent "Oh? Well, say hello to your father."

JASMINE

The uppermost A Deck on the *Xin Jian Zhen* had eight first-class cabins. Aki was the only first-class passenger from Kobe. Along the way, the boat docked at Tempozan Port in Osaka and picked up a dozen or so Chinese passengers, together with a large amount of luggage and freight containers. A well-groomed Chinese gentleman took the cabin across the passageway and down from Aki.

The *Xin Jian Zhen* turned its bow south, heading through the quiet water of Osaka Harbour under skies that threatened rain. The steamer had a gross tonnage of 14,543 tons and measured 156.67 metres in length, with a maximum speed of 21 knots. It could accommodate 345 passengers and 242 containers. The paintwork was white, the smokestack had a crimson band, and the decks were green. Once a week, the ferry made the trip from Kobe and Osaka to Shanghai in fifty-one hours.

Aki was 1.75 metres tall and weighed 62 kilograms, with long, bony limbs. He could still run 100 meters in 13 seconds flat. His eyes were a very dark brown, his nose slightly aquiline, his cheekbones slightly high. His face was tanned. He played no golf. He was 37 years old.

All was quiet. There were no more than sixty passengers on board, if that many. Perhaps because of the travel advisory put out by the government, Aki was the lone Japanese.

As the outline of the Rokko mountains receded on the starboard side, the gentle shape of Awaji Island began to define the boundary of Aki's view. Rising on the port side were the graceful lines of Mount Ikoma, Mount Kongo, and the Kisen mountains, scarcely distinguishable from cloud-peaks.

He was the only passenger on deck. The man who'd boarded in Osaka never left his cabin. Everyone else was travelling below decks in second or third class, and none of them came up to A Deck.

The sky had been overcast for some time, and as they went through the Kitan Strait and entered the Kii Channel, it began to rain in earnest. The drops fell hard, in dense sheets. Aki walked over to the port side facing the Kii Peninsula and squinted, trying to make out the Gulf of Tanabe and the town where he'd played as a boy, but rain and fog obscured all view of the peninsula.

A wind sprang up and the ship began to rock slightly. Now and again a thick layer of sheer white fog wrapped itself around the bow like an enormous curtain. Still, Aki remained where he was. A deckhand heaved a big mop to and fro, looking askance at him as he did so. Finally he came over and advised Aki to go inside: they would soon be in the Pacific Ocean, he said, and the wind and waves would only get worse, making it dangerous to be out on deck.

The wall of his cabin had a large porthole in it. When he pulled back the faded yellow curtain, he saw plumes of fog come flying towards him from across the deck. With nothing else to do, he wound up dozing on the sofa.

The sun set in the fog. He went down to the dining room for dinner. Set out on a counter were cold plates of stir-fried meat and vegetables. He selected one, paid for the meal at the register, took it to a table, and began to eat. The food tasted awful. So much for the anticipated pleasures of beautiful scenery and fine dining.

The other first-class passenger was seated alone in a corner by a porthole, drinking beer. Their eyes happened to meet, and they could not avoid exchanging perfunctory bows. *Who is this guy?* Aki wondered with a bit of suspicion.

He soon retreated to his cabin and stretched out again on the sofa to read, sipping Scotch from a leather flask he'd brought along. The book was a collection of poems and paintings depicting the fountains, rugs, and gardens of Arabia and Persia. A good five hundred pages long.

Had the tip of the column not bent in shame,
The fountain would have returned all its bounty to the rain.

He read the lines aloud.

The ship lurched about as it left the Kumanonada Sea and entered the Tosa offing. The cabin lights began to flicker; now reading was impossible. Nor was that all. When he went to take a shower, there was only a dribble of hot water, and when he called the purser to inquire about it, he was subjected to a long lecture about shipboard rules regarding water use. Fine. That made four pleasures he would have to forego. Resigned, he got into bed. The ship continued rocking as it surged along.

Time lagged until finally, like a car with a stalled engine, it ground to a halt. Or so Aki started to believe. Must he do without the pleasure of sleep as well?

It was the film director Xie Han who had told him: *Waki Tanehiko might still be alive.*

As chief director of the Special Research Group for Huxley Associates in Japan, Aki was involved in research on Official Development Assistance (ODA) projects relating to China.

In 1972, acting on the assumption that war with the Soviet Union was inevitable, Mao Zedong had moved quickly to establish diplomatic relations with the United States and Japan as a strategic ploy vis-à-vis the USSR. Despite their ideological differences, China and the United States were fellow victors who had fought side by side in World War II, and so relations were re-established with little difficulty. But with the vanquished nation of Japan, the issue of war reparations was still unresolved. The money involved was sure to be a whopping, unheard-of sum. Yet Mao chose to abandon reparations claims in order to normalize diplomatic relations with Japan in a hurry. That's how urgently the Soviet threat had loomed.

Japanese ODA to China, which began in 1979, was widely perceived in both countries as a quid pro quo.

The amount of assistance rose annually until, in 1986, China became the top recipient of Japan's bilateral ODA, and in 1987 the annual total of all aid, gratuitous and onerous, reached 170 billion yen. How was this enormous amount of money being used? Recently, concern over the invisibility and inefficiency of fund distribution was increasing. Every year, the Foreign Ministry issued a white paper on ODA, but regrettably, the report was made under the influence of interested parties. The situation called for a fair and accurate assessment by a third-party body. Based on a survey of the actual situation, Aki's team was expected to suggest a more effective and efficient scheme of disbursement. Almost half of the ODA projects in China were based on yen loans and, as financing arrangements restricted contracts to Japanese businesses, his team's proposal was bound to attract attention among Japanese firms eager to be involved. Moreover, he'd also been asked to look into the presence of projects based on development financing by the World Bank. The idea was that the Chinese would be less wary of dealing with capable Japanese partners than with white people. The voluminous report was almost finished.

Huge amounts of government financing inevitably gave rise to vested interests. In Japan, this meant conservative politicians known as the pro-Chinese faction and businessmen with connections in the Conservative Party; in the recipient country, this meant the top echelon of Mango and their sons and daughters. They were known as *taizidang* ("princelings") or "China whites." Naturally, Aki's investigation took in special interest groups in both countries, affording him glimpses of various corrupt practices.

The northwestern province of Xinjiang was an area of desert, underground mineral resources, and nuclear testing, inhabited by a Muslim Turkic people called Uyghurs. In the eighties, several pro-independence uprisings had taken place. With the support of seven hundred million yen's worth of gratuitous funds, a "high-quality cottonseed plant" was supposed to be under construction in the farmlands of the Tarim Basin – yet there was no sign of it anywhere. When asked, people said only, "Oh, there's nothing there. You shouldn't move around this area without permission, either. You never know where there might be a forced labour camp. You could be hauled in as a spy."

Aki's team decided to draw up a side report addressing such opaque, questionable issues. An essential part of all such surveys, the side report was given top-secret status within the organization, and any external use was strictly prohibited. Side reports drawn up by the eighty-three company branches located in forty-four countries around the world were housed deep in the Information Management Centre of the main Huxley office in New York, known informally as "Pandora." The accumulation of innumerable such reports from past surveys had given Huxley an almost mythical authority.

Two years ago, before getting started on the ODA survey, Aki had received a phone call from his friend Shuichi in Beijing.

"You know the movie director Xie Han?"

"Sure, he's famous. I saw one of his movies in Tokyo once."

JASMINE

"Well, he's now making a spy flick set in Shanghai in the 1930s, and guess what? Your old man – Waki Tanehiko, right? – is one of the main characters. I went to Shanghai on a lead the other day, and while I was there I visited the film studio and interviewed Xie Han. I heard it straight from him. He and your dad went to college together, and they worked together at Huaying, too. When I told him Waki Tanehiko had a son who's a friend of mine, he got all excited. I gave him your address. I have no doubt you'll be hearing from him. By the way, Mitsuru's coming to Beijing next week."

"Yeah, first time for her. Thanks for showing her around."

It was on this trip that Mitsuru's romance with Shuichi had begun.

In due course a letter came from Xie Han, and Aki wrote back to answer the director's questions. Mostly they concerned the house where his father was born and his life in Kobe after the war.

Aki picked up a curious piece of information from that first letter: Xie Han was unaware that his father had gone back to Shanghai in 1955 – this despite the fact that the director had never left Shanghai himself. In his second letter, Xie expressed great surprise at this revelation. Then it was Aki's turn to be astonished: apparently his father had appeared as a comic actor in a dozen or more movies for Huaying, under the name of Han Langen. This certainly came as news to him, and to his mother as well.

In the course of these exchanges, his ODA survey had begun, taking him back and forth to China frequently.

After graduating from college, Aki had gone to work for a major trading company, only to quit in less than two years to enrol in a graduate program at his alma mater. Once there, however, despite encouragement from his advisor, he became disenchanted with the academic side of economics and dropped out to join the prestigious firm of Huxley Associates at its Tokyo office. He had studied Chinese fairly intensively in college and grad school, and he always made a point of conducting in-house meetings with Chinese staff in their own language, so he had little difficulty with the language on site. His work mostly took him to Beijing and Shenyang, Changchun, Dalian, and other places in the north and northeast, or out to the western regions of Qinghai and Xinjiang, but never as far south as Shanghai. Finally, last spring, he'd had occasion to visit the Baoshan Iron and Steel Company there. He stayed for only a couple of days, and was able at last to meet Xie Han on his last afternoon there.

Aki remained sceptical that some Chinese comedian named Han Langen could really have been his father. During the Cultural Revolution, Xie Han had burnt all his old scripts, letters and other papers, as well as his old photographs. He could offer no proof that the two men were the same.

"How much time have you got?" asked Xie.

"About two hours."

"Let's go then."

With that, he bundled Aki into the studio car and drove off at maniacal speed. They crossed over Suzhou Creek and entered the Hongkew district. The car stopped at the entrance to a dimly lit alleyway in a *lilong*, an old neighbourhood with a maze of narrow lanes. Two- and three-story brick row houses stood packed together in a haphazard way, a cross between local farmhouses and London working-class housing. Narrow channels threaded through the length and breadth of the *lilong* like fine Shantou embroidery.

Xie Han led Aki into the heart of it. They climbed dark, narrow stairs to a third-floor room where, under a skylight in the sloping ceiling, an old man sat dozing in a chair. His name was Zhao; originally Kawakita Nagamasa's chauffeur at Huaying, he'd served later as company gatekeeper.

"Zhao is the only person who still has secret photos of Huaying," said Xie Han; he then rapidly explained to the old man who Aki was.

Zhao nodded and gripped Aki by the hand. From the depths of a bureau drawer, he brought out a photo album. The spine was worn to shreds, bare linen fibres exposed. Aki peered at the album where Zhao opened it. There was a large oblong photograph spread over two pages. Printed at the top was the caption, "In commemoration of the first anniversary of the establishment of Chinese Film United, Ltd. May 12, the 33rd year of the Republic of China, Shanghai." The 33rd year of the Republic would be 1944. Overall, the picture was slightly reddish in tone, and here and there it had swelled and cracked, the surface flaking off to reveal the white ground beneath. Even so, each person's face was clearly visible.

Kawakita, Zhang Shankun, Fuwa, Hanawa, Yanagida, Tsuji, Shimizu: one by one, the old man pointed to the faces and recited their names. Sometimes he would dart a look at Xie Han, seeking confirmation. One after another they were summoned forth, the principal directors and actors, male and female, from the prewar Shanghai film world. "This is me," he said, indicating a young man in suit and necktie at the right end of the back row.

When Aki informed him that Kawakita had died seven or eight years back, Zhao rested his fingertip on the photograph and stared up at the tiny skylight. On returning his attention to the photo, he pointed to a man seated at the left end of the first row. Then he swung his finger over to the figure of a man standing in the same row at the extreme right with his hands behind his back.

"Can you tell who this is? See – the two faces are exactly the same. Take a good look."

Aki knew instantly that this was his father as a young man. But how could there be two images of him in the same picture?

Xie Han explained. They had not been able to fit three hundred people into one long photograph using an ordinary camera. This photo was taken by panning slowly from left to right with a special camera that was the pride of Huaying. While the camera panned, the man had raced around behind from the left edge to the right, so that the lens caught him twice. It was actually one person. At the same time, it was two different people.

The man on the left had a wide grin on his face; this was Waki Tanehiko. The man on the right was sullen, his face set in a scowl as if nothing ever amused him; this was Han Langen. He had modelled himself on his idol, Buster Keaton.

Aki checked his watch and realized he would have to cut the visit short if he meant to catch his plane. With abbreviated thanks, they got back in the car and sped off to Shanghai Airport, arriving just in time.

The third letter from Xie Han had come just two weeks ago. Old Zhao had died, he wrote. Then he reported some more surprising news: Aki's father might still be alive.

The Tiananmen Square protests came to a sad end, but as it turned out, that whole business brought a peculiar piece of news my way. From the founding of the Republic through the Korean War, then during the Great Leap Forward and the Great Cultural Revolution, Mango built a series of secret prisons which they used for not just Chinese citizens but a good number of foreigners, too. After the Tiananmen Square protests – of course, plenty of students and pro-democracy activists are still on the run, even now – some people escaped to the Loess Plateau. With its yaodong, *cave dwellings carved right into the mountainside, it's an ideal hiding place for people in the underground movement. The caves have been inhabited since ancient times.*

There's a secret Mango prison in that area, too. Lodged in one of the caves, apparently, is an old Japanese man who was transferred there about ten years ago from a secret prison in Beijing. I heard this from someone who escaped recently to Shanghai. He says he never met the old man face to face, but the villagers call him "Xie," using the second tone. There are seven or eight different characters that this sound could represent, but only two of them are likely to appear in a Japanese surname – including the one in yours (which I regret to say doesn't have a very good meaning in Chinese). There's no telling which one it is. If it's true that your father, as I learnt to my surprise, came back to China after the war and was arrested here, then there's a good chance that it is him. But for now there's no way to be sure.

The postmark on the letter was not Shanghai but Nagasaki. Fearing the censors, Xie must have entrusted it to someone travelling to Japan. At the end of the letter, he urged Aki to return to Shanghai as soon as things calmed down.

Aki got out a Chinese-Japanese dictionary and found that the character in his name was derived from a similar one meaning "to threaten." And yet, he thought, the character was a common enough element in many Japanese surnames: Wakisaka, Wakimoto, Wakimura, Wakita, Kadowaki...

His second night on board, he dreamt he was being chased around by the character for "waki" in his name, until the efforts he was making to escape woke him up. It was the middle of the night. He told himself, *I am adrift on the rough waters of the East China Sea.*

JASMINE

There was keen pleasure in the thought. His irritation and his nausea had vanished. He couldn't feel the ship tossing about anymore. He opened the curtain and saw the deck sparkling like glass in the moonlight, while on the calm surface of the water moonlight flowed and undulated like a dragon's scales. The quiet was unbelievable.

Stepping out on deck, he saw with surprise that other passengers were gathered in the bow area, talking among themselves in low voices. The engines had been cut. The ship was floating, motionless.

An impression, oddly real, rose in his mind: he was aboard the mutinous *Hispaniola* in *Treasure Island*. Or was this a continuation of the dream in which he'd been chased by a Chinese character? No, mutiny was brewing. The *Xin Jian Zhen* had been seajacked. After the violence in Tiananmen Square, something could easily happen here. The passengers would be taken to Taiwan or Hong Kong, or maybe Singapore. Who was the ringleader? Who would play the one-legged cook, Long John Silver?

Someone tapped him on the shoulder from behind, and he turned to find the other first-class passenger standing there in green striped pyjamas. The fellow smiled, pushing up rimless glasses on his nose. The smile came from his mouth rather than his eyes. So this is the cook, thought Aki, still in Treasure Island.

"A beautiful night, isn't it?" said the newcomer in fluent Japanese.

"What are they doing?" Aki's voice was slightly blurred.

"It's the full moon. And the sea is finally calm."

The two men walked shoulder to shoulder along the deck. They were nearly identical in height and build.

"Why has the boat stopped?"

"Boats get sleepy, too."

"Seriously."

"They have to adjust for the time. If we kept straight on at the rate we were going, we'd reach Shanghai before dawn. You're travelling alone, I see. It's rare to see a Japanese person going to China alone by ship – all the more so at a time like this."

Who the hell was this guy, and why was his Japanese so good? The eyes behind his glasses had intensely brown irises. A trick of the moonlight? The man removed a business card from the breast pocket of his pyjama top and handed it to him. Odd of him to be so well prepared.

"My name is Cai Fang."

According to the card, he was a director of the Beijing People's Foreign Friendship Association and responsible for entertaining visitors. Aki, wearing a T-shirt and chinos, had no business card on him to offer in return.

"Actually, we're already slightly acquainted. I remembered last night." Cai Fang took off his glasses and rubbed his eyes repeatedly. "I believe it was last summer. You came to the government offices to inquire about plans to expand the railway service between Beijing and Qinhuangdao."

True enough. Aki had been taking a close look at the implementation of those plans, which numbered among the most important projects financed by ODA yen loans. But though he had certainly visited the government offices, he had no memory of meeting Cai Fang. His investigation had run into repeated obstacles.

Aki shook his head slightly to indicate he didn't remember, then said, "Reversing the comment you just made about me: it's unusual for a Beijing government official like yourself to be returning to China unaccompanied, by ship, at a time like this."

Cai gave him another of those mouth-only smiles and said nothing.

Out on the calm waters were the winking lights of innumerable fishing vessels. The passengers leant over the railing and then, in clusters of two and three, they began singing quietly – now a Japanese popular song, now a folk ballad he'd heard before, from one of the ethnic minorities in China's western hinterland. One couple started to clap their hands and dance in time to the singing. Little by little, others joined in; a circle formed. Moonlight poured down on them. The ship was stopped in the middle of the East China Sea.

"Nice song," said Aki. "What's it called again?"

"It's a folk tune, 'Song of the Yellow River Boatmen.' I've heard it once before."

I'll often remember this scene afterwards, and I'll tell someone about it. Who will that someone be? Wondering, Aki felt a strange thrill at the thought. Yet he also felt a premonition that by then he'd no longer be able to believe that this scene, this moment, had ever been real...

Jasmine

Later, he woke again because the rocking of the boat had altered. From the regular, small sideways motion that he'd given himself over to as he fell asleep, the ferry had definitely shifted to something more complex and elusive. Not only that, the low reverberations that were attached to the bottom of his sleep, vibrating with a satisfying rhythm (whether from the engine or the screws, he didn't know) like a knife on a chopping board, were subtly different now.

The ship had left the ocean to enter the mouth of the Chang Jiang or "Long River" – better known as the Yangtze. Here, muddy water running off the mainland merged with the clear water of the East China Sea. Mullet migrating in from the sea against the river current had to adapt to the new environment by adjusting the movement of their gills and using their tails and dorsal fins for freshwater swimming. The 14,000-ton *Xin Jian Zhen* was performing a comparable manoeuvre. Aki slipped back into sleep, surrendering himself to the new throbbing motion.

With the first rays of sunlight, he leapt out of bed. The sun was climbing higher and higher above the horizon every moment, stretching its long legs and scattering sparks on the tip of each heavy-looking, brown, triangular wave. He could hear a swell of voices calling out the river's Chinese name: "Chang Jiang, Chang Jiang." A pink-tinged fog began to form, mingled with soot and smoke. Coal blazed, oil burned, any number of chemical agents mixed and exploded. Odours of garlic and fennel hung in the air along with a vague stench of decay. It was the ripe smell of the continent.

The *Xin Jian Zhen* tilted heavily to port and swung around into the Huangpu River. They were now in Shanghai. The Huangpu marked the start of the city's harbour. Travelling up and down the river on either side was a jumble of large Panamanian freighters, leaf-shaped sampans, warships bristling with gun barrels, and junks like bats with their grey wings folded. On the pier a crane had stopped moving, dangling some heavy dark object in mid-air.

He was out on the starboard deck.

"Six hundred million tons." Cai Fang stood next to him and addressed him in Mandarin, muttering between his teeth. So it wasn't a trick of the moonlight; his eyes really were brown. "That's the amount of silt carried here by the Yangtze every year."

Aki was seized by the thought, *Why does this man keep coming up to me?* They had only spoken twice, so this impression was in itself rather odd.

"But not all of it gets washed out to sea," Cai continued. A large portion sank to the river bottom, he said, trapped by backflow from the ocean. The entire Yangtze River Delta was formed tens of thousands of years ago by the deposit of alluvium at the mouth of the river. During spring tides and at full tide, silt accumulated as far in as the Huangpu. Left alone, the steady build-up would gradually choke off the river, making it too shallow for ships to navigate. For Shanghai, the problem was a matter of life and death.

What to do? The three currents of the Yangtze, the East China Sea, and the Huangpu all ran together in a constant three-way struggle. No easy solution presented itself. Finally, after computing the permutations of the three currents by factoring in variables of time and season, engineers had designed a five-kilometre-long bypass channel extending from here approximately as far as the Yangshupu thermal power plant, visible on the left bank. There it was – the Chinese version of Oregon's Astoria Channel. Its addition had altered the flow of the three currents enough to drastically reduce the alluvial deposit.

Though Cai's voice was flat, his account was not difficult to follow. By now the sun, after rising above the horizon to cast light on land and water, had hidden itself again. Raindrops the size of poppy seeds flew through the air by the gunwale.

Soon, up ahead, the Bund came into view, once counted among the world's most beautiful boulevards. One hundred and sixty years ago, Shanghai had been a riverside fishing village where reeds grew in thick profusion. England, ruler of the seven seas, had developed the place. Back then the catchment of the Yangtze, over two million square kilometres in all, supported a population of 180 million, one-tenth of the world's population. Nowhere else in the world could you find a population of such density supported by a single river and its busy harbour. Following the Opium War and the Treaty of Nanjing, the harbour was opened to unrestricted trade. Residents proceeded to erect a row of buildings in a polyglot of architectural styles from Paris, London, Berlin, and other leading cities of the day. This was sometimes referred to as the "false front."

JASMINE

Shanghai became a Far Eastern Babylon, a place where virtue and vice coexisted and prospered with no impediment. People went there to make their fortune, or to escape poverty, or simply to forget. Europeans and Orientals lived side by side, inseparably intertwined, the city thriving like a dragon.

But starting in 1949, the dragon was slowly but steadily buried in desert sands stirred by the wind of communism. No longer did vice flourish, no longer did different people and different worlds collide. The central government, its power concentrated in Beijing, stifled the foreign presence by siphoning off every bit of wealth stored in Shanghai, without actually destroying the foreign structures that housed it.

The Japanese journalist Ozaki Hotsumi, in prison awaiting execution for his role in the Sorge spy case, wrote to his wife and daughter of his memories of entering the city for the first time:

> [Miyazaki] Toten[1] wrote that when he finally began travelling back up the Yangtze and saw Shanghai, he wept, overcome with emotion. I can sympathize. My own excitement on first seeing the city was greater than on any other occasion in my life.

That was in 1928. The Bund that nineteen-year-old Waki Tanehiko first glimpsed in 1936, also from a ship, and that his son was now gazing at fifty-three years later, had the same false front, its skyline unchanged.

The *Xin Jian Zhen* slowly turned to port. Aki had been staring down at the surface of the water, but now he raised his eyes. They had already reached midtown. With Garden Bridge close by, the engines slowed down as the ship approached Waihongqiao International Pier. *Time to go ashore*, he thought. The act of stepping ashore was, in itself, enough to stir a sense of high adventure. *Hello, yellow Babylon!*

The gangplank was drawn to the side of the ship. On the pier stood a lone woman in a white dress, turning a slate-violet umbrella

---

[1] (1871–1922). A Japanese political activist, adventurer and lifelong friend of Sun Yat-sen – who devoted his life to the cause of Chinese revolution. He first visited Shanghai at the age of twenty-two.

over her shoulder as she looked up at the gangplank. For a second, Aki saw in her a vision of Sato, before a gust swept the illusion away. He peered at her again. Definitely not Sato. Good-looking, though. Was she here to meet someone? This place was probably off limits to the general public.

A man and a woman wearing public security uniforms came scurrying up the gangplank. Aki went back to his cabin to prepare to disembark.

He stepped off the gangplank and onto the rough concrete of the pier. The woman was gone. Amid the other passengers, he walked down the pier and then on some two hundred metres farther. No sign of Cai Fang. Not in Immigration, either, so he must have been waved through. It occurred to him that the woman had probably come to meet Cai Fang.

He trundled his suitcase out to the taxi stand and heard someone call his name. In front of him stood the taxi driver Chen Ying, with his inimitable happy grin.

3

The hotel was the Broadway Mansions, rechristened Shanghai Mansions in the 1940s; in recent years its English name had been changed back again. Built in 1934 by Shanghai's real estate king Victor Sassoon in typical Art Deco style, the hotel had once offered long-term foreign residents the finest apartments anywhere in the city. The Shanghai representative of a major advertising agency in Tokyo, a friend of Aki's, was renting office space there; he was located in an executive suite overlooking the river, with combined office space and living area.

In the wake of the Tiananmen Square violence, his friend had temporarily returned to Japan, leaving the rooms vacant. Hearing that Aki was going to Shanghai, he had suggested he stay there and keep an eye on the place while checking which way the political wind was blowing. The desk was equipped with a private phone and fax. In Chinese hotels you generally had to go through an operator; to be able to make direct calls was a great convenience. Aki decided to take his friend up on the offer.

He checked in and went up to the suite, which was on the fifteenth floor, overlooking Suzhou Creek with a superb view of the Garden Bridge and the Bund. The door opened on a combined office and living room, although lounge would perhaps be more accurate. Off through a door on the left was a bedroom with twin beds. Aki, who had expected something like a suite in a Japanese hotel, was staggered by the vastly greater space and substance of these surroundings. He walked around to adjust to the unfamiliar dimensions of high ceilings and airy rooms, collapsing onto each bed in turn, several times, and taking deep breaths. The high ceiling was plastered, with a cornice. The tiled walls of the bathroom, which opened off the rear of the bedroom, were decorated with a design of roses. *Probably British-made*, he thought; they looked the same as the "Kobe rose" tiles in *ijinkan*, foreign residences in Kobe dating from the late nineteenth and early twentieth centuries. Although everything was apparently unchanged from the old days, the rooms were immaculate and pleasant, which was a relief. All this space for one person – *God, what a waste*, he thought, and then showered, changed into a suit, and set off for Shanghai Film Studio.

The recent turmoil and subsequent imposition of martial law had had little apparent effect on the place, which was bustling with activity. Even though Aki had turned up with no appointment or letter of introduction, the guard was undismayed, promptly picking up the phone and getting Xie Han on the line. "Go right on in," he was told. Xie was in Studio 4, rehearsing scenes for his new film *Paoying*, "Moving Shadows." What would be a good equivalent in Japanese, wondered Aki. *Utakata* – Fleeting Dreams?

He pushed open a smaller door in the corner of a large steel door, stepped through it, and was instantly enveloped in darkness. After four or five seconds, before his eyes could grow accustomed to the dark, a bright light suddenly came on.

"Li Xing, not like that. Turn your face more towards me. I want cruelty but softness, too. The expression of a wild animal. I know, try twitching your nose. Go ahead. Twitch it. That'll solve the whole thing."

This from a man in a white sports cap worn at a slant. Beyond him, in a pool of bright light, stood a woman. *That's the same one!* Aki almost said aloud in his surprise.

Yet, she was dressed very differently now from the way she'd been on the pier. Now she was wearing washed jeans and a silk blouse, without a trace of makeup. Her hair was bobbed, with a blue band wound around the brow.

The room was oppressively hot. Several large electric fans were humming with no discernible effect. Everyone was fanning themselves with round or folding fans; the effect was that of giant butterfly wings moving in a fitful dance. Stealing looks at this actress named Li Xing, Aki headed towards the white sports cap, approaching it from behind, but just as he came within hailing range he realized that this guy was too young to be Xie Han.

"Twitch my nose?" said the actress in a clear voice. "I can't do that."

"Do as you're told. Your character's a spy who trades sexual favours for information. Twitching your nose oughta be a cinch."

"I just can't."

"What do you mean, you can't! Concentrate and make a face. Then move the muscles around your nose… Damn. You really can't? Look – here, I can do it."

The guy in the sports cap leapt into the ring of light and twitched his nose. The actress slapped her thighs and laughed out loud.

She addressed a dimly lit corner of the studio. "Director, do I really have to do this? And please, can we turn off the light?" She sounded cheerful, her voice punctuated by laughter. Aki made out the figure of an elderly man sitting in a canvas folding chair with a cigarette dangling from his mouth. The spotlight went off.

"Xingxing, it's all right. No twitches. Let's move on to the next scene."

The old man exhaled cigarette smoke as he spoke, looking down, so that his face was wreathed in fumes and his voice was a raspy cough.

Aki quickly walked over, bowed, and said hello. Xie Han got up and held out his hand.

"Well, well! What a surprise, for you to come so suddenly, and at such a time … and this morning I heard you came by boat. Anyway, *huanying, huanying*. Welcome, welcome! Your father's in the next scene."

The spotlight came back on. A young man had appeared out of nowhere and was leaning against a black upright piano smoking a cigarette. When he finished, he tossed the butt on the floor and ground it out with the heel of his shoe before turning and seating himself at the piano. From beyond the spotlight, a couple opened a nonexistent door and entered the scene. The woman was the actress Li Xing from the scene before, escorted by a middle-aged man wearing a dark blue Mandarin gown.

"Which one's my father?" whispered Aki. Holding his cigarette between his fingers, Xie Han pointed at the young man, now affectedly adjusting his cuffs. Aki was shocked by the actor's youth. Since the movie was set in the Shanghai of a half-century before, it was only natural that his father should be portrayed as someone quite young – yet the sight was momentarily unsettling. A person much younger than himself. A mere youth, with no notion of what the future might hold for him, full of eager dreams.

"That's Ding Mocun." The director pointed to the man in the Mandarin gown.

"What's my father doing here?" Aki asked rather bluntly.

"Wait and see. This is the scene where he and the spy Zheng Pinru meet up again by accident."

Entering the cabaret, the woman looked at the pianist with a faintly startled expression, eyes wide and bright. The pianist, sitting with his back to the entrance, was unaware of this. The man in the Mandarin gown, noting the change in the woman's expression, looked suspicious as he told the waiter to take them to a table. While he was speaking the pianist began to play, singing to his own jazzy accompaniment the words, not in English but Chinese: "In every town, on every hill..."

The woman got up and walked over to the piano.

"...here, there, and everywhere, it's Shanghai Li Lu." As he sang, the pianist turned his head to look at the audience and found the woman standing by his side. "Hello, Lili!" he said, as if the words were part of the lyrics.

"Hello, Li Lu. It's been a long time."

He nodded and continued singing: "...the dream of love I dreamt that day, the devil's dream; with every passing day I remember, those eyes, in every town, on every hill..."

The assistant director went up to the actors to make various requests, but Xie Han looked on from where he was, remaining seated in his folding chair and saying nothing. The rehearsal went on.

Suddenly Xie leant forward and said "'It's been a long time.' Let's have Lili say that line in Japanese: '*Ohisashiburi ne.*'" That can be the signal for the hidden gunmen to open fire. How about it?"

The actress nodded and proceeded to practice the line several times, in a surprisingly natural accent.

A volley of pistol shots rang out. *Bang!... Bang!*

Xie Han stood up. "Okay, everyone, that's enough for today."

To Aki's acute embarrassment, Xie then announced that "We have a special guest" and introduced him to the cast and crew, causing a small commotion when they learnt that he was the son of one of the characters in the movie. This soon turned to applause.

Outside the studio, in blinding sunshine and to the shrill cries of cicadas, he asked the director again, "Why bring my father into it?"

"Because it's a true story."

"Even that scene just now?"

Xie Han shook his head. "Not in every detail. I embellish the story as necessary. That's only natural, isn't it?"

Aki nodded, watching as little boys dressed in Peking opera costumes crossed in front of them, kicking a soccer ball, and disappeared inside another studio through a small side door.

"But that actor doesn't look anything like my father."

"No, he doesn't. And your father was a better actor."

I'm glad he doesn't look like him, Aki wanted to say. He scarcely remembered his father, but he'd seen several pictures of him as a young man. One was the commemorative photo taken here at Huaying that he'd been shown last year by Zhao.

If the actor had been a ringer for his father, he would have felt even worse. As it was, he had to face a flesh-and-blood version more than fifteen years younger than himself. Fictional or not, that sort of inversion was hard to take. This was what lay behind the acute discomfort he'd felt earlier. And yet, if his real, other father, the one with an old and feeble body, was now confined somewhere deep in China's vast interior, in the heart of the Loess Plateau... His discomfort changed to vexation. To distract himself, he looked up, and caught sight of the actress leaving the studio and walking off in the opposite direction.

"She's very pretty. What's her connection with my father in the film? Are they lovers?"

Xie Han nodded, exhaling cigarette smoke without removing the cigarette from his mouth. In the movie, the man's name was Li Lu, the woman's Lili. "I've made her a communist spy for Mao, but Zheng Pinru was actually a spy for the Nationalist Party of Chiang Kai-shek. Otherwise... you see the problem, don't you? A sort of Shanghai Joan of Arc."

Xie Han had been engaged in filmmaking without a break for the past half-century, surviving by adapting the calibre of his work to changing political circumstances. His way of thinking, which he would never have publicly avowed, was roughly as follows: writing you could always do on your own; even if you had no readers, even if you were in prison or hiding, you could still carry on. But filmmaking without a studio was impossible. Film didn't last; it involved a fragile interplay of light and shadows. Particularity of time and place meant everything. Even under Hitler, he would have gone on making motion pictures.

"How did my father and Lili get together?"

"He was a spy, too – a double agent, in fact. So was she, for that matter. Here's what happened: Waki Tanehiko infiltrated the Plum Blossom Agency, Japan's military espionage organization in Shanghai, as a spy for the Comintern. Lili spied for Chiang Kai-shek, infiltrating Agency No. 76, the secret service of his enemy Wang Jingwei. The Plum Blossom Agency and Agency No. 76 were like an older and younger brother. But those two didn't meet as spies, they'd already met years before, as a boy and girl who both loved the theatre. These are actual facts."

They were already approaching the gate. The same kindly guard was standing there, smiling.

"This place has hardly changed from the old days. Your father appeared in several movies made here. Old Zhao used to stand right over there as a guard. And look – the spires of the cathedral, the same as ever."

The twin belfries of the magnificent French Gothic cathedral of St. Ignatius, commonly known as Xujiahui Cathedral, rose easily sixty meters into the air. The church had been destroyed in the Cultural Revolution and then rebuilt in 1985.

As Aki looked up, the sun, which had just begun dipping to the west, poured dazzling light out onto the two spires as if suddenly pierced through by them.

"I'm not out to learn everything about my father's past. I'm here because I got that letter from you indicating he might be alive... What about the person who might have seen him in the Loess Plateau? Where's that person now?"

"He escaped to Hong Kong. Probably in Paris by now." Xie Han looked at his watch. "Oh no, I'm late. A meeting. Let's have dinner tonight. Where's your car?"

JASMINE

Aki indicated Chen's Cedric, parked outside the gate. Xie went over and got Chen to roll down the window, said something to him rapidly, and came back.

"I told him where it is; he'll take you there. Let's say seven o'clock."

The two men shook hands, their palms damp with sweat, then quickly disappeared—Xie into a building, Aki into the recesses of Chen's cab, having decided to return to Broadway Mansions for the time being.

Aki had not exactly chartered Chen Ying's services, but Chen Ying was a hardworking, useful cabbie. On his last visit, Aki had happened to ride with him from the airport, and continued to rely on him almost exclusively for the duration of his stay.

For his part, Chen, awed at having been spoken to directly by the famous film director, was in a state of excitement. He was ready to talk to an actress next.

"Haven't you ever given a ride to one?"

"No, but at this rate, if I keep driving you around I might get my chance."

The cab was heading east on Huaihai Road. Aki let his eyes meander over the flood of people moving along under the arching plane trees that lined the street. So his father had been a spy in his youth. How did that tie in with his arrest on charges of espionage? A funny coincidence, if that's what it was.

Those were the thoughts swirling in half his brain. In the other half was the swirling figure of the actress Li Xing.

4
―

Xie Han's *Moving Shadows* was based largely on an event commonly referred to as the "assassination attempt by a pretty girl." The girl in question was Zheng Pinru, whose father was chief prosecutor in Shanghai's Supreme Court and whose mother was evidently Japanese, although her surname and other details of her identity remain unknown. In 1937, at the age of sixteen, Zheng Pinru joined the anti-Japanese resistance in Shanghai. She was assigned to a terrorist operation designed to obstruct Japanese political manoeuvring, underwent training, and then infiltrated Hongkew, the Japanese area in Shanghai's International Settlement, home to some hundred thousand Japanese. Zheng approached the upper echelon of the Japanese forces, seeking to trade sexual favours for information.

Around this time, Wang Jingwei, the leader of the left-leaning faction of the Nationalist Party, parted company with Chiang Kai-shek. Saying he was going to unite China through peace with Japan, he has gone down in history as a notorious collaborator with the invading Japanese. With him went the also notorious Ding Mocun who took a leading role in setting up the Security Service headquarters of Wang's faction in Shanghai. Because it was located at No. 76 Jessfield Road, this became known to all Shanghainese as "Agency No. 76." The name was further simplified to "No. 76" or just "76." An all-out terrorist organization, for a time it had the upper hand over both the Nationalists and Communists. Wang Jingwei had fled to Hanoi, but the success of No. 76 enabled him to move to Shanghai, where in August 1939 he began laying the ground for the establishment of his collaborationist regime.

One day, Ding Mocun encountered Zheng Pinru on the Garden Bridge. He had trained her as a spy, and so she seemed more than willing to renew their acquaintance, but she claimed to have given up spying. Ding, who had a high-strung, sickly wife, took Zheng as his lover and installed her in No. 76.

She became a core member of the agency, spying ostensibly for both Wang Jingwei's lot and the Japanese. Actually she was more active than that – she was spying for Chiang Kai-shek's side. Zheng was beautiful, and because her mother was Japanese, she spoke the language fluently. Maids and geishas in the Japanese-style luxury restaurants of Hongkew dubbed her "Otohime-sama," after the daughter of the sea king in Japanese legend.

In December 1939 the order came down from Chiang Kai-shek's officials for Zheng Pinru to have Ding Mocun assassinated. She wheedled him into buying her an Astrakhan coat and took him to an expensive furrier, but there her accomplice's shot missed its target and the plot fizzled. Ding escaped back to Hongkew. In his coat pocket he found a woman's calling card with a note scrawled in pencil saying, "Rest in peace, Ding."

Arrested by the Japanese Military Police for attempted murder, Zheng was handed over to No. 76, and in February 1940 she was executed by firing squad on the Shanghai execution grounds.

After the war, when the Japanese were defeated, Ding was put on trial in Shanghai, as were many other collaborators. Ironically, among the crimes he was charged with was the killing of Zheng Pinru. On 5th July 1947, at two o'clock in the afternoon, the sentence of execution by firing squad was carried out.

At that time, the traitors' trials proved a lively diversion for a Chinese populace exhausted from war and civil strife. Enthusiasm ran wild as the trials became a show. The visitors' gallery in the courtroom was filled to overflowing, and newspapers featured extensive daily accounts of individual trials and their outcomes. People cheered and applauded as, one by one, leading members of the puppet government were convicted, sentenced to death, and executed. Ding's trial stirred up particular curiosity. Of all the crimes mentioned in the indictment, the most sensational was his affair with Zheng Pinru and the assassination attempt.

Throughout that time, director Xie Han had been in Shanghai himself and had known Zheng Pinru personally. In 1939 he became the last graduate of the Chinese Department of the East Asia

Common Culture Academy. Even after graduation he continued to lead the student theatre group there. He also remained active in the Shanghai Communist group, which included Japanese members. Waki Tanehiko, two years Xie's junior, had been involved in the same activities. Eventually, dissatisfied with the campus theatre group, the two of them founded the left-wing amateur troupe Hushe (Tiger Society), advertising widely for members. Among those who responded was Zheng Pinru. Both youths fell in love with her at the same time.

When the war was over, Xie kept turning over in his mind plans for a film with Zheng Pinru as the lead character. But though she was an actual person, and her mother's nationality was also a matter of record, the mere recitation of facts doesn't make for drama. Waki Tanehiko had been Xie's best friend and his rival in love, but in the script he wrote, Xie altered things so that only Tanehiko and Zheng were in love; himself, he kept out of the story. He would manipulate the other two from outside the film.

Quite a surprise, thought Xie – *Tanehiko's son turning up here in Shanghai all of a sudden. And that look on his face, when he came in and saw Li Xing in the spotlight! As if he knew her from before. Not just knew her, but had fallen for her. Definitely love at first sight.*

5

Around 6.40 p.m., after riding in Chen's cab along the Bund, which was shrouded in a yellowish fog, Aki arrived at an old-style Chinese restaurant on Fuzhou Road. Inside he found Xie Han and his assistant director Gao Yong waiting for him. The first floor was filled with all the bustle and noise of a railway terminal. Every table, round or square, was fully occupied, and people were moving ceaselessly from one to the next. Some were eating and drinking standing up. The three men were ushered through the crowd and upstairs to a private room where some twenty people were already seated at two large round tables. As soon as Aki walked in the door, they all straightened in their chairs, then stood and applauded. An in-house party for the *Moving Shadows* cast and crew had already been planned for this evening; the event was not in Aki's honour. Nevertheless, the sudden appearance of this guest from Japan caused quite a stir, especially as his father was a character in the film.

Aki was seated next to the director. Li Xing was at the other table, the one reserved primarily for cast members. She had changed into a white sweater with an openwork design and black stretch trousers, and her hair was pinned up at the back of her head. Aki had on the same blue cotton suit as in the afternoon.

He was introduced once again to those in attendance.

"Of all those here, only Mr Yin," Xie Han mentioned, pointing at a plump man with a bald, pear-shaped head, "is not a member of the cast or crew." He added with a little laugh, "In fact, he's nobody. So why is Yin Dan here, you ask? All I can say is, it's because he's always around. Our own squatter..."

That explained it, thought Aki, looking at the man in question. In China, pointing was considered impolite; but if the person was a nobody, then apparently it was all right.

Whether he was listening or not, Yin Dan turned on Aki a gaze as bold and expressionless as a pair of binoculars with the caps on. He alone had already spread his large, stiff napkin in his lap, in readiness for the drinks and food to come.

Xie Han then thanked Aki for coming and toasted him with *laojiu* rice wine. Gao Yong served him some appetizers. Soon a couple of dishes arrived: rice paddy eel, fried to the point of charring, and stewed sea cucumber. Four or five bottles of *laojiu* were emptied straight away.

"Mr Waki's Chinese is perfect." Someone – it was hard to say who – came out with this opinion, which quickly became the consensus. Hands bearing food and drink moved without cease. Lavishly steaming baskets were brought in, piled high with shrimp. These were river shrimp from the brackish waters of the Yangtze River Delta, found especially in the backwaters around the lock. You grabbed a handful and put them on your plate. Then you peeled one, held it so the tiny white body with the brownish-yellow entrails hung down, dipped it in soy sauce laced with red pepper, and popped it in your mouth. After that, you dabbed your fingers in a bowl of oolong tea, and started on the next one. Yu Ming, the production manager on *Moving Shadows*, was a middle-aged woman who wore her hair in a mushroom cap and had no sex appeal whatever, but as she performed these actions in a smooth repetitive sequence, her hands looked oddly seductive. From time to time, Aki glanced at Li Xing, seated at the next table. She hadn't touched the shrimp, he noticed.

Everyone became pleasantly drunk. As their stomachs got heavier, filling steadily with greasy foods, their tongues wagged more and more freely. People said anything, whatever came to mind.

"We have a saying: the only times a Shanghainese will stop talking are in early summer, eating these shrimp, and again in winter, eating Shanghai crab," said Xie, raising his glass and drinking to Aki's health again. Gao inquired about the nature of his work. Aki offered a brief explanation, whereupon everyone unanimously agreed they'd never heard of any such thing as ODA from Japan. What *was* ODA, anyway? This general ignorance came as no surprise to Aki. The Party and the government saw no need to inform the public that large-scale infrastructure projects such as the construction of harbour facilities, railroads, expressways, and airports were financed by foreign loans. "Is this a kind of war reparation?" That's what Aki was often asked at the sites he visited.

"Does the money have to be paid back?" asked Gao Yong.

"A portion of it is a grant, but the rest has to be paid back, of course," he replied with a certain hopeful finality. Starting up a debate over Japan's war responsibility and the issue of reparations would only lead to endless argument. Besides, the Japanese government, following in the footsteps of Western countries that had imposed sanctions against China in the wake of the Tiananmen incident, had just decided to terminate ODA loans to China at the end of June.

For a moment, a pall fell over the room. For ordinary conversation to start up again, Aki needed to inject some appropriate comment here, but alas, Chinese was a foreign language. Nothing suggested itself. Then, as if drawn by some invisible force, his eyes came to rest on the face of Yin Dan. A peculiar expression rose in Yin's eyes – a combination of shrewdness and candour. After a short pause, Yin ventured, "*Malantou* is a weed, Han Langen was a ham, ..." Then he chuckled and added, with a kind of whistle between his teeth, "And you are his son!"

Malantou, Han Langen. It made no sense. Han Langen was his father's stage name, but who or what was *malantou*? Aki cocked his head and gave a strained smile, although deep down he was relieved to be off the hook about ODA.

"You knew my father, then?"

"Never had the pleasure. I've heard all about him from Xie, though," said Yin, indicating the director. "Lousy actor, but one of the funniest people who ever lived..."

The food kept coming, dish after dish without end. A communist who was a buffoon, one of the funniest people who ever lived? This was a far cry from the image of his father Aki had formed from listening to his mother. Taciturn, uncompromising, principled. You never knew what was going on in his mind, she used to say. Weren't they two different people, after all, Han Langen and Waki Tanehiko? Or was it possible for a man to have two distinct personalities, one in Japan and the other on the continent?

"Mr Yin, who or what is *malantou*?"

"*Malantou* is *malantou*. Like I say, a weed."

They were now drinking clear maotai liquor. Yin drained his tiny glass and laughed.

Xie Han intervened. "It's an herb that grows wild all around the Yangtze Delta in early spring. As Yin Dan says, it's really a kind of weed – you see it everywhere by the side of the road. First you boil it a little, then you stir-fry it with dried bean curd in rapeseed oil. A simple dish, but not one to be underestimated. When Spielberg came to Shanghai to film *Empire of the Sun* I brought him here, and he seemed to like it. You know, why don't I see if they still have it on the menu?"

He summoned the waiter, but the *malantou* season was over.

Countless glasses of maotai were raised and drained. The heavy, throat-scratching fumes of Chinese cigarettes hung in the air, wreathing everyone in smoke and making them speak in raspy voices.

"Lin Xiao is still young, but he uses '101' on the sly," Yu Ming let on to the cameraman Yang Jun. "After all, once a handsome actor gets thin on top, his image is never the same." Lin Xiao was the young actor in the role of Han Langen/Waki Tanehiko.

Yang turned in his seat and said, "Mr Waki, I understand that '101' has been popular in your country, too."

"Yes, for a while, it caused a sensation. It was selling for twenty or thirty thousand yen a bottle, and even at that price, people would fight to get it."

Yu Ming clucked loudly. Compared to a Japanese cicada, the Chinese cicada sounds loud and brazen, and the tongue-clucking of a Chinese woman is harsher still. "They're all snake oil, these hair restorers," she snorted. "How much is thirty thousand yen?"

Aki did a swift calculation and came up with the corresponding figure in yuan. Eyes widened in surprise. Imagine that, six thousand yuan for a bottle of hair restorer! What a country! And who was it that laid our own country bare? Let's demand reparations after all!

Yang Jun leant forward. "Until my grandfather's generation, my family served as court cosmeticians. The imperial consorts were obsessed with their hair – once it got thin, they lost favour, you see – and my grandfather left us the secret formula for a hair restorer. A whole lot better than '101,' if you ask me. That stuff relies on a kind of shock treatment – sulphuric acid and sulphur give a powerful jolt to the scalp and hair roots, so temporarily you do get some hair growth – a bit of fuzz, that's all. It's like setting fire to someone's bottom as a prank; it can cause serious burns. The main ingredients in our family's formula are dates and – no, that's all you're getting – it's a secret. Mr Waki, do you think our stuff would sell in Japan? I'm willing to let your company have the patent and marketing rights."

"Yang needs the money," Xie Han whispered in Aki's ear. "Poor guy – he has a five-year-old daughter with cancer."

When a large, steamed, blue-skinned fish was brought in, the director swiftly used his own chopsticks to serve the fish head – a choice bit – to Yang. After expressing his thanks with droll exaggeration, Yang conveyed a morsel to his mouth with evident appreciation.

Yin Dan gave a groan. "Some people put '101' on their scalp, others say thank you for a fish head, some smoke opium. Oh, this is a land of freedom, all right. Free even to spit on the floor!" His eyes were on Aki. A genial light in them belied the harshness of his words.

"Freedom, gentlemen," he said, after actually spitting on the floor, "does not exist in a country like Japan that has lots of money but nothing else of any value. And where there's nothing, there's no memory of anything. Freedom is from the Almighty. From the Party! Ah, my friends – you know, a 'friend' in Persian means a 'god' – our misery has great scope! My own heart sinks, right down into my boots."

Just then a platter even larger than the one with the blue-skinned fish on it arrived at their table; at the sight, Yin fell silent.

"Beggar's chicken!" someone shouted.

Everyone jumped to their feet at once, as if on cue, and peered at the great plate. This was a dish that Aki had never seen before. He was bewildered, as it seemed to consist of nothing but an enormous piece of baked clay.

Xie Han explained: You clean a chicken and stuff it with delicacies like shiitake mushrooms, ginkgo nuts, walnuts, and bamboo shoots, then seal it with crepinette and wrap the whole with lotus leaves. Next you add salt and wine to clay, mixing it to the consistency of paste, and spread it thickly all over the wrapped bird before baking.

Long ago, a beggar in Changshu first came up with the idea of cooking a chicken this way, and so it's called beggar's chicken.

"Go ahead, Mr Waki, please crack it open," said Xie. "That job always goes to the guest of honour."

Aki accepted the mallet offered him, but he couldn't bring himself to swing it down. People called out encouragement. Not knowing how much strength to use, he tried giving the thing a light tap at first. It emitted a *konk*, and that was all. The clay shell was surprisingly hard. Next time he swung harder. This time, bits of clay flaked off. Uncertainty over how much strength to use threw off his timing. He gave an embarrassed laugh.

Then something unexpected happened. At the next table, Li Xing got up and came striding over. She picked up the mallet, swung it high over her head, and brought it down with all her might. The beggar's chicken broke open beautifully, pieces of clay flying through the air. After a short, startled silence, everyone burst into applause, Aki joining in with the rest. Li Xing quietly slipped the mallet back in his hand and hurried back to her seat. Her warmth lingered in the handle, and Aki hung onto it as Xie Han peeled off the lotus leaves with a practiced hand, carved the chicken, and divided it up on small plates. Servings were carried over to the other table as well.

"It's good, isn't it?" said Xie. "In Guangzhou we call this 'nobleman's chicken.'"

The beggar's, or nobleman's, chicken was gobbled up in no time, leaving only clay shards and lotus leaves. The seal was broken on yet another bottle of maotai. As the strong drink took its effect, people spoke out more and more openly.

Gao Yong said with some bitterness, "Yuan Mu said there are only criminal offenders in China, no political offenders."

Other voices chimed in. "Mao Zedong pretended to be dead, and then jumped up and swam across the Yangtze. Fifteen kilometres to the other side, and he made it in an hour and five minutes! A world record if ever there was one."

"Zhou Enlai had nude photos of Jiang Qing. That's why he was the only one she could never lay a hand on."

Slightly tipsy, Aki half listened to these remarks while mentally tracing the plot of *Moving Shadows*. The two former lovers, Han

Langen and Zheng Pinru, meet up again as spies. Although they are on opposing sides of the conflict, their love revives. What would that be like, living the thrill of espionage and the thrill of romance at the same time? If he pursued the story beyond the limits of the film, would he find his real father somewhere at the end of it?

Encouraged by the drink, Aki put this last question to Xie.

"Whatever happens," he was told, "my movie will never go that far. As a matter of fact, the script still isn't finished. As you can see, I've assembled some top people for the cast and crew. Financing should be okay, too. It's only the storyline, the crucial element, that's unresolved – still being rewritten. The writer, Guo Fuhai, is about at the end of his rope. You see, in China, the political situation has a direct impact on the story, in subtle and not-so-subtle ways. When we started this project, the reformer Hu Yaobang was still in good health. He'd have let us do as we liked. Right, Mr Guo?" he called across the table to the scriptwriter, who sat downing maotai, his left hand at his temple.

"Yeah, well, whatever we do," Guo replied, "it won't hold a candle to the Great Wall. The desert's better than a sidewalk, a thief's better than a barber. Stands to reason. Tell you what I'm gonna do, Director. First I'm gonna crumple myself up like a used napkin, then I'm gonna knock myself out." He stood up, took the napkin from his lap and crushed it in his hand, then tossed it on the table; the next thing they knew, he crashed to the floor with a thud. Everybody laughed; no one got him up.

Li Xing was saying something to the other actresses in a low voice. Now and then a quick little smile would appear on her face, lighting her features with gaiety.

Sweetness and charm, murmured Aki to himself. Could one steer it in one's own direction, keep it for oneself? That was the thought that had struck him back when he first laid eyes on Sato. *Ready to try again?*

"What do you think of Li Xing?"

Aki jumped at this sudden query. Had the director read his mind?

"You saw how she cracked the beggar's chicken," Xie continued. "She's clever. As she should be – she is a spy, after all."

Li Xing was from Taiyuan, and her Japanese was good – better than his own, even if he was a graduate of the East Asia Common

Culture Academy. Her command of the language went well beyond what you could learn in school.

Aki asked why that was.

"She doesn't like to talk about it."

"Why not?"

Xie just shrugged. The question was left dangling.

"I saw her this morning at the pier."

"You did?"

"Yes, at Waihongqiao International Pier."

Xie looked dubious, but said nothing.

Aki stood up, screwed up his courage, and went over to Li Xing at the other table. He thanked her for her help with the chicken, but this was only a pretext. "I saw you this morning," he said in Japanese.

She tilted her head quizzically.

"At Waihongqiao International Pier. Weren't you there to meet someone arriving on the *Xin Jian Zhen*?"

Slipping out of her chair, she stood and looked Aki straight in the eye. "No, I wasn't at the pier."

"You weren't? I beg your pardon. My mistake."

After that, he found it difficult to keep the conversation going and had no choice but to beat a retreat. On the way back, he noticed that Yin Dan's seat was now empty. The empty plates and cup were neatly stacked, with a carefully refolded napkin laid ostentatiously over the top. Fantastic. The fellow had simply disappeared, like a well-behaved ghost. When had he gone? No one else seemed to have noticed his departure.

Jasmine tea was brought in. Xie Han poured it out carefully into fine porcelain cups. Aki, with his passion for jasmine tea, had caught the fragrance while the tea was still being carried down the corridor and had felt an immediate prickle of recognition. This was very like the tea served last year by old Zhao. Stronger smell, though. "Curious," he murmured to himself.

The director heard him, and peered into his face. "Are you familiar with this tea?" he asked.

"What could it be? It's similar to White Snow Bud... but no, not that..."

JASMINE

"If you know about White Snow Bud, then you obviously know a thing or two about the subject. This particular tea is handmade by our Yin Dan. Whenever he's invited to a party like this, he brings some along as a treat. It has no name yet. I invite him just for the sake of this stuff."

Apparently, Yin Dan had once been the ablest cameraman in Shanghai Film Studio. During the location filming of *Empire of the Sun*, he'd served as an assistant cameraman. Five years ago, after suddenly abandoning his camera in the middle of a shoot, he built a little shack in a corner of the studio and settled in there. Everyone loved him – even Mango. One day, he abruptly started digging holes all over the studio grounds. Crew members would go around and fill them in. Then one time he broke through a water main and nearly drowned in the hole he was digging. This caused such a ruckus that he gave up hole-digging and took to gardening instead, planting jasmine all around his hut.

The jasmine tea he made by hand was of outstanding quality. He used the finest grade leaves, Dragon Well green tea leaves fresh-picked in April. To scent them, he picked jasmine buds before dawn, while they were still drenched in dew, and then mixed them in with the tea leaves he'd set out to dry, thus permeating them with their fragrance. Later, he removed all the buds, repeating the procedure seven or eight times, being careful to leave no petals behind. One brewing of Yin's tea was enough to fill a room with the aroma for days, and there was never a single petal in the cup.

Yin Dan himself had left, but behind him he left the redolence of a tea that Aki thought he would never forget and could detect from quite far off. The banquet continued. He told jokes, knocked over his glass, fell silent, and smiled sardonically at their tales of incidents taking place under martial law.

He tried to get up, and staggered slightly. "Too bad I couldn't try any *malantou*," he said.

"You must come again in the spring," said Xie Han jovially. "All right, everyone, let's call it a night, shall we? All good things must come to an end, even banquets. Time for me to take my sly old head home and lay it on my cheap pillow."

They trooped noisily down the stairs and exchanged handshakes in the vestibule. Moist hands were laid atop dry hands, hot hands atop cold. Aki searched casually for Li Xing with his eyes, while shaking the actors' hands. At some point, however, she had vanished. Feeling let down, he started off on foot in search of Chen's taxi.

Even after ten at night, the congestion along Fuzhou Road showed no sign of letting up. Families and sweethearts, all-male and all-female groups, blended into one common whole, eating and drinking, then out on the sidewalks talking, joking around, and arguing, as pangolin sellers wove back and forth through the crowd. The pangolin, also called the scaly anteater, was a food animal, but Aki had never tried its meat. From ships and steam launches on the Huangpu came the sound of chugging engines and whistles, so near that it seemed the boats might come all the way into the street.

Jostled by the throng, Aki searched for Chen's cab. Finally he spotted it on a dark corner some way off, and after elbowing his way through the crowd, he reached it and got in. However, the cab was unable to make much headway. Chen blasted away on the horn. In aggravation, he opened his window, stuck his head out and yelled, but to no avail. As aggressively as it could, the Cedric inched ahead.

Someone rapped on the rear window. The sound reminded Aki of the tapping the mallet had made on the beggar's chicken. Thinking it was someone angry at Chen's driving, he turned around. The darkness and a large, racetrack-style sun visor kept him from seeing right away but in a moment he recognized who it was.

Hastily, he opened the door. Li Xing slid into the slowly moving car. A pleasant scent filled the air. Aki breathed it in as he closed the door.

She was breathing hard. Aki felt as if he had captured a rare animal.

Taking off her sun visor, she said, "Thanks. I got separated from the rest. I hope this isn't too much trouble."

Aki answered in Mandarin, "Hardly surprising, in this crowd. No problem at all. Let me take you home."

"That would be wonderful. I'm staying in housing on the film studio grounds."

Aki told Chen the change in destination. The studio was in the opposite direction from his hotel. Chen furtively adjusted his rear-view mirror, checking out the new passenger. "It's Li Xing," he said under his breath, his voice just audible. Then, with a determined nod, he leant heavily on his horn and lunged forward as if making a run at the pedestrians, picking up speed. It was amazing he didn't run anybody over.

The car cut across Fuzhou Road, turned left by People's Park, went south on Xizang Road, and then crossed Canton and Yan'an streets to come out on Huaihai Road. The fog thickened. Li Xing leant back in the seat and stared out the window. Neon signs rose up blurrily, one after another, and fell away again behind them. A moment ago Aki had been muttering about the fog, wishing it would clear away, but now the simple thought that it lay directly in her field of vision was enough to lend it a certain charm.

"Where does this fog come from?" he asked Chen. "From the sea, or the Yangtze?" He felt the need to impress upon her that Chen was a close friend of his, someone who could be trusted at the wheel.

"Neither. It comes from Lake Taihu and the creeks. It's a damn nuisance."

"Feels like being underwater, or floating in air, don't you think? Unsettling. Do you ever get lost in it?"

Chen did not reply to this, still using his horn as he wove through the traffic. In no time they left Huaihai Road, turned a corner unexpectedly, and were zipping along another street that seemed to be taking them farther and farther away from the film studio. Having a film actress as his passenger must have gone to Chen's head.

Aki said foolishly, "Thanks again for doing such a brilliant job of smashing the beggar's chicken." He would have liked to talk to her in Japanese, but that wouldn't have gone down well with Chen.

"I'd never had beggar's chicken before, either, you know. I just wanted to try my hand." Li Xing gave a little laugh. His tension eased a bit.

"Would you mind telling me something about your father?" she said. "I need to know more about the character I'm cast opposite. It would help me flesh out the part. Do you mind?"

Aki looked momentarily perplexed, but answered with a smile: "Actually, I hardly know anything about him myself. Not much more than you do. That's why I came to Shanghai, to find out what I can."

She studied his face. The look in her eyes was much livelier now than when she was staring out the window. Unable to resist, he told her what he knew:

"There's a report that he may be alive."

"What, he's alive!" The words slipped out in Japanese. "Where is he?" Back to Mandarin.

"Somewhere on the Loess Plateau, evidently."

"But that's where I'm from. My parents are both dead, but my *nainai* lives there alone. She's eighty now. It's a place called Yangquan, in Shanxi Province."

"Yangquan?" He'd never heard of it.

"What about your father?"

"I don't know exactly where he is. The information isn't one hundred per cent reliable, anyway."

Suddenly a section of fog cleared, and they emerged into the moonlight. Overhead loomed the twin spires of Xujiahui Cathedral. Aki realized that their driver had taken not a detour, but a shortcut.

When they arrived at the gate of Shanghai Film Studio, which was naturally closed, Chen honked his horn three times and the same guard as before came out. On ascertaining that Li Xing was in the car, he opened the gate and waved them on through.

Li Xing issued rapid instructions to Chen. They went past two traffic circles and five studios, coming to a drab, oblong two-story building. Chen pulled up at the entrance. This was the actors' guesthouse. Every window was dark, and even the entrance was unlit. Li Xing got out of the car, and Aki followed unhesitatingly behind her.

"No one's back yet," she said. "Even though I got separated from everyone, it looks like I made it back first after all. Thanks to you." In the beam of the headlights, she bowed gracefully in the Japanese style.

"I'll see you to your room. I can't leave you here alone in the dark. Besides, there's something I wanted to ask you."

She fumbled in her bag for her key as they walked into the building. She reached out a hand, and there was the click of a switch; then, after slowly flickering several times, a feeble fluorescent light came on. They walked side by side down the hall.

JASMINE

"Let me get this straight. Are you positive you weren't at the pier this morning?"

She stopped and turned to him with what seemed to be a look of real bafflement. "I'm quite sure – it's a case of mistaken identity. I mean, I don't even know where the pier is."

Aki smiled weakly and shook his head. So he had seen a vision not just of Sato, but of this woman, too? How could that be? How could you see a vision of a person you'd never met?

She came to a halt at one of the doors. Her key rattled in the keyhole. He felt a momentary urge to see her room.

"There's something else, too."

"What is it?" she said, pulling the door open. A stifling smell seeped out, heavy with summer humidity and just a hint of jasmine.

"Can you tell me a bit more about the Loess Plateau?"

"Well… it extends on the east from Taiyuan across Shaanxi Province in a crescent shape, on the west as far as Ningxia and Gansu Provinces, with the Yellow River running vertically down the middle. It was built up over millions of years from sand blowing off the great deserts in the northwest. Since ancient times people there have lived in caves in the cliffs called *yaodong*, which have arched roof and no pillars—"

"That answer I could find in a book," he interrupted with a smile. Did she want him to come into her room, or not? Tentatively, he said, "I'd like to tell you some more about my father."

They fell silent. He felt he'd made an ass of himself. Then she vanished and the door closed in his face. It was so sudden, he almost had the impression that her figure remained visible by the door.

On the way back, a wind sprang up and blew off the fog, but clouds veiled the moon. Amid the foliage of a plane tree, an owl hooted. For some time, Chen's fingers had been beating a tattoo on the steering wheel. He was worked up about something.

"What is it, Chen?"

Ignoring the red light, he shot across the intersection of East Yan'an and Middle Huaihai roads. "Her boyfriend's a fugitive on the most-wanted list. Everybody knows it. All you have to do is turn on the TV news," Chen said matter-of-factly.

"Who is he?"

"Name's Liu Hong. Sounds like a woman's name, but of course he's a guy."

"What kind of a guy?"

"Watch the news."

The twenty-one people placed on the government's wanted list in the wake of the Tiananmen Square incident included many reform-minded intellectuals and pro-democracy activists of international reputation, but the name Liu Hong was new to Aki. He nodded, understanding that Chen had given his first-ever ride to an actress, and as if that wasn't enough, she'd turned out to be the girlfriend of a wanted political offender. No wonder he was in a state.

Aki began fitting more pieces together. He had never, in all his life, seen a ghost or anything of that sort. Without a doubt, there'd been a woman standing on the pier. Since no one could be standing in that spot without connections, it seemed a sure bet that she'd gone there to meet Cai Fang – yet Aki found it impossible to believe that the lover of a wanted fugitive could have been standing there in the open.

His foot touched something. Bending down, he saw it was the sun visor Li Xing had left behind. Now here, he thought, was proof that the woman sitting beside him till a moment ago – even if she herself claimed it was another case of mistaken identity – had been no phantom.

He picked the visor up and held it protectively under his arm.

They were on the Bund, heading towards Garden Bridge. A heavy, dust-filled fog now hung over the Huangpu. Not a fog that came down from Lake Taihu and the creeks, but one generated by the river itself. They entered the intricate silhouette formed by the truss of the bridge. Lining the bridge stood a platoon of the People's Liberation Army, dressed in uniforms of the same dusty colour as the fog. The silhouette of the iron framework fell over them as well, like a net.

The Cedric crossed the bridge and pulled up at the entrance to his hotel. Aki sent Chen home and stepped into the elevator, with the sun visor firmly in his grasp.

His suite was on the fifteenth floor, and the windows facing south were open. From the confluence of Suzhou Creek and the Huangpu

River below arose this sinister yellow fog that enveloped the Bund, crawled up walls, and crept through his windows. A resinous odour stung his throat.

As he closed the windows and switched on the air conditioning, he realized he was still holding the sun visor. He was about to toss it onto the wicker chair between the sofa and the window, but then stopped short. When he checked in that morning and entered the room for the first time, there'd been no wicker chair. To get ready to see Xie Han, he had quickly showered, thrown on a robe, and then walked around the sofa, drying his hair. Had a chair been there then, it would have gotten in his way; he would certainly have noticed it. The wicker had a quiet, amber warmth, silently urging him to sit. He did so and heard a pleasant creaking sound. He found he was at the perfect height and angle to sit and look out on the streets of Shanghai.

He felt tired, but with no expectation of sleep. Settling back, he let his thoughts roam slowly over the day's events, squeezing them out like water from a sponge: coming ashore, the woman on the pier, Studio Four and Li Xing in the role of a spy, jasmine tea, the door to her room, his driver's excitement...

Suddenly remembering, he sprang out of the chair and, grabbing the remote control, turned on the TV. He clicked back and forth between Shanghai Television and Beijing's China Central Television. Both channels were showing live relays of Party-sponsored variety entertainment: seated rows of the Party elite being treated to comic dialogues in Beijing and, in Shanghai, to panda stunts. For over thirty minutes, he was forced to sit through comedy too rapid for him to follow and tiresome panda tricks.

The eleven o'clock news began. One after another, the names and faces of China's most-wanted flashed across the screen. Captured offenders underwent interrogation. A young man with a moustache was led away to the scaffold – an unemployed teenager, to be executed for attacking a tank with a bamboo pole.

Of the twenty-one people on the list, twelve had already been arrested, the announcer said. The remaining nine had either fled China or were on the run within the country.

Liu Hong – Aki was sure he caught the name.

"There he is!"

He stared intently at the screen. A face appeared. A close-cropped head, a small moustache, eyes looking up at the camera. This was apparently an enlargement of a small snapshot; the facial outline was blurred.

As the announcer's voice continued, subtitles at the bottom of the screen supplied additional information: *Liu Hong, born in Qinghai Province, age 36, head researcher at ESRIC, the Economic System Reform Institute of China, a wanted fugitive. Charged with supporting the pro-democracy movement, inciting riots, leaking state secrets to foreign media…*

The announcer began reading from a leaflet Liu Hong was said to have distributed:

I, along with the university students and a broad spectrum of Beijing citizens, am unalterably opposed to the bringing in of troops. I want to know: when a Communist tank crushes the body of a Communist Party member, what sound does it make?…

The announcer went on to state Liu Hong was believed to be … *hiding out at present in a cave in the vicinity of Linfen, Shanxi Province.*

Liu Hong. Aki said the name over softly to himself. It sounded like a woman's name.

6

The previous evening's fog turned to rain. Aki passed the morning reading from the book of Arabic and Persian poetry he'd brought with him. Now and then he switched on the television. Every time he did so, Liu Hong's face appeared on the screen. In the afternoon, he walked around the old Hongkew district with a map in one hand and an umbrella in the other. Old Zhao, who had shown him the photo of his father that day, was dead. He felt an urge to go and see his house. He paused for a while at the corner where North Sichuan Road turned west into Duolun Road, then followed his memory down the twisting lanes of the *lilong*, getting thoroughly mixed up before he finally located the place. What might have become of that photo album? He would have given a great deal for another look at the souvenir photograph in which Waki Tanehiko appeared twice as two different people. Had Zhao had any family? There'd been no sign of anyone else there before, and the dark entrance remained quiet, though this only made it seem more likely that the old man's tall, stooped figure might emerge at any time. Aki stayed another few seconds, eyes closed, before turning on his heel and leaving.

With some apprehension, he entered a dingy eating place nearby. On a sudden impulse he ordered *malantou*. As Xie Han had said, the dish was simple, made by stir-frying the greens with dried bean curd and a pinch of salt. As he ate, he found the flavour to be developing subtly. A dish his father may have loved, sampled more than half a century later by the son. He had the odd sensation of having caught his father out. Strange – this hadn't been his intention in coming on this journey.

The next morning, on his third day in Shanghai, amid a rain that bore signs of returning to the fog of two days earlier, he phoned for Chen to take him back to the studio. Chen was a different man today, having recovered his usual calm demeanour and way of speaking, but somehow he had a glum air of resolve about him. He never once honked his horn, and his driving was remarkably smooth.

Aki, however, sat jiggling his knees and twiddling his thumbs, as if Chen's earlier agitation and excitement had transferred to him. He was in the grip of an anxiety that was part tiredness and part jitters. The reason was plain: Liu Hong. Every time he turned on the TV, there the man was. He tried to stop watching, but before he knew it his hand would reach for the remote control. *I want to know: when a Communist tank crushes the body of a Communist Party member, what sound does it make?* Aki could now reel off the words from memory; they spun round inside his head like a pinwheel.

"Damn. I forgot the sun visor."

"Do you want to go back?" Chen slowed down.

"No, forget it. But, hey, you're certainly driving differently from the other night."

"Think so? I'm not doing anything different." Chen was offhand.

"Sure about that? You haven't honked your horn once."

"It's the difference between evening streets and morning streets."

Well, that might well account for it, Aki thought, then said, "I saw Liu Hong on TV all right – enough to be sick of him already."

"That so?" Another brush-off.

"Is it widely known that Li Xing is his girlfriend?"

"Yes. When she got the lead role in *Moving Shadows* and they knew she'd be coming here from Taiyuan, they ran a big article on her in *New Star*."

New Star was a weekly in the Shanghai area devoted to celebrity news. So far, Chen had responded to Aki's questions by meeting his eyes in the rear-view mirror, but now all of a sudden he half turned around and blurted out, "*Xiansheng*, what's the best place in Japan to live?"

"Where'd that come from? I'm talking about Liu Hong."

"Liu Hong is Liu Hong. Let him run away if he wants to and take Li Xing with him, wherever he wants to go…"

"Take Li Xing?"

"She's his girl, isn't she?"

Ah-ha, the thought popped into Aki's head, *Chen Ying is in love.*

"Chen, I was born and bred in Kobe. I live in Tokyo now because of my job. They say Sapporo and Fukuoka are nice, too, but for my money, it's Kobe all the way. You know what they say? Transfer an employee to Kobe and he'll never want a promotion."

Chen tapped the steering wheel and gave a small, appreciative laugh, nodding to himself several times.

The tunnel of plane trees, whose dripping leaves had splattered the cab with raindrops, came abruptly to an end.

"Looks like the rain has stopped," said Aki.

Sunlight straggled through a thin layer of clouds the colour of dishwater, making a rainbow along the edge. In no time every window in sight was in full regalia, laundry-decorated poles sticking out at right angles. Soon the spires of the cathedral came into view. This area was all built on landfill, to replace creeks. In the old days, people came and went not in automobiles but in skiffs and junks. Aki closed his eyes and imagined Chen's taxi was a boat.

Aki saw assistant director Gao Yong come running out of the office just to the right of the studio gate. The uneven ground was full of puddles, each iridescent with motor oil. Stubby-legged Gao skirted some and bounced over others as he tore along tos Studio Four. Twice Aki called out to him, but he didn't hear and disappeared inside.

Aki hesitated for a minute before making up his mind and pushing open the little side door. The big electric fans were groaning, and the round hand fans were waving. In spotlights here and there, motes of dust sparkled and drifted lazily upwards.

"Why doesn't anyone know where she was going?" Yu Ming's shrill voice rang out.

Hands thrust deep into his pockets, Gao shrugged. He was breathing hard. "You can't expect us to know. Just because she's the lead actress doesn't mean we can keep a twenty-four-hour watch on her."

"What if she's collapsed somewhere? In the bathroom maybe…"

"It's two days now. We've searched everywhere."

"Or what if it's… you-know-what?"

The murmurs died instantly. The hand fans paused. Everyone was thinking of Liu Hong. With their lead actress missing in unsettled times, they couldn't help tying her disappearance to the fugitive.

"Shall we notify public security?"

"Wait a minute now," said Xie Han, seated in his folding chair. "Think what you're saying. That's out of the question. Listen, everybody. Do you have any idea what would happen if they found out she wasn't here? Yu Ming, why are you blinking like a cat? For one more day, anyway, we'll go on as if nothing's wrong. Li Xing is a bright and sensible young woman. She'll be back. Where's my megaphone? Ah, Mr Waki," he said amiably to Aki, who had quietly approached.

"Director, I need a word with you."

His manner was so guarded that Xie, taken aback, stood up. His megaphone rolled to the floor. Picking it up, he held it to his mouth and called out, "That's all for today. We'll pick up tomorrow at nine. Don't be late."

Yu Ming repeated this, eyes blinking: "Be here at nine o'clock, people. On time." They started filing out of the room, followed by the property and lighting crews.

Xie Han sank back onto his chair, motioning for Aki to use a nearby metal one. "Have a seat. We can talk right here."

Aki sat, then leant forward. "Actually, the other night, I brought Li Xing back here to the studio in a taxi."

Xie Han inclined his head. "After the banquet?"

"Somehow she got separated from everyone else."

"Funny, they waited for her quite some time. Nobody's seen her since then."

That made Aki the last one to have seen her.

Xie Han nodded lightly and got up. They were alone in the studio. "Mr Waki, it's way too early, but let's go for a drink. There's somewhere interesting I want to show you."

Side by side they walked into the blazing heat. Aki headed towards Chen's cab, but Xie said something about a detour, and on the way they took a left turn in the direction of the scenery storehouse. After continuing a while, they turned left again, this time entering a passage between two storehouses. Suddenly the air was sweet with jasmine. Behind the storehouses in an unused lot about a hundred metres square was Yin Dan's garden. The tiny, narrow white flowers, tinged with pink, were in full bloom. Clinging like a barnacle to the concrete wall of the storehouse was a lean-to fashioned from scraps of lumber and cardboard boxes.

"Chez Yin. Let's have a look-see, shall we?"

The front door was a board made up to look like the door of a fancy hotel for a movie set. Xie knocked on it. It wobbled and swayed. No answer. He turned the knob and pulled, and the movie door swung open easily to reveal a tidy interior.

"Not here. That's unusual."

They walked back through the field of jasmine.

"Every once in a while I stop by for a cup of Yin's tea. The other day I brought Xingxing with me, and she loved it. She started coming by herself."

"And now she's nowhere to be found, and he's gone too."

"It does look that way, doesn't it?"

"May I ask a question?"

"Fire away," said Xie, stopping to light a cigarette.

"It's something Mr Yin said the other night: 'My own heart sinks, right down into my boots.' What did he mean?"

"Nothing much. It's just a way of saying he's disappointed. A pet phrase of his, that's all."

"Disappointed? In what?"

"As I said, it's a pet phrase. He might have meant the food on the table. Or the wine, or something bigger. I wouldn't worry about it. He's always disappointed in one damn thing or another."

They got into Chen's taxi. With Xujiahui Cathedral on the left, they went east on Hengshan Road, eventually merging with Middle Huaihai Road and entering the plane tree tunnel.

"It's nice after a heavy rain," said Xie. The people there and the air itself were stained green by the lustrous, overlapping foliage. "But see over there on that corner, and in the shadow of that building farther down – tanks."

Before long the cab stopped as instructed at the intersection of Fuzhou and Middle Jiangxi roads, letting them out at the corner. The Bund was close at hand; up ahead, a great ship was floating by. Aki followed Xie into the basement of a dilapidated hotel with its name in neon lights, "Xincheng Hotel." Inside was a long counter covered in stains. Ten round mahogany tables were lined up, each one piled with chairs.

Xie and Aki sat down at the bar. Xie ordered champagne and some pine nuts. The bartender, a man thin as steel wire, his face alone round and full, served them brusquely. They clinked the rims of their long, narrow champagne glasses.

"This used to be the Metropole Hotel," said Xie. "This bar was the second longest in the Orient. The longest one was in Shanghai, too, in the Shanghai Club. It's still a hotel, but foreigners hardly stay here anymore."

In the old days this was the centre of Shanghai, he further explained, what they called "the City." The Metropole had been one of a handful of glamorous hotels, along with the Park Hotel and the Cathay.

"Your father lived on the seventh floor of this hotel, right upstairs. Commuted every day to Hamilton House, a stone's throw away."

An ironical smile hovering on his cheeks, Xie Han looked at Aki as if to say, *Isn't that something?* He was in an unusually loquacious mood. It pleased him enormously to be giving a tour of old Shanghai to a man from the old aggressor nation, a man who was also the son of his longtime friend.

Leaning against the second longest bar in the Orient, he began to tick off buildings still standing in the City district and elsewhere that had been built in European neoclassical style.

The former Shanghai Club was now the East Wind Hotel, with the longest bar in the Orient. The former Hong Kong and Shanghai Bank building with its colossal dome now enshrined Communist Party offices and City Hall. Sassoon House, named after the opium and real estate magnate, was now the north wing of the Peace Hotel.

As Xie Han continued his recital, the Shanghai conjured up by the original names of these landmarks began to waver and shimmy. The disconnect between contours and content, slight though it was, created a double focus. Xie's eyes were like specially treated lenses through which, thanks to that disconnect, the city took on a 3-D quality. The Shanghai of legend, nowhere to be found yet undeniably real, rose into being. Xie aimed to fix that image on the evanescent medium of film. *Moving Shadows* would be his final film.

Xie saw everything in a dual aspect. Was this simply old age? A twilight state in which things appeared twofold by nature? No. He had studied and mastered the art from youth. A required subject for survival in this country. First, the duality inherent in the city of Shanghai itself. Then ideological duality – the Kuomintang-Communist alignment, the Sino-Japanese collaboration. Cinematic light and shadow; the Chinese language and the Japanese language; fact and fiction. Xie himself had assumed these dualities, thereby surviving a harsh regime.

In the Great Proletarian Cultural Revolution, his two sons had become Red Guards and attacked his duality head-on. He was censured, dragged to criticism meetings, physically assaulted. The boys were twelve and thirteen. Later they became embroiled in an internal struggle in the Red Guards. The elder boy was murdered, the younger one stuffed in a garbage can which his tormentors beat continuously with wooden sticks. He was released on the fifth day, a wreck.

Revolution was something you were better off avoiding if you could. With every revolution, the country got worse. At the end of the world, if God handed out awards for the three harshest prisons ever devised by human beings, China's labour camps would be a shoo-in.

In the world of politics, barbarians won. Chiang Kai-shek and Mao Zedong were barbaric, brutal bumpkins – poles apart from Wang Jingwei and Zhou Enlai, both of whom had been wounded. A sniper's bullet got Wang Jingwei in the back, lodging near his spine, and Zhou Enlai was badly injured falling off a horse, so that his left arm hung useless. Wang died after suffering excruciating pain from that bullet wound, making an early exit from the stage of history. Just as well: sooner or later Japan was bound to lose, and he'd have been tortured to death as the worst traitor of them all. Nobody ever took seriously his talk of peace between Japan and China. Castles in the air.

Though certainly no glorious war wound, Zhou Enlai's injury had a curious effect on people. After the war, he took to posing for the camera with his right arm bent somewhere near his navel, and everyone assumed that this arm was crippled. The word spread: Premier Zhou gave his right arm to put food on our plates. And yet it was his left arm that was immobile. Miraculously, he managed to hang onto the premiership of the People's Republic of China to the bitter end. How did he do it? Was it thanks to his good looks and his bad arm? A mystery.

Xie shook his head to rouse himself from this train of thought. He glanced at his companion, reflecting that he was about the age his sons would have been if they had lived. Then, in a slow, deliberate way, he began to talk about Waki Tanehiko.

"Shanghai is smack in the East Asia monsoon zone, so we get a lot of sudden showers. But people here hate carrying umbrellas. Japanese are much fonder of them, aren't they?"

"I wonder. I hardly ever carry one, myself. Getting wet doesn't bother me."

"When it rained, your father would make a dash for it, no umbrella, going from the front of this hotel to Hamilton House across the street in only fifteen steps. He was proud of that – fifteen steps. Only in a *baoyu*, a real downpour, would he have the hotel porter escort him over. An Indian with a little moustache and a turban. The perfect servant. He'd hold up an umbrella as big as a beach parasol, with stripes like a barber pole. Blue and white and red. If your father was going home, he'd stand in front of Hamilton House and signal by raising an arm, and the porter would charge over with the umbrella."

Aki absorbed this before asking, "Why did it take my father an extra five years to go back to Japan after the war ended?"

Xie Han picked up a little pine nut in his fingertips, held it up as if to peer through it in the faint light, and then placed it between his lips and rolled it around. The skinny, round-faced bartender was polishing a glass with a cloth, creating sharp squeaking sounds.

"Do you know the word *hanjian*?"

The squeaky sounds overlapped neatly with the word. Aki nodded noncommittally. *Hanjian*, he thought: someone who sold out his country by collaborating or colluding with the Japanese.

"As soon as Japan lost the war, what do you think became of the Chinese working at Huaying, the film studio that was a pet project of the Japanese military?"

"Arrested? And, okay, my father was Han Langen, the Chinese comedian …"

Jasmine

Starting the year after Japan's defeat, the traitors' trials took place over a period of two years and five months, from April 1946 to September 1948, in the high courts of cities across the land: Nanjing, Jiangsu, Shanghai, Hebei, Tianjin, Ji'nan, Amoy.

Huaying's operations were taken over by the Nationalist government of Chiang Kai-shek, and all the company's Chinese workers, actors, and production staff became targets of the hunt for traitors; many were arrested and imprisoned. The managing director and three honorary directors had all held key positions in the puppet government of Wang Jingwei and so were sentenced to death. Xie Han received a sentence of three years in prison.

Xie said, "There was an actress named Li Xianglan. That was her Chinese name, but she was actually Japanese. You must have heard of her."

Just then a man entered the bar. He was wearing a rumpled, dark blue suit and a big, loud, red-and-blue striped necktie that looked out of place. He sat down at the other end of the bar and ordered coffee in a quiet voice. After being served, he slurped his drink noisily.

"The first two people in the Far East to see *Citizen Kane* were probably Tanehiko and me." The change of subject was so abrupt that Aki was a bit startled. "August 1941."

"The same year as Pearl Harbor," said Aki. "Amazing that you could see *Citizen Kane* in Shanghai so soon."

"The New York premiere was in May. Which means that Shanghai movie fans saw the film before almost anyone else in the world, New Yorkers excepted. It was splendid. Orson Welles was only twenty-five. A young man like us."

Aki had never seen *Citizen Kane.*

Xie quickly scribbled something on the back of a paper coaster and slid it over the counter to him, his face turned innocently towards a corner of the ceiling.

He's from the Public Security Bureau, foreign affairs section. Let's switch to Japanese.

Aki gave a barely perceptible nod.

"*Citizen Kane* played in the Grand Theatre, Shanghai's top venue," Xie remembered. "That's also where Li Xianglan earlier held a song recital produced by Huaying, in May 1945. The event was billed as a 'Fragrance of the Night Fantasia,' after her signature song. It was a big hit. For three days she sang twice a day, afternoon and evening, before sellout crowds. Tickets sold at a premium."

"That's your connection?"

"Sorry?"

"The link between Orson Welles and Li Xianglan."

"Yes, indeed. The Grand Theatre. For Welles's movie the theatre was almost empty, for her there was standing room only."

Aki sensed that the guy at the end of the bar was all ears. "You know, her Japanese name is Yamaguchi Yoshiko," he said. "She's married to a foreign diplomat in Tokyo now. She herself is a member of the House of Councillors... Now there's a woman who was a Japanese and became famous as a Chinese actress. I guess you could say my father was a male version of her. Not as big a star, of course."

"Never was any demand for his work. He never achieved any popularity at all," said Xie with apparent approval. "Anyway, as I was saying before, we were all caught together and put in Tilanqiao Prison in the Hongkew district. Your father, me, Li Xianglan..."

Aki's eyes widened in surprise.

"You have to realize, except for those of us in the film business, everybody thought she was Chinese. To escape the charge of treason she had to prove she was a bona fide Japanese national. Kawakita ran around and finally managed to track down a copy of her family registry in Beijing. So in February 1946, she was cleared by a military court. A fate just the opposite of Kawashima Yoshiko's."[1]

"The Oriental Mata Hari."

"Exactly. Executed in 1948, in Beijing."

Just as they were getting back to Aki's father, the customer at the end of the bar stood up. "Well, if it isn't Mr Xie!" he called out with phony surprise, as if he'd just noticed them. He came over. "How's your latest movie shaping up?"

---

[1] (1907–1948). A Manchu princess brought up as a Japanese and executed as a Japanese spy by the Kuomintang.

Xie Han twisted around to answer. "Fine, thanks," he told the man, giving him an easy smile.

"Your companion is Japanese, I see."

Aki turned to the man as well, to find his eyes fixed on him.

"People in Japanese firms that left China are gradually coming back, aren't they? Your Chinese is excellent, sir. Are you here on business?"

Aki shook his head, then turned to the bartender. "I'd like some kind of cocktail. What can you make me?"

"You name it. Pretty much anything."

The man backed off, paying his respects to Xie Han as he went. Just as he seemed in danger of knocking into a table, he turned around and headed for the exit, then stopped and, facing them again, said confidentially, "By the way, they say Liu Hong made it to Jiangsu." Looking in their direction, he backed out through the double doors and disappeared.

Xie said to the bartender, "Wang, old fellow, I'm a little hungry. Make me a sandwich?"

"Yes, sir. What about the other gentleman's cocktail?"

"I'd like a gimlet," said Aki. "Can you do that?"

"You bet," said Wang with a wink.

It was ready in no time. Sipping his gimlet, Aki murmured in Japanese, as if to himself, "Liu Hong. Li Xing's boyfriend. I wonder if public security knows she's missing?"

"Who can say?" Xie shrugged.

Wang produced a sandwich, which Xie began to eat with gusto. Mouth full, he mumbled, "Who do you think that guy was spying on, you or me? Almost certainly you."

"You've got to be kidding!"

"Of course it's you. No doubt about it. After all, he's in their foreign affairs section. The rest of us know we're under constant observation everywhere we go, anyway. No need for such heavy-handed reminders."

Aki shook the crushed ice in his glass. It might just be true. At a time of domestic crisis, a Japanese national travelling by sea enters the country alone, with no clear purpose. Immigration isn't likely to overlook that.

"Funny," said the old director. His eyes had a slight squint. "He looked like the fellow playing Han Langen."

"Kind of, yeah."

"You don't look much like your father, do you?"

"I'm told I take after my mother."

"That must be it." He paused. "That guy might've been able to understand Japanese, for all I know. Well, we didn't say much of anything. Wait a minute – maybe he knows something about your dad that we don't, maybe that's why he's following you – no, I'm joking.

He propped his cheeks on both hands, so that his voice came out muffled. "Let's get back to the past. Now, thanks to Kawakita, Li Xianglan was able to show that she was Japanese and get safely back to Japan – but your father wasn't keen on proving his Japanese nationality."

Surprised, Aki raised his eyes, and happened to meet the bartender's gaze. Xie's words rang inside his head. While waiting for whatever came next, he wondered how old this bartender might be. He looked young, but there was something older about him, too. It might be those deep furrows in his forehead.

"He wanted to become Chinese… while staying Japanese." Xie's voice was still muffled. "And so he used both names, Waki Tanehiko and Han Langen. Not just as private name and professional name, either. There was more interplay between the two identities. He couldn't really separate them. You could say he was defined by the very ambiguity of his position, of his attitude. When they arrested him, I doubt if he was able to make a choice on the spot."

"What happened at his trial?"

"He was perfectly calm. Kawakita worried about your father, too, but saving the big star, Li Xianglan, was a higher priority. As was only natural. But your father went out of his way to refuse Kawakita's help, politely but firmly. He got indicted as the Chinese Han Langen, but he remained ambivalent throughout the trial. His attitude must have had a negative effect on the judge. Here's the proof. Except for the Chinese executives, the other actors, directors, and crew from Huaying were all let go, one after another. I was sentenced to three years for making 'slave movies.' Only Han Langen got a five-year term. He did time for treason as a Chinese, then went back to Kobe as a Japanese.

Which seems logical enough, too… By the way, that cocktail of yours looks pretty good. Wang, old fellow, make me one, too."

A slight distance away, Wang swung the cocktail shaker energetically.

"How old is he?" asked Aki.

"About your age. He was in my son's class in middle school."

"Then why do you call him *old* fellow?"

"That's what we always called him. Look at his face – it's always been that way."

Wang calmly set the gimlet in front of Xie Han, who took a sip and smiled appreciatively before commenting, "If the charge of espionage had held, your father's punishment would have been far more severe."

Aki quickly finished off his drink." Double agent?"

"Yes. In the movie, that is. How it really was, there's no way of knowing. Although as far as Zheng Pinru is concerned, her trial established that she definitely was a double agent."

"Which side do you suppose my father was actually spying for?" Aki asked, aware of himself being drawn deeper into the web of duality that Xie Han had introduced. Everything appeared double. Shanghai, his father, Xie himself. And weaving through his thoughts were two Li Xings: one on the wharf, dimly visible in the rain, the other in the spotlight, surrounded by golden, dancing specks of dust.

"The truth? Who's to say? Only he knew, of course, and he never would have told. Everyone who knew his real character is dead, friend and foe alike: Ding Mocun, Zheng Pinru… and Zhou Enlai."

"You're kidding! I wasn't expecting that name to pop up."

"They must have met somewhere along the line. Zhou set up the communist secret agency in Shanghai, and later kept close track of the Party's secret operations through an underling."

The clean-cut, intelligent features of the Zhou Enlai that the world knew overlapped with those of a special operative bent on murder and deceit.

"The crushed ice is what makes this so good," said Xie Han, and asked Wang for his recipe.

Wang obviously knew his stuff: "It should be made with lime, but since there are no limes in Shanghai, I make do with lemon."

"It's true," said Aki, "lime does taste better. But you have quite a knack. This is excellent."

The bartender's eyes crinkled with pleasure at the compliment.

Everyone in the know was dead, Xie had said, but this wasn't quite true. He himself was alive… The director mulled the two names over: Waki Tanehiko and Han Langen. By now he felt they represented two separate friends of his. No matter what he did, he couldn't get the two to converge in a single personality.

The fellow had spoken Mandarin as easily as if it were his mother tongue. Wrote it, too. That alone qualified him as a spy. And he hadn't seemed to belong wholeheartedly to either camp, had seemed rather to enjoy the ambiguity of his position. Xie remembered a film in which Han Langen had played the part of a Japanese youth. Though he wasn't a great actor, on that occasion his performance had been riveting.

The director's thoughts continued to run on. Tanehiko had had no principles. Not communism, not cosmopolitanism, not patriotism. What did he have, then? A kind of neutral detachment. Yet how could someone like that fall in love, father a child? A child sitting here now, grown up. What about him? He claimed to take after his mother, not his father. Probably true.

Turning to Tanehiko's son, he said, "The indictment was for being a Japanese spy – that was a shock. The same as a death sentence. If he could have proved he was spying not for the Japanese, but for the Comintern, or for Chinese communist counterintelligence, he might have been spared. But in those days, Shanghai was completely under Chiang Kai-shek's control. There was no one, and nothing, to vouch for him."

Aki was quiet, listening intently.

Records of the military trials, especially the traitors' trials, were lost in the turbulent shift from Chiang Kai-shek to Mao Zedong. Yet the traitors' trials were the focus of attention among Shanghainese, covered daily by all the papers in full detail. When Huaying film stars were subpoenaed, the Shanghai High Court was filled with a horde of fans. Xie Han had been in prison at the time, but after his release, he'd been able to read all the newspaper accounts thanks to a friend who saved them.

"...And yet the Japanese spy and Chinese comedian Han Langen didn't get the death penalty," said Xie in conclusion. Abruptly he stopped talking, and with his lips pursed, he rolled his eyes upwards and shook his head. Then, taking a toothpick, he stuck it in one section of his sandwich.

Aki grew impatient. "Why not?"

"*Wang le*," said Xie Han. Meaning, I've forgotten. He stuffed the sandwich in his mouth, with the toothpick sticking out. Chewing, he continued to speak as if reading from a script.

"What is the defendant's name?"

Han Langen. In Japanese, Waki Tanehiko.

"Where was the defendant born?"

Wang le.

"When and where did the defendant first meet Major-General Kagesa Sadaaki in the Bureau of Military Affairs of the Japanese War Ministry?"

Wang le.

"Where were you on 8th May of the 28th year of the Republic?"

Wang le.

"Isn't that the day when the traitor Wang Jingwei sneaked into Shanghai from Hanoi, aboard the Japanese ship *Hokko-maru*?"

Wang le.

"Well then, is it true that you know the female student Zheng Pinru?"

Wang le.

Xie Han took the toothpick out of his mouth and reverted to his natural voice. "What do you think? Pretty good, isn't it? I read the account in the newspaper. I can remember the cross-examination almost word for word."

The summation by the government-appointed defence lawyer took place on 17th September 1946. Concerning the criminal charge of a war crime lodged against the defendant, i.e. acts of espionage, he stressed the defendant's innocence, questioning the legal appropriateness of any attempt to hold him responsible for relevant actions in the past of which he had no recollection whatsoever. When the time came for the defendant's final statement, Han Langen uttered not a word.

Sentence was handed down on 20th September: five years' penal servitude.

"So the defence plea of not guilty by reason of forgetfulness didn't hold up – but then, if the trial had been held in Shanxi or Hebei or any of the other Communist-controlled areas, he'd never have gotten off with only five years. Still, every time he answered *Wang le*, the crowd must have gone wild."

Xie Han sighed deeply and stretched his neck again. There were unshaven whiskers on his throat.

"*Wang le*? So my father pretended to have forgotten. Was it all an act?"

His eyes still upturned, Xie nodded slightly.

Okay, thought Aki to himself, but then why, after finally making it home to Japan, should he have returned to Shanghai a mere five years later? Five years in prison, five in Japan. Like a neatly executed turn on skis. Or a piece of paper folded cleanly down the middle. Xie never knew that his old friend was back in town. Who, or what, made him come back?

Tanehiko had moved on to Beijing, where he was arrested again on suspicion of espionage – this time by the Communist government – and locked away. Had he said *Wang le* then, too?

Do I need to know? Aki asked himself. Not every son in the world had the responsibility of clarifying what sort of person his father had been. What one's father had done, whom he had betrayed, or killed, or loved... compared to issues of environmental destruction, famine, and refugees, or a car illegally parked in front of one's house, or which restaurant in Kobe had the best Cantonese cuisine, such things were insignificant, surely; no need to bother about them at all. He tried to convince himself that a son might forget that his father had ever existed, that doing this was forgivable. It could well be that his father would prefer having his existence forgotten. *Wang le*: I have forgotten and I want you to forget me, too.

"What about the films of Han Langen, are they—"

"None survived. There isn't a single one left," said Xie Han, looking at his watch now for the first time. "Four o'clock already. Sorry, I have to go. There's a meeting coming up. With the Film Bureau. The prospect is discouraging. The situation with your father does concern me, but I must say, right now I'm more worried about Xingxing."

Same here. I'd rather find her than him, murmured Aki inwardly. He slid off his stool, asked the bartender for the bill and paid it, overriding Xie's protests.

When they came out again on street level, another dusty fog had rolled in from the river. Like a ship, Chen's cab emerged slowly from the mist. Aki told Chen to take the director to the Film Bureau.

"Your father is being held somewhere on the Loess Plateau," said Xie Han. "I'm obviously concerned about him, but you must understand that this isn't a good time for me to be involved. I'm sorry."

"That's okay. Will I be able to see you again?"

"Yes, feel free to drop by the studio any time. You have a free pass."

He dropped the director off at a large mansion on West Nanjing Road in the old French Concession. Aki watched through the car window as he disappeared inside the entrance. His attention was then caught by the sight of a man in the hallway, crossing from the left wing to the right. He was tall and wore rimless glasses. It was his shipmate, Cai Fang. What could someone from the Beijing People's Friendship Association be doing here? Aki checked the plates on both sides of the front door. Shanghai Film Bureau; Shanghai Foreign Affairs Department; People's Friendship Association, Shanghai Division. Okay, Cai must have stopped here on business, he told himself, feeling reassured.

On the way back to the hotel, they drove alongside Suzhou Creek. On every bridge stood hundreds of soldiers, row upon neat row, rifles shouldered. They seemed partial to bridges.

"Chen, how about having dinner with me tonight? It's no fun eating alone."

The driver explained regretfully that his older brother was in the hospital, and tonight was his turn to sit up with him.

"Is it serious?"

"Incurable," Chen replied briskly.

7

Although Aki had told Chen that it was no fun to eat alone, in fact he was little bothered by it. He rather enjoyed sitting by himself at a table with an array of dishes spread out before him and something to read, whether a newspaper, a magazine, or a hardcover book. He drank hot saké or *laojiu* with his meal. Ever since his wife's death, he tended more and more to dine this way.

Forgoing the elevator, he walked up the three flights of stairs from his suite on the fifteenth floor to the restaurant on the eighteenth. Shown to a big round table with a stiff white tablecloth, the hem of which nearly reached the floor, he took his solitary seat and opened the heavy, leather-bound menu. At such times he often heard Sato's voice in his ear ("Guess what?"), felt her leaning over to peer at the menu in his hands. And so, as often happens when memories are vivid, the past was brought forward. She was joining him; it was her company he would be enjoying.

He ordered an assortment of dishes. "Won't that be too much?" the young waitress inquired innocently. He shook his head, smiling, and said no, that would be fine. Mentally he added, *I may look like one person to you, but there are two of us here.* That was why he needed to order enough for two. He selected a good *laojiu* before closing the menu with a bang. In so doing, he sealed Sato within. *Okay, I'm alone*, he thought. *I'll have myself a feast.*

He gazed out through the tall, perpendicular window. Thick fog gave the Garden Bridge arch and the Bund skyline the appearance of an India-ink painting. He dropped a hard, dried pickled plum in the bottom of his glass and then poured hot *laojiu* over it; after a minute or so, he slowly drained the glass. Then he got deliberately to his feet, went over to the window and, spreading out his arms, pulled shut the heavy taffeta curtains to right and left.

JASMINE

After an hour or so, he went back to his suite, where he perched on the desk and phoned his sister in Ashiya. He reached her answering machine. *Don't be angry with me*, he remembered her saying. *Don't give up on me, be my friend.* You bet I will, he promised silently before leaving a recording of his telephone number and hotel room number.

Sitting down in the wicker chair, he closed his eyes. He felt unfocused, like a person preoccupied who thinks of something one moment and can't remember it the next. He thought about Liu Hong.

He got up, picked up the remote control, and pointed it towards the TV. The public security man in the bar had said that Liu Hong made it to Jiangsu. That was the province adjacent to Shanghai, to the north. The television was relaying a live acrobatics show. While a voice trumpeted "The most pliant human being on earth!" a young man came on stage dressed in a costume of red and blue stripes. He bent himself around until his hands were grasping his ankles behind his head. In the blink of an eye he bent himself still further, until every joint in his body was dislocated and he could roll himself like a ball. A little girl then came out, jumped up lightly on the human ball, and began to dance and do balancing acts.

Abruptly the program switched to a news bulletin. Alongside a drab concrete fence, a middle-aged man was being led away in handcuffs. He was described as a worker in a plastics factory in Changsha who had travelled alone to Beijing on 20th May and taken part in the uprising at Tiananmen Square. After fleeing back to Changsha, he told people there what he'd seen.

The screen began displaying photographs of people on the most-wanted list who were still on the run: Yan Jiaqi, Chen Yizi, Wan Runnan, Su Xiaokang, Liu Hong, Yuan Zhimin, Wuer Kaixi, Chai Ling. So Liu Hong had not been captured yet. Step by step, he seemed to be getting closer to Shanghai.

The phone rang. It must be his sister. He quickly picked up the receiver, but said nothing.

"*Wei.*" Hello. No, not his sister, but a woman's voice.

"*Wei*," he replied.

This time she said hello in Japanese. "*Moshi moshi. Waki-san?*"

"Yes?" Aki gulped.

"I'm so glad! You're there!"

"What's up? I was worried about you. Shall we go on talking in Japanese?"

"Yes, in Japanese."

"Where are you?"

A brief silence, as if she were holding her breath. Aki held the receiver away from his ear, looked at the numerous tiny holes in the mouthpiece, and then slowly fixed his eyes on the TV. Liu Hong's face was back on the screen. Unlike before, he showed up now with peculiar clarity, perhaps because Aki was standing back, at a distance. Or because the receiver in his hand held Li Xing?

"Would it be all right if I came over now?"

Aki hesitated for one millisecond. "Sure. It's fine with me." Ought he to ask first why she wanted to come?

"Thanks. Actually, I'm calling from a pay phone on Zhapu Road."

"That's just around the corner." *What happened, did you get separated from everyone again?* he almost said out of timid curiosity.

At the hotel entrance, the doorman kept a strict check on the comings and goings of registered guests, and close by the elevator on every floor was a service counter staffed by eagle-eyed hotel employees. While supervision was not as intense as in the days when room keys for the entire floor were kept at the service counter, a guest's movements were still carefully monitored, making the entry of any suspicious character impossible. Chinese visitors to guest rooms were required to show ID and to record the purpose of their visit, their name, and their affiliation.

Prominently displayed on the desk in every room was a circular from the Shanghai Public Security Bureau with a long list of rules. Any guest who broke these rules or committed a crime would be prosecuted and punished according to the laws of the Chinese People's Republic. The list included "changing rooms without permission, setting off firecrackers, committing acts of violence, gambling, engaging in drugs or prostitution, putting up pornographic pictures or photographs on the wall, making lewd noises, watching lewd movies..." et cetera, et cetera.

Would it be all right if I came over now? Li Xing had asked. But Aki hadn't yet mustered the courage to risk admitting a Chinese woman to his rooms. A contradiction, since the day before yesterday he'd had courage enough to try getting into her room.

Li Xing had said, "We aren't allowed in the hotel, so in fifteen minutes please wait for me by the revolving door at the entrance. I'll be coming from the direction of Zhapu Bridge."

What on earth? Surely she wouldn't go to all this trouble just to retrieve a forgotten sun visor. "All right," Aki had replied. Then, out of nowhere, a thought flashed across his mind: *Maybe she's been with Liu Hong.* She went missing because she was in Jiangsu. Public security got word that Liu Hong was there. Naturally they'd be keeping a watchful eye on her. Could they have learnt of Liu Hong's whereabouts by following her? But in that case they would have arrested him. Which meant that she went to Jiangsu and back without being able to see him. Having failed in that attempt, she was coming to see Aki instead. The logic was imperfect, but his thoughts took that course. At least the story made a certain sense. What kind of sense, he couldn't have said.

He checked the wall clock. Already five minutes had passed. Without further delay, grabbing the sun visor off the sofa, he opened his room door; at a normal pace, he stepped out and proceeded down the corridor. He exchanged a few words with the woman at the service counter and got in the elevator.

The hotel was located at the foot of Garden Bridge, between Zhapu Road and Da Changzhi Road. As Aki pushed his way through the revolving door and stepped out onto the fogbound street, a young man came towards him, appearing suddenly from Zhapu Road on the right. As Aki stepped aside to let him pass, the youth stopped.

"Mr Waki," he said.

It took two full seconds for Aki to penetrate Li Xing's disguise. Wearing pale green sunglasses and a stylish dark blue drape suit, she was got up as Han Langen, his father, the one who was younger than his son. As this sank in, he felt a rush of admiration for her. More than that, he found her irresistible.

With slight affectation he coughed twice and then said in Japanese, purposely loud enough to be overheard, "Hey! Long time no see." He clapped a hand on her shoulder. His fingers and the final syllable of the phrase both trembled. Quickly they pushed through the revolving door and went inside. The doorman and the security guard patrolling the lobby glanced their way briefly, without apparent suspicion.

Recognizing the sun visor in Aki's hand, Li Xing smiled wryly. When he began to steer her towards a sofa in the lobby, she said in a low voice, "Your room." His heart beat hard with presentiment. Her disguise was a tribute to her powers of acting, but this was no time for admiration. Irresistible or not, she was up to some game. First he had to find out what it was. The day before yesterday, she'd slid into his car out of the blue. Tonight she showed up on his doorstep dressed as a man.

Eyes all around them were sharp. The least sign of hesitation or friction would attract notice. They moved along briskly and stopped at the elevators.

"Okay then, I'll show you some samples upstairs," Aki said loudly in Japanese as he pushed the elevator button.

They were alone in the elevator, and fortunately could zoom up to the fifteenth floor nonstop. He kept turning the situation over in his mind until the elevator doors opened.

At the service counter was an employee on a new shift. Aki gave her a cheery smile and a nod. She nodded back and then looked straight at Li Xing, but there was no follow-up. To Aki the distance down the corridor to his suite seemed twice as far as usual.

He stood before the door. Inserted the key in the keyhole. She too had stood like this, opening her door, he thought. The door swung inward. There, it had opened outward. He reached out and switched on the light. She'd gone alone into her room and left him standing there, shutting the door in his face. *The door she shut, I'm now opening.*

Li Xing stepped cautiously inside. The door shut. Aki swiftly locked it. They were alone together in the same room.

Even with the door locked, service personnel could easily unlock it with their own key and come barging in at any time; but he let out a long, deep breath anyway. Li Xing saw this. Aki was unaware of being seen. He offered her the sofa, and remained standing. She made no move to sit down, but took off her sunglasses and then hesitated, not knowing where on her person to put them; she wasn't used to carrying sunglasses, or to wearing that suit, either. Aki for his part was still holding onto the sun visor. He too was stuck, unable to think what to do with the damn thing. Its large, racetrack-style visor was almost the same colour as her sunglasses, he noticed. He felt like a total jackass. His heart was pounding like a drum.

The TV was still on. The news bulletin over, the acrobatics show had resumed. Two giant pandas were starting to do tricks. *She and I and two pandas, all together now.* Nothing made sense. He tossed the sun visor onto the sofa.

"Please sit down," he said. "Otherwise I can't hear properly what you have to say." He busied himself making tea, with his back to her. Silently, in the interim, she brought her own breathing under control.

"Here you go."

"Thank you," she said in a small voice, and finally sat down beside the sun visor. It tilted and swayed like a leaf. Swept again by apprehension, she kept darting glances at the performing pandas.

"So where'd you go off to, after getting separated from the others again? You look terrific, by the way. The beautiful young woman impersonating a man. None of the hotel guards or service people caught on, and they must be pretty good at seeing through disguises."

His attempt at jocularity backfired, coming out like sarcasm. The bedroom door stood ajar. He hurried over to close it.

"Shall I turn off the TV?" he said. It wouldn't be long before the news came back on. Then the three of them would be together in this room – himself and Li Xing and Liu Hong. No thanks. He switched off the set and turned around to face her.

As was only to be expected from an actress trained in the People's Liberation Army Song and Dance Troupe, her stride and gestures as they cut hurriedly through the lobby and came down the corridor had been credibly masculine, enough to carry off the masquerade. But once they came in the room and he saw her sitting still on the sofa in the bright light, unable to hide her nervousness, her appearance was unmistakably feminine, the contrast with her getup almost comic.

"Jasmine tea," she said with pleasure, lifting the teacup lid.

"I bought it here at the hotel. It's nothing special."

Li Xing shook the drops from the lid with easy grace, and took a long, slow sip. He liked the sound she made.

"Mmm, it's good."

She was sitting on the side of the sofa nearest the door, the left side of her body pressed against the armrest. Aki was seated diagonally across from her, on the edge of a chair three meters away. Li Xing tilted her head and looked at him with a wan smile. He meant to look away, but instead looked at her harder. For some time now she'd been eyeing the telephone on the big desk. Finally she worked up the courage to ask, "May I borrow your phone?"

"Certainly, help yourself."

"It's long distance."

"That's fine."

So she was here to make a long-distance phone call. This explanation satisfied him just a little. A call to Liu Hong?

She put on the sun visor, stood up and, moving swiftly over to the desk, scooped up the receiver. After pressing the buttons with some care, she stood waiting, biting her lower lip, face a blank. No one was answering. Aki swallowed hard and waited. She moved the receiver away from her mouth, covered the mouthpiece with her hand, and said, "It's really hard for us to call long distance. But—"

Just then the other person came on the line.

"*Nainai*! It's me, Xingxing."

So it wasn't Liu Hong. With lowered voice, sounding out of breath, she began to talk to her far-off grandmother.

"I'm so glad I got through. Sorry, I wanted to come home, but I couldn't. Yes, yes, I'm fine. So public security did come. *Nainai*, do you remember my father's cricket box? That's right, the one I gave you before I came to Shanghai. Yes, that's it. Then it's safe. Great! The hollow in the walnut tree? I remember. You hid it there, good. But I want you to do something else for me now. Take out everything inside, the notebook and the letters, and burn them right away. Yes, all of them. Right away. Be sure now."

Li Xing abruptly broke off and transferred the receiver from her right hand to her left, holding it now to the other ear. At the same time, she tucked some stray wisps of hair behind her ear.

"*Nainai*, goodbye. Be careful. No, I'm all right. Don't worry…"

Gently, as if setting a block of tofu in water, she laid the receiver back in its cradle. Aki was leaning against the wall by the window.

She went back to the sofa and curled up gracefully, then asked if she could have a glass of water.

Aki took a bottle of Perrier out of the refrigerator, poured some into a glass, and handed it over. Slowly, she drank half of it down in one breath.

"That was my grandmother. She's all I have now. It was a relief to talk to her."

"Won't they be listening in?" He meant this half jokingly, but she nodded calmly and gave a serious reply.

"I know, but even if they are, I think it's all right. She's a very courageous woman. Before they can get there, even now, she'll be setting fire to the cricket box."

"Miss Li..." said Aki, haltingly.

"Xingxing. Please, call me Xingxing."

"Xingxing..."

"That's right. That's what I call myself. 'Good for you, Xingxing,' or, 'No, no, Xingxing.' My *nainai* calls me that, and so did my parents."

And Liu Hong, he thought, but didn't say it aloud.

Leaving the wall by the window, he crossed the room with his arms still folded. She followed him casually with her eyes. As she did this, for the first time she was able to take a good look around.

"What a huge place. And the bedroom is separate. May I take a peek?"

"Be my guest."

She opened the bedroom door and peered in cautiously without going inside.

"Lovely. You're staying here alone? The *yaodong* we live in has four rooms, but this is bigger. Ten people could live here easily. Goodness, what big beds!"

She quickly withdrew, gently closing the door behind her. Aki stood next to the sofa, looking at her. She cast her eyes down.

"A *yaodong*?" he said. "I'd like to see one of those sometime. I know — we can pretend this is one."

"Lovely. A cave in the sky."

Diffidently, thinking in a corner of his brain, *This isn't what I really want to ask at all*, he said, "Did you ever hear of anyone Japanese out there?"

"Anyone Japanese... you mean, your father?"

"Yes, somewhere on the Loess Plateau."

Li Xing bent her head slightly, thinking. "The plateau is enormous. We used to live in Beijing, but at the time of the Cultural Revolution my parents were forced to move. My father was sent to Yangquan, my mother to Longzhong – on the east and west sides of the plateau. The distance between them was 1,300 kilometres. But how did your father—"

"Never mind, it's all right. The information's unreliable. Let's see, the distance between you and me right now is what, five metres? One two-hundred-and-sixty-thousandth of the distance that separated your parents."

"You did that awfully fast!"

"Mental calculation is my specialty," he said, shortening the distance by a meter. "Now it's one three-hundred-and-twenty-five-thousandth."

"Don't shorten it any more, please. I have to be going. But can I ask you just one question?"

From the safe distance of four metres, Aki nodded and smiled at her. Yet he felt as if he stood on the edge of a cliff.

"Are you a Japanese spy?"

His smile stiffened. "Good grief! I wondered what you would ask. Sorry, the answer's no."

"I'm not joking. I heard you worked for a Japanese intelligence agency."

"Who told you such a crazy thing?"

"I got it from one of the most reliable sources in the country. After all, you're not here on business, and you've chosen to come over alone at a particularly tricky time. You *must* be here to probe something or other. You said yourself you've been conducting some sort of investigation…"

"I see. Public security told you."

"I thought if you were a Japanese spy, I could trust you. That's why I—"

"How so?"

"My enemy's enemy is my friend. That's what they say."

"It's not that simple. Miss Li, I'm afraid you—"

"Xingxing."

"Then, Xingxing. You're making a mistake. There are no spies in Japan."

"Why not? They're everywhere here."

"Japan has no army."

"That's not true."

"Yes, it is. And it's Japan's policy not to have state secrets. Even if we do, we like to think that we don't. So in principle, there's no need for us to probe the secrets of other countries. You could say I've come from the country with the least secrets in the world to the country with the most."

"Having secrets gives you an advantage."

"So does getting hold of other people's. It takes more energy to maintain a secret than it does to let it go. What about in our case?"

"What about it?" Her expression didn't flicker. A pause. "I see. Well, too bad you're not a spy. Your father was one. And I'm playing the part of one."

"Sorry to disappoint you."

Aki put down the cup in his hand without looking at it and, trying to seem casual, said, "I've got one question – no, two – for *you*, if you don't mind."

She smelt so good. Where did it come from? Was it the clothes next to her skin? He was on the point of remembering something, but the fragment of memory vanished.

"Yesterday and today, where were you?"

"Public security. Yesterday morning I tried to board a plane for Taiyuan, so I could go home to get the cricket box. I got as far as the boarding gate at Shanghai Airport before they caught me."

"Did they give you a hard time?"

She shook her head, moving slowly along the wall. As he followed her progress, her shadow on the wall revealed plainly that she wasn't a man. He would dearly have liked to uncover the soft, very feminine body beneath the borrowed clothes.

"Is the box really so important? Then call her back. I'll make some coffee. Not instant, either."

"I can't drink coffee. Keeps me from sleeping. You shouldn't bother. But I will tell you about it."

She sat down again on the sofa. Seeing her settle back against the cushion, legs tucked up neatly on one side, Aki thought that yes, a sofa was something only a woman should ever sit on.

"The box contained my diary and letters. It belonged to my father. His only hobby was *qiudou*, or 'autumn fighting.' Do you know what that is?"

He shook his head.

"Cricket fighting. It used to be all the rage, and people would bet money on it. My father was a scholar, so he raised crickets to listen to them sing, mostly, and only entered them in fights every now and then. There are lots of props involved. Mostly tickling implements, things that are used to get the crickets to sing or fight. The handles are made out of ivory or bone or reed, with mouse or jackrabbit whiskers attached, or the soft throat hairs of Kashmir goats. Isn't it strange – tickling implements? He kept a whole set of them in his precious cricket box. The box is made of rosewood. After he died, I used it as a letter box."

Just before leaving for Shanghai to audition for *Moving Shadows*, she'd gone back on a rare visit to Yangquan and entrusted the box to her grandmother. It contained letters from Liu Hong and copies of her letters to him, as well as her diary. After the audition, whatever the outcome, she'd intended to go back there to retrieve it. Fortunately, she passed the audition and was chosen for the lead role. Then, just as she was making plans for a triumphant return home, the Tiananmen Square massacre took place. Immediately, severe restrictions were placed on travel, leaving her stuck in Shanghai. But Shanghai Film Studio's involvement in the local democracy movement at least gave her access to information not reported in the newspapers or on TV.

In May, the steering committee of the students, workers, and intellectuals gathered in Tiananmen Square had drawn up a membership list of the organization.

On the night of 3rd June, after martial law troops had opened fire, one person bravely returned to the headquarters tent in the square to burn and destroy that list. It was Liu Hong. That list was what Mango was after, more than anything. Ever since the uprising, Mango's greatest fear was that various democratization groups would unite in a national organization. The Party and the government issued nationwide orders to round up all suspected of having the slightest connection with them, to search their homes, and to confiscate any such lists. The hunt was already underway in Shanghai, and some people at the film studio had been detained and subjected to house searches.

Liu Hong's letters to Li Xing were basically silly love letters, with occasional unguarded references to comrades' names or the existence of an underground movement. Open criticism of Mango was scattered throughout. "What they've done over the past forty years is as bad as Hitler and Stalin, if not worse." That sort of thing.

Mango was bound to search the dormitory of her old song and dance troupe, as well as her old home in Yangquan. Her grandmother knew nothing about it. How to get word to her?

Use of the one telephone in the studios from which long-distance calls could be made was strictly limited, and kept under constant surveillance, while any mail she sent would inevitably be intercepted at the local post office. Her only hope was to beat them to Yangquan. Frantic, hoping somehow to board the local plane, she had gone to Shanghai Airport.

Li Xing told him all this in beautiful Mandarin, but her Japanese was almost as good, he knew. "Where'd you learn your Japanese?" he asked.

"At home."

"You learnt to speak Japanese at home?"

"Yes. My mother wasn't a native Japanese like Zheng Pinru's mother, but she was born and raised there. She died, though."

Her hand was on the doorknob. Aki cut her off.

"You mustn't go out first, alone."

"Sorry."

"I'll call you a cab. The same one as before. I'll do it now, so please wait."

"No, I'll walk. It's safer. Chinese women are great walkers. The sun visor would stand out, though, so may I leave it here?"

"Of course. But no walking. It's an hour and a half from here to the studio. I'd worry."

Quickly, Aki rang Chen on his pager. There was an immediate response, and although the driver seemed a bit out of sorts, he agreed to be at the hotel in fifteen minutes.

Her hand still on the doorknob as she turned to look at him, Li Xing was back in character as a young man.

"Xingxing, your sunglasses."

She'd forgotten them. Flustered, unable to remember what she'd done with them, she searched all her pockets with no luck. When this happens it's best to look somewhere farther away, Aki told her. He walked over to the desk, promptly found them by the telephone, and brought them back for her.

"Xingxing, one word of advice. Your disguise is perfect, but I think you should use it only at night."

She gave him a quizzical look over the rims of her sunglasses.

"In the daytime, I'm afraid you couldn't fool anyone. Your skin is too good. It stands out at a distance more than any makeup – beautiful bare skin."

"Thank you."

They went down to the lobby without incident. As she was getting into the cab, for a second she made as if to lean lightly against his shoulder.

A half hour later, Chen phoned to report that he had delivered the passenger safely to the film studios. A bit unusual to see a young Japanese guy staying in that neighbourhood, he added, apropos of nothing.

8

What if I fall in love? He awoke with this thought on his mind. He got out of bed and leant out the window, where in the park across the river he could see a group of people doing their *tai chi* exercises. He was unable to take his eyes off the intricate, ever-changing, elegant motions. However Communism and bureaucracy might impinge on the national consciousness, the people of this country possessed something you could only call a different kind of freedom, an untrammelled spirit all their own. You could see it in their painting and calligraphy, too.

He spent a pleasant while at the window, his sleepiness wearing off. Then he headed to the studio in Chen's car. The unexpected news that his father had been tried as a Chinese traitor and escaped severe punishment only by steadily repeating the words *Wang le* had come as a shock. Xie Han knew other things about his father, too. More revelations would be forthcoming. One intriguing question was the unfinished screenplay: what shape would it take in tracing the arc of his father's life? Zheng Pinru was doomed to execution, but what would be the end of Han Langen?

Yet his main interest, the real reason he was on his way there, lay elsewhere: Would Li Xing show up at work today?

Chen was again the Chen of three days ago – irritable, preoccupied. Aki fell in with his mood.

At the studio there was no sign of the director, and rehearsals were proceeding under his deputy's guidance. Li Xing was there. Yet she neither greeted Aki nor looked his way. Following instructions in a memo left by Xie Han, she was being made to practice acting with her eyes alone. "There are no scenes of high emotion," Xie Han had written. "For a female spy, only the eyes count."

Yu Ming walked around commenting out loud to no one in particular that since her return, Xingxing was prettier than ever – had she been with her boyfriend?

Yes, she was with me, he would have liked to say out loud.

Even when she had a break, Li Xing stood laughing and talking with other cast and crew members, continuing to ignore his presence. He could only console himself with the unlikely explanation that this might be an extension of "acting with the eyes." To top it all off, while he was having a word with the actor playing his father, she left the studio.

Aki almost wondered if her coming to his hotel in disguise the night before might have been a figment of his imagination – the way she materialized so suddenly out of nowhere, just like the time she showed up outside his taxi.

Rehearsals soon got underway again, and Li Xing reappeared. Aki stood watching with a thoughtful air, taking everything in.

Her style of acting was by no means professional. Yet, she had a quality unmatched by any actress in Japan. Beyond any question of talent or skill, all Chinese actresses, not only Li Xing, gave performances invigorated by a determination to relive their lives differently through cinema. It took guts to do what they did. He looked on in fascination.

He hung around for two hours. Then Yu Ming reported that although the director had planned to come in today, that was looking less and less likely. So Aki gave up and left.

For a while Chen drove east on Hengshan Road. Around where it merged with Huaihai Road, he began frequently checking his rear-view mirror.

"Something wrong?"

"That black Peugeot behind us – the kind they make in Guangzhou, they're always breaking down. It's following us. The number plate is public security."

Aki turned to look through the rear window. A slanting ray of light on the windshield of the Peugeot obstructed his view of the driver.

"I don't know – you think so?"

Chen nodded with conviction. Aki felt his mouth go dry. They entered the long tunnel of plane trees.

"What do I do?" asked Chen.

"Try to shake it. That way we'll know for sure."

JASMINE

Aki was only half serious, and he didn't think the man had that much nerve, but suddenly Chen gave the wheel a sharp tug left and they plunged into a side road. Lining it were the dark brick walls of the former French Concession.

"The car is still there."

Aki turned to see the black Peugeot coming up directly behind them. Then, *clunk*, it hit them. Chen honked his horn and stopped the car. The Peugeot slipped past on one side and sped off with a squeal of tires. In the front passenger seat was the man who'd been in the bar of the Metropole Hotel.

Chen got out, went around to the back, and bent down, running a finger along the place where they'd been hit. He reported little or no damage. Collisions like this were a commonplace of life in Shanghai, he said, usually resolved with a brief row and the exchange of a few bills. This time the other driver was clearly in the wrong. Chen could only cluck his tongue in protest.

The collision meant that the level of surveillance had been ratcheted up a few notches. What Li Xing had said suddenly seemed more plausible. But him, a Japanese spy? It was crazy. His protest was like Chen's, but done silently.

This was a warning. No sooner did he have any contact with Li Xing than they came up and growled in his ear. The idea of being treated as a spy was ludicrous, but in terms of his involvement with Li Xing, he'd probably better take the message seriously: *Don't tangle with her.*

At the thought he smiled dryly. It was as if they were acting at Liu Hong's bidding. *Hands off my woman.* Maybe this was the answer to the question tantalizing him: What would happen if he fell in love with a stranger, a Chinese?

He remembered something his friend Shuichi once shared with him: "To stay safe in a despotic country, you have to do two things: keep under the radar of the authorities and stay away from local women."

Even an intrepid international scoop artist like Shuichi, who'd come unscathed through countless scenes of havoc, claimed that the night he was chased by bicycle-riding public security officials in Beijing, his heart nearly stopped. Bicycles? "That's right, ordinary two-wheelers. But they came flying out all around me from alleys in the *hutong*, chasing after me with their bells ringing. It was intense, man."

As the taxi started up again, Aki sat back, rigid with tension. Here, too, the gnarled branches of tall plane trees lining the road reached out and intertwined overhead, forming a long arch that stretched into the distance, supported by a colonnade of thick trunks mottled white and green. Peeping out from between the trees were the elegant old buildings with peaked roofs of the French Concession. A dense, scruffy crowd flowed by in the street and on the sidewalks. On wires strung between the trees, clothespins held up newspapers and gaudy magazines for sale – among them *New Star*, the one in whose pages Chen had read about Li Xing.

Chen slammed on the brakes, just avoiding a man who'd run out into the street, ignoring a traffic signal. Small and middle-aged, in a white, open-necked shirt, the man banged furiously on the hood and held out an index finger, pointing, while he yelled something unintelligible. The finger was aimed not at Chen, but at Aki.

Chen stuck his head out the window and bawled at him while blasting away on the horn. The man jumped up on the hood but was just as quickly flung off onto the ground. Aki looked back to see that he'd picked himself up and was again pointing straight at him.

He closed his eyes. The streets of Shanghai, once so friendly and welcoming, had been transformed. Hostility and intimidation filled them now.

They had crossed Garden Bridge and were just pulling up in front of the hotel when the oppressive atmosphere was broken by a sudden burst of rain. A haze arose from the pavement and from the surface of the river. They were caught unawares.

"It's a *baoyu*!" A downpour. All around, muffled voices flew back and forth. Aki felt a sudden urge to drink with Chen tonight.

"Why not come on up, have one for the road?"

Chen again begged off. "I have to pick up Anli at the hospital."

"Who's that?"

"My brother's wife."

"Oh. Is he still bad?"

"It's a long illness."

After expressing his sympathy, Aki went through the revolving door into the lobby, shutting out the sound of the rain behind him.

Back in his rooms, he opened the window, and the furious sound of pelting rain returned. Thinking that this deluge might serve to contain the hostility in Shanghai's streets, he breathed a little easier.

As he leant against the narrow cast-iron frame of the window, which reached almost to the ceiling, the part next to his bare skin felt cold. The frame had been here since 1934, when the building was erected, close on sixty years ago. Apparently, the more years that piled up in a substance, the colder it felt to the touch.

A ship's foghorn sounded, unexpectedly loud and close. A wind sprang up and raindrops dashed against the window frame, ricocheting on into the room. The tieback on the curtain came loose and the curtain billowed out like a sail. For an instant Aki had the illusion that he was back on board ship. Where was this ship taking him?

Behind him, he thought he heard two or three light raps on the door. Hastily he closed the window and stood still, listening. Nothing.

He fell asleep on the sofa. When he first woke up, he didn't know where he was, and his eyes shifted restlessly like a baby's. As he was a traveller in an unfamiliar place, and as he had dozed off in the evening, it took a few seconds for him to reorient himself. It was now pitch dark, with no letup in the rain.

A light knock came at the door. It sounded the same as before. Hotel employees, when they bothered to announce themselves, always rang the doorbell, which had a sharp, intimidating sound. Who would knock? Director Xie? Maybe Chen had driven his sister-in-law home from the hospital and was ready now for that drink.

Aki tiptoed over and waited for the next knock to come, but there wasn't another sound. Perhaps the knocking had been at some other door.

He opened the door a crack, and recognized the sopping wet figure of the "man" from the previous day. He let "him" into the room, swiftly closing and locking the door.

"I made it." Li Xing was carrying a black suitcase in her right hand. Rainwater was dripping from her coat and the suitcase. "I don't think anyone followed me."

"Why didn't you take an umbrella?"

He could have kicked himself for this idiotic question. Awkwardly, he fled into the bathroom and brought out all the big and little towels he could lay hold of.

"Thanks."

Li Xing set her suitcase down and dried off her hair, bending her head to left and right. Aki took her coat and hung it on the bathroom door, then went behind the sofa to the window and looked down. At a short distance from the hotel, on the bank of Suzhou Creek, was the black Peugeot.

"Looks like you *were* followed."

This was a slightly smarter remark. Yet for all he knew he might be the one the car was tailing.

With a towel wrapped around her hair, Li Xing came over and stood next to him. There it was again, that scent, so hauntingly familiar.

"See the black Peugeot down there? It belongs to the foreign affairs section of public security. It rammed my car on purpose earlier, coming back from the studio."

Li Xing only nodded slightly, without evident surprise. A smile played on her lips.

She's not afraid of being followed, he thought. *I'm the one who's scared. Who knows? Maybe she's not even afraid of the people who run this country.*

"Did you come and knock before?"

"No."

Avoiding eye contact, he stared down at the suitcase on the floor, from which drops of water still trickled hesitantly.

"I'm moving," she said

So frank and casual was her tone that Aki responded automatically, "Oh, where to?"

"Here."

Here? he parroted under his breath, and glanced around. Then, finally, he looked her in the eye. She nodded, wide-eyed. He was left with a strong impression of eyelashes fringing dark pupils.

She turned off the floor lamp she was standing next to. Her figure floated, wraithlike. A moment later there was another click, and amid the soft, new, reborn light, she said, "I need help.

Please help me. Let me stay here. I'm counting on your kindness and friendship."

"What is this, a movie?" Shaken, he could think of nothing else to say.

"No." She shook her head and said in a small voice, "This is real." She used the English word. It sounded like a line of movie dialogue. Aki's supply of words, meanwhile, was drying up. He said stiffly, "You'll catch cold like that."

Li Xing opened her suitcase, took out a change of clothes, and disappeared into the bathroom. While she was gone he made a pot of jasmine tea. His hands shook slightly.

Friendship, he muttered to himself, as he listened to the faint hum of a hair dryer coming from the bathroom. *This is real.*

And so began their strange time together under one roof.

9

Li Xing's cricket box had contained dozens of letters – thirty-two from Liu Hong, sixty from her parents after they were relocated – as well as four volumes of her diary written in notebooks with ruled lines; the diary included copies of her letters to Liu Hong. All of this she'd been forced to tell her grandmother to destroy.

Sitting in her room in the studio guesthouse the day after her first visit to Waki Akihiko, she could only wonder: Had yesterday's call home been in time? Assuming that it had, she was gripped by sadness. Losing the letters and diary showed her what a mainstay they'd been. The earth at her feet had fallen steeply away, leaving her on the edge of a void.

Was there no way to retrieve the things that had been burned or confiscated in Yangquan? Then and there, she decided to salvage what she could by writing it down again herself. From the time she was a little girl, she'd prided herself on two things: her dancing and her powers of recall – yet now, faced with blank sheets of paper on which she was attempting to recover her past, she realized that memory was of all things most fallible.

What Li Xing had in mind was more than usually difficult. She was pursuing memories not of events but of the written word, trying to summon up and recreate long passages in their entirety. Nor was that the only problem she faced: there was also outside interference.

Recently there'd been signs that while she was off at rehearsals, someone was sneaking into her room and examining her notebooks. The guesthouse was run by a *bangongshi*, or general administration office. Every large workplace or work unit had its *bangongshi*, the primary responsibility of which was supervising the staff; it also had authority to issue work permits, which functioned as personal ID cards, as well as permits for domestic travel and so on. Anyone in the *bangongshi* had ready access to her room.

JASMINE

So when her director quietly passed on to her the news that Liu Hong was now close by, in Jiangsu, Li Xing thought hard. Needed urgently was a refuge, a place for her to focus quietly on writing and remembering. She turned her mind inside out in search of an answer, until one farfetched plan occurred to her: to move in with Waki Akihiko at his hotel.

It's my best chance, she told herself. *But would he let me do it – just to suit myself? He looked so smug and stuck-up at the afternoon rehearsal. Every inch the rich, intellectual Japanese. There in the studio, I toyed with the idea of asking him, but in the end I couldn't bring myself even to look him in the face. He'd only say no. What Japanese man would take that kind of risk for the sake of a Chinese girl? But then, the comedian Han Langen was Japanese, and he had a Chinese lover; Waki Akihiko is his son, and I'm Han's lover in the film... Doesn't this make us related in a way? Can't I somehow get through to him?...*

Outside her window, fat raindrops splashed onto the ground. A ring of oleanders swayed and rustled, red flowers peering like eyes from between the pointed leaves.

She looked abstractedly around. On one wall hung the suit she'd borrowed from the costume department. He'd been so accommodating yesterday when she wore it over to his place and phoned her *nainai*... But would it really be safe there? Two days ago, when they took her into custody at the airport and spent all day interrogating her, they'd told her flat out he was a spy. If that's what they thought, they'd be keeping an eagle eye on him, have easy access to his suite. All the same, she thought she'd be a little safer there than somewhere else.

Waki himself laughed off any such suggestion, treating it as a bad joke – something he could do only because he was Japanese and had never lived under an autocratic regime. The system wasn't something you could choose, nor could you choose to ignore it. When a regime was based on constant surveillance and informing, then any foreigner who exposed himself to it the way he had would inevitably be seen from a spy-like angle. He'd be continually watched, liable at any time to be arrested as an enemy spy or declared persona non grata, to be summarily deported or locked up.

Many Chinese resented the fact that Mao Zedong, in his haste to restore diplomatic ties with Japan, had abandoned claims to war reparations. A popular-level movement was underway to push for them. That such a groundswell might serve to increase discontent with Mango and develop over time into an organized antigovernment movement, joining forces with the push for democratization, was entirely possible. In some quarters the two activities in fact overlapped.

From the point of view of the authorities, Aki's firsthand research into ODA in China fully constituted an offensive activity by a foreigner. Surveillance of him had begun eighteen months ago.

Aki was under the impression that Li Xing had sneaked out of the guesthouse in disguise and come to the hotel unnoticed, yet actually lots of people at the studio saw her walking along without an umbrella, lugging a big suitcase, in the rain. Some were further baffled to see she was in costume, dressed not as Han Langen's lover but as Han himself. She didn't seem to be afraid of attracting attention – quite the contrary.

Meng, the properties man, jumped off his bicycle when he saw her and called, "Li Xing! Is that you? It's pouring!"

"Yes, it is, isn't it?" she returned loudly, in high spirits.

"Where're you off to in that getup?"

"Never you mind."

Her behaviour was eye-popping in its boldness. Yet Aki was aware that she was driven by neither love nor intrigue. Or rather it *was* love, he told himself reluctantly; it was all about her involvement with another man, and had nothing to do with him. His was a secondary, comic role.

Nevertheless, though nervous about this peculiar, unexpected situation, he was inclined to enjoy it, to lap up the sweet taste of adventure. Having come this far, he couldn't turn back, and he resolved not to do so. Not even if it meant ending up like his father.

There was no telling when a hotel employee might come barging in on them, so Li Xing kept up her male impersonation for the time being. With no particular business to attend to, without even knocking, hotel staff would bring out their long, heavy iron key – unchanged from sixty years ago – and rattle it in the keyhole. For anyone on the inside, this was unnerving. After opening the door a third of the way, they would call out politely, "*Xiansheng?*"

Aki decided, instead of dinner on the eighteenth floor, to go down to the snack bar in the lobby and pick up some instant ramen, crackers, and chocolate. That was all there was.

When he got back, Li Xing had changed into a shirt and a pair of his linen trousers, and was settled on the sofa. Dinner promised to be a meagre affair, but the combination of the things he'd bought and her own contribution of Yin Dan's jasmine tea made for a surprisingly pleasant meal. In the relaxed atmosphere of the room, she told him her reasons for imposing on him like this.

"Xingxing," he said eventually, "you can only go on pulling the wool over people's eyes here for a day and a half at best. You don't need to write out your diary right now, do you? Why not wait till the movie's finished, when your time is your own again and you can go wherever you want?" He said this pretending to believe her explanation, which he found only half convincing.

"No." She turned pleading eyes on him. "It has to be now. I'm afraid that if I don't do it now, I'll never be able to remember anything at all."

Her upper body swayed on the sofa. Aki got up and looked down out of the window. No sign of the Peugeot. Behind him, he sensed her getting up, moving off. He swung around to see her standing by the door, suitcase in hand. In a firm, almost harsh tone of voice, he said, "Stay here. You can use this desk all you want. And take the bedroom. It's yours. I'll sleep on the sofa."

For a fleeting second, he imagined her running toward him and throwing herself into his arms, but that of course didn't happen. It was another man she had come here for.

10

The next day, Li Xing could not get out of bed. Due to her soaking in the rain she'd caught a cold and was running a fever. This morning the Peugeot was gone from its spot below the window. After straining to lift the receiver of the bedside phone, she had production manager Yu Ming paged, and then explained that she wanted to be excused from the day's rehearsals. As shed gone missing only recently, Yu Ming asked her where she was.

"I'm at Mr Waki's place in the Broadway Mansions Hotel," she answered boldly.

Her voice carried as far as a surprised Aki in the anteroom.

Yu Ming told her to get better soon and hung up. Then she turned to assistant director Gao Yong, who had just walked into the room, and whispered, "Xingxing's taking the day off with a cold. Want to hear something interesting? She's dumped her boyfriend for a Japanese moneybags. She's such a sweet-looking thing – you never can tell about people, can you? It goes with being an actress, I guess, that sort of cheek. People will talk, but I doubt if she'll end up committing suicide the way Ruan Lingyu did."[1]

When he returned to Studio Four, Gao Yong passed the news on to the crew. The director had not yet arrived.

Meanwhile, Li Xing swallowed some Japanese cold medicine Aki gave her and slept for a couple of hours before getting up. Her fever had gone down. She changed into a bright orange dress, abandoning the masquerade, and with visible pleasure tucked into a sandwich Aki had ordered from room service. A maid came in, her presence

---

[1] A prominent Chinese silent film actress in the 1930s who took her life at the age of twenty-five after vindictive coverage in the press compounded by personal problems.

giving Aki the jitters, but Li Xing lost no time in smoothly engaging the woman in familiar conversation.

Then she made a pot of Yin Dan's tea, and the two of them drank it together. Notebook and ballpoint pen in hand, she indicated the wicker chair by the window and asked, "Would it be all right to move that chair into the other room? I don't think I'd be able to relax at the desk."

Aki immediately picked up and carried the chair into the bedroom, setting it down between two windows.

"There you are."

"Thanks."

When she sat down, the chair creaked pleasantly. Yesterday's rain having cleared up, the sky over Shanghai was serene and blue for the first time in a while. Li Xing quietly spread out the notebook in her lap and, with an occasional glance at the portion of sky visible through the windows, set to work on the recreation of her lost letters and diary.

Aki sat on the sofa and opened his unfinished book of Arabic and Persian poetry. Page after page of compass poetry.

> *Beloved, you and I are a compass.*
> *Although we have two heads, we share one body.*
> *Although now we turn, describing a circle around a*
> *point,*
> *In the end we draw our heads together as one.*

For a brief spell, Aki forgot the situation he was in. Then, suddenly concerned that he'd heard nothing from his sister, he tried calling her at work. She had quit her job as of yesterday. In the Ashiya apartment, her answering machine was still on. Had she run off to Belgrade in pursuit of Shuichi? *Those wicked thoughts will go away*, he had said. *How?* she had asked. *Give in to 'em*, he had told her.

Notebook in hand, Li Xing came into the room. "I'll make some tea."

Yin Dan's jasmine tea again. The marvellous smell of it spread throughout the room.

"Making any progress?"

"So-so." She put a hand to one cheek and shook her head. "Who did you call, your wife?"

"My wife died six years ago."

"I'm sorry…"

"I've all but forgotten her. There's the ambience she left behind, that's all."

"Ambience… I see. I think that's what I need in my writing, too. What are you reading?"

Aki showed her the thick book and read aloud the compass poem he'd just come across. Quietly she let the notebook slide out of her hand.

"I told you a little bit about my dad, didn't I?" said Aki.

She looked him in the eye and nodded. The compass poem was still echoing in her head. *In the end we draw our heads together as one.*

"He was arrested as a Chinese, under the name Han Langen, and tried as a traitor. During the trial, they say he answered every charge with *Wang le*, claiming he'd forgotten."

"Purposely?"

"Probably."

"I wonder. Because I can't remember even yesterday very well… Actually, it's funny that we do remember what happens to us every day. Even things that happened hours ago."

"That's true. There is something mysterious about the ability to remember. Xingxing, you aren't making much progress, are you?"

She looked down and leafed through the pages. Aki also took a casual look and then exclaimed in surprise, "It's in Japanese!"

Again she put a hand to her cheek and smiled. "Yes, didn't I tell you? I write my diary in Japanese."

"I didn't know. That's really amazing. How is it that your Japanese is so good, again?"

"My mother was a Chinese born and raised in Japan, a *huaqiao*. Didn't I mention that?"

"Yes… But don't tell me her name was Xiaolan."

"It was. How did you know?"

"And she was born in Kobe…"

"Yes. But why?"

"Your grandfather's name is Xu Liping. I know him very well."

"What? That's incredible! I have no idea what he even looks like."

Just as Xu Liping's mother had said that night in Teite on Tor Road, holding a handkerchief with Shantou embroidery to the corner of her eye, Xu Liping's second daughter Xiaolan had left Japan for China soon after graduating from Kobe College.

The founding of the People's Republic of China on 1st October 1949, sparked a growing trend among overseas Chinese to participate in the building of a new homeland. Among young *huaqiao* in Japan with hopes pinned on a new China, return to the fatherland became immensely popular, and many made the journey over the protests of their parents and other family members. Japan and China did not have diplomatic relations then, and there was no direct sea route between the two countries, so returnees jumped aboard repatriation ships dispatched by the Japanese government to bring home Japanese left behind at the end of the war. Between 1953 and 1959, 3,754 *huaqiao* returned to China on board these ships. Of that number, 675 were from Kobe. Most were young. Among them was Xiaolan. With few exceptions, they subsequently endured the Cultural Revolution and, simply for being returnees from Japan, were branded as antirevolutionary and subjected to ugly, harrowing experiences.

"Your grandfather is alive and well in Kobe," Aki told her. His voice shook a little. "He doesn't know about his daughter's death, and he certainly doesn't know he has a granddaughter named Li Xing."

Her mother had given her strict training in Japanese and, during the Cultural Revolution when the family was split up by relocation, sent regular reminders never to forget the language. Her mother had wanted her to write letters in Japanese, but this wasn't permitted.

Li Xing looked down and began to scribble in her notebook.

"Did your mother tell you anything about Kobe?"

Li Xing held out the page for him to see. He read aloud: "Rokko, Arima Spa, Suma Temple, Kobe College Chapel, Awaji puppets… ah yes, *joruri*."

"*Joruri?*"

"Puppet plays. Awaji Island is between Osaka Bay and the Seto Inland Sea – the second biggest of Japan's lesser islands, and the birthplace of puppet theatre in Japan. Someone must have taken your mother to see it when she was a little girl."

"Is it still going on?"

"Oh, yes. There's just one troupe left, though. It's not what it used to be."

The telephone rang. It was Xie Han, wanting Aki to come over to the studio.

"All right," he said, his eyes on Li Xing's face. "Right away?"

"No, not this minute. Toward evening would be better. How about five or so?"

"I'll be there."

Li Xing quickly realized who the call was from, and when Aki hung up she said worriedly, "It must be something about me."

Aki gave a noncommittal answer and looked at the wall clock. Still plenty of time before five. Checking out the window, he saw that the black Peugeot had returned. He lit his first cigarette of the day and blew smoke into the sultry air by the window, wondering as he did so whether they knew that Li Xing was with him. No way they wouldn't know a thing like that, he had to accept.

He tried several times to summon Chen on his pager but got no reply, so he was obliged to take one of the taxis camped out in front of the hotel. As they slid past the Peugeot he peered inside, but saw no one there, nor was he followed.

"Have a seat," said Xie Han in his office, indicating a small round stool. An air conditioner taking up half the window was rattling away, but the air in the room remained warm and damp. Aki looked at the director, feeling tense. Xie's jaw was dark with five-o'clock shadow.

"Xingxing has unloaded herself on you, I understand." There was an ironic undertone to this.

"Unloaded herself?"

"You must find it inconvenient."

"Not at all. I discovered she's the granddaughter of a friend of mine."

"Is that right? Who?"

Aki gave a concise account of the connection.

"Huh. That explains why her Japanese is so good. By the way, I've found out something about your father."

"Is he alive?"

"Very much so. What Tao said was true. He's in a kind of prison out in Jixian."

"Tao? Who's that?"

"The man I wrote you about before, the one who escaped from there to Shanghai."

"So he really is on the Loess Plateau."

Xie nodded. "It was 1955 when your father came back to Shanghai after the war, wasn't it? Someone sent for him."

"Who?"

"Zheng Pinru."

"That's impossible! She was executed way before that, by Agency 76 and the Japanese."

"She was alive. All along, that was the rumour. Supposedly, somebody else was executed in her place. But nobody knows for sure. She was alive, and *she* asked Han Langen – is it all right if I call him by his Chinese name?"

"Of course. After all, he became a Chinese comic."

"Han Langen was urged to come back to Shanghai by Zheng Pinru. That was his story. Whether she was the one who really contacted him, who can say? From her supposed execution in 1940 to this day, no one has ever seen her alive. It might have all been a setup. In any case, after that he went to Beijing, got arrested on suspicion of spying, and was imprisoned without a trial. Do you know about Ito Ritsu?"

"Oh yes. It's a well-known story. A leader of the Japanese Communist Party, held for twenty-seven years in a Beijing prison. Word got out that he was long since dead, so when he finally came home, it caused quite a commotion."

It was on 3rd September 1980, that Ito had appeared in Narita Airport in his wheelchair. Aki had watched it on TV. Ito's two sons went to the airport to meet their father, who by then was deaf and nearly blind.

Xie Han turned melancholy eyes on his visitor. Having gone only one day without seeing him, Aki was struck by how much the man had aged overnight. What could have happened?

Yesterday he'd received a summons from an old friend in the central committee of the Shanghai Communist Party and, together with the results of the investigation regarding Waki Tanehiko he'd requested, had been given an order to cease filming *Moving Shadows*. Well, worse things can happen, he told himself. On either side of this event, the flow of days would continue with little change. As the song says, "Everyone dies, everyone dies…"

"After Zhou Enlai and Mao Zedong died one after the other in 1976," Xie said, "Deng Xiaoping was gradually rehabilitated, as you know, and Hu Yaobang became General Secretary of the Party. Hu set about clearing the names of people who were branded as antirevolutionary or as spies and killed or imprisoned at the time of the Cultural Revolution. He undertook a survey of all the prisons and labour camps around the country, granting amnesty to everyone confined on a trumped-up charge. In Qincheng Prison in Beijing they discovered a Japanese national named Ito Ritsu. Who was this? That's how Ito came to light. But there'd been another Japanese prisoner in Qincheng, before that. After leaving Qincheng, he was transferred from prison to prison over a period of years, and so he slipped through Hu's net. It's been established that a few years back he was moved to a secret prison in Jixian, near Hukou waterfall. The middle of nowhere. His cell is a cave carved into a cliff. They say he's still there…"

Xie Han stood up, went over to the window, and stood as if sunk in thought. When he returned, he said huskily, "They say he can't remember anything at all. Even his own name."

"He has two," put in Aki quickly, the statement a question. "Han Langen and Waki Tanehiko."

"Neither one. So of course he has no idea whether he's Japanese or Chinese, either. No identity."

"Like the Man in the Iron Mask," murmured Aki. "I want to get him out." The murmur was more of a groan.

"I know. But not now. That's not a place that ordinary people can easily get to at the best of times. And tension is running high just now. Long-distance travel is under strict limits for Chinese and foreigners alike. It would be different if Hu Yaobang, the reformer, were still around. He would've ordered an immediate investigation and done whatever it took to free him."

"Roughly, how do you get to Jixian?"

"It's about two hundred kilometres west of Linfen…"

Slowly Aki raised his head, a thought forming in his mind. "Even if they were both accused of spying," he said, "my father's case has got to be different from Ito's. After he went back to Japan, he had nothing to do with the Japanese Communist Party. Whether Zheng Pinru sent for him or somebody else, I can't believe the Japanese Communist Party smuggled him in, did they?"

Xie explained: "Back then, there were various routes. One was through the Japanese Communist Party, others were the intelligence agencies of the Chinese Communist Party, and then there was the *huaqiao* route, through overseas Chinese."

"The *huaqiao* route!" he couldn't help exclaiming.

Like a mole bringing up dark earth, he dredged up a memory – a remark his mother had once made: *Xu Liping and the others are very kind, but I can't get over the feeling that they're hiding something about your father's trip to Shanghai.*

"In Beijing, was my dad arrested because of the old prewar charge of spying?"

"No. That was already dealt with in the traitors' trial. And anyway, who was he spying for? Japan, the Comintern, the Kuomintang? No, it was something else. In a despotic regime, when they pin a crime on you it's always espionage. That's what happened in the Cultural Revolution… Tanehiko was lured back by someone claiming to be Zheng Pinru. Naturally, he was prepared to risk everything. He'd received a letter from the woman he loved, a woman he thought was dead. Even if he still had his doubts, he would – ah, I'm sorry, this whole episode must have been painful for you and your mother."

"It's all right," said Aki.

The melancholy in Xie's eyes deepened. "This is how I see it. Han Langen may indeed have forgotten everything, as he said at his trial, but *they* hadn't forgotten *him*. They asked him back, lured him back out of his quiet life. Something like that must have happened."

"Who is *they*?"

"The top echelon of Mango could be involved. I can't be specific, but even if I had some idea, in this country it's not possible to name names."

Aki lit a cigarette and said nothing until he'd smoked it through. With his mouth twisted out of shape, Xie stared down at a pool of sunshine on the desk. He looked as if he'd have liked to curl up in it.

"Is it true that no copies of my dad's films have survived?"

"Yes."

"Not one?"

"Not one."

"What about other Huaying films?"

"There may be a few. Some say the Kuomintang hid a large number of confiscated goods from Shanghai somewhere in Xian. They could be there. Nothing's turned up so far."

"Then why do you say that no copies of *his* films survived?"

"Because he destroyed them himself."

"My God." His head slumped, then slowly came up again. "Why do you think he ever became a comedian?"

"Hah! I was sure you were going to ask why he burned all his films." Xie Han closed his eyes. He seemed to be going to sleep. Yet when he spoke, his voice had strength in it:

"That era, from about 1930 till the mid-1940s, was a time of great folly. One would have expected an actor, under those circumstances, to choose a tragic role for himself. Only an exceptional man would choose comedy. The person who takes a hard look at things, who tries to think them through, is drawn to the comical side of human nature. He develops an apprehension – no, that's not right. What is the word…?"

Aki joined him in searching for it. "Acumen? We usually use it in a rather different sense." The Japanese word he suggested was used to describe a child reaching the age of discretion.

"Yes, good. Acumen."

"How would you say it in Mandarin?"

"*Dongshi*… So, the question is whether one passed through that period of great folly or without acquiring a certain acumen. Once when Tanehiko was drunk he told me: 'The ideal life would be to live in Shanghai embracing a woman, and one's conscience, with both arms.' He was a spy and a comedian, and on top of that he loved a female spy. Did anyone ever survive an age of folly with as much acumen as he did? And now, fifty years on, we're going through a similar time."

"You're not thinking of turning *Moving Shadows* into a comedy, by any chance?"

"Who knows what could happen?" The director sidestepped the question with a bitter smile, knowing the order to cancel the film was already in the works. "These things can only be understood, my friend, through the prism of experience. For a young Japanese like yourself, there may be no way to understand." He gave a small, reedy laugh. "The film's been stopped. The new general secretary used to be the mayor of Shanghai. A spy film set in Shanghai during the Japanese occupation, and not an out-and-out anti-Japanese film, either – it's not something he's likely to appreciate. Or so the city fathers have judged, and made their decision."

"Does Xingxing know?"

"No. Nobody does."

Aki dragged hard on the cigarette he'd lit. Exhaling smoke, he said with bleary eyes, "You say someone Japanese like me wouldn't understand. Has that got something to do with the question of war responsibility?"

"Nothing whatsoever. If it seems otherwise to you, go ahead – draw your own conclusions. My father was killed by a Japanese soldier in Nanjing. Responsibility is something that can only be verified through actual experience. In that sense, maybe I was thinking about that."

"You mean Japanese people haven't acknowledged their own responsibility?"

Xie Han neither nodded nor shook his head. Just then a roll of thunder sounded along the edge of the sky. The two men remained silent, listening.

"Let's all stop bandying words about. We Chinese are at fault, too. For one person to tell another forcibly not to forget this or that, and keep pushing for an apology, is undignified. Not that there's any reason to expect Mango to behave with dignity. I believe that true religion was devised to confer dignity on mankind.

The holiest rite in the Christian faith has to do with the removal of sins from the book of memory. And Buddhism teaches that in the final days, all the scriptures themselves will disappear. So there we are."

He changed the subject. "Incidentally," he wanted to know, "what in the world is Xingxing up to? What's she doing at your place? Is she smitten with you?"

"Hardly! I suppose she needed a quiet place to learn her lines in."

Xie took it for granted that the two were already lovers. And he hadn't the slightest intention of complaining about it. In fact, this development was one he was inclined to encourage. Even if the movie was cancelled, he'd like to see the actress he'd cast in the role of heroine fall in love with his old friend's son. Now that Liu Hong was on the move, heading this way, their story might actually be more exciting than the film.

"She learnt her lines long ago. Poor thing, when she hears the movie's been cancelled, she'll probably fall to pieces. Mr Waki, there may be trouble ahead. How will you cope?"

"With great acumen, I hope." Aki smiled weakly and stood up. "By the way," he added, "I insist on hosting a return dinner. I'd like to invite Yin Dan, too."

"Unfortunately, he's no longer around. He's hidden himself away somewhere. You must have noticed at our dinner the other night – the fellow's a master of sudden disappearances. And our cameraman Yang Jun was arrested last night."

Just then Yu Ming came bursting into the room without knocking. "There's been an order to cancel the film!" she announced, before noticing Aki, whom she greeted in surprise. Pursing her lips, she recomposed herself and said: "Xinxiang's caught a cold, has she? What's good for a cold is mushroom soup. The kind she needs is called silver wood ear. You can get it at Ronghuaji, and they have takeout, too. That's on Kunshan Road. It's a little out of your way, but do get her some."

Aki shook hands quickly with Xie Han.

"When are you leaving?"

"Not sure yet... as soon as possible. I do want to host that return dinner first, though."

"That's good of you. You should probably delay your search for your father, I'm afraid. As soon I can, I plan to go to Jixian myself. I'll let you know. And... tell Xingxing to come back soon."

"I will. Thanks."

He gripped him by the hand again, this time more tightly. The thought crossed his mind: *This may be the last time I ever see him.* It came from gripping his hand so tightly, he decided.

11

Do I want to meet my father? Aki asked himself. *No,* came the answer. There was something bogus in the notion of conducting a serious search for a father whose living face he could not recall. Why not act on the assumption he was dead? Better to forget about him. *Forget me.* His father's own words were borne to him on winds sweeping from the ends of the Loess Plateau. *I have forgotten myself. You forget me, too.*

Then why this desire to see the films of Han Langen? Hearing that not one foot of them remained had only spurred his interest.

It wasn't because of any interest in his father per se. Rather, he wondered about the kind of performances given by that Japanese youth turned Chinese comedian. What kind of vernacular did he speak, how did he eat, how did he spit? Questions like these aroused real curiosity in him.

His taxi arrived at Ronghuaji on Kunshan Road, the place Yu Ming had told him about. He got out, looked around, and saw to his surprise the back of his own hotel only a short distance away, rearing up.

Like a cathedral in a European town, the hotel with its distinctive setback silhouette was visible from almost everywhere. It looked like a great eagle that was either just landing or about to take wing.

Figuring it would only be a ten- or fifteen-minute walk back, he decided to dump his taxi.

The shop was crowded, and he had to stand at the end of a long line. Before him, in a file stretching all the way in, were some thirty customers. Another five or six pushed up behind him right away, shoving him forward. An array of smells filled the air, enveloping him: male sweat, female sweat, old cooking oil, face powder, rotten fruit, briquette smoke, and more.

"*Waihin! Hei, waihin!*" came the voice of the female owner. Everyone swung their heads to look at Aki. *Waihin.* Foreign guest. How could they tell he was a foreigner?

"We can't keep a *waihin* waiting. Come on up here," called the woman in a white chef's cap and jacket, beckoning. He took a diffident step forward.

"*Kuai, kuai.*" Hurry, hurry.

People all around raised their voices in encouragement, urging him on: "*Chin, chin.*" Please, go ahead. He got her to ladle some of their special mushroom soup into a large plastic container to go.

"Are you Japanese?"

"Yes."

"Well, our soup has cured plenty of Japanese colds, going way back. You're getting a special discount. Tell your wife to get better soon."

As he left the establishment with his soup, drops of rain began to fall. On the sidewalk, a fruit vendor was yelling at the top of his lungs: "*Mangguo! Mangguo!*" Aki paid for two mangoes, and as he took them, the patter of raindrops quickened. No sign of a taxi. He regretted having sent the other one away. Too late now.

Out of a dark, cave-like lane children came chasing after a soccer ball; by a steaming roadside ditch an old woman sat scrubbing out a *matong* potty. Clutching his soup and mangoes, Aki headed for the Broadway Mansions looming just ahead. Seen through the rain, it was dark and unprepossessing, like an old duffer. His suite was on the opposite side, overlooking the Bund. Li Xing was there now, sitting in the wicker chair with her notebook open in her lap, retrieving lost memories.

Tell your wife to get better soon. Aki repeated the words softly to himself, turning his face skyward. He could make out individual drops as they fell. Getting wet would be okay, he decided. Summer rain in Shanghai. For some reason it filled him with nostalgia. His father had bounded between the Metropole Hotel and Hamilton House in fifteen steps, dodging raindrops. Yet here he was walking slowly through the rain on his way to a woman on the fifteenth floor of his hotel, straight ahead, bearing mushroom soup and some nicely ripened mangoes.

Dark splotches on the newspaper bag holding the mangoes appeared, then more and more of them. A few drops fell also on top of the shiny persimmon-coloured fruit inside, and lingered there.

Feeling that he'd walked quite a way already, he looked up – to find the hotel no closer than before. It seemed in fact to have receded the exact distance that he had covered. He looked to his right and left. Without realizing it, he'd picked up an escort of two bicycles, one on either side. He quickened his pace, but they stayed with him. Casually, he checked the riders out; they were both wearing wide-brimmed plastic rain-hats and plastic raincoats over white open-necked shirts, and sticking out of the breast pocket of each was what appeared to be the antenna of a small two-way radio.

Now the distance to the hotel seemed to shrink. If he took a left at the next light, he'd be at Triangle Market. Then if he turned into a lane and ran for it, he should be able to make the rear entrance.

He turned left. The bicycles turned left along with him. As the road narrowed, they drew in closer on either side. The sounds grew louder: the squeak of pedals turning, the swish of tires on wet pavement, the squawk of the radios. When in front of him he saw another bicycle heading his way, with a rider in the same sort of raincoat, he was no longer in any doubt as to who these people were. That he was surrounded by bicycles, not cars like the black Peugeot, only made the sense of menace more personal.

He felt his throat constrict, his knees go weak. He looked up, then around; but although it should have been right at hand, there was no sign of the hotel, as if the building had magically flown away.

The man pedalling leisurely towards him was saying something into a hand radio. Just then, seeing the handlebars and front wheel wobble, Aki dived into a still narrower side lane, an alleyway little better than a crack between two buildings. It was so long and crooked that he soon had no idea which way he was running. Finally, a way out appeared. When he recognized the Peugeot blocking the exit, he almost felt a glow of familiarity. Over his shoulder, he saw the bicycles had increased to five or six and were coming towards him in single file. The riders seemed to be in a playful mood, taking their hands off the handlebars or standing up off the saddle. The brims of their hats were too deep for him to make out their expressions. His stomach clenched.

How did I stir this up? he wondered. He remembered Shuichi saying something about the panic he'd felt on being surrounded by bicycles in a Beijing *hutong*. This was what he'd meant. *What did I* do? What do they want with me? With Li Xing? Don't tell me they've taken her off somewhere already.

He started sprinting towards the Peugeot. She might be inside. Then the rear door swung open, and the man he'd met in the basement bar of the Metropole Hotel slowly got out, manoeuvring around a puddle. Again he was wearing a wide, loud necktie that looked completely out of place; whipped about by the wind and rain, it lay draped over his shoulder.

"Get in," he said, grasping Aki by the arm. "You're so wet, you'll catch cold. Like somebody else."

"Where are you taking me?"

"Where do you think? I'm escorting you back to your hotel."

As they pulled away, Aki glanced back at the lane he'd just come out of, but the bicycles had vanished without a trace. The car's interior was pleasantly cool. The ride, however, was far from smooth; the cushions were in a shocking state, and it felt as if the seat was scraping along the ground.

"Do you mind if we take a slight detour? I'd like to talk with you about something. My name's Ma. Ma Zuqi."

After entering North Sichuan Road, the driver swung right and headed west along the left bank of Suzhou Creek. Aki's hotel slipped farther and farther behind them on the left.

"What've we got here? Mushroom soup from Ronghuaji. Ah, yes. It's famous, you know. Just the thing for a cold. And you got some mangoes, I see – two of them. Of course. Mind if I open the window a bit?"

Ma lowered the window a few centimetres, letting in rain and smoke and the stench of the river. Breathing in deeply, he said, "Whatever anyone says, I love the smell of Shanghai. Care to read the paper? It's today's evening edition." He took a folded copy of the *Shanghai Evening News* out of his pocket and held it out. Aki took the paper and laid it on his knees without looking.

"You ought to have a look," said Ma, and pointedly opened up the newspaper in front of him. Even in a Communist country like this, there were tabloids devoted to gossip and scandal. Today's front page was taken up by a large photo of Deng Xiaoping and Jiang

Zemin, along with the contents of their speeches. Aki turned the page. Li Xing's face jumped out at him.

> Actress Li Xing has left her lover Liu Hong, a fugitive on the most-wanted list in connection with recent antirevolutionary unrest, and taken up with a Japanese man recently arrived in Shanghai.

They had thoughtfully supplied Aki's name and the name of his hotel.
"Damn fools," Ma said scornfully.
Who did he mean? Aki cocked his head, unsure.
"With a population of 1.1 billion, a quarter of who are illiterate and a third starving, who else but Mango do they expect to feed this country?" he demanded.

Hello, a member of the establishment just said "Mango."

"The idea of democracy in this country is a joke. It could only lead to a worse mess."
Aki turned towards the man and tried to read his expression, but found no sign of his true intentions.
Ma looked down, flexing his fingers affectedly and fiddling with the knot in his wide necktie. "Mr Waki," he said, "you've done something pretty remarkable. Before the war it was different, but since the war no Japanese who's come to China has had the balls to do what you've done."
Aki cautiously swallowed the lump in his throat. He felt that the sound could be heard throughout the vehicle.
"You know why Li Xing came to your room?"
Aki emptied his head of all thoughts and stared at the driver's profile, as pockmarked as a peanut shell.
"You may think we leaked the information in this article, but you'd be wrong. She gave it to them herself."
Aki turned to look out the window. The car had reached Shanghai Station and was about to make a U-turn in the plaza with the clock tower. The sun was just setting, urged on its way by the rain. Aki had to go on listening to Ma.
Public security authorities had picked up Li Xing at Shanghai Airport trying to board a plane to Yangquan. They questioned her

politely. Through her boyfriend, she knew the headquarters of the underground organization and the names of its leaders, but this was only a tiny fraction of the whole. The authorities had already ascertained that Liu Hong was in hiding in the province of Jiangsu. They were dead set on arresting him. He was certain to try to contact Li Xing. So, the day after her arrest, they let her go. A decoy.

For Li Xing to contact him herself was impossible; she had no way of knowing where he might be holed up. He would have to make contact. Then where should she wait for it to happen? Where could she? Nowhere in all of Shanghai was safe, nowhere could she avoid surveillance. Even if there were such a place, how could she notify Liu Hong?

"You see it now, don't you? That was her whole reason for cozying up to you. She could get the *Shanghai Evening News* to headline her whereabouts in big letters. It's the biggest-selling evening paper not just in Shanghai, but in Zhejiang and Jiangsu, too. That way, he'd get the message wherever he was. Even if he himself didn't see the article, somebody looking out for him would, she figured, and would let him know. Frankly, not even we have control over foreigners – we'd naturally be cautious around them. So the best place, the only place for her to go into 'hiding' was your suite, and creating a scandal with you was a golden opportunity to let him know where she was. You see, she could've gone off with a famous filmmaker like Zhang Yimou or Chen Kaige and the *Shanghai Evening News* wouldn't have written one line about it."

It's not true, thought Aki. *She came to my rooms to write, and remember.* It seemed useless to argue the point. Either way of looking at it was plausible. Either way, he came off as a patsy.

"He might figure it's a trap."

"Yes, he might. There's a fifty-fifty chance. After all, it is a trap in one way, and in another it isn't. I'll grant you, the lady's got guts. Throwing herself bodily at you, a short-term Japanese visitor, that way."

Not true again, he said to himself in anger and frustration.

"Of course, any time we wanted, we could take you into custody and have you deported."

"I haven't broken any of your country's laws."

"Haven't you? In this country, couples aren't allowed to stay together in a hotel unless they've got a certificate of marriage or engagement. As I'm sure you know. It's all there in the hotel regulations."

Aki kept silent. So that was it. The hotel staff had been instructed to turn a blind eye to the presence of a woman in his room.

After making a U-turn at Shanghai Station, the car was now travelling back along the east bank of Suzhou Creek.

Ma continued: "That's the law, anyway; whether or not it's always upheld is another matter. High officials go unchallenged, and we know that a Hong Kong prostitution ring operates in foreigners' hotels. We can't go after every little misdemeanour… so in short, sometimes we look the other way and sometimes we don't. Listen. Liu Hong is bound to send word to Li Xing, any day now. When he does, we'd like you to let us know right away. Here's the number of my pager. If you cooperate, nothing will happen. Li Xing won't be arrested. Nothing, absolutely nothing, will happen."

Aki felt he'd been battered down.

"From now on, you won't be followed anymore. Your phone won't be bugged. We trust you. We trust Japanese people. And here we are at your hotel. Li Xing is waiting for you."

Aki opened the car door and stepped out into the rain. Raindrops hit spitefully against the back of his neck. By now it was quite dark out. The Peugeot drove off. He looked up almost vertically at the hotel room windows above him, counted with difficulty to the fifteenth floor, and picked out his suite. A light was on. No doubt about it, that was the floor lamp Li Xing had placed next to the wicker chair. He slowly walked the short distance to the hotel entrance, getting soaked in the malevolent rain. Twisting reds, yellows, and blues projected by a neon sign in the bar next door gleamed on the surface of the road. A handcart loaded high with something or other was coming this way. The shafts dug into the sides of the old man pulling it, who was leaning so far forward that his naked torso was virtually parallel with the ground. The neon sign shone on his back, where rain mingled with sweat.

In front of the revolving door, Aki was stopped by the old man's voice: "*Xiansheng.*"

Aki didn't want to see anyone else but Li Xing. He felt no desire ever to speak a word of Chinese again. Of all things, he had become that lowest of creatures, a Japanese national trusted by Mango.

The old man turned out to be Chen's father. The night before, Chen had run off with his brother's wife, Anli. They were headed for Japan. An underworld network had arranged, for a price, to smuggle them out of the country. Aki thought back to the East China Sea that he himself had crossed, imagining the two of them crossing that same vast area in the cramped quarters of a fishing vessel.

The old man had come looking for him because Aki was his son's temporary employer, and Chen Ying had often said how well he was treated. Also, since Aki was from Japan, he wanted to let him know that his boy had arranged not just to elope, but to head in his country's direction. Talking about it made him feel a little easier. His other son was still hospitalized and knew nothing yet.

"*Xiansheng*, how can I tell him?" the old man wailed, hunching over even further. "*Xiansheng*, if you ever come across that rascal in Japan, I want you to give him what-for. I know I can trust you – you're Japanese..." The rest was lost in noisy sobbing.

So once again I'm a trusted Japanese, am I? He thought with fondness of the taxi driver. He'd always been on the lookout for Aki, and when he spotted him, he would thrust his hands into his pockets, hoist up his trousers, and come striding over.

12

What on earth had happened to her memory? It was like a house eaten away by termites.

Her father's death, for example. In the old notebook, her account of it had taken up thirteen pages. There were thirty-six lines on a page, making thirty-five spaces to write in. Her father had loathed the horizontal writing style of the *People's Daily* and so, following his lead, she wrote vertically. Even without lines going the other way to form squares for each character, her writing generally came out to an even twenty-five characters per line. That made 875 characters per page, which at thirteen pages amounted to 11,375 characters in all. This was how much she had written about her father's death. Her memory of the substance of what had occurred was intact, and yet the number of characters she'd been able to write so far in Aki's hotel room was only 2,275 – barely one-fifth of her previous total.

She remembered how on his deathbed her father had run trembling fingers over her face, how he had recited some French phrase over and over like a Buddhist incantation till his dying breath. He was from Hefei, Anhui Province, and graduated from the Department of Foreign Languages at Tsinghua University in 1940, studying abroad in 1942–45 at Oxford and the Sorbonne. From 1953 on, he conducted research at the Institute of Literature of Peking University under the scholar and writer Qian Zhongshu. After the Cultural Revolution got underway, in 1966 the Red Guards stormed their house, which stood on a traditional lane facing a courtyard. Her parents were strung up over the goldfish pond with dunce caps on their heads and their hands tied behind them, and eventually dunked in the pond. Li Xing, then six years old, had trembled in her *nainai*'s arms.

About her mother, she was able to write an even paltrier number of lines. She remembered the date of her death: 21st October 1975.

But was it a sunny day or overcast? Or had there been scattered showers in the morning that cleared up suddenly in the afternoon? This sort of weather was common in autumn on the plateau. But no, even this she couldn't remember.

Her memory was a house that appeared solid enough on the outside, but whose beams, pillars, and walls were so worm-eaten that it was on the verge of collapse.

Concerning Liu Hong, letters from him and copies of her letters to him would easily have filled an entire notebook. The rate of reconstruction was thus lower still. Today she had written this:

A group of intellectuals from Beijing sat at the restaurant table next to ours. Their conversation was so interesting, I couldn't help listening. To my amazement, they turned out to be famous – all pro-democratization, pro-reform leaders. From the names they called each other, I figured out who they were: Su Xiaokang, Yan Jiaqi, the writer Zheng Yi, and Liu Hong. They were all in high spirits, and absolutely dazzling. But they were thrown by the house specialty, steamed bread in mutton soup. Pretty soon one of them – a rather good-looking boy (Liu Hong, that's you) – got up and came over to where some of us were sitting, and asked how to eat it. I showed him the proper way, by tearing the bread in strips from the right as you go.

And then he had the nerve to stand there and ask me for my address. I didn't give it to him.

It had taken her half the day just to write this much. Something peculiar was happening. Of the passage she remembered, all she'd been able to transcribe was this little bit; and as she worked it out, her ballpoint pen travelling slowly over the page, Liu Hong's image had grown fainter, then started peeling and falling away.

Some things came back to her readily enough, and she was able to get them down quite easily. Things that were of no consequence, mostly. Like the time when his classmate and friend from Peking University, Cai Fang, came to see the troupe on a mission from the Central Committee. But to her surprise, she found next to nothing to say about Liu Hong himself. He was fading.

She looked up with a start, shocked at how quickly darkness had come. Outside, large drops of rain were falling. Had Aki taken an umbrella? "He's coming back," she said to herself softly. But she had run out of things to write. Why had she ever dreamt this up – retrieving her diary and letters like this, turning her own head into a kind of cricket box? What in God's name for? So she could know who she was, stand tall?

Just then the doorbell rang with their prearranged signal: three short rings in a row, a pause, then two longer ones. She quickly scribbled, "He's come back to me." Then she ran to the door.

"God, you're soaked to the skin!"

"Yes, now I'm the way you were yesterday."

Her slim figure was wrapped in the same orange dress as this morning. The sight warmed him. Her notebook with the blue cover lay open on the sofa, the ballpoint pen lying crosswise on the curling pages, barely able to hold them down. With his good eyesight, Aki could read what was written there: "He's come back to me." *So Liu Hong came back*, he said to himself. When and where might that have been?

"You'll catch cold."

She flew off and returned with an armful of towels. Next she poked at the bundle she'd taken from him and exclaimed, "Oh good, mangoes!"

"The other package is a special mushroom soup from Ronghuaji. Ms Yu told me it's good for colds."

"Great. Let's have it right away. For your sake, since you got wet in the rain."

She poured the soup from the container into teacups and they drank it cold. The pale mushrooms waved about in the liquid as if bending in the wind. The broth was clear and sweet, with a hint of sage. She put the two mangoes on a saucer. They were almost the same colour as her dress, and when she picked one up and started paring it neatly, he lost sight of it for a second against the material.

"How's your writing going?"

"It's not. I've forgotten things. See, the pages are still blank…"

Could she really forget? He doubted it. Who had leaked the news of her presence here – she herself, or public security? It could have been either one. This was probably her only way of meeting Liu Hong, and public security would do anything to arrest him.

Aki felt as if he were locked alone with her in a tower visible to all Shanghai.

Wang le, she'd said – pretending to have forgotten. She'd never had the slightest intention of reduplicating her lost papers, but was only playing for time while she waited for her friend to contact her. If she was going to take advantage of him, Aki, then he could return the favour. He could forget about maintaining a respectable distance and topple her onto the sofa. That's what sofas were for, wasn't it? *Now's your chance, close the gap*, he told himself. Just go over to her by the window. Two people gazing out together – that should be enough to set the mood.

Yet he stayed standing on the other side of the desk, frozen in place.

Li Xing lingered by the twilit window. It seemed too far for conversation, but he couldn't help saying, "Forgotten? But surely not all – you haven't forgotten it all, have you?"

Li Xing shook her head. Her figure blended into the view of the Bund framed by the long, vertical window.

"I can see you did write something. If you don't mind… I know I shouldn't ask, but I'd really love to read even a little of it."

"You've every right to ask."

"That's not what I meant."

"Something happened, didn't it?" She looked thoughtful, eyes cast down.

Aki walked a little way towards her, and stopped when he had measured off three meters. Still a respectable distance.

"The film's been cancelled, hasn't it?"

Caught off guard, he could only nod helplessly.

"I knew it. When I was picked up at the airport, that's what they said. That *Moving Shadows* would be scrapped. And also…"

"What?"

"The *Shanghai Evening News*. It was in your coat pocket."

Li Xing moved slowly away from the window, along the wall. He turned, following less her face than her gaze. Her shadow on the wall had a forlorn look, the shoulders slumped. Then abruptly she vanished into the bedroom.

Before long the door opened. *No doors stay shut,* he thought. Li Xing stood there again with her suitcase in her hand.

"I'm sorry. And thank you very much." She bowed her head. It was a nice, polite Japanese bow. She walked toward the door.

With a catch in his voice, he said, "What about your promise?"

"What promise?"

"You forgot already? You promised to read me something from your notebook."

"I never said that."

"Yes, you did. Please, open your bag and read something to me. One section from the salvaged diary of Li Xing."

She turned wide eyes on him. The suitcase fell with a thump at her feet. She bent over, undid the clasps, and pulled out a rolled-up notebook. On the spot, she read aloud:

A letter from Liu Hong finally came. Hadn't heard from him for a whole week, so I was getting nervous. At the Tang Dynasty Theatre Restaurant, our team was asked to perform at a banquet for the provincial Party Secretary. We did "Pamir Rejoicing" from the Uyghur ballet. I missed several steps even though I was the lead dancer, and I faltered during the allegro and the fouetté – there was nothing good about my performance at all. Liu Hong's letter was –

Here she broke off and stole a look at him. He was listening, arms folded. He looked up and signalled with his eyes for her to continue. Out of nowhere, she felt a flash of pure affection for him.

She began reading again:

Hearing about the death of former General Secretary Hu Yaobang, students have started gathering in Tiananmen Square. It was the same when Prime Minister Zhou Enlai died. Oh, and Cai Fang came by before noon. He was showing someone around – a Japanese VIP named Saionji. Apparently, he was on close terms with Zhou Enlai. We did some songs and dances from the Loess Plateau at the theatre restaurant and afterwards, Cai came backstage, alone, and made himself a pest. Telling stupid jokes and puns. He calls me the "dancing girl from the plains." His eyes looking out from behind those frameless glasses are very Uyghur-ish, a beautiful brown. He said, "Xingxing, tell Liu Hong to look out for himself, will you?" It really was a dreary day.

"Xingxing, please sit down," Aki said. She sat down on the sofa. "Good, that's the way. Everything's going to be okay." He couldn't conceal the note of false heartiness in his voice. Li Xing shook her head. She closed the notebook, rolled it up, and held it tight.

"Well, I kept my promise. Thanks. You've been very kind."

"Kind? Oh yes, I'm famous for my kindness. The fairy godmother!" He deliberately tried to keep his tone light, but it came off as sarcastic.

"Let's go eat," he said. "I'm hungry. The place on the eighteenth floor serves Chaozhou food. Let's have pigeon. It'll lift your spirits to go up there. Afterwards, we can climb up to the terrace at the top and get a bird's-eye view of Shanghai. See here – " He gestured at a framed photograph hanging on the wall. "Zhou Enlai went there, too." He proceeded to read the caption aloud:

The late Prime Minister Zhou Enlai often brought foreign heads of state and leaders to the terrace of Broadway Mansions to give them a bird's-eye view of the city. This photograph was taken on the afternoon of October 20, 1971, when he escorted the Ethiopian emperor, Haile Selassie, to the nineteenth-floor terrace.

He paused, then turned and said, "From that height, you might be able to see Liu Hong on his way here."

She gave him an odd, flushed look. "How mean you are. No, thank you. I had that mango, so I'm not hungry. I don't want anything to eat and I don't want a bird's-eye view of Shanghai."

Tears glistened in her eyes. Aki saw them and assumed they were from angry disappointment. He apologized sincerely. After that, the two of them dined on pigeon. When they'd finished, without climbing up to the terrace, they went back down to the fifteenth floor. Aki unlocked the door with his key and let Li Xing in, then followed her in and locked the door. She disappeared into the bedroom without turning around, but left the door open. All was quiet. Aki hesitated for one millisecond, and went in.

13

The slope Aki was standing on lurched again.

The next morning, he stayed in the sitting room while Li Xing sat in the wicker chair; they didn't see each other once. Every so often he would stand with his forehead pressed to the wall, absolutely still. He was careful to leave her alone, and when he needed to use the toilet he went all the way down to the first floor. Around eleven o'clock, a man and a woman came to clean the rooms, but he sent them away, saying he had a cold. He coughed violently to prove it.

Aki felt restless. Just when he'd finally gotten a taste of her, he seemed likely to lose her. Liu must be well on his way. Through the *Shanghai Evening News*, he knew by now where she was. Aki could scarcely take his eyes off the cheap beige telephone sitting on the desk. He listened for footsteps in the corridor.

How would Liu make contact? Aki opened the window. The many sounds of Shanghai rushed in aggressively, instantly occupying every corner of the room. Eventually, he was able to sift out individual noises from the din. More annoying than the hubbub of cars, boats, bicycles, and factories were the cries of human beings: each one carried some meaning. Mixed in with them might be Liu Hong's voice.

Given the chance, Aki would have gone down and walked around with a finger on his lips, begging everybody in the city, one by one, to please shut up and leave him and Li Xing alone.

The Peugeot was parked in its usual spot. Li Xing was by the window. Her every movement made the wicker chair creak, the sound faint but audible to Aki in the next room. Silent pleasure welled up inside him. At the same time, he was struck by a stupid thought: *There's only one thing truly criminal a woman can do – to be with one man while thinking of another.*

In her wicker chair, Li Xing was following a similar line of thought: *I'm a horrible person, really. There's only one thing worse than giving yourself to one man while thinking of another — and I'm doing it. I came here for Liu Hong's sake and now it's Aki I've turned to. Body and soul.*

Li Xing was sure of her own inclinations, but she didn't know how to handle them, nor did she yet have a clear notion of how Aki felt. Suddenly she had an idea. Yes, that would help her to decide.

Checking on her tiny wristwatch that it was now noon, she banged shut the notebook on her lap, stood up, and took out from her suitcase something carefully wrapped in newspaper. A reddish pottery teapot, small enough to hold in the palm of her hand, and still smaller matching teacups. She set them out on the nightstand, boiled some water in the electric kettle, and then called to Aki to come in.

Entering, he saw a teapot and three cups laid out in a particular pattern on the nightstand. The pot contained Yin Dan's jasmine tea.

"Please sit down there."

He did so, looking dubious about the whole procedure.

"This is called the Challenge."

What in the world?

"I learnt it from my *yeye*, but my mother knew it too."

Yeye meant paternal grandfather. The maternal grandfather was called *laoye*. Her *laoye* was Xu Liping, back in Kobe.

"*Yeye* was a member of the Nationalist Party, but before that he was involved in the Heaven and Earth Society. Have you ever heard of it?"

Aki shook his head.

"An old secret society. It even played a part in the Taiping Rebellion. When two members met for the first time, they used a password to see if they belonged or not. One would ask, 'Art thou blind?' The other would answer, 'No, mine eyes are bigger than thine.'"

She swallowed. Eyes shining, she went on, "Okay, let's begin. This is the induction ceremony. Suppose someday you and I meet somewhere far away, and have forgotten each other. This way we can remember it's us again. Do you want to join the Heaven and Earth Society?"

Aki nodded.

"All right, then I'll show you how."

She reached out for the teapot. The three cups were lined up in a row, facing the spout. She poured tea into each one. Aki's eyes took in every movement her hands made.

"Offering someone tea this way is an invitation for them to join the cause. To accept, you choose the cup in the middle and drink from it. Go ahead."

Her eyes were right by him. Aki unhesitatingly picked up the middle cup and took a sip. Questions, though, occurred to him: *Join the cause ... on whose behalf? What for? Against whom?*

As he was about to take another sip of the hot amber liquid, he saw a tiny white petal rise swiftly from the bottom of the cup, curling open as it did so. Yin Dan's method involved transferring only the fragrance of the flowers to his tea leaves, without mixing in any petals. Was this a bad omen or a lucky one? He was on the point of mentioning it, when she spoke again.

"Have you got any idea what I was really doing all morning in the wicker chair?"

"That's obvious, isn't it?" he said pointedly. "Writing in your notebook, waiting to hear from Liu Hong."

Li Xing closed her eyes and gave her head a little shake. Then, mischief in her eyes, she said, "Guess again."

Out in the corridor, several guests went by, talking loudly in English. Mixed in was the thump of heavy suitcases being dragged along. *Keep it down, will you?* Aki said under his breath. Then, to answer her, he shrugged. "Okay, what were you really doing?"

"Being in love. With you."

Aki sucked in his lips. He took her in his arms, so clumsily that it might have been the first time. Uncertain how to hold her, he was ill at ease, shifting his weight from right to left and back again. They both still felt the events of the night before were scarcely real; everything now was awkward. There was something jittery about the way they kissed. Li Xing's sweet, wild gaze wavered before him close up, swaying like a boat at its mooring.

When the phone rang, he felt her give a start. "It's him!"

Aki reached slowly for the phone, his other arm still encircling her waist. The sensation of her touch lingered on the hand reaching out. He picked up the receiver, but for some reason his hand went numb and he dropped it in the cradle. Snatching it back up, he called, "*Wei, wei wei,*" but the line was dead.

The taste of her was still on his lips. He put the receiver back and looked around the room in a daze. Seeing the window open, he closed it and drew the curtains. The phone rang again. Li Xing backed off, standing in the shadow of the half-open bedroom door.

"*Wei*," he said brusquely, and waited for someone to speak.

"Mr Xie, is that you?" said an excited voice in Beijing dialect, using the Chinese pronunciation of his name.

"Yes."

"I won't give my name, but you know who I am." He spoke rapidly. "This line's probably bugged, so do as I say. I'll call back in thirty seconds."

Li Xing again came closer. He looked up at her and nodded. Precisely thirty seconds later, Liu Hong called back.

"Listen. After this, make sure you always pick up in the middle of the third ring and hang up in fifteen seconds. That way the bug can't work. I'll call back in one minute this time. You hang up first."

Li Xing sat down on the sofa and crossed her arms and legs. A slipper dangled from her toes, about to fall off. She set it swaying. Watching the slipper out of the corner of his eye, he took off his watch and laid it beside the phone. As instructed, he picked up on the third ring.

"Is Li Xing there?"

"Yes. I'll put her on."

"No. I want to talk to you. I'll be blunt. Get some money ready. Fifty thousand yuan."

Aki counted off fifteen seconds and silently hung up. Li Xing was squarely in the centre of his vision. On the other end of the line was Liu Hong. The phone rang again. At the third ring he picked up.

"*Wei*. You Japanese still haven't paid us any reparations. Li Xing is my wife."

"Your... wife?"

"As good as."

"Then you're asking for double reparations. That's extortion." The last bit was going too far, he thought, but it was too late. With Liu's suppressed, self-mocking laughter sounding in his ears, he quickly put the receiver down.

It would take five calls to complete Liu's business.

The Hong Kong-based network that helped political criminals flee China had so far successfully smuggled seven major wanted criminals overseas by way of Hong Kong, but a week ago, a number of their people were arrested in Xi'an and Shenzhen. For the time being, they had been forced to withdraw their operations from the mainland. That was four days ago. Liu had reached Shanghai the day before yesterday; two days earlier and he'd have been in time. As a wanted criminal, he would have trouble heading further south incognito. It was imperative that he leave the country immediately. His only recourse was to rely on the underworld – the snakehead gangs who, naturally, demanded payment up front. Seeing dictatorships and democracies alike as a means of doing business, they alone could ignore the authorities and survive.

Aki thought of his old driver, Chen Ying. Had he made it safely to Japan, or was he still afloat on the East China Sea? Probably he, too, had paid fifty thousand yuan to a snakehead gang.

Aki hadn't yet been able to explain his arrangements with Liu to Li Xing, but she seemed to get the picture anyway – and was visibly upset. Though he held the receiver out to her several times, she refused to take it. Yet midway through the fourth call, from a short distance away she called, "Liu Hong!" The anguish in her voice was plain, and carried across the space that separated them. It registered squarely with Liu. Abruptly his pushiness vanished and his tone changed to one of supplication.

"None of us have any money. There's no one to turn to but you. If you can't help, I'll go to a friend's place further south. I can only stay in Shanghai another day and a half."

Fifty thousand yuan was, what, about a million and a half yen? The helplessness and uncertainty that Chen and Liu must feel infected him as well. If his money could buy Liu's freedom, it might serve also as a kind of personal reparation. It was a persuasive thought. He began to work out how to raise the cash.

He had about 600,000 yen in travellers checks with him. There was a Citibank branch on the first floor of the Peace Hotel. Using his Visa gold card, he could probably take out a loan of US$7,000 to make up the difference.

"Xingxing, could you come over here," he called out. "He's going to phone back one more time. This last time, you should talk to him. Tell him I'll get him the money. He has to decide when and where the transfer will be made."

Li Xing shook her head but moved nearer, as far as the window, sliding her back along the wall. "God, for him to be asking *you* for money! But please… please, let him have it."

The words were wrung out of her. Requests for money can ruin things; they're like a blast of cold wind. Yet, hers had the opposite effect: it blew the things he loved, and wanted to possess, toward him.

The phone rang.

"I won't talk. Don't make me." As she backed away, he could see in her eyes a crisscross pattern of light and shadow from the lace curtain.

"Fifty thousand yuan. All right."

The handover would be tomorrow morning. He would phone later with details.

"Is Xingxing there?"

"I'll put her on."

She turned her back to him. Through the narrow gap in the curtains, she stared outside. What was there to see out there, besides the black Peugeot? The figure of Liu Hong?

"I'm taking her with me," the voice on the phone said.

Aki replaced the receiver. "He says he's taking you with him," he told Li Xing, her slim figure still facing away from him. His tongue was dry; the words came painfully.

He had only forty minutes till the bank closed. He grabbed his jacket, made sure his passport and credit card were there, and tore out of the room. Once in the corridor, he forced himself to slow down. The Peace Hotel was on the Bund, a little way past Garden Bridge. He turned left outside his hotel and was approaching the bridge when Ma Zuqi caught up with him and said familiarly, "Where you off to?"

"The bank. Then I'm going to buy my plane ticket home."

They walked abreast across the bridge. The day was overcast and muggy.

"No word yet?"

"Nothing."

"It'll be tonight then, count on it. Believe me, we want this guy. Two others have already gotten away from Shanghai. Remember, Mr Waki, it's one thing to feel sorry for the fox – but whatever you do, stay out of the way of the hounds."

"I will. I'm a foreigner here after all, a guest in your country. But I'll say this, Mr Ma: I can see you mean business, but you strike me as someone who enjoys the hunt."

He felt as if he'd walked down this street before in his dreams, as if all this, now, was itself a bad dream. *Let it end, if I'm dreaming, but leave me Li Xing.*

"Watch it," murmured Ma, grabbing his elbow and pulling him back onto the curb at a corner with no traffic light. A black Crown zoomed past, sounding its horn. The sudden commotion took Aki by surprise, but failed to really wake him up. Only twenty-five minutes left.

He was now racing against time, and he was in luck. When he left Citibank, there were seven thousand dollars in his pocket. Ma was nowhere to be seen.

Briskly he retraced his steps across Garden Bridge. Ma was leaning back against the iron railing, smoking a cigarette. Seeing Aki, he casually raised his right hand, cigarette between his fingers, and waved. For a moment, Aki had an urge to blurt out everything. If he did, the nightmare and Li Xing both would be *suan le*. Done and gone.

She was standing in the same place by the same window in the same position as when he'd left. For a ballerina, the feat was easy.

She was playing with a tassel she'd pulled off the curtain. She spotted Aki. A man approached him and crossed the bridge alongside him. Someone from public security, she thought. He must have – no, he couldn't…

He came back.

"I got the money," he said.

Li Xing flushed with shame at having doubted him. Angrily, she said, "Don't you hate the way this country works?"

"What way?"

"Everything you see and hear, everything around you. All of it. Me, Liu Hong with his demand for money, public security always watching us, opium and Hami melons and *malantou* and mangoes."

Jasmine

"I like it all. Why, I even like Mango. Because it represents you, even if it makes you suffer, Xingxing."

She let out a tiny sound midway between a sneeze and a laugh.

They had to seem free and easy for the benefit of eyes watching them. Li Xing and the Japanese guy were sleeping together, the story would go; she was *his* woman now.

For dinner, they dressed nicely, went up to the restaurant on the eighteenth floor, and had Cantonese cuisine. They looked and acted like people in love. But they fooled no one. That's because they were, in fact, in love.

On returning to the suite, they shut themselves in the bedroom. The only lights were a single bedside lamp and a floor lamp with a green silk shade by the window, both turned low so that their two moving shadows showed hazily on the walls, as if the room were filled with a fine mist. They changed from shoes into cloth slippers and sat on the edge of the big bed. Ever since last night, in bed, they had spoken entirely in Mandarin.

Li Xing dangled her slipper from her toes. "It's like we're on a pier," she said. "Below us is the water."

"The Yangtze?"

"Yes."

She had never seen the sea. With a half-smile playing on her face, she swept up her hair in her left hand and gazed off into space. As though this were a signal, Aki toppled her back on the bed. After a long kiss, hot breaths and saliva mingling as they struggled like two enemies, they undressed. They stared into each other's eyes while their four hands roamed at random, quick, awkward, and impatient. Eventually a sturdy arm held the linen sheet high and their two naked bodies, slightly damp with sweat, slid underneath.

For a while they had no chance to look into each other's eyes. They were intent on following instead the way their fingers and tongues covered every corner of their bodies. Like the viewfinder of a camera touring a battlefield or disaster site, they saw themselves from above. Then, gently yet unmistakably, their moving shadows coalesced.

The night before, when it was over, Aki had been surprised to realize that he had never fantasized about what it would be like to sleep with a Chinese woman. The discovery puzzled him and pleased him at the same time. That he loved Li Xing simply for herself, without regard to any aspect of her background, he'd been able to confirm not only in his heart, but with his body. If asked, "What was it like to sleep with her?" he would have answered promptly, "It was good," with no unnecessary commentary. Asked, "Was it all you imagined?" he would simply have nodded. It was against his nature to exaggerate; when he chose to emphasize his words, he usually did so by lowering his voice.

For Li Xing, the sensations that she'd had last night, and that continued even now to resonate slightly inside her, were a new experience. Her pleasure was mixed with wonder. And yet... she wasn't confident. Although her ballet-trained body was lithe, strong, and beautiful, she wondered: could he really like such a poor, thin thing?

As she'd done the night before, once again Li Xing whispered in his ear: "Be careful – please don't come inside me."

The Mandarin for "be careful" was *xiaoxin*, written with the characters "small" and "heart" – a combination that in Japanese meant "timid." In the echo of the word as she said it, the subtly different meanings collided, to his delight.

When the time came to sleep, Aki returned conscientiously to the sofa. As he buttoned his pyjamas to the neck, he asked himself what he was going to do. Was there any way he could spirit her away, take her to her grandfather in Kobe? The effort he might devote to such a scheme hinged on the amount of energy this affair generated. Once it reached a certain heat, he wouldn't stop, even at the risk of his life. There was something not quite rational in his determination.

Odd that now, of all times, he should inwardly turn for help to his wife. Perhaps when people are stretched to their limit, it's not the living to whom they cling for support, he thought, but the dead.

Certainly the most natural thing to do, and the easiest, would be to let Li Xing leave the country hand in hand with Liu. In any case, there was no avoiding a clash with the Chinese authorities. Would he, Aki, be arrested? Of course he would.

A thought occurred to him: exactly the same drama might have been played out here in Shanghai fifty years ago. He was thinking of his father, whom Xie had quoted as saying, "The ideal life would be to live in Shanghai embracing a woman, and one's conscience, with both arms." What sort of conscience did he mean?

Aki stretched out on the sofa, wrapped himself in the sheet he had pulled off one of the twin beds, and closed his eyes. Tomorrow – everything would be settled tomorrow, decided one way or the other. *Suan le*, done, that was the best way. Time to forget it all till then.

But he couldn't sleep. He thought of what Xie Han had said. He was dead right. Threats never to forget the past, demands for reparations – this wasn't dignified. Yet being Japanese, he could never say so. Liu's remark about the war was more acceptable. Japan's efforts to make amends were still inadequate. The postwar Japanese were aggressors awakened to a sense of themselves as victims.

> *I had nothing to do with the war and it's not my responsibility, but everywhere you look in Japan today, you find prosperity. Money's all anyone has. What else forms the mainstay of each Japanese individual? It's sad. If reparations had to be paid, and someone asked me how, I'd have to say by putting to use the personal wealth of each individual. Xie Han said responsibility is something verified only through actual experience. ODA is certainly a laudable use of Japanese wealth; but since it can't lead to individual self-awareness, the concept of responsibility never gets through.*

His own money was going to be used to finance a couple's flight abroad. Responsibility here *was* getting through to him. For him. *This is putting my personal wealth to good use all right*, he thought... a thought that was like a bomb strapped to his chest.

Before he knew it, he was asleep. When he woke up, he could tell he had slept surprisingly well, feeling physically and mentally refreshed. He got up and went into Li Xing's room. She awoke, pushed back the linen sheets with a sleepy, faraway look, and stretched her arms up over her head. Pale soft hairs in her armpits were lit faintly by the sunshine filtering through the lace curtains.

"It's morning."

"So it is."

"What about breakfast?"

"My breakfast is you," he whispered in her ear.

Aki felt as if until now he'd been walking alone through a Shanghai shrouded in fog, and that suddenly the loneliness and fog had been dispelled, opening up a view of things he'd never seen before.

On her side, Li Xing had come to a decision – one reached before she'd begged him to give Liu Hong that money. The first night they were together, she'd thought, *This man is kind, and good*, and wanted nothing more than to make him happy. Last night, after making love, her decision was reaffirmed. But she couldn't tell Aki about it, because she loved him.

This was what she had resolved to do: leave Liu Hong; see that Aki got safely back to Japan; and remain alone in China, a fugitive.

That was only half of her decision, though. What the other half was, not even she herself clearly understood yet.

The telephone rang. Aki, who'd been dozing beside her, sprang out of bed. The male voice on the phone wasn't Liu's; someone else gave him the instructions, perhaps a member of some gang. Thirty minutes from now a taxi would be parked behind the Broadway Mansions Hotel, across from the west service entrance. A red Tianjin Charade. Li Xing was to get in that taxi with the money.

She came and stood at his elbow, neatly dressed and ready to go. Wanting to curse and swear at someone or something, he gave her a bleak smile and relayed the message. "I'll go with you downstairs," he added.

"No, I'll go alone."

His mind registered automatically that she'd switched to a formal level of Japanese. "Why alone?"

"If I'm caught, and it's just Liu Hong and me, that'll be the end of it. We'll be sentenced to fifteen years in a forced labour camp in Chaidamu or Tarim. People don't usually come out of that alive. I couldn't bear it if you were caught, too. And besides…"

"Besides?" His voice choked on the word, and he tasted something bitter at the back of his throat.

"I'm a Chinese woman. Not weak, like Japanese women." An impish smile was on her lips.

He handed her the envelope.

"No, don't. I've got ten thousand yuan of my own saved up. That's enough to get by on."

"Don't be stupid! He needs fifty thousand. It's right here."

"He shouldn't have asked for it. Money is to have fun with. I can't have you throwing yours away like this."

"You're being unreasonable. Listen, what's good about money is that you can use it any way you like. I don't know if Liu Hong meant it that way or not, but if he wants this as a kind of war reparation, that's okay with me, too. Just think of me as someone from Japan you met in passing, and remember me sometimes."

As he said the words, a protest swelled inside him. *The hell I am. I'm no such thing.*

"Met in passing? Oh, no, no..." That's all she could say.

Aki forced the envelope into her hands. "You've only got fifteen minutes. Hurry."

He had made sure that by using the emergency staircase, she could go straight out through the service door without entering the lobby. If she cut across the corridor quickly and timed it just right, no one would even know she had gone.

Li Xing left.

Aki stood staring vacantly at the door she had opened and closed behind her without looking back. He remembered how she'd shut the door on him in the guesthouse at the film studio. Remembering, he told himself, *That's that.*

The hands of the wall clock pointed to the time she was supposed to get in the car. He shivered and looked around. Time to clear out. He picked up the phone, called JAL, and reserved a seat on the evening flight to Narita. The planes were all flying virtually empty, so getting a seat was no problem. Then he started to pack. Reminders of her were everywhere. The sun visor. The borrowed suit, which she had ironed and hung on a hanger. He dialled Xie Han's number, but the operator only snapped, "*Bu zai.*" Not here. He'd have to leave without keeping his promise to host a return dinner.

The telephone rang. It was Yang Jun, the cameraman. He'd been released.

"Heard you're going back to Japan. I wanted to talk to you about that hair restorer. What would you be willing to pay for the marketing rights?"

Without a knock, the door opened. Li Xing reappeared.

"Would it be all right if I came over now? I have some samples I can bring with me. I'd really like you to—"

Li Xing slowly set down her suitcase as if back from a trip somewhere, and let out a long breath.

"Mr Yang, the boom in Chinese hair-growing products in my country is dying down. I don't think it'll work." Aki stared into Li Xing's eyes as he spoke. "They say if you really found a cure for baldness, you'd win a Nobel Prize. Not only that, it's next to impossible to get an import permit from the Ministry of Health and Welfare." *Mustn't blather.* She was standing with her back to the door.

"How about smuggling some in, then?"

"No."

"Then I'll sell you the list of ingredients. How about manufacturing it yourself in Japan?"

Gently Aki put down the phone, and went over to Li Xing.

"I'm back," she said.

"Hey, there."

"Is that okay?" She sat down on the sofa. It made the old familiar sound. "I decided to stay in China."

Her smile was resolute. In front of her and a little off to one side, maintaining a respectable distance, Aki stood with a stupid look on his face.

"He didn't come. I gave your money to the messenger."

I broke it off with Liu Hong. This unspoken message showed clearly on her face, but Aki, unsure, said only, "You like it here."

"No, that's not it. If I went away—"

There was nothing handy around him, but as if looking for something to lean on, he turned fully towards Li Xing and tried to read her face straight on.

"—I wouldn't be able to see you again."

"But I was going to leave the country tonight."

"That's okay. I'm happy just to see you here like this."

"What will you do now?"

"Run away."

"Alone?"

"Yes, alone. If I can make it to the *yaodong*, I'll manage."

"But can you get there?" *All I do is ask questions.*

JASMINE

"They gave me a message from Liu Hong. A way to reach him if anything happens."

"He must have guessed you wouldn't come."

She nodded and got up from the sofa. "You, I can feel, Liu Hong, I can only remember. When you have to force yourself to remember someone, it's no good." She took his hand, let it go with a sigh, and sat down again. With a strange expression of relief, or fear – one couldn't tell – she said quietly in a strangled voice, "Liu Hong, Liu Hong." But it was Aki she was calling out to as she tumbled down the slope. He was listening carefully, and he heard it.

Looking out the window, he saw that out on the ledge two sparrows were chasing each other in the sunlight. One of them would chase the other into a corner, then they'd both turn around and dart off in the opposite direction. They did this again and again. As he watched, he came to a decision. It was settled in the most natural way possible: he would never leave Li Xing.

They would go together to the Loess Plateau. Across the whole continent, there were untold numbers of political prisoners in hiding, tens of thousands of them, all fugitives from the law. No reason why he and she couldn't do that, too. And maybe somewhere in that area was his father.

"What was the message?"

"Go to the cricket seller in the street market on Jixiang Road. When you find him, say 'Jasmine.' That's the password. Liu Hong probably got into Shanghai the same way."

"Where's Jixiang Road?"

"Near where the writer Lu Xun used to live."

"That's not far from here. Xingxing, let's hurry. They may come charging in here any time."

All she had to do was pick up her suitcase and she was ready. Aki hastily tossed the bare essentials into a travel bag. Watching, she said in surprise, "*You* don't have to hurry."

"I'm coming, too."

Her eyes widened. The decision she'd taken was firm, but where it might lead she didn't know. As she started to speak, he interrupted: "Damn it. Forgot to pack my pyjamas." He opened up his bag again and tried to stuff the things inside, to no avail.

"That's right, even when you sleep on the sofa you wear them, don't you?"

"Can't sleep without them. And they have to be the kind that button to the neck."

She shrugged and giggled. He managed to squeeze the pyjamas in. The leather flask and the sun visor would have to go.

Like any two travellers about to check out, they stood in the doorway and surveyed the room a last time. It was full of things left behind. Too bad. The phone was ringing.

They slipped quickly across the passage outside, and started down the emergency staircase.

"This makes it twice I've done this in less than an hour."

They emerged onto Changzhi Road and walked north for a bit before catching a taxi. The smaller Shanghai taxis were all red Charades. He told the driver to take them to Lu Xun's old residence.

They'd been lucky. That morning, Ma Zuqi had succeeded in tapping the phone call from Liu Hong's messenger. After Li Xing got into a red Charade with the money, she was followed – until at the corner of Kunshan Road, just when a big trolley was blocking her pursuers' view, she slipped out of the cab and hurried back in the opposite direction on the sidewalk. They missed this manoeuvre and kept on following the Charade.

Since it hadn't occurred to Ma Zuqi that she might return to Broadway Mansions, the building and its environs were left temporarily unguarded. Aki and Li Xing were able to take advantage of this lapse to arrive safely at the outdoor market on Jixiang Road.

The lane was crowded on both sides with free-market street stalls. They found the cricket seller right away. Inside little cages hanging from a pole over a handcart were insects in full cry. A middle-aged man and woman were seated, fanning themselves on stools between the shafts.

Li Xing went up to them and quietly said the password. The man immediately got up, stepped outside the shafts, and signalled with his eyes for them to follow.

He took them to a house in a bleak section of the old *lilong* north of Lu Xun Park, and told them to wait there until nightfall. Then he asked for a credit card. Having left almost everything else behind,

Aki refused to hand it over – but seeing the man's reaction, which clearly implied the deal was off, he reluctantly held it out. The Visa gold card was stuck unceremoniously in the breast pocket of the man's sweaty shirt.

The room they were in had once been used as a kitchen, and in the corner was a damp pile of pulverized charcoal. They sat down on wooden stools, propped their elbows on the edge of a rickety table, and looked at each other in the lingering twilight. On top of their anxiety was the stifling heat. There was nothing to say.

"There's a cricket singing somewhere," said Aki, although he wasn't entirely certain whether he'd picked up the sound or not.

"I don't hear anything."

"Really? I must have gotten that chirping sound on the brain."

They fell silent again. Now and then they exchanged a glance. He noticed something odd: whatever way they looked at each other, his eyes and hers never seemed to align perfectly.

At some point Li Xing laughed out loud, as if to lighten the air in this room where darkness was slow to fall.

"What's so funny?"

"Nothing."

The vicinity grew noisier. Having been warned not to go outside, Aki crossed to the edge of the window and peered out. Fat women sat on stone steps in doorways, their legs stretched out heavily on the stone pavement. Charcoal briquettes flared, and over the fires, metal ladles and cooking pots made an angry racket, as if quarrelling. Men home from work slammed on their brakes and hopped off their bicycles, making the kickstand squeak as they shouted out teasing remarks to children who came running.

At almost the same moment, Aki and Li Xing were seized by the same thought: *Where are we now?* It was like being a kid again. As if they could run outside and find old playmates waiting for them, all the same height as long ago.

Li Xing stood up with a small yawn. The moment seemed to stretch and stagnate. Then all at once darkness fell, locking them in fast.

"Why does it get dark suddenly like that? It's the middle of summer," said Aki.

She knelt down on the floor in front of him and leaned forward on both arms. She hadn't anticipated this, his coming along. It would have been safer if he'd gone straight home, even though she'd wanted to stay with him for as long as she could.

"You're the first truly gentle person I've ever known," she told him. "I can hardly believe a Japanese man could be like this. But you've done enough. You really must... go back." She forced the words out.

He felt a spurt of anger. "But I've made up my mind! There's no turning back." It was partly because he saw himself being forced to do things whose outcome was beyond his control. *Once I handed over the credit card I was sunk*, he wanted to say, but it would have sounded too mean.

"No, you can still go. You mustn't come with me. I left Liu Hong and chose you. And I chose China, not another country. I've no regrets. That's why I'm here with you now... Let's say goodbye here."

"Xingxing, listen. What you're saying is full of contradictions. You chose this country and me; I chose this country and you. Why say goodbye?"

"I love you, really I do. But it's impossible, isn't it? – this romance we're having. I can't explain. You just mustn't come. Are you going to do the same thing your father did?"

For a second he flinched, and in his mind's eye he saw the Loess Plateau open up behind her. He tried to embrace her but she moved away, and the vision vanished. Her shoulders shook. She was crying.

When the cricket seller reappeared, he told them to get ready; they were going to take a boat. Aki stood up first.

They left the lane and walked along a narrow creek, its tar-black water shining. The fog tasted like cold copper coins. Far away, a tiny lantern described a circle; it was apparently a signal. "That's it," murmured the cricket seller, and quickened his pace.

They went down a steep, narrow, U-shaped flight of stone steps towards the water. The lantern on the boat's gunwale below lit up the way before them.

The boat was a solid-looking scow with an awning. The man with the lantern urged them to jump on board. Light entered the water like a snake. Li Xing hesitated, and turned to face Aki with an angry gesture. He gave her a determined look; privately, he was thinking, *Okay, here's where I get cut off from the world of comfort. Goodbye to Tokyo and Kobe and that scenery I love in the northern foothills of Chokaizan.* Strangely, he felt no regret. Inwardly, he apologized to Sato: there'd be no memorial service this year.

He took Li Xing's hand, squeezed it hard, and together they jumped aboard the scow. Li Xing said nothing more. In the bow was a woman with a pole in her hand. In the stern, holding the oars, was the lantern man; the cricket seller had silently departed.

Aki and Li Xing slipped under the awning. As the woman pushed the end of her pole against the stone steps and manoeuvred the scow away from the bank, they seemed to rise up in the water, and without delay the man began straining hard at the oars. The boat took off down the narrow, twisting creek. Where it might be headed, they weren't told.

Shortly afterwards, the semi-diesel engine in the stern kicked in, and with a loud knocking sound, the boat picked up speed. They had entered Suzhou Creek. Aki tucked up the edge of the awning, poked his head out, and took a look around. One after another, sampans and junks cast off from the little docks lining both banks, crowding into the waterway. Only some fifty meters wide, the creek was so thronged with boats going up and down that it seemed a miracle they didn't bump against each other. Those going back upstream were headed towards Suzhou and Wuxi, those going downstream, towards the Huangpu River and on to the Yangtze. The water smelt foul. Added to it were the chemical odours from factories along both riverbanks. The boat with Aki and Li Xing aboard was moving upstream.

14

China is a land of rivers. The shortness of the Chinese coast is in inverse proportion to the width and depth of the interior. With the Yellow River, the Yangtze, the Pearl River, and other such vast waterways as axes, a transportation and information network of large canals and creeks arose during the Sui dynasty, linking Beijing in the north with Hangzhou in the south. The network expanded in all directions, becoming ever more exhaustive in reach as it was perfected through the Tang, Song, Yuan, and Ming dynasties. For travellers heading north, the southern point of departure in any period of history was Hangzhou.

At one time, a traveller could undertake a three- or four-thousand-kilometre journey south to Guangdong and west to Jiujiang or Chengdu – all in one boat. But in the twentieth century, the advent of steamers increased the popularity of ocean transport, and the further advent of railroads and automobiles increased the popularity of land transport, so that the canal system declined in status.

Vessels plying the canals were of two types, those active in daylight and those active at night. The Green Gang, a secret organization that controlled the black market in prewar Shanghai, operated boats and oversaw boatmen using separate troops for day and night. The night vessels carried contraband such as privately grown rice and opium.

The great canals gradually fell into disuse, but in the region of the Yangtze Delta, canals remain an important means of transportation to this day. East of Lake Taihu, in the Taihu Plain, creeks branch out like capillaries, with rowboats, sailing vessels, and motorboats moving constantly to and fro.

In earliest times, the land of the Yangtze Delta, including the Taihu Plain, was unmanageably soft and swampy. From around the Qin dynasty (221 BC–206 BC), as creeks were opened and land drained, the area was transformed into fertile farmland. The creeks and rivulets still function primarily as a means of drainage and irrigation, beyond their role in transportation.

At waterway intersections and harbours, and at river crossings, vessels, people, and goods would gather, forming population centres and markets; then, as commerce and manual labour flourished, towns came into being. Of the twenty-three riverside towns in the Taihu Plain, the largest is Suzhou. Even now, one can travel by water to Shanghai or Nanjing from any of these towns without ever setting foot on land.

Such towns also afforded convenient hiding places for the Green Gang. The connecting waterways are woven together in a complex and subtle network. Public security officials found it impossible to patrol the creeks at night.

15

The fog appeared again. The man sat in the stern, adjusting the engine or plying the oars, and the woman in the bow wielded the pole, using it to push back sampans that seemed about to bump into them and occasionally plunging it straight down to the riverbed to measure the depth of the water. The bowl of the pipe she was smoking glowed red. The smell from it drifted in under the awning, faint yet distinct.

"Opium," whispered Li Xing.

Leaving behind the outskirts of Shanghai and parting with Suzhou Creek, the boat entered a small tributary. They were surrounded by fields of tall hemp. Aki tried asking the man in the stern where they were going, but got no reply. Was it all right to trust him? They had no choice, said Li Xing. Eventually the boat came out onto a broad area like a lake, the swirling fog deepening. The awning was rolled up a third of the way. A wind came up. All around the boat in the pitch darkness, little waves were whipped into small surges. Typhoon coming, said the woman in the bow.

They headed back into a creek that bent like a crank, intersecting with other channels again and again. Hemp and alder branches from the banks on either side pressed in around them with a loud scratching noise.

"We're lost," the man shouted hoarsely to the woman, in a tone of frustration. "Which way is Zhouzhuang?"

"So that's where we're going," murmured Li Xing.

Aki repeated the name inquiringly, but she shook her head. She was from northern China. The geography and place names of the Yangtze Delta were largely foreign to her.

All at once, from overhead came the angry shouts of several men. A voice called out "Who are you?" and a floodlight came on, the beam rapidly crisscrossing the boat. People were running about on the bank. The boat was ordered to stop.

Out in a field, the orange rooftop light of a patrol car was spinning around and around. The boatman in the stern called back: "What's going on?"

"A political criminal from Beijing is on the loose in the area. We're searching all boats."

"We've got a woman in labour on board here. We're on our way to the maternity hospital in Wujiang, but I lost my bearings in the fog. I could sure use some help, officer. Where are we?"

The boat normally carried hemp that had been soaked in water, beaten, and dried. Under the awning were bundles of the stuff. Li Xing quickly reached out and grabbed a handful, then rolled it up and stuffed it under her clothes. A uniformed officer leapt on board, making the boat roll heavily to one side. The light from a dimmed flashlight swept across Li Xing's belly where she lay stretched out. Aki held her hand, playing the concerned husband. For a moment it seemed to him as though she really was carrying new life, that the light on her belly came from inside her.

"Sorry for the trouble," said the officer to them both. Aki bowed his head in reply. "This is Tongli-zhen. You're not lost. To get to Wujiang, just go straight for another five kilometres. So, head that way, and be careful. Have a safe delivery, ma'am."

Engine off, the boat glided forward with oars. Wujiang was a big town on Lake Taihu with an emergency hospital, so the pretext of taking a woman in labour there was plausible. The boatman had come up with this story on the spur of the moment; his ingenuity and Li Xing's quick-witted response had saved the day. Yet if they kept on as they were, they would end up in the wrong town – just the opposite direction from Zhouzhuang. And if they turned around, they would attract suspicion.

The fog steadily deepened. Time after time, the man swore and spat into the haze. The woman in the bow kept insisting they find another route. If this was Tongli-zhen and they were on their way to Wujiang, it meant they were headed west. Zhouzhuang was some twenty kilometres west-southwest of Wujiang. The thing to do was find a cross-creek as quickly as possible and change direction; they had to get further south.

They travelled another couple of kilometres before finally coming to another creek that crossed theirs at an angle. The man swung the boat to port and switched on the engine.

For nearly two hours more, they continued to wander lost in the watery maze, the sound of the engine echoing over ponds and the surface of the lake. It was already three in the morning. They had to get where they were going before daybreak. By morning their names would be on the wanted list not only in Shanghai, but all over the surrounding countryside. Not even the creeks would be safe then. Once the sun came up, their escape route would vanish like the dew.

The boat was swallowed up in a waxy fog. With his arms held straight out in front of him, Aki couldn't see the tips of his fingers. They cut the engine again. The woman in the bow stopped smoking and laid aside her pole. With the unsteady light of an oil lamp at her side, she squatted, her arms around her knees. The man talked fiercely to himself as he rowed on, giving an impression of unreliable determination.

Hand in hand, Aki and Li Xing came out from under the awning. Sometimes locks would loom up out of the thick fog, blocking the way, and the boat would have to turn back. The two of them lost hope. The fog seemed to have fallen on them from another world.

Now and again it would suddenly thin to reveal the meagre lights of a village or a stand of hemp on the bank, swaying in fantastical shapes. The next moment, a heavy white cloud would fall like a curtain. Then no matter how they rubbed their eyes, they could see nothing, not even the water beside them. It was as if the boat were floating mid-air.

And it was too quiet. The only sound was the scraping of the oars in the oarlocks. Why no croaking of frogs, no chirping of insects? Not a fish jumped.

"We're lost on the face of the earth." Li Xing's voice was steady. "But it's lovely. Because for all we know, we may have died and won't ever be apart again."

Their faces were largely hidden from each other, but as her words suggested, she was in a buoyant mood, with a smile just visible, like a pale moon at midday.

Aki, for his part, barely managed to keep his spirits up by playing with her fingers.

The man at the oars said something.

"*Shenma?*" asked the woman.

"I said the typhoon must've missed Shanghai, must've swung off in another direction. Otherwise this damned fog would blow away."

"Went to Japan, like as not."

Abruptly Li Xing raised her head. "Smell that? Where's it coming from? It's jasmine."

Aki thrust his nose into the air and sniffed, inhaling a lungful of air mixed with fog. He shook his head. "Xingxing, that's the fog you're smelling."

"No, I'm positive. It's Yin Dan's tea."

This time he leant over the side of the boat, above the water. A distant, faint ribbon of scent was barely distinguishable. Yet the smell of Yin's jasmine tea was quite recognizable; make one pot of it and your room would be redolent for days. No mistake about it, she was right.

"Comrade, go straight on here!" she called out. "A bit slower. That's it, now to the right. Go on. Left here, that's the way."

The smell of jasmine strengthened imperceptibly. After a time, lights along the banks began to seep through the darkness. Ahead were the dark forms of houses.

"It's Zhouzhuang!" shouted the man in the stern.

Slowly they passed under an arched bridge. Up ahead loomed a three-story building – a teahouse – with stone steps descending straight into the water. The man manoeuvred the boat to the foot of the steps. The scent of jasmine came from here, conveyed to each particle of fog as surely as if Yin were doing it by hand himself.

The hard bow of the boat scraped against the steps.

"We're there." Aki picked up Li Xing by the waist and lifted her towards the side of the boat.

"Kiss me," she whispered. "As if it were the last time."

She leant down and pressed her lips to his.

Noboru Tsujihara

The riverside town of Zhouzhuang was lovely. It turned out to be on an island some thirty kilometres southeast of Suzhou. A central north-south canal was intersected by another pair, forming the town's axis. In its present form, Zhouzhuang dated back to the late thirteenth century. Two- and three-story wooden buildings stood overhanging the grid of canals side by side, each with space enough in front to secure a boat lengthwise. In all, fourteen arched stone bridges spanned the canals, where small boats with sails passed up and down. Clustered near the bridges were teahouses, pharmacies, inns, and barbershops; an outdoor market was held every morning in a square at the foot of one of the bridges.

Here, roads were canals. On dry ground, narrow lanes formed an intricate maze where you could wander around and around before coming again to the sparkling water of a creek. At strategic points there would be stone steps leading down to a rowboat. Before the construction in 1986 of a bridge to the north, waterways were the sole connection between Zhouzhuang and the surrounding area.

For the Green Gang, the town was an important base, as local authorities were unable to police the creeks at night. Other underground organizations opposed to the Chinese Communist Party had followed its lead.

The son of a prominent calligrapher, Yin Dan had graduated from the Nanjing College of Painting and Calligraphy before getting into the Shanghai motion picture industry and distinguishing himself as a cameraman. People used to say: In Beijing there's Zhang Yimou, and in Shanghai, Yin Dan. Little by little, he cultivated a reputation for eccentricity that allowed him to devote himself, undetected by Mango, to the creation of an antigovernment movement with a secret base of operations in Zhouzhuang. The director Xie Han was completely in the dark about this.

Their reunion was friendly and heartening. Here in Zhouzhuang, Yin was no different, the same watchful little man who had greedily attacked the beggar's chicken in the restaurant on Fuzhou Road. Wearing a scruffy, open-necked white shirt with the sleeves rolled up, he made them a pot of jasmine tea. His habit of stroking his pear-shaped head or pulling on his ear gave him an air of studied nonchalance. His small, bleary eyes were the eyes of a monkey feeling the cold. He looked nothing like a man who had single-handedly built up an underground organization in opposition to the most heavily policed state in the world. Though he could be as rough as the rapids of the Yellow River, he seldom showed that side of his personality. In his presence, people let their guard down and relaxed. Yin Dan himself provided all the camouflage needed to fool Mango.

Aki, too, settled back. However, after a mere ten or fifteen minutes of desultory conversation with Yin, and despite being fortified by the jasmine tea, all at once he felt an overwhelming drowsiness.

Li Xing said little or nothing, sitting with her head drooping. The fog on the creeks had left her looking pallid. That Aki would come with her this far was something she'd never expected. Yet now this much was clear: *All I can do is leave everything in Yin's hands. He'll do what's best for all of us, what's best for Aki.*

They would discuss their next move after getting some sleep, they decided. An old woman who'd been standing invisibly in a corner of the room led Li Xing and Aki off to their sleeping quarters, her gait suggestive of bound feet. Down a corridor with earthen walls, around a small inner garden, and up creaking wooden stairs they went till they came to their rooms. He and Li Xing would share the same room, Aki had assumed, but to his disappointment that wasn't to be. He felt disgruntled that on the first night of their new life as fugitives they would not be sleeping together under a single sheet. Her kiss still lingered on his lips. Later, he told himself, he would slip into her room.

The decorative window in his room was a simple carved wooden frame fitted with ground glass. Just outside was a canal. He heard drain water gurgling in a stone trough and falling onto the broad surface of the water below. Far away, oars squeaked. He remembered Li Xing settling herself into the wicker chair. Though still heavy, the fog was turning pale, showing signs of the approaching dawn. With every step he took, the wooden floorboards creaked. Li Xing was next door, her floor creaking faintly, too.

He took his pyjamas out of his bag. Remembering Li Xing's teasing, he smiled ruefully. Without putting them on, he fell into bed as he was.

Though this extraordinary day had been exhausting, sleep would not come. A green frog and a wall lizard crawled around on the ceiling. It was hot. Next door, all was quiet. Had she gone to sleep? He got up and went out into the corridor.

"Xingxing," he called softly. No reply. He reached for the doorknob and tried to turn it, but it wouldn't move. The key was still in the lock – no, the door was locked from the inside. He went hot with exasperation and disappointment. Yet, willing himself to think rationally, he had to concede that the teahouse contained not only the two of them but also Yin Dan, the old woman, and no doubt assorted other people as well. Locking her door was surely only reasonable.

Going back to his room, he decided to lock his own door, but was puzzled to find it had no lock. He lay down again and, closing his eyes, tried to empty his mind. Sleep came in light snatches. In his sleep, or rather as he lay drowsing, drifting in and out of sleep, he heard all sorts of sounds: the grate of something being dropped or dragged, the near-whispers of urgent speech. Underneath it all, in a ceaseless accompaniment, flowed the various water sounds unique to a town in the river district.

In a dream he saw the interior of the room next door. Much like his own room, with an iron bed. But of Li Xing there was no sign. He awoke in surprise, sprang up and ran to her room. Reached for the doorknob, which turned with disconcerting ease. The door opened on a scene exactly like his dream. She was gone. Her suitcase was gone. The bed-sheets were folded neatly with no sign of use.

Yin Dan had come up behind him. "She's not here anymore. You go on back to Japan," he said flatly, as though it needed no explanation. Then, rubbing the top of his head, he turned on his heel and walked away.

Aki followed him and waylaid him in the courtyard. But he was too wrought up to talk sense.

"Calm down," he was told. "Here, here's your credit card back. No one used it, don't worry."

"What do you mean, she's not here? Where did she go?"

"It was what she wanted, and we thought it was the only way, too. Just ask yourself, Mr Waki: what kind of life could you, a Japanese, have with Li Xing in this country? A life on the run is no life. You would've had to get out, go overseas. Right now that's not possible. What would you do, seek asylum in the Japanese embassy?"

A look of aversion filled Aki's eyes, and he shook his head. Inside him, he was cursing and yelling. His face was drawn taut, the outline of the bones showing prominently. If only he had someone else to blame for this disaster, this humiliation and heartache, he could have breathed more easily.

Yin Dan swung open a heavy door and led him into his private quarters. "Sit down," he said. On rare occasions Yin had a nasty tongue — mostly when speaking about Japan and the Japanese. "I used to think that you people were shallow and stuck-up. But you, Mr Waki, are a little different. I should have expected no less from a son of Waki Tanehiko. You're actually the first Japanese ever to come to this setup of ours."

Yin got up from a rosewood chair carved with peonies and walked over to a large open window. His cloth shoes made no sound. The window had a balustrade and a curved-back seat. The fog had finally lifted; sunlight reflecting off the surface of the water shimmered and danced.

"Why don't you come and sit here? This kind of window seat is called a *meirenkao* — a beauties' bench. Until the Qing dynasty, young women of good families were forbidden to leave the home without good reason. Their daily lives were confined to the innermost courtyard and the sitting room, and they could look outside only from a seat like this."

Meirenkao, murmured Aki. A bench for a young beauty to lean back against. He had assumed this teahouse facing the creek was a single, independent structure, but in fact it extended far back in a linked chain, building upon building. He now saw that Yin Dan's room looked out on a different, smaller creek to the rear. Could she still be somewhere on the premises, hidden away back there?

"Mr Yin, I understand what you're saying. But please, could I just see her one more time?"

His voice was choked with emotion; but Yin, still looking like a monkey out in the cold, made no direct reply. "Last night they arrested Liu Hong." He offered the remark with studied casualness.

"And she found that out, did she?" said Aki, the words sounding like a groan.

Yin nodded. From his rear pocket he took out a bundle of paper folded in half. Aki had seen it somewhere before. Yin tore off a page, crunched it up to soften it, then spread it out and blew his nose loudly.

Aki lunged forward and snatched Li Xing's notebook away. Forced to leave in a hurry, she must have run down the corridor, never noticing when she dropped it. Later, the old woman probably picked it up and handed it to Yin. It was covered in unreadable Japanese writing. The paper was fine and soft, perfect to use as tissues or toilet paper. Several other pages had already been torn out and disposed of in this way.

Back in his room, he read on one page in the bedraggled notebook, "He's come back to me." The words were a hasty scribble, the handwriting fast and fluid. He thought, *I know when she wrote this. That time I came back to the hotel soaking wet, after being chased by public security officials on bicycles. All along, it was me she meant.* The next day she'd spent all morning in her room, and in the afternoon, after showing him that business with the teacups, she'd said, *You know what I was doing all morning? Guess.* What had she been doing, he asked, and she answered, *Being in love.*

With who?

With you.

Her voice seemed to hang, echoing, in the air. He knew then for a certainty that she was gone.

Aki made his way back to Shanghai, where he was arrested by someone from the foreign affairs section of public security.

16

He spent the anniversary of his wife's death in a foreign jail.

He found himself mulling over Li Xing's question: "Are you going to do the same thing your father did?" There was an odd sort of comfort in the idea.

Since her notebook was unlikely to escape the attention of public security, he'd thought of tossing it in the water, but in the end decided to return it to Yin Dan. If it had to be thrown away, Yin might as well have the thing to blow his nose on.

The Public Security Bureau was located inside the former Shanghai Public Works Building, a substantial, old-fashioned structure. From across an intersection, it stood facing the Metropole Hotel, his father's onetime residence, and Hamilton House, where Huaying, the film company he worked for, had been located. Aki was not handcuffed. Ma Zuqi began by addressing him in a menacing tone, then set to work interrogating him about his escape route and the location of the organization that had assisted him.

The interrogation went on from nine in the morning till five in the evening, with a two-hour break for lunch. At precisely five o'clock, Ma abruptly ended the session and went home.

"Where did you come into contact with this underground organization?"

"*Wang le.*"

"How did you travel, by car or by boat?"

"*Wang le.*"

"Don't make a joke of it."

"I'm not joking."

"Where did you arrive?"

"*Wang le.*"

"Who was there?"

"*Wang le.*"

"Were you intimate with Li Xing?"

"*Wang le.*"

Ma stared into his eyes. Aki gritted his teeth, determined not to look away.

Sometimes it felt as if he were being squeezed to death, and yet he was still confident in his ability to get through it, for his ears rang continually with the echo of Li Xing's voice asking, "Are you going to do the same thing your father did?" The fantasy that his father was shouldering half this ordeal made it possible to continue. But if Ma Zuqi had used torture, he knew for a certainty that he could not have withstood it.

Six years earlier, death had carried Sato off. Now Li Xing had disappeared, as if she'd been abducted.

Li Xing was alive, somewhere in this more immediate world, and he clung to the hope of seeing her again. If luck was with him, it could happen. But if he gave in to Ma Zuqi now and revealed the escape route and the location of Yin's organization, she was lost to him. It was hard to explain, but he was quite sure of it.

The building he was in was large, with a flagstone courtyard, sounds from which continually reached his cell. Oddly, these consisted mainly of the wails of children and the voices of their scolding mothers, the *chop-chop* of cooking knives, the clatter of runaway washtubs, the squeal of bicycle brakes. The riddle was soon explained – part of the building was set aside as residences for the families of civil servants with offices here. "I live right above here," Ma Zuqi told him.

On the morning of the seventh day of his detention, after a muggy, sleepless night, Aki sensed all of a sudden that he couldn't take these conditions any longer. He had reached his limit. The desire for relief was bound to break through during questioning. He would not be able to resist.

Yet when Ma came in that morning, his attitude seemed completely changed. Suddenly he was using polite speech and, without referring to the charges against Aki, he talked genially about all sorts of other things: his hometown, his wife and two daughters, the time he saw the Snow Festival in Hokkaido. His wide, striped necktie was sporting a large brown stain from coffee or soy sauce. Aki interpreted the change in tactics as a signal that the investigation was proceeding to another level – harsher interrogation, mixed with physical abuse. He resigned himself to what was to come and kept his eyes fixedly on the stain on the tie dangling in front of him.

The next morning, he was led out of his cell and taken outside the building. Was he going to be put on trial? Or sent off summarily to Chaidamu or a *yaodong* prison? He was bundled into the black Peugeot. As he was looking at the Shanghai cityscape, thinking it might be the last time he ever saw it and trying his best to imprint it on his memory, the car went over Garden Bridge and pulled up in front of the Broadway Mansions Hotel. He was then taken up to his old suite on the fifteenth floor – "This is the room you and Li Xing ran away from, hand in hand," said Ma with a touch of malice – apparently to resume his old life as a hotel guest.

The rooms themselves were not the same as before. Everywhere he looked, there were obvious signs that things had been ransacked, torn up, ripped apart, and hastily thrown back together. The sun visor and the drape suit she had worn had both been carried off somewhere.

Ma opened the window. The door to the corridor outside was standing open, so the wind blew straight through the room. Papers sticking out of drawers and lying on shelves rattled noisily. The wind swept away the last traces of Li Xing's presence – yet the fact that she had once been here only hit him all the harder, and he propped himself against the wall for support.

Ma spoke slowly and distinctly. "You are free to use these rooms. But no telephoning. You are welcome to dine in the restaurant on the eighteenth floor. For the time being, you will not be able to go to any of the lower floors. And of course you may not set foot out of the hotel... Would you like to contact the Japanese consul general?" he ended.

"No," said Aki shortly.

Ma nodded. "Good. As a matter of fact, we haven't gone public with any aspect of your case. No one knows."

"Why not?"

Ever since his arrest, Aki had been subjected to steady questioning; this was the first real question of his own. Ma's only answer was a vague smile. Then he looked down and lit a cigarette, frowning deeply. With difficulty Aki managed to suppress the urge to say, *Send me to the secret prison in Jixian, Shanxi Province, where my father is being held.* If that ever happened, he thought cynically, he would have succeeded brilliantly in tracking him down, wouldn't he?

The lines between Ma's eyebrows seemed fixed in place.

"We've temporarily requisitioned these rooms."

"To confine me in?"

"Think of it as a type of house arrest."

"Residential surveillance."

"As you say."

"When will the trial be?"

"There probably won't be one."

"Why not? You're sending me to prison without a trial?"

"No. At present I'm waiting for instructions from above."

"Above?"

"Yes, from the Central Committee. *Xiansheng*, it turns out you're a very important man. You surprise me."

"What do you mean?"

"I can't answer that."

The frown lines on Ma's face finally dissolved into a little smile. He took off his necktie, rolled it into a ball which he stuffed in a pocket, then leant back on the sofa. Aki remained standing. Ma sat, not with legs outstretched, but like a proper gentleman. So began their strange time together under one roof. It would continue until the instructions from the Central Committee came, Ma said.

"I'll use the sofa. You go ahead and make yourself comfortable in the bedroom."

The housekeeping staff blinked in surprise, which was only natural. His roommate was no longer a beautiful actress but a sweaty, vulgar, middle-aged man.

A week passed. Ma turned out to be surprisingly good company. Every morning, the prisoner would look out the window at the locals doing tai chi in the park across the way and mimic their movements in his room. The warden joined in. It was good exercise, and they made rapid progress. In that ironic sense, he gained some physical freedom.

One morning Ma said: "You're being released. You're to be deported. So get ready to go back home."

He drove Aki to the airport in the black Peugeot. The springs had gotten even worse; now it seemed as if his own bottom, not the car's, was scraping along on the ground.

"What happened?"

"*Mei yo.* Nothing at all. It's been decided that nothing ever happened. You'd do well to take that view, too."

"I would've liked to say goodbye to Director Xie Han."

Arms crossed, Ma said nothing.

Since Ma stayed glued to Aki's side the whole time, baggage inspection was waived, and at Immigration, Aki used the counter reserved for diplomats and other VIPs. At the gate, the two men shook hands like two old friends who had just renewed their acquaintance, and went their separate ways.

17

Why had he been let off, allowed to return home without fanfare? When Aki found himself back home, pinching himself to see if it was real, just two weeks remained of his sabbatical. He used the time to recharge his batteries and to hold belated memorial services for his wife, and then went back to work. No one in Japan, at any rate, had any inkling of his deportation. With no indictment hanging over him, he had nothing to worry about.

He poured all his energies into the ODA report. By immersing himself in it, he hoped for a while to forget, and he did forget. Copies of the completed 570-page report sold well. Specialists praised it, and the number of times it was quoted in print set a new record for his company, Huxley. In the report, Aki marshalled all his powers of logic to press the case for a swift resumption of ODA to China. Nor, of course, did he neglect to file the secret side report. Containing, among other things, the results of his investigation into the suspicious "high-quality cottonseed plant" in Tarim, Xinjiang – which despite an outpouring of funds, had never been built – his side report was sent to the head office in New York and sealed away in Pandora.

Around the same time, he was asked to join the Study Group on Assistance to China set up by the Japan International Cooperation Agency. The group was headed by a bigwig – a onetime foreign minister now serving as advisor to the Ministry of Foreign Affairs. They were commissioned to investigate the state of yen loans to China, and weight was given to Aki's opinions, which meant he was soon involved in the writing of this group's report, as well.

Why had he been permitted to return safely to Japan? In the end, he didn't know. It was impossible to go easy on a country for something you didn't understand. Nor did he mean to do so. While he had no idea what the Chinese might be thinking, it was apparent that China could not manage without ODA. Since Aki had a strong desire to see his father and Li Xing again, he recognized that it was necessary to forge friendlier personal ties between himself and the country where they were living as virtual hostages.

At the end of July 1990, roughly one year after the Tiananmen Square crackdown, Japan became the first nation in the Western alliance to remove sanctions against China, and November saw a full reimplementation of ODA. This enormous political decision was influenced by the report of the Study Group on Assistance to China.

Some people view all world events as part of a conspiracy of some kind. Everything in the world is connected in a vast spiderweb, and every event, however insignificant, has a hidden meaning. *If only I'd picked up that crumpled flier on the road that day*, says such a person to himself, *the message it contained might have solved the whole mystery*. Others hold that events are the result of coincidence, and seek to apprehend them on their own terms.

Aki, a political sceptic, belonged to neither camp. Conspiracies exist, but only for those who believe in them: this had always been his attitude. Yet, since returning from Shanghai, his view had changed slightly. There was no doubt that some things were indeed easiest to account for as part of a conspiracy.

For example, the 1955 letter summoning his father back to China. Thirty-four years later, a letter again had brought the son to Shanghai. The author of the first one was ostensibly the spy Zheng Pinru, but at the time, she'd been officially dead for fifteen years. None of the comic actor Han Langen's papers survived, nor any copies of his films. Had he really existed? What about Liu Hong's solo escape and capture, and Li Xing's subsequent disappearance? What did all this mean?

The conclusion was inescapable: that he, Aki, had been co-opted on the orders of the Chinese public security authorities, or possibly someone even higher up. He had cooperated only by doing his job conscientiously and honestly and in accordance with his personal creed of political scepticism, putting aside any prejudice as much as possible and allowing his abilities full play. He had nothing to be ashamed of.

Opposition was strong: reimplementation of ODA now would play straight into the hands of a Communist dictatorship that had used military force to oppress the students, workers, and intellectuals who rose up in Tiananmen Square to demand democracy. At the same time, it would further fatten the swarm of Japanese politicians and corporations with a vested interest in ODA. Before the cut-off, Japanese ODA vis-à-vis China had been increasing rapidly, even surpassing aid to Indonesia, where the postwar establishment was formed by special interest groups supported by war reparations from Japan in the 1950s. The reparations business was sheer gravy to them. Now Chinese ODA was about to follow the same unsavoury path.

Aki voiced his opinion at various meetings. The decision of whether to reinstate ODA or cut it off should not be based on a simplistic sense of justice. People locked away in work camps and secret prisons of course deserved our sympathy, as did anti-establishment activists on the run, and the greed of special interest groups was abhorrent. Yet it was also true that the lives, the very existence, of hundreds of millions of Chinese depended on ODA-related projects. Moreover, swift reinstatement of ODA would provide Japan with a golden opportunity to seize the initiative in relations with China.

What if he had ignored the letter from Xie Han hinting that his father was alive and had never gone to Shanghai? Presumably, his pride as a member of a world-class team and his conscience as a researcher and analyst would have induced him to write up the same report from the same perspective. As a result, ODA would have started up again in the same way. Nothing would be any different – though the difference in his own state of mind would be as night and day.

What was his present state of mind? Sometimes he was seized by the fancy that everyone else was walking through a lobby with the soles of their shoes flat on the floor, while only he was tiptoeing. The feeling came to him when he was immersed in paperwork, when he was attending meetings, when he was reading foreign poetry.

Everyone with a secret feels that way, to a greater or lesser extent, but in Aki's case the sensation was rather more pronounced. Whenever it occurred, he had another, parallel thought: *Li Xing is alive. Somewhere, in some dim interior, she too is walking on tiptoe.*

Shortly after this, Aki was promoted. Huxley was not listed on the stock exchange, but operated as a partnership. Huxley Japan had four partners. Before his sabbatical Aki had been a senior consultant, but now he was singled out to become a fifth partner, leapfrogging over eight men.

The important and the trivial, he learnt, tiptoe side by side.

He sealed away all that had happened in Shanghai. Suppressed it, distanced himself from it. One day the receding tide would bear it all away. Yet, to forget something was not to lose it. Even if he forgot it, "something" might remember him.

Three years passed.

18

"Something" reappeared first of all in the form of another letter from Xie Han. After returning from Shanghai, Aki had sent the director a letter of thanks. Naturally, he was silent about his deportation and about Li Xing, only expressing appreciation for the many kindnesses he had received during his stay and asking him to send him any news of his father's whereabouts.

Xie's reply was written vertically in the old way, a style of writing one seldom saw in China anymore. The stationery was handmade paper from Duo Yun Xuan Art Studio.

There had been a great change in Xie's own circumstances: he had been forced into retirement. *Old soldiers just fade away*, he wrote, and continued:

> *In the end,* Moving Shadows *proved as ephemeral as its title. Now, in the solitude of my hospital bed, I let the movie unreel on the screen inside my head.*
>
> *The tedium of each day makes me think how much I'd love to see your father. Yet there's been no further word of him. I have cancer, and I can see in my doctor's eyes that I've little time left. "Our misery has great scope. My own heart sinks, right down into my boots." That's pretty much how I feel.*
>
> *What inspired me to make the effort to write this letter was something connected with your father. I told you about* Citizen Kane *showing in Shanghai. This happened about the same time. A curious event was staged in the city. Back in 1920, a fellow called Archer Samler in Philadelphia founded something known as the Memory Association. When people needed to memorize things, they could call on the association for advice. For a fee, of course. A branch was set up in Shanghai in 1938, and to commemorate the occasion a big tournament was held in the Great World amusement hall to test*

JASMINE

people's power of memory. Anyone could participate. Tanehiko won. I'd forgotten all about it.

The Memory Association had branches in Tokyo, Beijing, Rio de Janeiro, and other cities. They were planning to set one up in Tel Aviv as well, but the local populace were up in arms. How ignorant, how insulting, they said. The Bible consists of a single volume, War and Peace *five, but the Talmud has thirty-six! We Jews learn all thirty-six by heart, and we never forget. So pack up your association and leave town.*

By the by, I was delighted to hear that Liu Hong and Li Xing were able to get away. I gather they are both in Paris.

Coming to this last sentence, Aki gave the letter a sharp flick with the back of a finger. Yin Dan had said that Liu had been arrested, and Aki still believed that this news had made Li Xing leave him. The twisting corridors of thought that had brought him to this conclusion were hard to explain, perhaps illogical, but it all came down to one thing: *If it was me, that's what I'd have done, too.* Which was a rather peculiar thing for a man in love to think. But to be rock solid, love must give rise to an emotion greater than itself, namely sympathy. This latest news opened cracks in the dike of Aki's sympathy.

Xie Han ended his letter with the words: "*Zai jian, wo erzi.*" Goodbye, my son.

The premonition he'd felt as he was shaking hands with Xie for the last time in the studio office, that he might never see him again alive, hit now with double force. What mattered, Xie had said, was whether or not one passed through the age in which one lived with *dongshi* – acumen. What did that really mean? Aki still did not know.

Xie's death was reported in the Japanese newspapers, although the write-up was small.

After a while, news of Liu Hong arrived from an unlikely direction: in September 1993, Shuichi met him in Paris.

Shuichi was home for the first time in a while after reporting on trouble spots in Europe and Africa. He and Aki got together at the bar Camellia, in the hotel in Tokyo Station. A long vertical window at one end of the bar offered a view of trains pulling into and out of the platforms beyond. They drank gimlets. It was still early in the afternoon, so they were the only customers.

Shuichi's articles from areas of unrest ran in the major daily papers and weekly magazines. Aki had read every one of them.

"I know you must have been worried about Mitsuru," Shuichi said. "Sorry."

"What about your wife and kid?"

"A mess."

"Another trouble spot, huh?"

An uncomfortable silence followed.

Four years ago in the summer, Aki had left Kobe by ship, heading for Shanghai, and three days later his sister had given in to her "wicked thoughts" and met up with Shuichi in Paris. From there she'd travelled with him to Berlin, where on 9th November they witnessed the opening of the Berlin Wall from East Berlin. In December they were in Bucharest. In their room in the Hotel Bucharest, not a hundred metres from the Ceausescu Palace, they had seen the bodies of the executed dictator and his wife on their TV screen.

Returning to Paris, they stayed a month, after which Shuichi went on to Belgrade and Mitsuru flew back to Japan to take up her old job with the industrial design firm.

The world is studded with as many romances as there are stars in the firmament. Each has its own size and radiance – and lifespan. Some burn out and disappear without a trace; others make a blazing trail of light before plummeting to earth and gouging out a deep hole on impact.

Both Aki and Mitsuru had fallen heavily to earth and ended at the bottom of a crater.

"Xie Han is dead, I hear," said Shuichi, and Aki nodded. Shared thoughts on this loss began to revive the warmth between them.

"He took me out one time for a really superb gimlet."

"In Shanghai? No kidding. I seem to remember you couldn't get a gimlet in the Peace Hotel bar, or in the Jin Jiang, either."

"This was the Metropole."

"Metropole? Never heard of it."

"That's the old name, from before the war. You know, the Xincheng Hotel, over on Fuzhou Road."

JASMINE

"That place. I'll stop in next time I go," said Shuichi, and then snapped his fingers. "What am I saying? – there won't be a next time, I'm on their shit list."

Actually, so am I, added Aki silently.

There was nobody behind the counter, and Shuichi leant over and called for the bartender. With no result. Resignedly, he twirled his empty cocktail glass in his fingers as he talked about the changes in Eastern Europe following the collapse of the Soviet Union. In his characteristic way, he spoke in the clear, distinct style of a schoolteacher.

Aki listened without comment. The bartender returned to his place. There was the brisk sound of the martini shaker, and then a second gimlet was poured out for each of them.

"I read your ODA report."

Aki nodded.

"Sounded like the only thing to do was reinstate the ODA. But there must have been a secret side report."

"No, there wasn't one... You just stick to the war in Yugoslavia. That and—"

"And what?"

"See that Mitsuru is happy."

"I know, I know. Did something happen to you in Shanghai?"

"Like what?"

"I don't know. It's a question."

"Nada. Nothing at all." There was a sardonic edge to his quiet voice. After a pause, he said, reminiscing, "There weren't any limes, so Wang made our gimlets with lemon."

"Who's Wang?"

"The bartender. Xie kept calling him 'old fellow,' though actually he's quite young. Xie said he was his dead son's friend."

"A lemon gimlet. It's years now since I got deported from Beijing." Shuichi said this with such evident warmth that Aki gave him a quizzical look, but Shuichi went on without reacting, one hand rubbing the nape of his suntanned neck: "It was that scoop."

"You mean Deng Xiaoping's speech in autumn 1988, the one he gave at the Central Working Conference of the Chinese Communist Party?"

"That's the one. I was so excited. Never thought about the consequences."

Aki had read Shuichi's article based on the scoop, without feeling the information it imparted was crucially important. But then, the Central Committee's documents were classified as top state secrets even if they read, "Military advisor So-and-so forgot to bring any tissues with him and blew his nose on some paper for official communiqués belonging to Whozis of the Politburo, seated next to him."

Shuichi said, "They came straight up to me and insisted I reveal my source. No use lecturing them on the freedom of the press or journalistic ethics – and the confidentiality of news sources – it wouldn't have sunk in. They badgered me for a month and a half. Then I was arrested, hauled in for questioning. The interrogation lasted three days – and then all at once they tell me I have three days to leave the country. I never did reveal my source."

"Ever feel yourself weakening?"

"No."

"You did get scared that time they came after you on bicycles, though, you said."

"Yeah, but that was different. Once you're behind bars, your nerves settle down."

Is that a fact? thought Aki. *Bully for you. Mine sure as hell didn't.*

"One thing always bothered me," said Shuichi in a thoughtful way. "Not a pang of conscience so much as a kind of thorn in my side. After Tiananmen, I heard he was on the most-wanted list. Feared the worst. But I shouldn't have worried." Shuichi rolled his eyes upward and chuckled. Gone was the thoughtful look. "The lucky bastard managed to get out of the country in one piece. Amazing!"

Aki turned towards Shuichi and stared at him.

"I saw him in Paris. In August of '89 he escaped through Yining, in Xinjiang Province, to Almaty in Kazakhstan. He was helped along the way by an underground organization supporting Uyghur secession and independence."

"Who's 'he'?"

"My source. A guy with a name like a girl's. Liu Hong. Didn't I introduce you to him in Beijing once?"

"No. Was it really Liu Hong?"

Shuichi nodded, looking puzzled.

Aki clenched his fist centimetres above the bar and slammed it onto the wood. *He lied to me after all. Yin Dan, that little shit with a face like a shivering monkey.*

In September 1989, refugees from China had gathered in Paris and formed the "Democratic Chinese Front." In 1993 Shuichi happened to return to Paris at the time of the group's annual conference and decided to cover it, in the process running into several old acquaintances among the pro-democracy activists. One of them was Liu Hong.

The effect of Aki's brooding silence was to make Shuichi go on talking as casually as before. But to Aki, what he said was anything but casual.

"Seems Liu intended to leave the country with his girlfriend, but that didn't pan out. She's an actress with a Shanxi troupe, name of Li Xing. I met her once, in the coffee shop in the Beijing Hotel. Very good-looking."

"What happened to her?" His voice was husky.

"Dunno. I heard she stayed in China, went underground."

Something flickered in Aki's eyes, like a pilot light.

"You know, actually," said Shuichi, "I thought she looked a little like Sato."

No way am I taking that bait. He reached for a far-off ashtray and flicked a long ash from his cigarette into it.

"I'm on my way to see Mitsuru after this," said Shuichi.

"Oh? She in town?"

"No, we're meeting in Gora. I'm off for Moscow day after tomorrow. Won't be back for a while."

Shuichi had received word that the Russian leader Boris Yeltsin, who seized power following the collapse of the USSR, had decided to open the archives of the Central Committee of the Communist Party of the Soviet Union. If so, this was a groundbreaking event. There would be information on Lenin, Stalin, and Trotsky, and the records of the Comintern as well; and since the CPSU controlled Party branches worldwide, there were certain to be secret documents about its Chinese and Japanese counterparts.

"You're in a hurry, right?" said Aki lightly. Like two rowers in a boat, they pushed away from the bar at the same time. They looked at each other, exchanging awkward smiles. The smiles were a sort of tribute to one other, a silent acknowledgment that while everything they had discussed today was certainly important, they were both middle-aged men whose most passionate feelings were elsewhere engaged, who were caught up in matters of less central concern.

It was still only three in the afternoon. They parted inside Tokyo Station, Shuichi to take the bullet train to Odawara and transfer to the Hakone Mountain Railway, Aki to return to the office and chair a meeting.

19

Aki presided over a series of meetings at Huxley, debating, persuading, making promises. He kept an eye out for who among his staff was decisive and who was merely self-important. He gave orders and noted how efficiently they were carried out. He attended government councils, patiently listening to long-winded speeches with no idea what point was being made until finally it would dawn on him that the speaker was merely boasting, or making empty, self-serving statements. He endured it all with good humour, but refrained from chiming in or nodding in agreement. Politicians and bureaucrats asked for time with him. He himself could see whom he chose, without an appointment.

The Chinese made no move to contact him.

Had anyone asked him what happened during these four years, his answer would have been, "Nothing." But if the next question was, "How did you fill the time?" would he have had an answer?

The years had been consumed in forgetting Li Xing. Was that filling time? He had met her around the sixth anniversary of Sato's death and, just like that, had let her slip away. He had loved two women and he'd lost them both.

Ironically, each time the anniversary of his wife's death came around it was the image of Li Xing, vanished in the fog of a boat journey, that haunted him. His time with the two women had not overlapped, and yet now they blurred together in his mind, creating the illusion that they were one person. There were moments when he would stop to look over his shoulder, and peer into a world bleaker than anything he'd ever known – yet comforting, in a way, too. This, presumably, was the world of the dead, the world that had swallowed Sato. To descend into it and fetch her back was the stuff of old myths. But the one that Li Xing was in seemed no less inaccessible, not the land of the dead, but a vast continent where all means of searching for her were closed off to him.

Back when China still lay behind the Bamboo Curtain, a crucial source of information about it for the West, apart from spy satellites, was the *People's Daily*, the official organ of the Chinese Communist Party. Every day, the CIA and Japan's Cabinet Research Office would dissect it, compiling statistics, making comparisons, trying to read between the lines – looking for signs of power struggles, natural disasters, famine, and so on.

The need for this sort of analysis had diminished. Even so, Aki regularly scanned, in addition to the *Wall Street Journal*, The *New York Times*, and other major papers, the *People's Daily*, the Beijing *Guangming Daily*, and the Shanghai *Wen Hui Bao*.

One day on page three of the *Wen Hui Bao* he found an article stating that the hideout of a dissident ring in Zhouzhuang had been searched by Shanghai Public Security authorities. The entire group was rounded up, it said, listing the names of over thirty detainees. With bated breath, Aki searched for Li Xing's name. It wasn't there. Neither was Yin Dan's – so the police had failed to get the ringleader.

After riding out the second Tiananmen Square incident of August 1989, the new leadership in Beijing had grown to a monstrous size, thanks to ODA and an enormous influx of capital from Japan and the West. All were in search of cheap labour and a market of 1.2 billion consumers. Despite the sensational collapse of the USSR and East Germany – or perhaps because of it – the regime had only grown harsher, its system of domination becoming increasingly refined. Political systems were like life forms, constantly evolving in order to survive. In modern China, a paradoxical form of government had come into being, one where the more autocratic the regime became, the more affluent the citizenry got to be. Ordinary standards of good and evil, right and wrong, did not apply. Later generations would see that Nero's reign was in fact beneficial.

Was it okay to breathe a sigh of relief that Li Xing's name wasn't on the list, or was this a signal that all was lost, that she was no longer alive?

A month later, Aki read in the *Wen Hui Bao* that five members of the dissident ring had been sentenced to death.

20

Xu Liping's mother had died. The family grave was in Kobe's Chinese cemetery. The body, packed in ice, had been flown home from Boston. The funeral would be held in the Chinese temple in Nakayamate, Kobe. Learning of these arrangements by phone from Mitsuru, Aki hesitated for scarcely a second before deciding to attend.

His last encounter with Xu Liping had been some time ago. During the four years since returning from Shanghai, he had made several trips to Kobe and always made a point of stopping by to say hello. He never failed to send him a New Year's card and seasonal gifts – but couldn't bring himself to talk about Li Xing. For a while, he'd been tempted, looking up the number time and again in his address book and reaching for the phone, only to think better of it. *Hello, Xu Liping? Surprise – while I was in Shanghai I met a young woman who might just be your granddaughter. Actually, I am sure she is. Unfortunately I lost track of her.* How could he say this? Her name's Li Xing; her mother, Xu Lan, died in 1975. "Xiaolan" was what they called her.

Old Xu Liping had by no means forgotten his daughter, but he had long since abandoned any hope of seeing her again. But Aki had by no means abandoned any hope of seeing Li Xing, even as he was trying to forget her. *So let it go.*

He took the bullet train from Tokyo and met Mitsuru in the lobby of the New Kobe Oriental Hotel. It had been a while. Seeing him, she said that he'd put on weight. Flustered, he came up with the standard excuse: "Middle-age spread, I guess."

"Better than skin and bones. Don't worry, you haven't lost your devilish good looks. One can still see your cheekbones."

"Devilish good looks? Sounds like something Mother would say."

Mitsuru was all in black. The second time he'd seen her in mourning, he reflected. *Should it be this becoming on a woman so young?*

"Shuichi still in Moscow?"

"I guess so."

"You mean you don't know."

Aki had reserved a room in this hotel, and while Mitsuru waited in the lobby, he checked in and went up to change. Then they got in a taxi, and he told the driver to take them to Kanteibyo.

"What's that, a hospital?" the cabbie asked

Aki was dismayed. How could any Kobe taxi driver worth his salt not know the old temple?

"Sorry," the man said. "I just came here from…" His words faded into unintelligibility.

"From where?"

"Wakayama."

Mitsuru tugged at her brother's elbow. Patiently, using the familiar local dialect, he gave the driver instructions, then turned back to her for confirmation. "Right?"

"Yes, fine."

The taxi went west along Kitano Street, turned up Kitano Hill, and entered Yamamoto Street.

"Look, Aki, the Xu family's old house."

He craned his neck to look up at a striking, white Western-style building behind a stone wall. A prime example of Kobe's *ijinkan* – foreigners' mansions from a bygone era – it had been converted into an Italian restaurant: Ristorante Siena. Kobe's basic design had been laid out by expatriate Westerners and Chinese. Xu's grandfather and great-grandfather had each played an important role in the city's formation.

By this stage, Yamamoto Street had turned into a narrow, twisting lane with the mountains on one side, the sea below. Xu and his wife now lived somewhere near here, on the mountain side of the street. The road suddenly widened again. Potted chrysanthemums lining the sidewalks to right and left were a vivid yellow, lit by the slanting rays of the early October sun. Flowers for the deceased. Mourners walked along in little clusters beside them.

"How pretty," Mitsuru said. "Look, the flowers go all the way to the temple. Makes a nice contrast with the dark clothes."

"Let's get out and walk," suggested Aki.

Jasmine

They left the taxi and, looking up, saw the white twin dragons on the temple roof in the distance. Blending in with the others, they moved slowly in that direction.

"Quite a crowd," he commented. "Just look at all these people – you can tell Kobe isn't really Japanese at heart. That's what I like about it. I wonder if the old lady was sick long?"

"I heard she was fine the night before, talking about the old days. In the morning when her oldest daughter went to wake her, she was gone, lying peacefully in bed."

A large Mercedes-Benz with a diplomatic license plate passed by with a light tap on the horn. Aki glanced over in time to make eye contact with two men who turned simultaneously to look out the rear window. They seemed to know him. Or rather, he had the impression that one of them had recognized him and informed the other, "That's Waki from Huxley."

"Aki, did you hear me?"

"Yes."

"Then you'll stop by?"

"Where?"

"Bad boy, you *weren't* listening. Stop by to see Mom."

"I was planning to go and see her."

"Was?"

"Am."

"Bet you don't remember how old *she* is."

"Seventy."

"Seventy-one. That's twice now. When was the other time? Oh right – when we had dinner at Teite, just before you went to Shanghai. You got it wrong then, too."

"Did I?" he said absently. "You know, I've got a little spare time. While I'm here, I might make a side trip to Awaji."

Before long they could hear the chanting of a sutra, and the smell of incense floated on the air. Merging in with the now denser crowd, Aki and Mitsuru filed through the gate with its bright red pillars and square, blue-tiled roof. Prayer beads in hand, palms pressed together, they proceeded towards the Mounting Dragon Gate, its pillars and lintel elaborately carved with images of the legendary carp that leapt through the Dragon's Gate of the Yangtze and became a dragon.

Beyond stood a great incense burner. They lit sticks of incense before entering the main building, where they knelt formally on cushions and bowed before the seated image. After that, they moved into the hall on the right. The altar was a mass of yellow chrysanthemums, with a photograph of the deceased and a plain wooden coffin. Amid the grieving relatives on either side was the figure of Xu Liping, his familiar monocle and stooped shoulders. A quiet calm seemed to radiate out from him to fill every corner of the hall. Time spent quietly like this was long gone from Japanese funerals.

Each mourner received a small yellow chrysanthemum at the entrance and then filed across the cool brown marble floor towards the altar, holding the flower by its long stem. Aki and Mitsuru laid their chrysanthemums on the altar and bowed their heads. Turning around, they bowed to Xu Liping, who smiled fondly at them. Quietly, he said, "Stay and see her off with us, if you can."

The remains would be cremated. In the past, the bodies of wealthy Chinese were encased in stout wooden coffins specially ordered from the mainland, then shipped back for proper burial in the home province. Not anymore.

People who were staying on after the service to see Mrs Xu off found seats in a courtyard enclosure or stood on the fringe in little groups. Crossing by the great incense burner, Aki distinctly heard someone whisper his name. One's name is audible even from a certain distance.

The sound came from the shadow of a pillar in the Mounting Dragon Gate. The younger of the two men in the Benz approached him. Aki likewise veered in the man's direction. He had already guessed that they were representatives of the Chinese government.

"I'm Zhang Liang," he announced, holding out a card. Consul in the Osaka Consulate of the People's Republic of China, it said. Aki offered a card of his own in return.

They walked off together towards the front gate where the other man – the consul general – was waiting.

The consul general greeted Aki then quickly took his leave, heading off towards the waiting car. Aki and the man named Zhang Liang remained where they were. Beside their heads was a carving of a carp being transformed into a dragon.

"I just got here in August, from Beijing. Cai Fang told me to look you up."

"Cai Fang?"

"Yes. He sends his best wishes. No better man, he said."

Aki thought back. Cai Fang was that brown-eyed fellow he'd met on the boat to Shanghai. "You mean the Director of the Beijing People's Foreign Friendship Association?"

"That's right. Actually, he used to be there, but now he's back in the head office." Zhang lowered his voice slightly. "Ministry of State Security. He's deputy director of the Department of Foreign Affairs. My direct superior."

Aki mentally steeled himself. *This guy knows all about me, then.*

Zhang's eyes were deep-set, and in their depths the pupils moved constantly, like minnows.

Maybe this had something to do with ODA? Aki cast about in his mind. A representative of Chinese intelligence would not single him out for no good reason, call out his name like that. Zhang had used a voice just loud enough to carry to his ears without attracting general attention. There had to be a knack to it.

"Congratulations on your promotion at Huxley. We look forward to continued good relations with you in the future. Although I work in the Osaka consulate, I often travel to Tokyo on business, so maybe I'll see you there one of these days."

Aki mumbled an answer, trying to figure out why Zhang, or his boss, had contrived this contact.

China's ninth five-year plan would begin in 1996. In step with this, Japan was now settling on a plan for its fourth yen loan to China as ODA. This loan would determine the total amount of capital aid to that country for the period 1996–2000; the deliberations of the General Council on Issues Relating to China would carry a lot of weight. The aid package was expected to total around one trillion yen.

There was one serious obstacle: China's plan to carry out an imminent A-bomb test. In Japan, with its persistent "nuclear allergy," public opinion inclined to the belief that unless China promised to call off such testing, all economic aid should be frozen – even though Japan itself enjoyed a peaceful existence under the US nuclear umbrella.

"You've stopped going to China, haven't you?" said Zhang. As his eyes moved, his upper body also swayed, giving the impression that he might at any time lean closer. *Funny thing to say*, thought Aki. *Of course I have, everybody knows that.*

Just then, from a slight distance, someone's voice called out to Aki. At some point the side doors of the funeral hall had opened, and there stood Xu Liping. Zhang took off.

It was time for the casket to be borne away. Mitsuru and Aki went back inside. The casket was now open, and again the mourners filed by one by one with chrysanthemums – blossoms only this time, no stems – and placed them around the body. Old Mrs Xu looked tiny and shrivelled, a dried-out walnut taken from its shell.

Xu Liping, his eyes swollen and his nose red, picked up the dark cloth slippers that his mother had worn and gently laid them in the casket at her feet, like a pair of black butterfly wings. Aki remembered seeing them before. A sudden thought flashed in his brain as though for the first time: *This woman was Li Xing's* lao popo. *Her mother's father's mother.*

Mitsuru stopped at a flower shop by Mikage Station to buy their mother an armful of chrysanthemums.

"More?" said Aki. "Haven't we had enough for one day?"

"She likes them."

"Surely she doesn't need so many."

"Oh, but she does. She eats them, remember?"

They walked on as far as the Hankyu Railway overpass, where they stopped as an express train bound for Umeda thundered overhead. Beyond, on either side of the tracks, a metre-wide space fenced off by railroad ties and wire was filled with a profusion of cosmos and chrysanthemums. Mitsuru had grown up near here, in a neighbourhood very much like this, and she looked back often as they walked up the steep hill towards Fukada Pond.

The lights were on in the nursing home. Seated in her wheelchair in the reception room, Yasuko was in good spirits. Nothing in her conversation seemed particularly off the mark.

"Your father just up and disappeared one day without a word, like a ghost with no manners. What about you?" This blunt comment was addressed to Aki, whose visits to her were irregular. She pulled five or six petals from the chrysanthemum in her hands and put them in her mouth. "Didn't I teach you any manners?" She eyed her two children suspiciously, each in turn. "And why doesn't either of you get married, I'd like to know."

"Mom," said Mitsuru, "have you forgotten Sato?"

Silence.

Aki said gently, "Sato was my wife, but she's been dead ten years. Mitsuru will be getting married any time now, though."

Mitsuru had been stroking her mother's arm as it lay on the armrest, but now she looked up at him. "Shuichi and I broke up."

Aki in turn was silent, only nodding.

His sister smiled. "You know who my heart belongs to? You, big brother. Or no – make that your father, one removed from you. He's the one I really love."

"Wouldn't surprise me if that man was a ghost from day one," announced Yasuko. She turned suspicious eyes on her son's feet as if checking to make sure he was flesh and blood.

Aki felt a draft around his ankles. Tapping his heels on the linoleum floor, he said firmly, "Dad was no ghost. The proof is, you gave birth to me, and see here? I've got two legs just like anybody else."

"You know something about your father? He didn't like scaly fish. Strange, considering he was born right on the sea."

Mitsuru murmured in his ear, "She's forgotten all about mine." Mitsuru's father, a law professor at Konan University, had died in a car accident. An unassuming man, not a great legal scholar.

Yasuko looked Aki up and down suspiciously several times. Impulsively he reached out, took the chrysanthemum away from her, and stuffed it in his mouth.

"For God's sake, Aki!" Mitsuru exclaimed, exasperated.

"Dad was no ghost – and the proof is, he's still alive."

"You saw him?" asked his mother with interest. "Where?"

He only shook his head, and took her hand in his.

"*I* know where he is," she said. "Shanghai. A woman there sent for him. He was cheating on me the whole time. You know what he was? A gloomy old lecher, that's what."

Aki looked down. He was thinking about the difference between his father's images in Kobe and Shanghai. Here, he'd been taciturn and gloomy; there, light-hearted, droll, and stylish. Dashed across the street from the Metropole to Hamilton House, dodging raindrops without an umbrella; made puns constantly; knew just where people were ticklish on their arms and legs. Yasuko was unaware that he'd ever been a Chinese comic actor.

Just then, in a frail voice his father called to him: *Help me.* Aki was certain that he'd heard it. Across a gap of thirty-eight years and thousands of kilometres, his father's voice came to him. His mother then reinforced the impression: "Didn't your father say something to you just now, Aki?"

Outside, the sky was dark. Light from the hotel on the hill outside the window streamed into the room through the treetops.

All at once Yasuko's head sank heavily onto her breast.

"She's asleep," said Mitsuru. "It's always like this."

21

Not alive, perhaps, but not dead, either. The idea of his father as a ghost was unsettling. Intellectually, he could accept the image of him as an abstraction, a lifelike construct. But when the door opened, the wind blew in, and darkness settled, who could go on saying this sort of thing seated calmly in his chair? And didn't reducing your father to a kind of mirage make you, his counterpart, something similar?

The next day Aki went to Awaji Island. It was his first visit there since a middle-school field trip, twenty-six years earlier.

On the island bus he chatted with an old couple from Kyoto who had come to see the sun go down over the Seto Inland Sea. Still plenty of time before sunset; they would get off at the next stop, Goshikihama Beach, and wait there. They talked about a "green flash." The Hotel Anaga had nine little villas, and from the terrace of just one of these, at dusk on a clear day in winter, supposedly you could see it on the horizon. Did he think it was true? Aki had no idea.

The time it took for the sun to climb over the Ikoma-Kongo mountain range and sink beyond the horizon of the Seto Inland Sea corresponded exactly to the time it took him to leave Kobe by boat, tour the island by bus, and make it back again. The place was the ideal size for an autumn day of exploring. In the course of circling the island, his thoughts had gelled into a decision.

As soon as he got off the boat, he went straight to call on Xu Liping.

The condominium building where Xu and his wife now lived was old, but substantial and luxurious. Xu was the property manager for the real estate he still owned after the liquidation of his business – including Suwayama Court, this ten-story building with eighty units. Xu was at home. Services for his late mother would continue for some time, but this afternoon the old man was taking a quiet break. Despite the suddenness of the visit, he seemed genuinely glad to see Aki.

Against two of the walls was mahogany furniture fitted with dark red velvet cushions and built-in ceiling-high bookcases. Comfortable-looking chairs were arranged around a large, oval rosewood table as though in readiness for guests. The keyboard of the black upright piano was exposed; Xu had just been playing.

Enveloped in a silvery grey light, the room was not very Chinese in decor. The discovery surprised Aki, but he soon realized that the Xus had not deliberately set out to exclude all trace of their origins. Undeniably elegant, the decor was intended not just to please the owners but to give pleasure to others as well. This was the home of people with the means and discrimination to indulge a sophisticated taste.

The old man listened in silence as Aki told him, with unconcealed pain and regret, about his daughter and granddaughter. When it was finished he said, "No apology needed. The story of your escape together in the night sounds like a fairy tale." He smiled, his fingers fumbling with the lace cover on the armrest.

Aki let out a long, slow breath. "You could be right. Maybe it was a fairy tale. But I won't let it stay one. Not anymore."

Xu shook his head. "Forget about her." He repeated the advice, then said, "I tried to forget Xiaolan, and I succeeded. You, too, must forget this girl."

"I should have told you sooner."

"No, it's all water under the bridge. At my age, I have no desire to burden my memory with sad things. I've reached the state of mind of Prospero." In his younger days Xu had put on a series of Shakespeare's plays in Mandarin.

There was a sound in the hallway.

"My wife's back. I don't intend to tell her what I've learnt from you today."

Aki nodded, and for a time the two men sank into silence.

Footsteps drew near. The door to the living room was open, so Xu's wife saw from behind that someone was seated on the sofa, but who it was she couldn't tell.

Aki enjoyed the sound of the soft padding of her cloth shoes. This was Xingxing's *laolao*, her maternal grandmother. He got up.

"Good heavens, we have a guest, and you're as quiet as if you'd been smoking opium!"

JASMINE

Xu Liping was no opium smoker. The figure of speech was similar to the French *un ange passe*, said when conversation breaks off and silence fills the room.

"Oh, I'm sorry. It's you, Akihiko!"

He rose and bowed respectfully. She was a silver-haired old lady with a full face.

"And you haven't even offered him a cup of tea…" With this reproach, she quickly excused herself. Aki and Xu Liping took advantage of the opportunity to step out onto the balcony for a smoke. Beyond the balcony lay a grove of large camphor trees, maples, oaks, and wingnuts; feathering brightly between them were the lights of Motomachi and the waterfront Meriken Park. If the trees were removed, there would have been a panoramic view of Kobe and the sea, but Xu preferred it as it was. He had a deep and abiding affection for these hills where his father and grandfather had lived before him, but to look down on the city the way Westerners liked to do struck him as in poor taste.

Xu propped his long cigarette in the ashtray and made a startling remark: "You kept quiet for nearly five years, but I've been quiet for more than thirty." He picked up his cigarette again, flicking off the ash, and put it back in his mouth. "A letter from a woman definitely came."

"A letter to my father, you mean. How do you know that?"

Without answering the question, Xu went on: "In those days, the Chinese population here was deeply divided between two factions, pro-mainland and pro-Taiwan – not just in Kobe, of course. The two fought bitterly for supremacy. My father had already taken Japanese citizenship before the war. He went to the Peers' School, where he became friends with Prince Konoe Fumimaro. The prince often came over to our house in Kitano."

"The one that's now the Ristorante Siena."

"That's right. Prince Konoe was an enlightened man, but he was also a member of the old nobility. Terrified of revolution. More than once he told my father, 'If revolution ever comes to Japan, I want you to hide me.' Our family had a villa on an island near Amoy where we used to go for three months every winter. The prince must have had that villa in mind." Xu paused before continuing.

"After the war, my father had nothing more to do with politics. Except for his friendship with Zhou Enlai."

"Zhou Enlai?" he echoed. *Him again.*

"Zhou came to study in Japan in 1917, and left Kobe in April 1919 to take part in the May Fourth Movement. While he was here, he stayed with my family. So you see, although we were anti-Communist, for him we made an exception." The many wrinkles in Xu's face seemed to tell not of old age or fatigue, but of determination. "The connection between Zhou Enlai and Kobe runs deep. Maybe even deeper than Dr Sun Yat-sen's connection with the city. If there's any possibility that your father is still alive…"

"Yes?"

"It may have something to do with the death of Zhou Enlai."

"Why do you say that?"

Premier Zhou died in Beijing on 8th January 1976. The cause of death was cancer. A gathering to commemorate the event had triggered the first Tiananmen Square incident.

"Your father went back to Shanghai in 1955 after getting a letter from a woman – or so a handful of us *huaqiao* believed. Back then, Communist China had all kinds of spy agencies engaged in clandestine activities in Japan. As you'd have expected, together with Stalin, they were on a mission to turn Asia red. But the US military was stationed here in Japan. There was also the struggle with Chiang Kai-shek. What to do with Japan? In any event, the promotion of revolution in Japan was a top item on the Communist agenda. And all the intelligence operations here were controlled by Zhou Enlai. Besides the various spy agencies in Japan, he – Zhou again – had another espionage organization, one that was essentially private. Call it Y Agency. Headed by a Japanese."

"My father?"

"No. Y Agency made deep inroads into the Japanese Communist Party and the Japan Socialist Party, as well as burrowing around behind conservative political leaders of the day. The boat your father took to China was a spy ship belonging to Y Agency."

"You mean they went to all the trouble of procuring a ship just for my father?"

"That I don't know. But I do know for a certainty that that ship could not have left port without instructions from Zhou Enlai."

Jasmine

"Assuming the name on the letter was really Zheng Pinru, as I heard in Shanghai, then Zhou must have known of their affair. But why did he have to use a dead woman – a ghost – to get him back to China? And then have him arrested? What on earth for?"

"That I don't know, either. I've told you all I can. I'm not hiding anything, I just don't know. My grandfather aided Sun Yat-sen, but my father was a supporter of Wang Jingwei. So you see, to both the Party and to Chiang Kai-shek, the Xu family were traitors."

Aki couldn't help recalling that his own father, under the name of Han Langen, was also tried as a traitor.

"In 1959, four years after your father left, our daughter went to China, wanting to participate in the building of the motherland. You know what my mother told her? 'Motherland? We have no motherland!' Her going was a shock. Then came the Cultural Revolution. Her letters stopped coming. We did all we could, but nothing, not one word, ever came from her after that. I even wrote to Zhou Enlai, although of course by then he was engulfed in the whole calamity himself. Thirty million people died. There she was, hailing from a family of expatriates living in Japan – and traitors, to boot. What chance did she have? We lost all hope. The Cultural Revolution broke my last tie with the mainland. Yet now you tell me that your father may still be alive and I may have a granddaughter."

The old man's eyes, though restless, stared straight at him. Aki wanted him to go on talking, if only to hear his voice.

"As far as I can see..." Xu's voice was slightly high-pitched.

As far as I can see, Aki echoed silently.

"...the Japanese take 1945 as the cut-off point for everything. When in fact it was no such thing. For a déraciné like me, the postwar world and the prewar world exist on a continuum. That's the only way I can look at things."

"And my father?"

He shook his head. Aki took in a deep breath, then let it out. "Shall we go in?"

They returned to the living room.

"There's one more thing I'd like to ask," Aki ventured.

The old man turned to him with a quizzical look. Their two figures were reflected on the polished surface of the piano. "What's that?"

"You said that if my father were alive, it would be because of the death of Zhou Enlai."

"Yes, and I'll tell you why. Suppose it was Zhou who had him arrested in Beijing and imprisoned. I have no way of knowing that, mind you; this is all conjecture. But supposing that is the case, then Zhou forgets about him. Forgets about why he had him arrested in the first place. As he would – just think of all that was happening on the mainland: the anti-right-wing struggle, Soviet-Chinese antagonism, the damage caused by the Great Leap Forward, then the Cultural Revolution. Each of these involved another purge. One false step and Zhou would be swept from power, thrown in jail. Political life was a tightrope. By around 1976 the Cultural Revolution had run its course. That must have been a big relief for him. And maybe then, in his relief, he remembered Waki Tanehiko, remembered that he'd had him lured back to Japan and arrested. Maybe he now regretted having done that."

Aki murmured his agreement, and continued the thought. "And then what? What could he have done, or tried to do, about my father? But whether he thought of him or not, before he could make any decision, sickness carried him off." He stopped. A tentative smile crossed his face.

"Yes, he died. They all died. Friend and foe alike."

Seated on the sofa, Xu stirred with a small, birdlike movement. They had exhausted all they had to say to one another. Aki got up to take his leave, but the old man held up a restraining hand.

"My wife is preparing tea. Brewed Gungfu-style. Please wait."

She came gliding in on slippered feet, carrying a tea set on a tray of red lacquer: three reddish-brown cups, with a teapot and water basin of the same colour. With graceful gestures, she poured hot water into the pot and removed the foam with the lid. Little by little she then poured tea into each of the cups, down to the last drop.

"This is Wuyi Rock tea," she said, "rare oolong from the Wuyi mountains. Did you know, Mr Waki, that oolong tea is called 'blue tea' in Chinese?"

"No, I didn't. It's different from green tea, obviously."

"Yes. Midway between green and black. There are several varieties of Wuyi Rock tea. This is one of the best, Shui Jin Gui. Golden Turtle. It tastes of the wind."

Jasmine

He took a sip. There was a slight acidity, which did indeed have an effect rather like wind blowing on the tip of one's tongue. After she refilled the pot, Aki gently took it out of her hands and placed it in the centre of the table. He then filled the three cups, arranging them first in a straight line facing the spout.

"Gracious! The Challenge! Where did you learn this?" she asked.

"From a friend in China."

"A young person?"

Aki nodded.

"Well, well," she said. "It's hard to believe any young person on the mainland today would know about it."

Xu Liping only gave a brief, tight-lipped nod. There was a certain tension between the two men. The person who arranged the teacups was inviting the other to join a cause with him. Whoever chose the middle cup and drank from it agreed to join forces with the other man.

Unhesitatingly, Xu picked up the cup at the end and drank it slowly dry.

After Aki left, Xu said to his wife: "You know, it looks as though Waki might still be alive."

"What a thing to say! What did you think, that we had a ghost come calling?"

"No, I mean his father, Waki Tanehiko. He's alive, still in prison on the mainland."

She leant a hand on the back of a chair, a confused look on her face.

"Sit down, my dear," he told her, and she perched on the edge of the sofa where Aki had been sitting. "He wants to rescue his father. It's probably hopeless. The man may even be dead... But do you remember how, years ago, we taught our Xiaolan the Challenge?"

"Of course. How could I ever forget?"

"The person who taught it to Aki was ..." He clamped his mouth shut. He'd made up his mind not to tell her about Li Xing. But he was torn.

"What's wrong? Why won't you go on?"

"In Shanghai, the person who explained it to him was an actress from Shanxi named Li Xing. Her mother's name was Xu Xiaolan. In other words, he met our *granddaughter* over there. And she's a member of the underground movement."

His wife pressed her hands together to her breast.

"As you know," he said, "in all this time I never had the slightest wish to get mixed up with either side, the mainland or Taiwan. I'm perfectly content here in Kobe, that's all. And now in my old age I'm confronted by this – Aki asking me to join in with him... It's too much."

His wife buried her face in her hands.

Just then, the intercom buzzed. Thinking their visitor was back, Xu felt a momentary sense of dread; but it was only a bill collector for the newspaper they took.

22

The consul Zhang Liang was waiting for Aki, leaning on the counter in the dimly lit bar Camellia.

A few days after their first encounter at the funeral of Xu Liping's mother in the autumn, Aki had called on Zhang at the Osaka consulate and put in a formal request for his father's whereabouts to be traced. Since then, the two had gotten together three or four more times to go over progress reports, steering clear of touchy subjects like politics and ODA. For these meetings, Zhang took advantage of his monthly trips to Tokyo for embassy briefings. He and Aki always met at this bar in the hotel in Tokyo Station. Zhang admired the setting with the view of the trains; he wished aloud that there was a bar like this in Beijing.

Zhang attached no conditions to Aki's request. But now that his ODA work was once again secret, and tricky, and fairly urgent in nature, Aki felt it was unwise to meet with him so often. Still, neither could he afford to hesitate. He did not have all the time in the world. The only way of reaching his father was to approach Cai Fang through this intermediary. He had no alternative.

In conversation, Aki was always astonished at how much Zhang knew about him: his wife's death in 1983, his studies in college and graduate school, his trips to China and other countries, his position and achievements at Huxley. And yet, to his still greater surprise, Zhang seemed ignorant of all that had happened to him in Shanghai. It was most peculiar. After a number of cautious feelers, he reached the conclusion that Zhang actually had no knowledge of those events. The portion of his life having to do with Shanghai was simply missing, a gap in his file. When he mentioned his summer there, all Zhang had to say was that it was "a curious choice – nobody born and bred in Beijing likes the place." And yet he was a member of the all-seeing Ministry of State Security. His boss was a senior official in it, had even travelled to Shanghai by ship with Aki, and was around the whole time he was there... so he *had* to know everything!

Clearly, Cai had given Zhang the specific task of initiating contact with Aki. Yet Zhang seemed genuinely in the dark about those earlier events. His boss had withheld the information. Why? What was he up to? Did he intend using that information against Aki, somewhere down the road?

Aki had hopes that Cai Fang would do all he could to track down his father. The man's current post certainly gave him the necessary authority to conduct such a search. He knew Aki's secrets, knew Aki better in fact than almost any man on earth. Only someone privy to a person's secrets could truly understand him, which was why Aki persisted in believing, naïvely, that Cai would do all he could on his behalf.

But there was another secret issue: who was the woman he'd seen standing on the wharf? Li Xing had dismissed the suggestion that it was her; yet over time, the figures of the two women had merged indistinguishably in Aki's mind again. If she'd been there to meet Cai Fang, then maybe the two were allies of some kind.

The initial response to Aki's request came after a five-month wait. In full, it said: "This agency was unable to confirm the existence of anyone named Waki Tanehiko within the borders of this republic." Short shrift.

The second response came three months later: "No record exists of a Japanese person named Waki Tanehiko having entered this country in 1955."

It was then that Zhang Liang brought up a personal matter, something unusual for him. He mentioned that he might soon be getting married. Due to the sensitive nature of his work, Party screening was extremely strict; his boss was using his influence on the couple's behalf, though, and it would probably turn out all right. How about telling him to use his influence on my behalf, too, Aki had said, half in jest. Will do, Zhang had said.

The third response came a month ago. There was no record of an arrest taking place in Beijing, nor did the names Waki Tanehiko or Han Langen appear anywhere in court records or on the list of prisoners in Qincheng Prison; also, there were no concentration camps or secret prisons in the Republic of China. The inquirer should take care not to be led astray by propaganda put out by forces intent on slandering China and overturning its political system.

"A year you've been waiting, and this is all you get? I see they threw in a little lecture at the end," said Zhang, driven to feeling sympathy for him. "The trouble is, you think of China as a country of written records. Sorry to disappoint. We also have a tradition of book-burning and burying scholars alive. People don't take notes, and our keeping of archives is sloppy. Every change in the powers that be, every set of new executives, means piles of papers get destroyed. I spent two years in Moscow, and the Soviet Communist Party was impressive. They're compulsive note-takers. Every written document, every last little scrap of paper, is kept. The archives are vast, and there are a lot of them. Their Central Committee has its own archives, of course, but so does every other government office. Not just documents, either. The number of film reels in storage is equally amazing. Films from all over the world, I've heard. Gosfilmofond, out in a Moscow suburb, is the Russian State Film Archives, and it's the size of a small village. They may be fellow Communists, but what a difference. You have to wonder, maybe the Soviet system collapsed from the sheer weight of all those records... Anyway, I'm afraid you won't get anywhere by looking for documentary evidence of your father's existence. Unfortunately, I'm not in a position to personally escort you to Jixian or wherever, either."

An hour ago, out of the blue, Zhang had phoned Aki at his office to say he had a spare hour before his train left, and could they possibly get together? Any news, Aki had asked. No, Zhang said, he just wanted to talk. He'd gotten hold of some good tea. Not a lot, but enough to share.

Ignoring the chairs along the wall, Aki sat one stool down from Zhang at the bend in the counter, and leant towards him. "Here," said Zhang, taking a small packet wrapped in tin foil from his pocket. Aki accepted it with a deliberately furtive air, commenting dryly, "You'd think it was marijuana," as he looked inside. "Oolong, is it?"

"Yes. The best. Genuine Big Red Robe tea."

"Wow."

"A friend of mine just became vice-governor of Fujian Province."

"An official perk."

"Right. I'm from Beijing, but somehow I don't go for jasmine tea. What about you?"

"I like them both."

Zhang nodded.

The bartender asked for his order. Glancing at Zhang's cocktail glass, Aki asked, "What are you drinking?"

"Between the Sheets."

"Early for a nightcap," he said, smiling. "Make mine a bourbon. Double."

When Aki's glass was set down on the counter, Zhang stared at it for a moment before saying in a flat, hoarse voice: "About the Tarim survey…"

Taking out a cigarette, Aki lifted his eyebrows to question if Zhang minded his smoking.

"Go right ahead. I'm no smoker, myself." Zhang paused, then said, "In 1988 you conducted a survey of a high-quality cottonseed plant in Tarim, Xinjiang."

Looking quizzical, Aki said nothing.

"Yet your final report – which was extremely well done, we were all impressed – that report contained nothing on that Tarim plant. Why not? I'd be interested in seeing that part."

"No such thing exists." Aki said this slowly and clearly, steadily returning Zhang's shifting gaze.

"Didn't you see anything in Tarim?"

"Yes, a farm in the middle of the desert. Quite an enterprise, in fact."

"Why isn't it in the report?"

"Look, it's not our policy to review every single thing we see."

"Is it in a side report?"

"There isn't one."

"Assistance for the plant amounted to seven hundred million yen, but it's vanished into thin air."

"Well, it's got nothing to do with me. Start looking for corruption in these situations and you're bound to find it, but that's not the job of a think tank."

"I see. All right." Zhang's mouth tightened, and he fell silent. This probably wasn't the reply he had wanted or anticipated. His gloomy face brightened as he pointed at the lone window in the bar and remarked, "Nice to see the trains come and go, isn't it? I wish we could get more tracks in Beijing. More trains, too."

There were cowbells attached to the door, and they rang clearly as a couple came in. They sat at the bar near the window; the man, middle-aged, ordered a Scotch on the rocks, the woman, who was much younger, a Cherry Blossom. She kept stroking her hair. Thanks to these newcomers, the view of the trains was now blocked off.

"Not bad-looking," murmured Zhang Liang. "Chest flat as a pancake, though."

Aki smiled politely, although he didn't enjoy this sort of talk.

"Let's drink a toast," said Zhang. "My wife is finally coming."

"Cheers," said Aki, raising his glass. So Zhang was now a married man.

"Finally! And more good news: I got my Japanese driver's license."

"Well, hey, good for you. Mind if I have another smoke?"

"Of course not. I don't smoke... but you know that."

"I haven't got a driver's license," said Aki.

"Really? That's unusual. Here, take a look at mine." He reached into his suit jacket pocket, took out a leather case, and showed it to him. "While you're at it, take a look at my wife." He took out a colour photo from the opposite side of the case, but before Aki could see it, he said, "Oops, wrong one, this is my mother." He put the photograph back and pulled out another one, holding it up before Aki's eyes like a trump card.

He saw it first at a slight angle. Then straight on. A gust of wind from a far-off pier swept straight through him.

"Mr Waki."

Hearing his name jolted him back to reality. Quickly, he reached for his glass of bourbon, meaning to drain it, but not a drop was left.

"She's a fine-looking woman. May I see it again?" His voice was as even as he could make it.

"Sure. Look all you want – you can't wear it out!"

But the light in Aki's eyes burned with sufficient intensity to reduce the picture, and with it the person photographed, to cinders.

"I'd like to get you something to celebrate, a gift. What would you like?"

"You don't have to do that."

"Oh, I insist. Please. Allow me to get you something. When is she arriving?"

Zhang slid the photo back into his leather case, looking happily excited. He flicked a finger repeatedly against the rim of his cocktail glass. "Next month. The year's almost over; she'll be coming the very last week of the year. So we'll be spending this Chinese New Year's in Japan."

"Are you going to Beijing to travel with her?"

Zhang shook his head. "Can't leave Osaka. It wouldn't work out, anyway. Li Yan — that's her name; it's written with the character for swallow, the bird — she's coming by boat. I was against it, but she wouldn't listen. It's just a hop from Beijing by plane. Only two hours to Kansai International Airport. Instead, she's taking three whole days! She says it's because she's never seen the ocean before. I told her once she gets here, she can see it till she's blue in the face if she wants."

"She'll take the Yan Jing ferry from Tianjin?"

"You'd think so, but she's insisting on taking the *Xin Jian Zhen*, the one from Shanghai."

Aki finally ordered another bourbon. He lit another cigarette, took two or three puffs, and snuffed it out between his fingers. He felt no pain.

Zhang kept stealing looks at the female customer. In a low voice he said, "I prefer breasts like mangoes." He dropped his voice further. "Like my wife's."

Aki said nothing, only closing his eyelids. Another gust of wind swept through him.

"I'll try a little harder to look for your father. Once my wife gets here and things settle down a bit, I'll go back to Beijing. I've got some reports to file there, anyway. Don't give up hope. Just be patient."

Aki was scarcely listening.

23

The ship that Zhang Liang's wife, Li Yan, was taking from Shanghai to Kobe in December 1994 was due to sail at one o'clock in the afternoon on Saturday, the 24th, and arrive in Kobe at ten o'clock in the morning on Monday, the 26th.

On 23rd December Aki flew from Narita on ANA to Shanghai Airport. He himself made the arrangements for airline and boat tickets and reserved a hotel; no one else knew about the trip. Still less could anyone have known his purpose. He obtained his visa in Tokyo. Since Zhang Liang worked for the Osaka consulate, there was no danger of immediate detection. *Top secret all the way*, he murmured to himself in the airplane.

At the airport he got in a taxi. He remembered his old driver Chen Ying. Every time he got off a plane or boat in China, Chen had been conspicuously standing around with a happy-go-lucky grin, his hands in his pockets. He'd never heard anything further from Chen. What had become of him? Were he and his Anli living happily ever after somewhere in Japan?

The taxi drove into the downtown area. Aki was riveted by the scenes outside his window. The city was being overturned. Everywhere he looked, another old neighbourhood lay dismantled, reduced to piles of rubble; those few that remained were under attack from great iron wrecking balls flung around by cranes. There were huge clouds of dust, with laths and girders sticking out of them, hanging perilously in the air.

The traffic was appalling. Aki got tired of looking out the window, and went through the city centre with his eyes shut. "*Dao le.*" We're there. At this comment from the driver, he reopened his eyes. There stood the Broadway Mansions Hotel, unchanged, an eagle with its wings half folded. The familiar sight was reassuring.

He was booked into a standard twin on the fourteenth floor, one with a view of Suzhou Creek, as he'd requested. It pleased him above all that the room was directly below the suite where he'd spent several days with Li Xing and nearly a week under house arrest. The coincidence struck him as a lucky omen.

Aki opened the curtains. It was a clear day, but where the sun was he couldn't tell for sure. Red-tinged light shone through the choking haze to fill his room. December had been unusually cold here, with occasional snow flurries, he'd heard, but today the air was warm. Underneath the surface reflections from its banks, Suzhou Creek wound along, black as tar. Flat-bottomed barges laden with coal entered on it one after another from the Huangpu, passing under Garden Bridge and heading back upstream. On to Suzhou, Wuxi, and Kunshan. *Yes, and Zhouzhuang too*, he thought. On ropes stretched over the piles of coal, colourful laundry fluttered in the wind like a signal.

The view had changed considerably. The row of pretentious, neoclassical European-style buildings was the same, but just behind them, steel-frame skyscrapers now jutted into the air. Along the riverside promenade was a strip of three-story concrete shops extending all the way to Pier 16, so unless you climbed to the rooftops, the surface of the Huangpu remained hidden from view.

Across the river, a queer-looking tower was under construction, shaped like a hairpin, a good five hundred metres high. All kinds of sixty-story buildings were springing up around it. Just a few years ago this had been agricultural land – nothing but some piers, a factory or two, and a scattering of workers' housing. Now it was being transformed into a financial centre, to amass the wealth of the world.

The city was pulsing and humming with activity, kicking up a pall of dust as it reinvented itself – and hidden somewhere in all this ferment was Li Xing, here to board the ship for Kobe. The thought made him restless. Wearing a sweater and a leather jacket, he hurried out into the street with three places in mind to revisit. Straight off, he went to Shanghai Film Studio, where the sole familiar face belonged to Yu Ming. When he asked her about Xie Han's house, she shook her head and said it had been torn down. His wife had died long ago, and Yu had no idea what had happened to his ashes.

He then went to the bar in the basement of the Metropole Hotel. The long counter was unchanged, but it had been converted into a karaoke bar. No sign of Wang. The market where the cricket seller had been was nearby. He began to drift in that direction, but soon thought better of it. If he allowed himself to revisit the corner in the alleyway where the man had taken them... then the road by the creek... the stone steps leading down to the barge... he might give in and go all the way back to the river town where he had lost Li Xing. What he was committed to now was facing forward, not backward, in the belief that time's natural unfolding of events would bring him to Li Yan, as apparently she was now called.

For dinner, he went to the hotel restaurant on the eighteenth floor – and to his surprise was turned away. Unaccompanied guests could not be served, he was told, so he withdrew without objecting. Going out to eat was too much trouble. He went down to the coffee shop in the lobby and ordered two kinds of sandwiches to go, picked up a bottle of red wine at the kiosk, and went back to his room.

The gaudy lighting of the buildings on the Bund made them look more than ever like a theatrical backdrop. Aki closed the curtains, munched his sandwiches, drank his wine. He made short work of the meal. There was still plenty of wine, but it seemed no amount of alcohol would get him drunk tonight, so he left off.

Anxiety reared its ugly head. Was Li Yan really Li Xing? After going underground, Li Xing must have resurfaced under a different name and resumed her life – and somehow or other become acquainted with Zhang Liang.

As Zhang had said, it was only a short hop by plane to Kansai International Airport, and yet his wife insisted on travelling by boat. Moreover, since she lived in Beijing it would be natural for her to sail from nearby Tianjin, but instead she was going out of her way to take the *Xin Jian Zhen* from Shanghai. *Tomorrow I'll see her*, he almost yelled. His eyes travelled around the room, looked up at the ceiling. *Up there was our room.*

Sitting back in the chair, he drank one more glass of wine. He opened his book of Arabic poetry, and quietly read aloud a couplet:

NOBORU TSUJIHARA

The watchmen know that Hafiz is in love.
Even King Solomon's councillors know.

The following morning, after a morning mist mixed with the dust from construction sites had cleared, the air tingled with a resinous smell that stung the tongue and nostrils. Aki checked out and tried to hail a taxi in front of the hotel, but was turned down by driver after driver, all of whom said his destination was too close. Giving up, he set off for the pier on foot. Fortunately, he had only one small bag to carry.

He turned left at the foot of Garden Bridge and walked along the Huangpu, arriving at the boarding area in twenty minutes. A lively crowd of young girls spilt out into the street. Dragging large suitcases and great big carryalls of heavy plastic with wide stripes of red and blue, they thronged into the smallish waiting room, which was poorly lit and stuffy. On his voyage from Kobe five years ago, there'd been barely fifty passengers in all, but he guessed there were a good three hundred now.

Aki got in line and waited for the processing for leaving the country. His eyes roamed about like a searchlight. Li Yan was here, somewhere in the crowd; the thought drove him to distraction.

The line began to move. Still no sign of her. Aki was duly processed and left the building, walking the two hundred metres to the ship. Everything was happening in just the reverse order from five years ago. The *Xin Jian Zhen* was anchored with her bow upstream. Both fore and aft, two thick hawsers stretched down from the side of the ship to wind around mushroom-shaped bollards on the pier. Aki came to a stop by one of them.

He walked briskly up the gangplank. At the purser's desk, he entered his name and passport number in the register for A Deck, where there were eight first-class cabins and one VIP cabin. The first-class cabins were twin rooms, the VIP cabin a suite. A consul's wife travelling alone would probably be in one of the first-class cabins, he thought. He cast a quick glance over the other names in the register, but hers wasn't there. No hurry. This was a ship, not a creek or an alley where she might slip away.

He was handed his key; it was just like checking into a hotel. The purser's desk was on C Deck, so to reach A Deck he climbed the spiral stairs in the central stairwell. His cabin was A5. Five years back it had been A4, directly across the way. He put down his bag and had a quick look at the bed and sink before going back out. After checking the vicinity of the stairs, he went out on deck near the gangplank.

He looked down at the pier. The group of girls was now camped out below, awaiting the signal to board. Their suitcases and carryalls were piled one on top of the other on a pallet covered in netting. The luggage was hoisted up on a hook suspended from a crane. The girls climbed noisily aboard.

A large, shiny black car approached. Was Li Yan inside? Aki followed the vehicle's progress intently. It drew alongside the gangplank, and the driver opened the passenger door. A man holding a black bag, the captain perhaps, got out.

All around the ship, buzzers were sounding.

"*Qi mao!*" Weigh anchor. The order boomed from the loudspeaker. The hawsers were detached from the bollards. The winch in the bow began to groan, hauling in the chain from the water. The dripping anchor rose into sight. The gangplank was drawn back from the side of the ship.

As the steamer had dropped anchor facing upstream, it would have to swing left in a wide U-turn as it pulled away from shore and re-entered the river channel. Still no sign of Li Yan. Aki left the railing and returned to his cabin. Was she on board? Or had she had a sudden change of heart, switched to a plane ticket after all? This seemed possible. He hadn't checked out every passenger, but still...

Aki stopped a passing crew member and verified that the first-class cabins were all occupied. If Li Yan was indeed on board, she must be in one of the curtained cabins. The range of possibilities was limited. Plenty of time. He sat down heavily on a bench on the portside sundeck, crossed his legs, and watched the continent recede. This would probably be his last view of it. *Farewell, Babylon,* he muttered under his breath.

From the riverbank came the sound of things being hammered or dropped, the clang of steel plates, the hum of engines. Smells, too. Scorched oil, rotten fruit, coal-fire smoke. The rank smell of the continent. Why did it stir him so?

A large crane on the wharf lifted an enormous steel plate and rotated it in the air. Eventually, the crane swayed to a standstill and a voice rang out: "Okay, *xiexie!*" Aki murmured his own thanks, to Xie Han and Shanghai.

A voice by his ear said, "You're Japanese, aren't you?" The next thing he knew, a plump, middle-aged woman was settling down beside him. Aki nodded.

"Me too," she said. "Been living in Shanghai three years now. I'm on my way back to Osaka to get my teeth fixed. No use going to a Chinese dentist. They're expensive and no good." As she laughed, she covered her mouth with her hand to hide her front teeth.

"Pretty extravagant, isn't it, taking a boat trip to go to the dentist?"

"You think so? Actually, this is the cheapest way to go. Round trip plane fare runs to 150,000 yen, but this way I only spend 20,000. The difference pays for the dental work and the hotel, both. It's cheap and relaxing besides. I always take a second-class Japanese-style cabin."

"They have those?"

"Oh, yes. Three, no, less; rather large. The Chinese passengers aren't interested, so you can really stretch out and get comfy. See how crowded the boat is today? I've got a large cabin all to myself!"

"You say you've been living in Shanghai for three years? Why did you move there, if you don't mind my asking?"

The woman smiled back at him in a friendly way. "Unusual, isn't it? It's because my husband is Shanghainese. We had a Chinese restaurant in Sakai City, but he was getting on and we didn't have any kids, and he really wanted to go back. The Communists are more broad-minded now, he said, and the cost of living there is cheaper – so next thing you know, there we were."

"And what do you think now, after three years over there?"

"It was the right move. It's a fun place to live. And the city hall back home in Japan sends our pension over like clockwork. We don't lack for anything – it's just the dentists that are no good. So once every three months, I take a ride on this boat. I do enjoy it, I have to say."

Up ahead, sticking out of the waves was a small white lighthouse, marking the confluence of the Huangpu and the Yangtze. A damp, chill wind blew. The Chinese girls were out on deck taking a stroll, practicing Japanese phrases as they passed by arm-in-arm: "Hello, my name is Cho." "Hello, my name is Kyo." "That is the sea. This is a mountain. That is a fish. Pleased to meet you."

"Those girls are from Jiangsu Province," said the woman. "They're going to visit a spinning factory in Okayama. That's the official story, anyway. Actually they're going to be working there and sending money home. For three years they make 55,000 yen a month, of which the company sends 10,000 straight back to their parents. Some of them manage to scrimp and save quite a lot, but others run away." She stood up. "Goodness, it's getting chilly out here. You can tell we're on the Yangtze, all right. I think I'll go below."

"See you later, then," Aki said. "Still plenty of time before we get to Kobe."

As he stood up to see her off, he sensed some movement behind him and, turning, noticed that two men in A3 had just opened the curtain and were standing looking out at the water, talking. That was the cabin diagonally across from his. Now he knew the occupants of cabins A8, A6, and A3. Four to go.

Suddenly the wind picked up, and the cold drove him back inside.

He lay stretched out on the sofa, head on one armrest and feet on the other, attempting to pick up the change in the boat's swaying as it left the mouth of the river and entered the sea. He listened intently to the sound of the engine. While waiting, he dozed off. The dinner bell roused him. It felt as if he'd slept barely a quarter of an hour, yet outside the porthole the sky was dark. Presumably, the ship's eastward progress shortened the hours of daylight. They were now out on the East China Sea.

He went down to the dining room and sat right at the back, by a window, remaining till the last possible minute. Li Yan did not appear.

Although the rolling was minimal, he gradually succumbed to seasickness. Neither the degree nor the quality of the boat's motion seemed very different from when they were on the Huangpu or the Yangtze, but once seasickness got hold of you, it tightened its grip and wouldn't let go. Like a fish, the boat made subtle adjustments in the transition from fresh water to salt. Each alteration had its effect and the effects were cumulative, his discomfort mounting steadily. "The purser is now distributing seasickness pills," came the announcement. Aki got up and went out.

In front of the purser's desk, the Jiangsu girls had formed a long line, waiting for their pills. Some were in tears.

He was handed a packet of white tablets and told to take them three times daily, before meals. He stuck the medicine in his pocket and went for a stroll around A Deck. The lights of every cabin were on, but he could see no sign of any occupants behind the curtains. He walked aft from the bow with a strange sense of speed, as if sprinting. His queasiness got worse. He returned to the cabin, took two tablets, and fell flat on his back on the bed. Overhead the fluorescent lighting was mercilessly bright. Still, little by little the nausea subsided.

Aki got ready for bed. "Tomorrow, it'll all happen tomorrow," he muttered as he buttoned his pyjamas to the neck and climbed into bed.

Sleep did not come easily. Things that Li Xing had said to him came back vividly, along with her gestures and expression. The words were all in Mandarin.

Have you any idea what I was really doing, all morning long? Guess. Eyes filled with mischief shone like dew on a leaf. *Being in love. With you.*

Despite everything, sleepiness finally came. *Right now, Xingxing and I are in the same boat, floating over the same water,* he thought, yawning. *Tomorrow... tomorrow is the day...*

He dreamt a stupid dream – "It's got no point at all," he said out loud. And woke up. It was morning. He'd slept soundly all night long. Soon came the tinkling of the bell in the corridor announcing breakfast. He had no appetite, but he swallowed two of the tablets he'd been told to take on an empty stomach and went down to the dining room.

Here and there on the floor of the forward lobby lay the Jiangsu girls, wrapped in blankets. Their faces had a uniformly greenish cast, their expressions full of distress, eyes closed. Poor kids. Not only the sea and the boat trip were new to them, but also this awful helplessness.

After a light breakfast of toast and coffee, he walked around looking for a crewman, intending to ask about Li Yan, and ended up out on the sundeck. The sun was not yet fully up, but its presence could be felt along the eastern horizon. No sign of an island anywhere. The search for a crewman took him around the entire circumference of the deck. He was stopped by the woman who was on her way to Osaka to have her teeth fixed.

"You've been doing a lot of walking since yesterday, haven't you?" she commented. "Keep circling around the boat the way you do, you'll end up like the tigers in *Little Black Sambo*, a big pool of melted butter!"

"I need the exercise."

"I have to say," she sighed, "by day two of this trip, it starts to feel like you've been on the boat forever. You know what I mean?"

"Um, now that you mention it," he answered, not focusing on what he was saying, his eyes scouring the vicinity.

"You're in first class, aren't you? All by your lonesome?"

He nodded.

"Fancy," she said mildly. "Some people know how to live, I guess."

She had a point; the first-class cabins were all twin accommodations, and occupying one alone was indeed extravagant. As this woman's whole motive for being on the ship was economy, he must have seemed a terrible spendthrift.

"There's another first-class passenger travelling solo, too, you know," she added. He perked up at this news, encouraging her to go on, and she jerked her right thumb over her shoulder at the window just behind them. "When I caught sight of her, I thought at first she might be your wife."

"You saw her?"

"Just the one time. At the purser's desk."

"Just one time," he repeated. The woman nodded. Aki looked away, far across the sea where flying fish leapt from the waves.

"Spends all her time in her cabin. But she's a real somebody – wife of the Chinese consul, I hear."

"How did you find that out?"

"Just ask the purser, he'll tell you. She's gorgeous, too."

Four or five seagulls glided towards them from the bow, skimming the side of the ship. On the horizon appeared the dark shapes of the Tokara Islands, each one capped with a winding cloud like smoke from a volcano. The lady was not done talking, but with scarcely a backward glance, he hurried to his cabin.

Why didn't she come out? What about her meals? There was no sign of them being delivered to her door. This seclusion was exactly the proof he needed that the person in question was not just Li Yan, but also Li Xing. She had discovered he was on board, and she didn't want to meet him. Why not? Because she was Li Xing. But in that case, why avoid him? His mind travelled endlessly in circles.

"We are now passing Kusagaki Island," came an announcement.

He lay on his back in bed and smoked a cigarette. He opened his collection of Arabic poetry, closed it again, had a swig of Scotch from the flask. He stared at the ceiling and focused on the rocking of the boat and the vibrations of the engine being conveyed to the muscles in his back, trying to calm himself. He went down to the dining room. No sign of her. He ordered a steamed bun, soup, and beef with green peppers. The food was piping hot and tasted far better than five years ago.

He got in line at the register, behind the ubiquitous woman from Osaka. Her turn came and someone began to ring up her bill. Aki glanced over casually towards the entrance. Just past the door he could see the curve of the spiral staircase connecting two stairwells. A light grey flared skirt came partway down the stairs, stopped at waist height and wavered uncertainly, then abruptly fled back up out of sight. Li Yan. He broke out of line, intent on pursuit, only to feel the Osaka woman clutch his arm.

"Sorry," she said, "I'm all out of coins. Could you change this for me?"

Hurriedly he grabbed a fistful of bills and coins from his pocket and laid it by the register. "Be right back," he said. "Go ahead and use this."

"Hang on, wait a minute, you can't leave all that!" She wouldn't let go. She was surprisingly strong.

Trapped, he stared at the spiral staircase with a baleful look meant rather for his captor. On the spot, he devised a plan. After good-naturedly providing change for a fifty-yuan note, he calmly settled his own bill and then mounted the stairs, hanging onto the banister like a kid.

This time, he was able to accost a female attendant. "Just now in the dining room, the passenger in cabin A7 left this behind. I don't want to disturb her, so I'd appreciate it if you could hand it to her." He passed over the retractable ballpoint pen he always carried in an inner pocket: red ink, blue ink, and a mechanical pencil.

After making sure the attendant was headed for Li Yan's cabin, he ran out on deck, went around by the bow, and ducked back into a corner of the passage leading past the VIP cabin. The attendant came down the corridor from the opposite direction, stopped in front of cabin A7, and knocked. Li Yan would probably open the door a mere crack, just enough to peer outside. If he timed it right, he could stroll by and get a good look at her face.

The attendant called out, telling the occupant she had forgotten something. Three times she identified the item: *yuanzhubi*, a ballpoint pen.

Aki waited several seconds and then, hearing the faint click of a lock being released, stepped quickly into the corridor and began walking aft. The door of A7 opened a fraction. The attendant held out Aki's pen towards the crack in the door. The crack widened.

Through the thirty-centimetre space peered the face of Li Xing.

"I didn't leave anything anywhere," came a small voice. As she spoke, she spotted a man behind the attendant, off to one side. With scarcely any change in her voice, she thanked the girl, snatched up the pen, and slammed the door shut. The lock clicked. There was a finality to it.

The attendant stood there rather taken aback, then turned to look in the direction the woman in A7 had been staring. There stood Aki, who cheerfully returned her nod before nonchalantly opening his cabin door, strolling inside, and closing the door behind him. Instantly his expression changed, and in his excitement, both arms went up in celebration. No doubt about it – it was Li Xing! A little thinner, maybe.

In the cabin next door, a little girl was sobbing. Her mother spoke to her sharply, and the wails increased. "*Bu shufu, bu shufu.*" I don't feel good.

Li Xing was in a cabin adjacent to the little girl on the other side. Realizing that she would also be hearing this, Aki's eyes unexpectedly filled with tears. He wanted the child to go on crying without stopping.

24

The moment she saw him, Li Xing hastily closed the door and locked it. She leant against the wall for support.

"He's come back to me," she murmured, wrapping her shawl around her shoulders. "But it's too soon."

The thought was a hollow one. Too soon? When they'd been apart for five years? If he ever heard her say this, it would break his heart; he'd never understand.

Li Xing had been aware of Aki's presence all along. She first spotted him on his way to the ship, as he paused on the pier by the bow. Having boarded early with a VIP pass, she was sitting in her cabin looking idly out the porthole. She looked down at a spot on the pier three metres or so from a bollard. And there he was.

The shock was huge. She couldn't believe her eyes. *How could it be? It's impossible. He can't be standing there!*

Wearing a dark brown turtleneck sweater and black leather jacket and carrying a black bag with orange trim, Aki glanced up at the ship. A second before he did so, she ducked behind the curtain. *I'm not his Li Xing anymore, I'm Li Yan. Zhang Liang's wife.* She pulled the curtain tight shut.

Now from the adjacent cabin came the sound of a child sobbing. *Bu shufu, bu shufu!* Poor little thing. But Li Xing had suffered from seasickness, too. Just like the girls from Jiangsu, this was her first boat trip, first-ever look at the sea. And yet, to keep him from seeing her, she had to stay holed up in her cabin. Which might actually have helped her seasickness. Her stomach was empty, she felt almost as good as new. She could go for days like this, easily. She'd been through far worse experiences. She once hid out in a cave for nearly a month with next to no supplies. Endured awful work conditions in a black-market factory. Survived solitary confinement in a forced labour camp.

Persuaded that his presence on board might be a coincidence, nothing more, Li Xing wavered, perplexed, unsure whether to thank her lucky stars or curse them. When she first made up her mind to go to Japan, this was the last thing she thought might happen.

Stepping away from the door, she went over to the porthole and leant to look out. Its back to the setting sun, the boat steamed steadily eastward. She didn't realize that travelling east makes the days grow shorter, and wondered why it was getting dark so early. It gave her an uneasy feeling.

A knock came at the door. Three faint taps, a pause, then two more. Their old signal. Back in the Broadway Mansions they'd used the doorbell. It was on hearing that signal that she'd scribbled in her notebook the words, "He's come back to me."

Li Xing stole towards the sofa and sat down, holding her breath. Her pale throat was flushed and her heart throbbed. "He's come back to me," she murmured again in the back of her throat. "But not now, not now. It's too soon." Clutching her elbows, she buried her face in her crossed arms.

Aki tried knocking on her door in the old way, and then left. He'd made up his mind beforehand to try it just once. The point being, beyond anything else, to convey his presence to her.

He went out on deck on the side away from her porthole. The fishing boats that had been scattered among the waves at sundown had become in the deepening darkness a myriad lights. At first he mistook them for stars, then saw the stars above him. Yet the horizon was invisible, so that sea and sky merged: fishing lights were stars, stars fishing lights. Each gave out a slim shaft of light that pierced the eye like an arrow.

At some point, together with suspicion and disappointment, a sense of deep frustration came boiling up in him, as if she were now the enemy. What in God's name was she doing married to Zhang Liang? Why go to such lengths to avoid him, Aki?

Arms clasped behind his head, he lay in bed staring up moodily at the too-bright light on the ceiling. Then all at once he sprang up. "I've got it," he said aloud. "This will be a brand-new romance!"

The key was not to see it as the continuation of something now five years old. His new love was Li Yan, a woman who merely happened to look like the actress Li Xing. To pursue her under the misguided assumption that she was an old flame of his would be a mistake. She was – had always been – Li Yan, the consul's wife. One chance shipboard encounter and he was smitten. Love at first sight. Just like that time with Li Xing in Studio Four. Granted, it was wrong to be falling for another man's wife, but love knows no boundaries, doesn't it?

He bent over the table next to the sofa and wrote out one sweet declaration of love after another on the ship's stationery. *From the moment I first saw you, I lost my heart...* He resisted the impulse to let the dam burst and spill out his true feelings, instead forcing himself to remember the days when he was a lovesick college student writing letters like this. But there was one important point he was careful to include: *I'll be waiting for you on 16th January in the lobby of Hotel Anaga on Awaji Island.* He also gave instructions on how to get there. He added a simple map showing the way.

He chose 16th January for their tryst because on that day only, in the town of Fukura, there would be a traditional outdoor performance of the Awaji puppet theatre. He had already bought two tickets, one for his sister. She'd have to take a rain check. He specified the Hotel Anaga because it was close to the town and also because he hoped possibly to be able to see the "green flash" from there.

He didn't know the telephone number of the hotel, but neither did he put down his own number. Let her come or not come. Better not to know which it was to be until the day arrived. It was a gamble.

He wrote: *Tomorrow morning, just after seven, please look out your window. Awaji is the second largest of Japan's smaller islands, located in Osaka Bay. It will appear very close. We'll go right by it, not a kilometre away. That's where the Hotel Anaga is and where the puppet theatre is performed.*

Quietly he slid the letter under the door of cabin A7, then went back to his room and put on his pyjamas. From now on, he decided, he would sleep with the top button unbuttoned. He set the alarm on his wristwatch for six and went straight to sleep.

Next morning, heavy clouds hung low over the Kii Channel, as if last night's starry sky had never happened. No sign of the Kii Peninsula or Shikoku in the distance, let alone of Awaji Island under their noses.

JASMINE

The *Xin Jian Zhen* docked at Wharf No. 4 in Kobe Harbour at nine in the morning, but the paperwork for the student workers took so long that no one was allowed to disembark for some time. The woman who'd come to have her teeth fixed developed a heart problem and was carried out to a waiting ambulance on a stretcher. As the siren receded into the distance, finally the announcement came: "All passengers, please disembark!"

Li Xing finished getting ready and looked out through the porthole at Japan in the rain. The most refined country in Asia appeared as a blurred and shapeless mass. The streets, the buildings, and the water were a muddy grey, the mountains a muddy purple. She entrusted her suitcase to the cabin attendant and descended the gangplank.

From behind his porthole curtain, Aki watched as the consul's lovely wife left the ship wearing a fur coat and hat. Hungrily, his eyes followed her every move. The consul himself would surely be waiting to pick her up, somewhere on the pier or in Immigration. He lingered in his cabin till the last minute.

By the time he cleared Immigration, the big room was deserted. He rode alone up the long escalator and hailed a taxi, going straight to Shin-Kobe Station and hopping on a bullet train. By nightfall he was back in Tokyo.

25

From 30th December to 3rd January, Mitsuru went to the resort of Akakura with five friends from work and skied till she could ski no more. The 5th of January, the first day of work in the new year, was a Thursday; after putting in another full day on Friday she had the weekend to relax, so she was able to bounce back quickly from the exhaustion of skiing. On Sunday afternoon she prepared potato salad and sweet *inari* rice balls to take to her mother. On the way, she picked up a jar of stewed figs and rosehip blancmange. All were favourites of Yasuko, who lately had stopped eating flower petals.

Her car, a dark blue Mini Cooper, climbed the steep hills of Mikage with ease. The car stereo was playing a Mozart string quartet. The day before yesterday, having heard of a new CD by the Alban Berg Quartet, she'd stopped off on the way home from work to purchase it for her mother. It contained the "Haydn Set," six pieces dedicated to Haydn. Yasuko loved them, and her appreciation had been passed to both her children.

"We're feeling rather cross today, I'm afraid," warned Nurse Sakiyama. Single and middle-aged, with a honeycomb of wrinkles on her forehead, she'd been looking after Yasuko for three years now. "But I'm sure she'll cheer up when she sees you. Mrs Tachibana, your daughter's here," she called, opening the door and poking her head into the room. "Oh, she's asleep. Well, come on in."

Mitsuru turned sideways and slipped through the half-open door, taking care not to bang the paper bags she was carrying.

Nurse Sakiyama straightened the foot of the bed. She looked at the bouquet of roses that Mitsuru had brought, comparing them with a vase of freesias on the sill of the bay window. "Those I just arranged yesterday, so why don't I go get another vase?" she said, and left the room.

Jasmine

The yellow flannel curtains were closed. Mitsuru put her various gifts on the coffee table and went over to her mother, who was sleeping with her right cheek on the pillow, snoring softly. It sounded like someone blowing into an empty bottle. The nurse returned with a slender-necked Czech crystal vase, already filled with water. Mitsuru quickly trimmed the leaves and stems and arranged the half-dozen roses in the vase. This she put on a shelf by the head of the bed, the glow from the flowers lighting up her own face as she did so.

"I brought some rice balls and other things," she said. "Would it be okay if I gave her those for supper?"

"Certainly. Then I won't take her to the dining room, I'll just bring a tray in here."

"That'd be nice. Thank you," said Mitsuru, with the polite bow she had learnt from her mother.

Mitsuru opened the curtains and inserted a disc in her mother's CD player, beside the vase of freesias. The volume was turned way down. Shortly after the performance began, Yasuko stopped snoring. Mitsuru bent down over her face to listen, but the old woman's breathing was quiet; all she could hear was the rumbling of her belly.

She made a pot of tea and laid out some paper plates on the coffee table for supper. All the while Mozart filled the air, as the sun outside crept lower in the sky.

She felt her mother stir, and turned around to find her lying with her eyes open, staring out the window. "Well, you had a nice nap," she said.

"Did you bring me this music?"

"Yes. Happy New Year, Mom."

"That's right, it's the New Year. What year is it now?"

"1995."

"Not the Western count—"

"Heisei 7, then."

"Not Heisei, either. I can't understand unless you use Showa."

"Showa 70." That era had ended in 1989 with the death of the emperor Showa, but her mother never had adjusted to a new emperor and a new name for his reign.

"Thank you. How old are you now?"

Mitsuru smiled and said nothing. Her mother lifted her head slightly and peered over at the coffee table.

"I brought some of your favourites, Mom. Rice balls and potato salad. Made them myself."

"Thank you. What's in that jar?"

"Stewed figs."

"I'll have some of that."

Mitsuru quickly pulled out the wheelchair, set it beside the bed, and raised her to a sitting position. She then put a sweater around her mother's shoulders and half-lifted her out of bed, helping her into the wheelchair.

"I'm not hungry."

"You're not? Your stomach was gurgling just now."

"Was it?" she asked in evident embarrassment. She ate two *inari* rice balls before reaching for the figs. "These are good."

"You used to make them for me all the time."

The shadow of a smile crossed Yasuko's face; then her eyes wandered back to the window. "Now who do you suppose that might be?"

Mitsuru saw no one. "I don't know," she said, and put on the second CD.

"Who's playing?"

"The Alban Berg Quartet."

"We used to have a recording by the Juilliard String Quartet. What became of it, I don't know. Toward the end of the Andante in D minor, it had a scratch and the needle would skip over about two seconds of the music. I don't know how the scratch got there, but it was quite noticeable. I didn't scratch it, mind you. But that's neither here nor there." She paused, then asked, "Whatever happened to that record? Do you know? You there."

"It's Mitsuru."

"Yes, you."

"Mitsuru, Mom."

"You... It's not my fault your father died, you know."

Mitsuru nodded, looked down, and fiddled with her watch for a moment.

"Why are you looking at me that way?"

But Mitsuru wasn't looking at her mother, and she knew that her mother wasn't looking at her, either.

Nurse Sakiyama returned with supper on a tray. She placed it on the wheeled table beside the bed and pushed it over, approximately where the old woman's blank gaze was fixed.

"All set now? I'll leave her in your hands then, Mitsuru. Call me if she needs to go to the toilet. Just bring the tray back to the usual place." Her rubber-soled shoes squeaked on the linoleum as she walked away.

Seated in her wheelchair, Yasuko craned her neck towards the door, listening intently to the receding footsteps.

"That woman has a huge gap in her front teeth, did you see?" she said in a low voice. "When she smiles, it looks disgusting." Spittle formed a tiny web in the corner of her mouth. "Watch out for her. She steals things."

"Mom—"

"Oh, yes, she does! That's not all she does, either. Late at night she sneaks in here and tries to strangle me."

Mitsuru turned her face away and let her gaze wander out the window. The sun had dipped quite low in the sky. The quartet was starting the second movement, Andante in D minor. The leisurely siciliano rhythm floated through the room. Mitsuru got up and walked over to the window as if reeling in her line of vision.

From the time she was quite small, she'd always believed that no one in the world was as good as her mother. Words she'd learnt in a college philosophy course, from Socrates, came back to her: *What harm can one person do to another? A good person cannot be harmed.*

Mitsuru felt sad for her mother. What made her even sadder was that somewhere inside she wanted to believe these accusations and distrust Nurse Sakiyama. She felt the stirrings of a notion that it would somehow be better if the woman actually *was* a thief.

"There, it skipped!" Yasuko burst out. Mitsuru had heard it, too. The old woman's eyes danced happily, while Mitsuru, feeling suddenly drained, leant her forehead against the wall.

During the coda, for two or three seconds there'd been no sound. An illusion? She and her mother had both heard the music jump. Mitsuru held herself perfectly still, savouring the moment.

Negotiating the steep, curving descent in low gear, with her hands kept fairly loose on the steering wheel, Mitsuru thought about the time she'd just spent listening with her mother to the entire "Haydn Set"; it had been like a pool of water in the forest, still and deep. She couldn't say what exactly, but something seemed definitely to have come to an end.

Back in her apartment, she made a cup of coffee, then sat down on the sofa with it and rubbed the corners of her eyes.

The intercom buzzer sounded. A package for her. She pushed the button to unlock the door at the entrance. Her room was on the ground floor, but getting there from the entrance took a couple of minutes because you had to take a roundabout route, skirting an inner courtyard.

It was the nice young man from that delivery service, the one with the zebra logo. He handed her a large envelope with the address printed in a window. The name of the company meant nothing to her. She wasn't wearing her contacts, so without checking the address, she opened it and took out the contents. Documents for a loan application. Taking her glasses out of a drawer, she looked at the packet again. She could make nothing of it. Puzzled, she inspected the address. Not for her after all. The name wasn't hers, the address wasn't hers. She lived in Hiratacho, Ashiya, but the envelope was marked "Higashi Nada Ward, Kobe." That was across the way; the narrow street she lived on was the dividing line between the two cities. She promptly called the number of the delivery service printed on the address slip.

About thirty minutes later, the delivery man was back, out of breath and full of apologies. He had a package for her from Aki. Somehow the two had gotten mixed up. Hers she could smell – it had the delicate fragrance of jasmine.

"Sorry, I opened the envelope," Mitsuru said.

"It's all right. I'll tape it up and explain what happened."

The young man was tall and slim; she remembered once watching him admiringly as he bounded up the steps toting a heavy-looking cardboard box with ease.

"That smells good," he said.

On 29th December, the night before she left for the ski resort, Aki had called to say there was a change of plans about going to see the puppet play on Awaji Island. Something must have come up at work, she'd assumed; but no, actually he would still be going, he said, hemming and hawing awkwardly.

"So what's she like, this person you'll be seeing the puppet play with?"

"Mumble, mumble," said Aki distinctly, to which she gave a little peal of laughter.

"I've picked up some good jasmine tea. I'll send you some," he said.

"When were you in China?"

"Last week. Shanghai. Flew over, sailed back."

"You mean you were here in Kobe and never came by? That's *bad*. What kind of a brother do you call yourself? It's funny, five years ago you went over by boat and took a plane back. What was it, something about your father again?"

"No. Tell you all about it next time I see you. How's Mother?"

"The same. You know."

The tea Aki had sent was a rather rare variety called Peony Rosette. Long, downy tea buds were hand-tied in small bundles using thin white thread, overlapping in layers like the petals of a peony to form a ball. Infused with hot water, the rosette would slowly open like a bud, swaying in the cup until deep within it one white jasmine flower appeared.

The following Saturday, around noon, Mitsuru went shopping at the co-op by Ashiya Station. On the way back she drove along the left bank of the Ashiya River and turned at an intersection under the expressway. Right in front of her, the driver of a small truck veered to avoid a cyclist who had jumped the red light, slamming on his brakes. The truck scraped against the pedestrian barrier and smashed its left front fender against the steel pole of a traffic sign before stopping. The cyclist, a middle school boy, never looked back, fleeing on his bike into the pine trees nearby.

The truck belonged to a parcel delivery service – one with a zebra logo. When the young driver stepped out of his cab, Mitsuru had a start of recognition. He was trying to make a call on his cell phone, but having no luck. Mitsuru got out of her car and walked up to him.

"Uh, hi there," he said, scratching his head with embarrassment. "I can't get the office on my cell phone."

"Maybe it's broken. Here, try mine."

Using hers, he got through right away.

"It was the kid's fault, running the red light," she said.

"Yeah, but I should have been more alert."

"I'll be a witness for you when the police come, if you want."

"Thanks a lot. That'd be great."

Before long a police car arrived on the scene. A support team from his company also came and transferred the packages scheduled for delivery to another vehicle. To both the police and the company representative, Mitsuru gave a clear account of what she'd witnessed, so the investigation wrapped up quickly and the truck was soon hauled off. Mitsuru was impressed by the calm, frank way the driver handled a difficult situation. There was more to admire about him than just his style in delivering packages.

She waved goodbye, got back in her Mini Cooper, and drove off. In the rear-view mirror she saw him standing with his head bowed in her direction. She adjusted the mirror slightly and began to whistle.

The next day was Coming of Age Day, the national holiday for young people whose twentieth birthday fell during the current year. It was also a Sunday, but Mitsuru went to work anyway. The deadline was fast approaching for goods for a new station building and plaza that her company was working on in conjunction with a construction company. Although not herself a designer, Mitsuru was knee-deep in work, acting as a liaison and drawing up estimates.

Monday was a substitute holiday, making up for the one that had fallen on Sunday, but once again Mitsuru went to work. She didn't get home, exhausted, until eight that night. Shortly afterwards, the intercom buzzed.

"It's Uchiyama from the Zebra Parcel Service. You have a package."

"Come on back."

"I'd prefer to wait here."

Why did he sound so stiff? The apartment building had a reception room just off the entrance hall, and she told him she'd meet him there.

Jasmine

The package he had brought her was his personal gift to her. "You really helped me a lot the other day. Thank you."

"Not at all. Is everything straightened out now?"

"Yes, I even managed to get all the packages delivered with no more trouble."

"You weren't hurt, were you?"

"Not a scratch."

"That's good."

"I'm from Izushi. Ever hear of Izushi soba noodles?"

"Of course. They're famous."

"These were handmade at noon today. Please try them. There's sauce and horseradish to go with them, too."

Diffidently, he held out a large bundle wrapped in newspaper and string. He'd gone home early that morning and gotten his mother to make the noodles, then turned around and headed straight back to Kobe.

"Hey, thanks! What a treat. And this is for you," said Mitsuru, taking out of her pocket a little Ziploc bag containing five rosettes of the tea from Aki. "From the package that got misdirected the other day. It's jasmine. All you do is put one in a big glass cup and pour hot water on it."

"Great. Thank you very much."

Uchiyama had other deliveries to make, so with a quick bow of his head he was out the door. Abruptly, there came the sound of a truck driving off.

Mitsuru had had dinner out, but she boiled up some of the noodles anyway, added the sauce, and happily slurped them down. Delicious. She put the rest in the refrigerator, wondering what to do with so much. Enough there for ten – no, fifteen people, easily. Maybe she'd better share them with the neighbours.

She took a bath and got into bed to go through the photos from her ski trip, just back from the camera shop. While looking at them, she decided: *I know, I'll have everybody over for a soba party!*

26

The outdoor performance of the puppet theatre began at 10:00 a.m. on 16th January in the compound of the Hoshinji temple, near Fukura harbour. At precisely 7:05, just as the sun rose, drumbeats from a large *taiko* drum had announced the grand event, the rhythmic tattoo resounding across the southern end of the island for the first time in some thirty years.

Li Xing was there!

Wind whipped wildly around the great roof of the temple's main hall, causing the dozens of streamers to flap, but around the stage and seating area scarcely a breath of air stirred. This was due to the carefully planned layout of the temple compound, fitted snugly in a small valley to the northeast of a hill shutting out the sea.

Around the edge of the compound were stands selling *oden* stew, grilled chicken on skewers, cotton candy, and masks. The stage building was made of logs and enclosed by straw matting, with reed blinds laid across the roof. At the entrance was a signboard with gold lettering reading "Japan's Finest, the Supremely Talented and Accomplished Puppet Troupe Founded and Managed by Uemura Gennojo." Paintings and prints depicting earlier performances were crowded together on display. Roughly five hundred viewers filled the pit and the stands.

It was around one-thirty when Aki and Li Xing passed through the entrance, the gatekeeper calling out a rousing welcome. Inside, families were sitting on rush mats, eating picnic lunches; junior high and high school kids were in the standing-room area, the boys in high-collar tunics and the girls in middy-blouse uniforms; men, with beer or saké in hand, and city folks, with their opera glasses, were seated in the gallery. Places were not reserved, so Aki and Li Xing, as latecomers, had to be content with squeezing in at the back.

JASMINE

Through the buzz and murmur of the crowd, they could make out the distant twang of the *shamisen* and the rhythmic singing of the chanter. The central stage was even further away, but as Aki and Li Xing focused on the puppets, the action took on such immediacy that it seemed to be taking place right in front of them. And as they were drawn in, the vocal and instrumental accompaniment also took hold.

These Awaji puppets were cast in a different mould from the refined and seductive world of *sewamono*, domestic plays in *bunraku*, the Osaka puppet theatre. The torso and head were a good deal larger, the face paint and costumes brighter, the eyes bigger and more mobile. Princesses and maidens had oval faces with lovely features, but female heads known as *dakki* and *menketsu* could transform themselves in a second – the former into a frightful demon, the latter into a ferocious, man-eating fox.

Both the Awaji puppet theatre and *bunraku* contained scenes of savagery: heads getting chopped off and flying through the air, a fox ripping open a woman's belly with its teeth and pulling out her bloody entrails. The use of dolls made possible the juxtaposition of extreme cruelty alongside fairy-tale enchantment.

A famous section of the "Morning Glory Diary" was now underway. While searching for fireflies on the Uji River, Miyuki, the daughter of a samurai, met and fell in love with a man named Asojiro. Later, rejecting the suitor urged on her by her parents, she fled her home in search of her beloved. Her constant weeping out of longing for him ended in her going blind. She became an itinerant *koto* player, taking the name Asagao, or Morning Glory, and gradually wandered further east. At an inn in Shimada, she came face to face with him, but he had changed his name and was not able to reveal his identity. Unaware of whom she was performing for, the blind Miyuki plucked the strings of the *koto* while singing the poem Asojiro had written for her in Uji:

> "The dew-fresh morning glory,
> struck by the sun's cruel rays, longs for a shower of rain."
> Yes, good sir, I thank you. I come from Chugoku,
> and I lived for a time in the capital.

One year ago, firefly-hunting on the River Uji,
I met a man and fell in love.
The time we shared was brief as a summer's night.
Our troth we pledged and then, unwillingly,
we were forced apart.
With no word of his whereabouts, I could not rest at home,
and journeyed from the capital in search of him.
I left Osaka and Omi behind,
wandered aimlessly to Mino and Owari.
Tears of longing ruined my eyes.
Sightless now am I,
sad as a water-bird roving overland…

Not that Aki could make out all the words, by any means. Li Xing understood the gist of the story from his explanation, but she had even more trouble trying to pick up the words of the classical text. At one point, however, she caught his arm and asked excitedly, "Is Miyuki Chinese?"

"Ah. Because she said, 'I come from Chugoku,' you mean? But the word doesn't mean China here, as you'd expect. It's the name of a region of Japan, it's Hiroshima."

For some reason she was disappointed.

The face of the puppet Miyuki was beautiful; yet, studying Li Xing's profile, Aki told himself that hers was much lovelier. The thought made him feel intensely happy.

Next was the famous scene from "Cherry Trees along the Hidaka River," in which Kiyohime, the spurned heroine seeking revenge on her former lover, suddenly takes on the face of a demon; she then transforms herself into a monstrous serpent and swims across the river.

Aki and Li Xing left at the intermission and descended the long stone steps of the temple. Below was a stream – just a lazy trickle – and beside it a flagstone path. As they set out on the path, a gust of wind picked up Li Xing's hat and carried it off. Aki gave chase, finally retrieving the thing after it snagged on the branch of a camellia bush. The branch next to it was covered with pink buds, and impulsively he broke one off and stuck it in the ribbon on the hat before returning it to her. The wind was still strong, so she removed the bud and wore it as a corsage, tucking the hat under her arm. The wind was blowing off the sea. Buffeted by it, they held hands for the first time.

They'd arranged at the hotel for a car to pick them up around three-thirty. The driver, a man around forty, had been a devotee of the local puppet theatre since high school. The best part came *after* the intermission, he told them; why were they leaving now?

Back at the hotel, Aki and Li Xing sat side by side in chairs on the terrace of their little villa. They had come back early to see the green flash. Conditions had to be just right. Ideally, you needed a wide view of the sea's horizon to the west and clear blue skies, with no clouds or boat traffic to block the view.

"Cold?" asked Aki.

"No, I'm fine."

Like Hoshinji Temple, the villa had been constructed with an eye to avoiding the sea wind; to the west, moreover, it afforded an unobstructed, ninety-degree view of nothing but the sea. They talked about the puppet theatre for a while. Then Aki checked the angle of the sun and looked down at his watch. It was not yet dusk, but a faint, fluctuating lustre filled the sea, which had begun to change colour. The air was so sparklingly clear that it seemed thin.

"Nearly an hour till sunset. At this rate, we may really be able to see the green flash. I think there's a good chance."

"I hope so." Li Xing turned her clear eyes on him.

Silence stole over them. Behind the privet hedge separating their villa from the next, a bird sang out shrilly. Li Xing started, then hunched her shoulders. "Things take their own course, don't they?" she murmured, as if roused to speech by the bird's outburst. "Even if something's realistically impossible, we go on hoping against hope, wanting it to work out. Five years ago, when I decided to run away with you into the heart of China – in that boat through the creeks at night – it was like that. We made it as far as Zhouzhuang, and then I heard from Yin Dan that Liu Hong had been arrested. I loved you – but with him in jail, I felt that my only choice was to be alone. There is no law that a woman can only live in tandem with a man, anyway. So to keep from letting either of you down, I decided I would live on my own. It was a hard decision, a lonely one, but I made up my mind to leave. Even though you were right there, close beside me… so close that on the other side of the wall I could almost hear you breathing."

"I went to your room. The door was locked."

"I know. I was right there, on the other side of the door."

"Later I dreamt of an empty room. Woke up in a panic and went to your room again. This time the door was open, the place empty."

"I know. I got back on the boat."

"But Liu Hong never did get arrested. Yin Dan was lying."

"No, he wasn't. He really was arrested."

The information Yin's operatives had picked up was accurate. Much later, Li Xing learnt the details from Cai Fang.

Liu Hong's capture occurred at a roadblock a hundred and fifty kilometres south of Shanghai. But as he and the gang member with him were being escorted back to Shanghai, their jeep driver took a shortcut, leaving the main road to go fast down a road parallel to a creek. Seeing his chance, Liu dived into the water. A strong swimmer, he swam underwater for nearly fifty metres, heading downstream. Along the bank were fields of hemp where it was possible to travel a long way undetected. He walked all night till he came to the city of Hangzhou.

Luckily for Liu, the gang had given him the fifty thousand yuan from Aki. Their plan had been to get him as far as Ningpo, then put him on a fishing boat and help him escape to Taiwan. The money was supposed to go to the local snakehead gang leader in Ningpo.

Opting for neither the southern route to Hong Kong nor the eastern route to Taiwan, Liu had instead headed west, arriving in Urumqi a month later. His reasoning was simple: the escape route to Hong Kong was too dangerous, and to the east lay the ocean; by heading due west he could perhaps go overland to Europe. There was something else he couldn't get out of his mind, what Vice President Wang Zhen had said at an emergency meeting of the Party's Central Committee to declare martial law: "To reform the four thousand Beijing intellectuals who're in opposition to the Party, we should pack 'em all off to Xinjiang!" This induced him to go there, to the Xinjiang Uyghur Autonomous Region – of his own free will.

JASMINE

The money was a godsend. Without it, he could never have made it all the way to Paris. Some public security officials in central China were sympathetic; others were amenable to a bribe. In Urumqi he got in touch with members of the underground separatist movement. They, too, wanted cash. He crossed the border at Yining and travelled on to Almaty, Kazakhstan.

Li Xing finished her account by saying, "So you see, Aki, your money was put to good use."

As for herself: following Yin Dan's instructions, and with the help of his organization, she had taken shelter with the underground Catholic Church in northern China. The Chinese Communist Party boasts a membership of fifty-eight million, but there are eighty million Christians in China. Guided by staunch Catholics, Li Xing managed to escape to the northeast, and began working in a handbag factory near the city of Shenyang. This black-market sweatshop, owned by a Hong Kong businessman originally from Shenyang, turned out imitations of deluxe brand goods from Italy and France and shipped them to Hong Kong. The local authorities were all on the take, and turned a blind eye. Most of the workers were women without proper documents; they were paid 1.6 yuan per hour and worked thirteen hours per day.

Having decided to make her way alone in life, Li Xing never thought of turning to Cai Fang for help. And if Liu Hong was behind bars, then even a man in Cai's position would be helpless to intervene on his behalf. She continued working in the handbag factory for a year and a half. Then the Hong Kong owner was arrested, and the resulting police investigation reached all the way to the sweatshop in Shenyang. And so, ironically, Li Xing was arrested, not for her participation in the pro-democracy movement or the Tiananmen Square demonstrations, but for involvement in illegal business activities and graft. She and two hundred co-workers were rounded up.

After a one-week trial, the factory management and the city authorities who had accepted bribes were all sentenced to death and publicly executed by firing squad. Most of the female workers were released, but a dozen heads of the various production lines, Li Xing among them, were sentenced to three years of "labour education" and consigned to a *laogai*, a forced labour camp, in Xining City,

Qinghai Province. This form of punishment, imposed without benefit of judicial procedure, was determined solely by local public security forces; no courts or prosecuting attorneys were party to it.

The *laogai* proved to be yet another black-market factory. Here, counterfeit brand-name leather goods and clothing were manufactured for export to Japan and Australia via the Shanghai branch of another owner based in Hong Kong. All that distinguished this factory from the previous one was that it was run by the state and its workers were prisoners. Li Xing and the others were sometimes forced to stand waist-deep in huge vats filled with toxic chemicals, tanning sheep hides.

Fifteen prisoners were housed in a cell fourteen metres square. There were no beds; everyone slept huddled on the damp floor with a single blanket. The air was filled with a fetid smell. There was one small window high on the wall through which a bit of natural light came through, but the burnt-out light bulb hanging from the ceiling was never replaced.

The Shenyang handbag factory incident went unreported at the time. A year later, however, early in 1993 when the Party and the government began a campaign to eradicate corruption, the press took it up as a model case. Details of the scheme received ample coverage, and the names of prisoners consigned to "labour education" were made public.

Cai Fang read the articles and found Li Xing's name among those mentioned. That she had parted company with both Liu Hong and Aki and was in hiding somewhere on the continent he already knew, but after her dealings with the Catholic Church in north China, he'd lost track of her. Now he set about appealing to executives in the relevant bureau to grant the female workers involved immediate amnesty, arguing that they had not participated directly in any bribery or corruption, they had simply found work at a black-market factory. The Party, he reminded them, should always deal harshly with those in authority but generously with the people.

Li Xing was released. Thanks to Cai's efforts, her old personal register was switched with a clean, fictitious one created in its place. Her new name was Li Yan. As she had officially ceased to be Li Xing, there was no further possibility of her being accused of the crimes of procuring funds for the pro-democracy movement or of harbouring a wanted criminal and abetting his escape.

It came as a relief to her to hear from Cai that Liu Hong had made it safely to Paris.

What had these five years of separation meant to her? Her feelings for Aki during their brief, intense affair had not been suddenly extinguished, nor had they burnt themselves out. But while her love for him had, if anything, matured with time, she understood that there was little chance of ever being with him again, and therefore felt no impatience or anguish. Rather than oblivion, she accepted resignation.

After she was rescued from the camp and freed from the rigors of physical labour, she became seriously ill. She couldn't eat, and developed a lingering fever. For six months she was in a hospital affiliated with the Ministry of State Security in the suburbs of Beijing. It was there that she heard of the death of her beloved *nainai*.

As her condition gradually improved, her spirits rose with it. The moment her feet were back on solid ground, she began to feel hope. She would go to Japan. To Kobe, her mother's birthplace. It was also where *he* was born and raised. What the world of overseas Chinese might be like she could scarcely imagine, but if her grandparents were still alive, she wanted to see them. And if she could, she wanted to live a life of her own, however modest, in that same world.

A few days before she was due to be released from the hospital, Cai Fang came to see her. She greeted him with surprise: "Goodness! You've put on weight, haven't you?"

"Yes, it's doubled over the last five years."

"No, really?"

"Really and truly."

"You look like Orson Welles."

"Who's he?"

"Listen to you. You sound exactly like an official in the Ministry of State Security taking me for an American spy."

"Good one. But now that you mention it, you've put on a little weight yourself, Li Xing. I'm glad."

She nodded, then asked diffidently, "I wonder if you could tell me something. Is... is he okay?"

"He's fine," said Cai, who then proceeded to fill her in on what had happened in Shanghai after she left Aki.

"Why wasn't he punished?"

Cai's only reply was a shake of the head.

Li Xing confided her plan to him. He promised to give it some thought, and left.

She was released from the hospital and, again at Cai's doing, stayed for a while in a guesthouse in an old part of Beijing. Her new quarters were located on a narrow lane lined with small *siheyuan*, the city's traditional courtyard dwellings.

After a couple of weeks, Cai appeared and asked, "Any change in your plans since we last talked?"

She shook her head.

"In that case, are you willing to get married?"

"To you, you mean?" she said with a burst of laughter. "You've already got a lovely wife and daughter!"

"No, no."

"You're saying that's the only way I can leave the country?"

He nodded. "If you marry, you can go to Japan."

"There's no way I could go there alone?"

"Absolutely not." This came with a vigorous shake of his head.

"Who would I be with?"

"An employee of mine, Zhang Liang. Works at the Chinese consulate in Osaka, in charge of intelligence."

"Would you mind telling me one other thing?"

Behind the rimless frames of his glasses, he rolled his eyes. His manner was not encouraging.

"Is he married now?" she asked in a smaller voice.

"I assume you mean Waki Akihiko, not Liu Hong."

Her head down, she nodded.

"Liu got married in Paris. Waki's unmarried. Still searching for his father."

That was all she needed to hear.

"Just one thing more. Why are you doing all this for me? Because you're Liu Hong's friend? I mean, here you are, a top official in the ministry—"

Jasmine

"Li Yan, let me be very clear. I'm not talking about a make-believe marriage, the kind that snakehead gangs arrange when they send women to Japan. You'd be Zhang's actual wife, and as the wife of the Chinese consul, you'd have a considerable role to play."

"I understand. When I think of all I've gone through recently, this is nothing... well, not nothing, but..." Her voice trailed off.

From the courtyard bench, Cai lumbered up and, with a little jump, grabbed a handful of silk-tree blossoms. He tried to throw them farther off, but they caught in the wind and ended up on Li Xing's shoulders. His bulk shook as he uttered a raspy laugh.

"I'm not the kind of man to swear mindless allegiance to the Party. I can't say more than that. It's the same with marriage, isn't it, Li Xing?"

Tacitly, he was telling her this: *Marriage, too, is an interim thing, just as my being a Party member is. Any time you want to leave your husband, you can. I'll gladly help you when the time comes.*

Li Xing understood and accepted this way of thinking. *That's how he's managed to survive. I'll do the same.*

"All right," she said. "Of course I'll work for you. Although I can't say I know who *you* may be."

And so they made a deal, shaking hands on it in the new Chinese fashion.

"When you get over there," he said, "I want you to see your friend Waki."

"All right. But not straight away. When do I meet your friend Zhang?"

"He'll be coming to Beijing soon to file a report. That's time enough."

"It's a horrible plan," she murmured.

"Not at all. For this country, it's better than most."

"Is it?"

"Oh, yes. Shall we go for a walk? The old *hutong* neighbourhoods are disappearing fast in Beijing, the way old Shanghai is almost gone. But around here, things are much the way they used to be."

Li Xing shook her head.

"You're quite free to come and go as you please, you know. No one will be following you."

She shook her head again, more forcefully. After a few seconds of silence, she said in a somewhat brighter tone, "You know, you've changed. You don't make jokes anymore, the way you used to."

"Don't I? I suppose I don't; you're right." With a handkerchief he wiped the sweat away from the folds of fat at the back of his neck.

Her husband-to-be Zhang Liang was a trial, a hurdle she must somehow get past. Words she'd first heard at a Catholic service slipped into her mind: *Unless a grain of wheat falls into the earth and dies, it remains by itself alone. But if it dies, it bears much fruit.* Not exactly comforting, and yet the message was useful, she thought.

In Japan she'd take her time, establish herself eventually on her own two feet, go back to being Li Xing. And when she was ready, Aki would be there, waiting for her. As the first step in this plan she decided to sail from Shanghai. Mentally, she said to her mother, *Mom, you made the crossing from Kobe by boat; now I'll go back by boat, in your place.* Following the same route Aki had taken, and his father before him.

But then, upsetting her orderly arrangements, Aki had suddenly shown up in person. That was why she'd murmured, *It's too soon.*

"It's too soon, you see." Her voice shook, and she bit her lip.

Aki couldn't hide a slight tremor in his own voice. "So that's why you came. Just... to tell me this?"

Without replying, Li Xing adjusted the mint-green shawl she was wearing, tied like a necktie. "I'm still Li Yan. It'll take me a little time."

"How much? Another five years?"

"Don't say that." She paused. "I've already told you everything that happened to me after I left you in Zhouzhuang. And I've listened to your story as we walked along. So many things have happened, so many detours before we could be together like this again. Plus I got to see the puppet theatre that my mother wanted so much for me to see. It was worth it, coming to Japan."

Aki's mood by now had given way to concern. Five years was not enough, she was saying. He understood her plan to become independent in theory, but the thought of her retreating from him was more than he could bear.

"Coming here was worth it, you think? Let's make it even better. You say it'll take time for you to go back to being Li Xing. Then how about this? Say I fell in love with you at first sight as you are now – with Li Yan. Just like I wrote in that letter on the boat. You call yourself by a different name now. Fine. Why do you need to go back to being Li Xing?"

"It's just not possible," she murmured. "We'd have to start afresh, all over again."

"And we will. We'll make a brand-new start."

"But as long as the past remains, the present can never be the way we want it to be. It can never be happy."

"There's nothing bad about our past."

"You know, I was sent here with a specific assignment – to keep tabs on you." She tossed this out almost as if it didn't matter.

"What's Cai Fang up to? Zhang could handle something like that."

"I wonder."

"Does Zhang Liang know that the Chinese authorities arrested me, then let me go?"

"I don't think so."

"He certainly doesn't seem to. Cai sent him to Japan and arranged for him to contact me. Yet, Zhang doesn't know the crucial fact that I was let off by the Chinese government. Cai withheld that information. Why? He left out the most important bit about me – or he's holding it close to his chest. I've been biding my time, wondering when he'll try to use it. And then you came."

"Ironic, isn't it? Considering it's my fault you got caught."

They traded smiles. But Aki's smile turned sour.

"Should I really feel grateful to him? Sure, the pardon was good news. But he set it all up for reasons of his own. And Xingxing, I'm happy about what he did in coming to your rescue and getting you over here in one piece. But the upshot is, I'm sitting next to a woman named Li Yan, who's another man's wife. Was that really the only way?"

For a few seconds, she covered her face with her hands. "His real reason..." Her voice trailed off, as if breathing were difficult. "I think his real reason for wanting me here is to keep an eye on Zhang."

"What? But Zhang's his number one guy. Why would he want him watched?"

"Something strange is going on. I have a feeling they're not on the same team. Or worse – they could be enemies. I've been in Japan for three weeks now. It doesn't sound like much, but…"

Aki gently laid one hand over hers, wanting to reassure her. She shook her head and slid her hand away, as if she meant to get up and go. But she didn't.

A sudden memory came back to him. The time he first learnt that she was coming to Kobe was the afternoon when Zhang had summoned him to Tokyo Station on the pretext of sharing some oolong tea with him. Out of the blue, with studied casualness, he had quizzed him about the Tarim survey. Why did the Huxley report contain no mention of the high-quality cottonseed plant there? Aki must have seen something of it. Then he had said something unexpected: documents on the Tarim project were missing from the Japan International Cooperation Agency. And seven hundred million yen in gratuitous ODA was gone, vanished without a trace.

The fact was, Aki had seen no sign of the cottonseed plant anywhere in the wilds of Tarim. The seven hundred million yen seemed just to have evaporated, like water on burning sand.

Perhaps Zhang, in connection with this business, had become suspicious of his boss and launched a private investigation…

Aki turned back to her abruptly, amazed at this possibility. She was staring off into the distance, her thoughts too far away for her to notice. *She's not a Japanese woman*, he thought. Put into words, it was ridiculously obvious, but the reality of it hit hard. A Japanese woman could go pretty much where she pleased, stay as long as she liked. When she grew tired of one place, she was free to move to somewhere else. But a Chinese woman travelled because she had a duty to discharge. Li Xing, deprived of the freedom to come and go as she chose, was here on a mission.

Better not to exaggerate the importance of that mission – and yet what if Cai was brought down by some scandal? What would happen to her then? Did he, Aki, have it in his power to protect her secret all the way, somehow get her mission revoked?

He pressed on with this line of speculation. Perhaps Cai was up to his ears in the Tarim project. Perhaps five years ago he came to Tokyo and, one way or another, managed to destroy the relevant records at the agency. He had to have an ally somewhere within the organization. All that remained on paper was Aki's side report, but that was buried deep in Pandora in Huxley's head office. Once a document went in there, not even the author was allowed to make or possess copies.

What *was* Cai's angle? Was he siphoning off vast sums of ODA and using them for his own purposes, behind the Party's back?

Before them, the sun tilted towards the horizon, its colour changing from burnished gold to deep orange. The wind had died down. From below came the rhythmic pounding of waves. The horizon was clear and empty, not a wisp of cloud or vapour to block their view.

"When the sun goes down, I'll go."

"To report back to Cai Fang about me?" The attempt at humour fell flat.

"I love you."

"You love me, but you spy on me?"

"No, I'd never do that. Cai Fang was purposely vague. I'm sure he wants you on his side."

"Fine with me. I don't know what he's up to, but he doesn't strike me as an embezzler."

"Of course he isn't."

"Tell him this from me: I'm his friend. That's because I love you so much, Xingxing."

"Yes. I will."

"Maybe it'll let you partly off the hook."

"Yes."

"Tell him as far as the Tarim survey goes, he has nothing to worry about. At least until the fall of the US."

Matching the irony in this, she said, "Right. When China defeats America."

Aki then explained about Pandora.

"I see. Once, quite a long time ago... though it feels like yesterday... I seem to remember we had a conversation like this. You said that of all the countries in the world, Japan had the fewest secrets. But there can't be a country without secrets, any more than there can be a person without secrets. So I wonder – not to make too much of your Pandora, but perhaps Japan has entrusted all its secrets to America."

"I remember," he said. "That was the time you came to my hotel to phone your *nainai*. Dressed up like my father. Not my real father, but his character in the movie."

"That's right. I was positive you were a Japanese spy," she said with a husky laugh. Aki laughed louder.

"What about Cai Fang?" she said. "He seems to have deep convictions of some sort. But he's not a pro-democracy activist like Liu. He doesn't strike me as sharing those beliefs on the same level, anyway. I think if it came down to it, he could order people killed without a qualm."

"Spies live in a world where beliefs matter less than the techniques of betrayal."

"Mmm. Betrayal. It's Zhang Liang's convictions I really wonder about. He may be loyal to the Party, but he's no diehard Communist. I guess I'd say he believes in getting ahead. What about you, Aki, what do you believe in?"

He smiled. "Convictions can be secrets. Because they're private. But I'm an open book."

She laughed again, a throaty pigeon sound, and said mischievously, "Really? I doubt it."

"You think? Then I confess. My secrets are two in number: my acquittal in China and my father. He may be alive over there. Now there's a man with secrets to burn."

Her eyes were bright, childlike. "I've got just one secret."

"Which is?"

"You. That's what makes me strong."

Their eyes locked. The crimson light of the setting sun began to fall on them.

She cocked her head quizzically, but didn't ask anything else.

"If Zhang's motivation is getting ahead, then what about Cai — someone you say could have people killed without it bothering him."

"I don't know. But if you ask me, Yin Dan could be a killer, too."

"Yin Dan. Whatever happened to him?"

She shook her head. "I don't know. I tried asking Cai."

Jasmine

Just as she'd said that, by the nape of her neck Aki thought he'd caught a trace of the lingering scent of jasmine. When he tried to make it out more distinctly, it was gone.

Unaware of this moment, Li Xing swung her gaze to the left. "Look, the lights on the suspension bridge came on."

"That's the Great Naruto Bridge. It goes to Shikoku. See all the white foam on the surface of the water? That's the famous whirlpool." Aki explained the principle of this swirling current, as the sun sank even closer to the horizon.

Li Xing listened, then searching for words, said hesitantly, "There's something my father used to say. 'A wide perspective comes only when you look at your own small dwelling after seeing a great expanse of land or sky.' The way we're sitting here looking out at the sea from a tiny garden. And the scenery – isn't it grand!"

The blazing sun continued its relentless descent. Here and there in the shadows of trees, on soil stained purple by sunset, birds in small groups were pecking for food. Li Xing swept her hair back, her profile now deep indigo in honey-coloured light. The same colours moved across the contours of Aki's face. The both of them, with her father's words in mind, stared out ahead, sharing a single focus.

The moment the sun brushed the horizon, Li Xing let out a tiny yelp, as if she'd been burned. In a twinkling, the sun spread out on either side, pouring light like lava on the surface of the sea. Through the light glided the dark shadows of fishing boats and freighters. Floating in the sky far above them were fragments of clouds lined in deep red and gold, with centres of sooty black.

Li Xing reached over and laid a hand on Aki's elbow. The pressure of her hand increased with the sinking of the sun. By the time the sun's orb disappeared from view, her fingers were digging into him. Then she gave another tiny gasp. Between sky and sea flashed a faint, green ray of light. For one millisecond, so briefly they hardly knew it was there, the green light filled the paper-thin boundary between time and space.

"It's gone," she said. Darkness elbowed its way under the long eaves of the gabled roof and down onto the terrace. Light seeped out from the floor lamp in the room behind them. Li Xing shivered and gathered her shawl closer around her. "I wish I could stay forever... But I have to go."

She spoke faintly, stood up, swayed slightly on her feet. He put out a hand to steady her, and said sadly, "If I let you go back tonight, I'll feel the same way I did in Zhouzhuang. I never want to feel that way again. Anyway, let's go in."

He got up and slipped an arm around her waist, one hand on the flare of her hips. When he closed the terrace door with that hand, the warmth in his palm seemed to spread out and around him. He drew the white lace curtains, plum-coloured darkness showing through the design.

"Oh, I forgot," he said. "For dinner we have to go all the way to the main building. It's a bit of a hike."

"You must tell me – how do I get home?"

"Let's have dinner. All you had for lunch was a sandwich."

"No. No dinner and no drinks. Just tell me how to get back."

Wineglass in hand, Aki parked himself lightly on the edge of the oval table with a token bouquet of flowers and a message from the hotel manager.

"So you really did come here to explain, and that's all." Disappointment darkened his voice, made it husky. He tried to produce small talk, anything to detain her, but the words wouldn't come.

She shook her head. "If I'm not home tonight, what will he think?"

"You said he'd be in Tokyo till tomorrow noon."

"He always calls at eleven."

"Do you think he suspects you're not Li Yan?"

"No, not yet."

"He's definitely fond of you. But what if he finds out you've been deceiving him? What happens then?"

"That's why I have to be careful, stay on his good side."

There was one thing she hadn't yet told Aki. Just before leaving Beijing, an envelope had arrived from Cai Fang; it in were official divorce forms. To complete them, each party needed the approval of an appropriate sponsor. Already Li Xing's column contained the signature and seal of a Beijing government official, someone she didn't know; Zhang's had the official seal of the Bureau of Foreign Affairs and the signature of Cai Fang. This was his way of ensuring that the divorce could go through at any time. All that was missing was Zhang's own signature. She had to avoid turning him against her, had to set things up so he would consent to sign.

This was her other secret. She carried the divorce papers about with her wherever she went, like a lucky charm. She had a feeling that if she told anyone about it, even Aki, the power of the charm would fade.

"Want to know my official history? It goes like this: Li Yan, born 14th May 1961, at 5–28 Jinhong Hutong, Dongcheng Ward, Beijing. That part is true – if I put down some place I didn't know, it might be reason for trouble. Father a travelling salesman, mother a cleaning woman in Tiananmen Square. That's a couple who lived two doors down from me once in Beijing; I just turned myself into their daughter. Then let's see, I did rather well at school, so I attended Beijing Language Academy, majoring in Japanese—"

He interrupted her. "Won't Zhang Liang find out about your communications with Cai Fang?"

She looked down. "There haven't been any yet. When the time comes, what should I do?"

"I'm in Tokyo, so I can't – hold on, I know. My sister. I'll introduce you to my little sister."

Hearing that he had a younger sister was reassuring. "I'd love to meet her."

"She lives in Ashiya. Works in Yodoyabashi, in Osaka. Not far from the consulate." He brought his face close to hers. His sister was the excuse for making intimacy easier. "I'll give you her address."

Li Xing got out a pen and notebook from her handbag.

"Isn't that—"

"Yes, it is. It's the pen you had the attendant give me on the boat."

"Right. Awfully nice of me, wasn't it? Okay, here it is. Ashiya Urban Life, Apartment 109, 2–6 Hiratacho, Ashiya. I can't wait for you two to meet. And here's her phone number. So," he said with finality, "I am not letting you go tonight."

"Peculiar logic," she murmured, her breath warm and inviting. Aki drank it in, his lips on hers. As the kiss became more passionate, their minds clouded over, blotting out all thought.

Li Xing pulled away from the long kiss as though rousing herself from sleep. "I really must get back." Her voice was faint, yet she managed to free herself and move behind the sofa. Three metres away from her stood Aki, lost, his hands gripping the edge of the table.

She looked away and retreated a few steps along the back of the sofa. Then a memory came to her of another room: She was alone in the labour camp, straining her eyes in the dark, trying to summon Aki's image to her side. The moment she pictured this, she knew she would stay.

Aki carried her towards the dimly lit room next door.

"Let me see your face." Still in his arms, she cradled his face in her hands. "*Wo ai ni*." I love you. She said the words with deep emotion, as if for the last time.

Deep in her eyes, tiny radial lights seemed to flicker. She slid out of his arms.

"Take your clothes off," he said, the words as much a plea as a command. Then, "You're a little thinner than before."

"Yes."

A flood of memories made him awkward. "It killed me to think I'd never be with you again." Her lithe body was in his arms, and her beautiful breasts. Not the shape of mangoes, but as firm and warm and sweet.

The bed was at the same level as the window, and in the calm, looking-glass sea outside the lovers could see the clear reflection of the full moon. The moon itself was far above the villa's gabled roof. The moon in the sea moved steadily to the right, peering in through the window, but neither of them noticed.

At about four in the morning, Li Xing awoke. For a moment she couldn't remember where she was, and lifted her head to look out the window, but the moon was no longer gazing in. She reached out and gently touched Aki; he mumbled something and turned towards her, fast asleep. Relief and happiness flooded through her. Tears stung her eyes. She couldn't go back to sleep.

As she lay drowsing, suddenly there came a violent jolting motion from below; her body bounced up fifty centimetres into the air. *I thought I couldn't sleep, but I must've dozed off.* The same thing had often happened in the labour camp, where she'd been in a perpetual daze, hovering between sleep and wakefulness.

JASMINE

Her body bounced as though on a trampoline; she came close to falling off the bed. With a shout, Aki grabbed hold of her and threw his body over her. He knew what was happening.

The up-and-down shaking continued. The wineglass on the bed stand fell over and broke. The walls and ceiling creaked, high-pitched cracks could be heard spreading in the windowpane.

"Earthquake?"

Aki nodded.

Li Xing knew little of the horror of earthquakes. Aki, for his part, had grown accustomed to earthquakes after living in Tokyo, but this one seemed terrible. He'd never experienced anything remotely like it. Funny there should be a major earthquake in the Kansai area – let alone Awaji Island, of all places!

"It's okay," he said. "It'll stop soon. Damn, this is a bad one! I'm so sorry."

She giggled. "It's not your fault."

"No, but still."

The rocking subsided. Using the bedside panel, Aki tried all the lights in the room. One lamp and the ceiling dimmer would not come on. The most fragile-looking of all, a tall floor lamp, stood untoppled and unbroken, emitting a soft glow.

They were taking a quick shower when the aftershock struck. Naked, Li Xing threw herself into his arms. He couldn't help feeling aroused, but then the phone rang: it was the manager, inquiring if they were all right.

"We're okay, thanks," Aki said. "But that was a big one. A window cracked. A wineglass fell over and broke."

An employee was on his way to check out the room, the manager said.

In their bathrobes, Aki and Li Xing put on their leather gloves and started to pick up bits of glass off the floor. They turned on the TV. Somebody was giving the weather forecast, while a banner across the bottom of the screen ran breaking news: *At 5:46 this morning there was a severe earthquake in the Kinki region. In Awaji Island and Kobe it registered 6 on the seismic scale, with a magnitude of 7.2. The epicentre was around the Akashi Strait, three kilometres northeast of Awaji. The danger of a tsunami is...*

"It was centred exactly where we are – unbelievable," Aki muttered. "No wonder it packed such a wallop. Magnitude 7.2. Damn." He threw on his clothes and told Li Xing he was going out to look around the hotel.

In the entrance hall to their villa, a large Bizenware vase had smashed to pieces. The colourful roses it had contained lay scattered on the floor, unnaturally vivid amid the pottery shards and spilt water.

Outdoors, the sky in the east was just beginning to lighten. The light on top of the main tower of the Grand Naruto Bridge was winking; the headlights of several cars were zipping along. Nothing seemed out of the ordinary. It was as if the tremors had never happened.

Then a hotel employee came running up the slope to him. "Is everyone all right?" he asked breathlessly. "Is anyone hurt?"

No, Waki hadn't imagined the earthquake. "We're fine," he replied. "How about at the other villas?"

"You were the only villa guests last night. I'm glad you're safe. You're welcome to come down to the main building for a complimentary breakfast."

"Any news of Kobe?"

"It's not good. The epicentre was at the northern end of Awaji Island. Kobe's in bad shape."

"Oh," Aki gulped, worry tearing through him. Then he told the employee they'd be along in a bit.

The employee sprinted back down the slope.

When he re-entered the sitting room, Li Xing was dressed, eyes glued to the TV. There were images of a city in flames, clouds of smoke billowing. This was Kobe.

Aki grabbed the telephone and pushed the buttons for Mitsuru's number. No response. He tried repeatedly. Nothing. He tried his mother's nursing home in Mikage, and this time the call went through. But no one picked up the phone. He tried Mitsuru again. Nothing.

They packed up their things and went quickly down the gentle slope towards the main building. The sky was now completely light. There was no wind, but the air was freezing and they turned up their collars. The automatic door at the entrance to the reception opened smoothly, and the warmth of the lobby enveloped them.

Jasmine

Hotel guests were milling around anxiously. Two other couples they remembered having seen at the puppet theatre. A large-screen TV in the lobby was showing more footage of Kobe. A middle-aged female guest burst into tears.

Everyone was itching to leave, their nerves on edge. A middle-aged man and a young woman, probably there on the sly, were both from Kobe; faces dark with worry, they each stood with a cell phone pressed to an ear, trying to get through to someone.

The hotel manager addressed the group. Aki couldn't help remembering the man's expression yesterday when something about the green flash had been mentioned. Again this morning, the guy was grim-faced. Stupidly, Aki wondered if the flash and the earthquake were somehow related.

"Except for Kobe City and part of Nishinomiya, the phone lines are working. We're checking information about boat service to the mainland now, so please be patient a little longer. Breakfast is available in the lounge. You're welcome to stay on in your rooms past checkout time at no extra charge."

Someone handed the manager a note. He read it over before announcing, "Unfortunately, all boats are cancelled, including service by ferry and hydrofoil from Sumoto to Kansai International Airport; Tsuna to Tempozan Port, Kobe Central Pier, and Izumisano Port; and Iwaya to Akashi. However, around 4:00 a.m. one ferry did leave from Tsuna for the central pier."

"Well, of course," said one of the guests. "That was *before* the earthquake."

"Yes, but don't forget, the people in that boat were heading into the middle of it." This from the woman who'd been weeping in front of the TV. One of the couples that had attended the puppet performance, as well as the weekend lovers, had come by car; these four quickly drove off to the harbour, just in case a boat might leave.

Aki hurried over to the public phones and tried Mitsuru's number again. Again, nothing. He was finally able to get through to the Mikage nursing home and verify that his mother was safe. Luckily, it was Nurse Sakiyama who answered the phone. The hilly parts of Kobe weren't much affected, she told him.

It then occurred to Aki to give Xu Liping a call. The line was busy. He reported this to Li Xing, who was sitting on a sofa, adding that her grandfather was probably all right.

"But your sister…" Her face was pale.

Aki's frustration mounted. There was Mitsuru's safety to worry about, but he also had to get Li Xing back to Osaka by tonight at the latest. Why, of all times, did such a disaster have to happen now? But then again, a disaster is good at no time.

There was no way back to the mainland but by boat. Temporarily, all departures were cancelled, but they might start up again at any time. Aki decided that they, too, should head for one of the harbours from which boats and ferries left for Kobe or Osaka. He asked the front desk to call for a taxi, but was told that none were available.

"How about the hotel courtesy car?"

"Of course we'll gladly provide you with transportation, sir, but as you know, the boats aren't running. Rather than be stuck waiting for hours at the harbour, we recommend that you wait here a bit longer."

Oh you do, do you? muttered Aki in annoyance. "Yeah, I see your point," he said. "Still, I think we'll take a car as far as Sumoto or Tsuna. If nothing turns up, we'll be back." Turning to Li Xing, he said, "Let's get something to eat while we can."

Hand in hand they went into the lounge and sat at a table. Out the window was the Grand Naruto Bridge. Cars were moving across it. "That's it!" he said suddenly. "All we have to do is cross that bridge." He explained: "See, the bridge will take us to the next island, Shikoku. From there, Takamatsu City is connected to the mainland by the Grand Seto Bridge. It'll be a big detour, but if there aren't any boats in action, we have two choices: swim, or cross that bridge."

Li Xing pushed aside her plate of French bread and poached egg, folded her hands on the napkin in her lap, and nodded. She looked nice and warm, and miserable.

"Sir, your car is ready," announced the bellboy. As they walked across the lobby towards the door, they heard one of the guests saying, "Well, what about the hotel motorboat? Can't we use that?"

"I'm very sorry, sir, but the boat is available only from April to November. There's no one on the hotel staff qualified to operate it at present."

"I have a license to operate light craft. I can do it?"

"I'm sorry, but that isn't something we can allow."

Before getting in the car, Aki tried calling Mitsuru again, without any luck. Xu Liping's line was still busy.

It was the same driver they had yesterday. As he pulled onto the road, he suggested they not try to reach Kobe or Osaka by boat. "All the ports are shut down. Nothing's doing. Things are bad, I tell you. Kobe's been wiped out. It's unreal. Even here on Awaji, the northern part of the island is a shambles. The dead are piling up."

It was a grim picture. "How about if we took the Grand Seto Bridge from Shikoku to Kojima. Would you drive us?"

The driver shook his head. "Too far for me. Sorry." He drove down a slightly elevated promontory and through the fishing village of Anaga. Some twenty fishing boats were anchored inside the breakwater. The area had sustained little damage, and there had been no tsunami, either. A dozen fishermen were standing staring out to sea, arms around each other's shoulders.

"Mr Uemura," Aki addressed the driver by name, "stop here, would you, please. What do you think about our hiring a fishing boat to take us across?"

"Not a bad idea if they'll do it."

"You mind coming with me to ask?"

Leaving Li Xing in the car, Aki and the driver approached the fishermen, several of whom knew Uemura and greeted him. "My customer here wants somebody to take him to Kobe in a fishing boat," Uemura said to the group. "What about it? Can one of you do it?"

An old fisherman looked them with a wry smile on his weathered face. "You crazy? Tiny boats like them – clear to Kobe? That's asking to be swamped."

A young guy sitting on the ground with his arms around his knees chimed in, "Yeah, these are wooden boats. The engine'd never make it."

"You know," said the old fisherman, "what if you took the *Tsunahiki-maru*? Might work."

"Ah, you could be right."

Uemura pointed beyond the breakwater to the left. Half hidden behind the concrete wall was a fairly large boat. The height and

thickness of its mast and windlass supports dwarfed all other boats.
"Where's Toru?" Uemura asked.

"Home," said the young guy. "Wore himself out last night, I reckon." There was general laughter.

Uemura took out his cell phone and put it to his ear, telling Aki that Toru was an old friend from high school. Toru came on the line, and Uemura explained the situation.

"He'll be right over," Uemura said to Aki, sliding the phone back in his pocket.

According to the radio, Osaka had suffered relatively little damage and its subways and loop line were all running. Toru had gotten them across the water to Kobe, and Aki was now considering asking Toru to take Li Xing on as far as Tempozan Port. But soon he thought better: this was no time to leave her on her own. First, he had to check on Mitsuru. Then, he would see that Li Xing got back to Osaka, one way or another.

The roads were impassable, and live electric wires dangled midair. A seven-story apartment building had collapsed, the dust still rising. Incessantly, out of nowhere, came the sound of muffled cries. People in their nightclothes walked around, stunned, blankets draped over their heads. A young man sat next to the unmoving body of a woman at the side of the road.

"It's like a bad dream," Li Xing kept saying.

"I know. But right now we have to stay awake."

They made their way to Ashiya. The familiar cluster of high-rise apartment buildings in Seaside Town looked the same as ever, towering above them. The sight was somewhat reassuring, but the relief was short-lived. The closer they got to the river, the worse the destruction was. The sky was dark, the air thick with falling ash. Helicopters hovered in the smoke. The smell of gas was everywhere.

The neighbourhoods of Isecho and Hama-Ashiya had a lot of old wooden houses. Some of Aki's mother's relatives had lived here; when he was small, she'd often brought him here to visit. Now, not a single dwelling stood. The body of an old man lay alone at the side of the road. There was no one else in sight, everyone else presumably buried in the rubble. The area was utterly devastated; the only way to tell where they were was from address plates on fallen telephone poles.

JASMINE

They came to the river. A small crowd of evacuees had gathered on the tennis courts, and people were warming themselves around a fire. Ahead was a concrete bridge, which led over to Hirata-cho. The bridge was intact. Here, too, people were camped.

Aki took Li Xing by the arm, and together they walked across. Never had crossing a bridge seemed so unsafe. Below them the riverbed was dry, as it often was in winter, streams supplying the mouth of the river with their flow.

On the other side, Aki, peering ahead, made out a beige structure of reinforced concrete. "There it is," he said. "That's my sister's building."

"Oh, good!"

As they walked closer, Aki was hit by a mounting wave of apprehension. The height of the building was wrong. He counted. There should be five stories, but he could see only four. They rounded a clump of shrubbery and stood directly in front of the building. The entrance was gone. The entire first floor had been obliterated.

They went around to the rear. A rescue team was digging with shovels. "People are in there, buried alive!" shouted a man who seemed to be a resident.

Eight years earlier, Mitsuru had taken out a loan to buy this condominium; she liked the design of the apartment, how it was situated. "It's on the first floor," she'd announced over the phone, cheerful and excited. "The garden's dinky, but it's got grass and hydrangeas, and sometimes even a nightingale comes by. Eighty-two square metres may sound kind of extravagant, but I like living alone, and I like being on the first floor."

Now, a tall, thin young man was making an impassioned appeal to the rescue squad even as he banged on a crushed front door with a wrench and tried to insert a jack. It was the door of Mitsuru's apartment.

For a second Aki closed his eyes and prayed that his sister had spent last night away from home. Maybe she had stayed over at a friend's house. Sunday was Coming of Age Day, yesterday was a substitute holiday; maybe she'd taken a long weekend, gone off on a ski trip. He could only hope.

Who was this young guy? Silently, Aki got down to work beside him. Together they struggled to break down the door and pry an opening. After a bit, Aki said, "I don't know who you are, but I'm Tachibana Mitsuru's brother. Can you hear anything?"

"No."

"I hope to God she wasn't home last night."

"She was here, I'm afraid."

"How do you know?"

"My name's Uchiyama. I work for the Zebra Parcel Service. Last night, just after eight o'clock, I brought her some soba noodles. She was definitely home."

Before long, reinforcements arrived, and members of the rescue squad pitched in with the effort. A resident lent Aki and Li Xing, who was doing anything she could to help, work gloves.

"I see something!" shouted one of the rescuers.

"No answer," said another. "Doesn't look good."

After a while the rescue called a break, afraid that too much digging might further weaken the upper floors.

It was night-time before Mitsuru was brought out. The members of the fire brigade shook their heads, indicating no hope. Aki and Uchiyama protested vehemently, but the firemen had to take off on another rescue mission.

Uchiyama picked Mitsuru up in his arms and raced over to his truck. Despite the grimness of the situation, he was careful not to jolt her as he ran. Aki couldn't help noticing and being touched by this. Holding Li Xing's hand, he ran to catch up with Uchiyama.

The traffic lights at the intersections weren't working. Cars fleeing in every direction clogged the streets along with ambulances, fire trucks, patrol cars, and Self-Defence Force vehicles on emergency duty. It took an hour and a half to travel the two kilometres to Ashiya Community Hospital and get Mitsuru inside. The hospital was running on emergency generators.

"I'm very sorry," the doctor told them, and bowed his head. Mitsuru looked alive. She had no external injuries; there was no bloodshed. She must have been asleep. The expression on her face was peaceful; it showed no sign of suffering. Aki laid a hand on her cheek; it felt warm. Beside him, Uchiyama was crying.

"Go ahead, touch her," he said.

"I have no right."

"Go on," he said.

Gently, Uchiyama laid a trembling hand on Mitsuru's face.

"May I, too?" asked Li Xing. "I can't believe I'm meeting your sister this way." She buried her face in Aki's chest.

Somehow Aki managed to pull himself together and do the things that needed to be done. Injured people and dead bodies were being carried into the hospital one after the other. He decided to move Mitsuru to the hospital mortuary, but it was crammed full. They barely managed to find a corner to lay her down in. The body of a sixteen-year-old high school girl, brought in after Mitsuru, was turned away; the girl's mother collapsed, distraught.

Uchiyama volunteered to remain and keep watch at Mitsuru's side.

"Thank you. Your staying with her would mean a lot. I'll be back later, even if it takes all night."

His brain operating in crisis mode, Aki thought next to phone Xu Liping, but there were huge lines at every public telephone in the hospital. Uchiyama quickly produced his cell phone, and Aki made the call. This time the line was free, and Xu picked up. He and his wife were safe, Aki was greatly relieved to hear. And then Aki explained, as succinctly as he could, that Li Xing was with him and needed somewhere to stay. He chose not to mention, not over the phone, anything about Mitsuru.

"What a time for her to come!" exclaimed the old man. "There are fires spreading east from Nagata Ward. I can see them in Shimoyamate, too. At night the wind blows in off the sea, which will probably fan them towards us. If that happens, escape for us will be impossible – my wife got sick last autumn and she's in a wheelchair. I've been preparing for the worst. But if you want to come here, come. Just keep an eye out for fires. Take care, and—"

He was cut off in mid-sentence as the line went dead. No matter how many times Aki redialled, he couldn't get through again.

Traffic was at a standstill. Roads had ceased to function. And even if an occasional fire truck did make it to the scene of a fire, the water mains were ruptured. Kobe was a city of many rivers, but now little water. It was past midnight by the time the rescue crews began scooping up seawater and dumping it on the burning city.

Aki and Li Xing set off on foot. The city lights were out, and yet the streets were bathed in a dim glow: the city was on fire. It was too dark to see clearly where they were going, but the flashlight Uchiyama had given them helped.

The roads were fissured and strewn with rubble. At first they held hands as they walked, but this made the going harder. Finally, only when they had to clamber over some obstruction, or leap over a crack or hole in the ground, would Aki take the lead and grasp her by the hand.

They passed a family huddled around a kerosene stove amid the ruins of their home.

Men sharing a blanket talked in low tones: "Buried, then burned alive. God almighty. Couldn't do a thing but watch and pray."

They came across a broken telephone pole. Aki turned his flashlight on it and made out the address: 5-chome Kitamachi, Motoyama.

"How much further?" she asked.

"Maybe ten kilometres. As the crow flies."

Aki put an arm around Li Xing's shoulders and drew her near. In the sky ahead of them, overhanging columns of dark smoke were lit below by the red glow of flames, like a sunset. Never in his wildest dreams had he thought he'd be guiding Li Xing around a Kobe that was a sea of flames. Never in his wildest dreams had he thought Mitsuru would perish – just like that. As he and Li Xing walked on and on, the wind blew cold, now a whisper, now a moan. In some shallow water, they observed someone incongruously washing a pair of jeans.

"Wait – who's that?" asked Li Xing, pointing suddenly to the man. Under the circumstances, the question seemed absurd.

Aki looked at the man, and to his utter astonishment, he recognized who it was. "Chen!" he shouted, shining his flashlight on the man. "Chen Ying!" It was his driver from Shanghai. They raced down to the riverbank. "Chen Ying! You're Chen Ying, right? Look, it's me!" Aki turned the beam on his own face.

The man glanced at Aki, then did a double take. "*Xiansheng!*" he cried. And with no further ado he joined the two of them as they walked on towards the Xu residence in Suwayama.

"*Xiansheng*, Kobe was just like you said it would be, a great place to live. But now it's finished."

JASMINE

"Where's Anli?"

"Dead. She died a year ago."

They had come as far as the Gomo Tenjin bus stop, where they stopped to help someone screaming that his daughter was buried alive. There were no tools available. But for perhaps a half hour they toiled in silence, getting bloodstains on their work gloves as they lifted pillars, dislodged planks, removed chunks of concrete, dug down in the dirt with their hands. They could hear a faint moaning. They kept digging.

The man's five-year-old daughter was alive! She'd been protected by a door that had fallen over a TV set. When Chen lifted her out of the rubble, she wailed. It sounded like the cry of a newborn child.

The Shinkobe Oriental Hotel stood intact, with lights in every window and its pointed spire thrusting up into the sky. The top-floor lounge, famous for its night view of the city, was lit up with flickering candlelight. For all Aki knew, there might be couples up there sipping cocktails as they looked down on the burning streets. But blaming them meant blaming all the people across Japan who sat staring, transfixed, at Kobe's fiery destruction.

They hurried due west along Yamamoto Avenue. The Kitano district was almost untouched. White *ijinkan*, the former residences of early foreign settlers, lay sleeping in the darkness. Aki's flashlight beam picked out the graceful outline of the old Graciani house where Xu Liping and his family – including Li Xing's mother – had once lived.

They got to Suwayama a little past twelve-thirty – after a hike of three and a half hours. The electricity was out in Xu Liping's apartment, but the living room was faintly illuminated by the reflection from the fires below.

The Xu family had survived the Great Hanshin Flood of 1938 and the bombing raids of World War II without loss of life. This time, however, things were different. Already they had been informed of the deaths of the husband and son of their third daughter, who lived in Takarazuka. Nor had anything yet been heard from a male cousin in Suma.

Xu Liping had had time to think about all he stood to lose. Although nothing in comparison to the losses his father and grandfather had sustained, it was a bitter blow. If only he'd made better, bolder use of his wealth while he could. He had donated one hundred million yen to repair Ijokaku, the former villa of a wealthy Chinese merchant in Maiko, near the Akashi Strait, and turn it into the Sun Yat-sen Memorial Hall. The scholarship fund established by his grandfather to aid resident Chinese and needy overseas students from China and Taiwan was an ongoing concern, and he had endowed a chair at the Kobe University School of Medicine. *Not nearly enough*, he thought. Maybe, if he lived through this, he would become a power broker for the dissident movement on the Chinese mainland.

"What do you think of that, Yumei?" he said aloud, but his wife in her wheelchair beside him made no response. "Ha ha. Just joking."

Or maybe he would work to revive *budaixi*, Chinese operatic puppet shows. They were all but obsolete in both Fujian and Taiwan. How about doing Shakespeare in *budaixi*?

The Taiwan president Li Denghui had said that after retirement he wanted to trace the route Basho followed in his *Narrow Road to the Deep North... Maybe I could go along, be his guide... Ah, if only I could have gotten Li Denghui together with Zhou Enlai. What might have happened? That would have been something.*

Waki Akihiko's phone call had interrupted these meditations. He was bringing Li Xing, his granddaughter, to him. *Live long enough and anything can happen!* reflected Xu. He wasn't bowled over by the news, but neither was he entirely calm.

When Aki, Lu Xing, and Chen arrived, Xu greeted them warmly: "Hello and welcome! I'm told the roof fell in on the main buildings of Ikuta Shrine and Kanteibyo. Here one or two things fell off a chest of drawers, that's all, and the only thing broken was one drinking glass."

And then without further ado he folded Li Xing in his arms, close to his heart.

27

At home in her kitchen, Li Xing dropped a wineglass, breaking it into pieces. She hastily gathered up the pieces and ended up cutting her finger on a sliver of glass. It started to bleed. At the hotel villa, she and Aki had picked up pieces of another broken glass, wearing leather gloves; remembering was painful in itself.

Surreptitiously, so Zhang Liang wouldn't notice, she washed off the blood in the bathroom sink, applied a herbal medicine, and wrapped her finger in a Band-Aid. After a quick sob, she went back to the living room where her husband was sitting on the sofa, drinking Hennessy VSOP, a gift from the Chinese community in Kobe. In China he'd never drunk the stuff, but lately he'd developed a taste for cognac.

Li Xing's hair was parted in the middle, and she wore an apricot-coloured cardigan draped loosely over her shoulders. Zhang had eaten dinner in the same suit he wore to work, then showered and changed into pyjamas and a dressing gown.

"Want to try some of this, Li Yan?" he said.

She shook her head.

She'd stayed at her grandfather's apartment for two days. The fires, having reached as far as Nakayamate, were brought under control during the night; knowing this, Aki had felt safe leaving her there and returned to Ashiya to attend to his sister's body. Chen Ying had nowhere to go, his home having burned down, so he offered his services to Xu Liping. Xu had a car, Chen was at home behind the wheel, and that was that.

The bullet train Zhang took from Tokyo on the afternoon of the 17th went only as far as Kyoto. There he transferred to the older line and got back to Osaka that evening. Not knowing the reason for his wife's absence, and unable to ask his colleagues or the consul general about her, or seek their advice, he was frantic with worry. Maybe she'd been badly injured in the earthquake and taken to a hospital. There was nothing he could do but wait.

Early on the morning of the 18th, as instructed by the consul general, Zhang and two staff members set off for Kobe by car to get in touch with the local Chinese community and gather information. Six hours later, they arrived at the Center for Overseas Chinese in Nakayamate, where they met the head of the association and heard accounts of damage suffered. They returned to Osaka the same day. The following day, accompanied by the consul general, they headed back to Kobe with a truckload of emergency supplies and the announcement of a one billion yen relief donation by the Chinese government to aid Chinese survivors of the quake.

At the Center for Overseas Chinese, walls had collapsed and the ground floor was badly damaged, but the building was still usable and the phones were working. Zhang borrowed a phone to call home; he played the messages on his answering machine and heard the one just sent by Li Yan. It turned out she was in Suwayama, less than a kilometre away.

Aki spent that same day running around trying to arrange his sister's cremation. Crematoria in Ashiya and Kobe were filled to capacity; to make matters worse, there was only one coroner to be found in Ashiya, and in Kobe, only four. Without a coroner's report, cremation was impossible. Uchiyama, the delivery service guy, managed to dredge up a supply of dry ice, enough to preserve Mitsuru's remains for four or five days.

That evening, Aki and Li Xing had a long talk on the phone. Xu Liping was also consulted in detail about what she should do. The next afternoon, Chen drove her back to Osaka, reaching her home in five hours' time.

"Quite a surprise," said Zhang, sticking his upper lip and the tip of his nose inside the brandy glass. "Who'd have thought you had distant relations in Kobe?"

"I know, I can hardly believe it myself," she replied. "My mother's surname was Xu, and apparently her great-grandfather came to Nagasaki long ago as head of a puppet theatre group that was popular in Taiwan. Anyway, three days ago I got a sudden phone call asking if I was the daughter of Xu Lan, from Beijing.

I said yes, and they invited me over. I meant to come right back, but they urged me to stay, and you were in Tokyo, anyway... Then there was the earthquake, and I was stuck. I'm so sorry. I know you must have worried."

"That's all right. Still, even if they did claim to be relatives, it was a bit risky, wasn't it – taking off like that after just one phone call? If they were Taiwanese, things could have gotten messy."

"Yes," she murmured, looking contrite, and refilled his glass. He seemed preoccupied. The way he watched her with hollow, shifting eyes made her feel like an interesting specimen of bug. She had to get him drunker. When he was under the influence, his eyes stopped fidgeting and his tongue loosened up.

"Inside Tokyo Station there's this little bar, nice atmosphere. I like to sit sipping brandy, looking down on the train platforms. Now and then I meet up there with a Japanese guy I know. Exchange a little information. Capable fellow, speaks really good Chinese. I phoned him the day before yesterday; thought we'd get together before I left, but he wasn't around, they said; he was stuck in Kobe when the earthquake hit. So I got on the bullet train, but it didn't go farther than Kyoto. Terrible thing about Kobe."

Zhang held his glass in his right hand; his left was in his dressing gown pocket, where he always kept it when talking face to face with his beautiful wife. It helped him keep a grip on himself, not be servile with her. The movement of his eyes slowed.

"Li Yan, hear me out, please. Don't get angry, okay? There's something I've been meaning to ask you, but I just... Tell me, were you Cai Fang's woman?"

Li Xing turned a level gaze on him, her eyes barely an arm's length from his.

"Lately that's been all the talk around the ministry. Even the vice-minister hinted it was true," he continued. "Is it?"

"I don't want to talk about it," she said coolly, nodding. Zhang put his brandy glass on the table and reached out for her right hand, holding it in both of his. Inside the cocoon of his hands she shifted her bandaged finger slightly.

"Do you still have any feelings for him?"

"No."

Amid the tissue of lies she'd had to tell tonight, this "no" was the lone truth, and she delivered it in a strong, no-nonsense tone of voice.

Zhang hung his head, directing a small smile of satisfaction at empty space. Then, slowly, he began to talk. He had stumbled on the surprising truth about Cai Fang: the man was a traitor to the Party and to his country.

The Party always comes first, doesn't it? thought Li Xing to herself.

"The investigation's nearly done."

"Oh? What investigation?" Her tone was offhand, as if to say, *I have no interest in this matter, but as you seem inclined to talk about it, go ahead.*

"An old friend of mine is on the faculty of Xinjiang University in Urumqi. I got him to do a little digging. See, I knew Cai spent some time in Urumqi before he went to Beijing. You wouldn't believe all the stuff that came out. That son of a bitch."

If Zhang brought up Urumqi, capital of the Uyghur Autonomous Region, he had to be hinting at something related to the underground separatist movement there. Calmly, she withdrew her hand from his grasp and said, "What you're doing could be dangerous. You can't dismiss a man like Cai Fang as easily as all that."

"I know. I'll be careful. I'm not going to make my move anytime soon. Now, if I can just get my hands on the side report in Huxley… Got to see that guy right away."

"What guy?"

"Didn't I tell you? The one I said before, the guy in the bar in Tokyo Station."

A half-smile played at the corners of her mouth. Without a doubt, this "guy" was Aki – which meant Zhang would never lay his eyes on any report. Knowing the connection between these two men was oddly reassuring, which explained her smile – an acknowledgment of the irony of the situation.

But Zhang saw the smile as a wifely expression of admiration and confidence. "I'll take off for Beijing soon as I can. Headquarters wants a report on the Kobe disaster. I know more about it than the ambassador or the consul general, so I'll go. I mean to settle Cai's hash then. He'll be history."

"This could mean a big promotion for you. Two ranks, maybe three."

Zhang drank the last of his brandy and nodded. He didn't see the irony in this comment, either.

"Be careful. He's tricky."

"I know. I won't send any documents by diplomatic pouch, or leave them lying around the consulate, either. Just because I work directly for him doesn't mean he hasn't got his spies out."

Relaxing, she let her bandaged finger uncurl with the others.

"What happened?" he asked.

"It's nothing."

"Good. Glad you got off so lightly, I mean." He was referring to the earthquake.

"Yes."

"That reminds me – what's the name of that distant relation of yours in Kobe?"

"Xu."

"Yeah, but Xu what?"

"Xu Liping."

"Oh yeah? Xu Liping? No kidding. I can't believe you're related to him!"

She looked at him quizzically.

"Xu Liping of Kobe is somebody. *Very* well-known family. I mean, the guy's held in the highest respect, both by us and by Taiwan."

"But he's just an old man."

Yeah, right, he thought privately. *He'll let you think so – which is what makes him such a tough customer. Cai Fang never let on about her being connected to the Xu family. Sneaky. No way he wouldn't know a thing like that, not someone that careful in checking every detail. Why didn't he say something? He deliberately hid it. Why?*

A vague foreboding came over him. It was like brushing against the edge of Cai Fang's net.

Among all the Chinese residents of Japan, those in Kobe occupied a rather special position. Elsewhere, in Tokyo, Osaka, and Yokohama, the residents fell into pro-mainland and pro-Taiwan factions, but in Kobe, there was a third faction as well – call it the Sun Yat-sen group – with ties going way back. Well-known writers and university professors, doctors, a former star of the Takarazuka revue, and others had formed what appeared on the surface to be a freewheeling social group – centred around Xu Liping.

Should he make an enemy of Xu, or an ally? For Zhang Liang, concerned above all with getting ahead, this was a serious question.

He set down his brandy glass and turned on her his shrewdest and most thoughtful gaze of the evening. "Let's go to bed."

"I've seen too much death today. I can't... I'm sorry."

"Right. It had to be a hell of an experience." He stood up. "Well, good night, then. You want to know something? I happened to go to the funeral of Xu Liping's mother a couple of years ago, in the autumn. Creates a bond, doesn't it?"

Li Xing remained seated on the stool for a while, feeling slightly weak.

28

Aki was waiting for Mitsuru's turn to be cremated, hoping it would come quickly. There was nothing to do but get through it. The supply of gas to all the crematoria had been stopped, and they were running instead on crude oil. Still, why this rush to reduce her body to ashes and bone? Why couldn't she linger awhile, go back to Teite, have some striped mullet with him one more time?

If only. The thought was taboo during a time of disaster, yet it kept returning to him. In the hospital corridor, an old woman had been quietly talking to her granddaughter. She'd used those words, and the girl had let loose with a wild shriek, alarming everyone around.

This was Aki's big regret: *if only* he'd taken Mitsuru to Awaji for the puppet show. A useless *if.* The person he'd taken was Li Xing.

Uchiyama used a motorbike to hunt for more dry ice. Even so, the body showed signs of deterioration. They somehow got through the coroner's examination, only to be told to remove her from the hospital mortuary. Schools and community centres, district assembly halls and public buildings were filled to overflowing with the living and the dead. Funeral halls and morgues were packed. Not knowing what else to do, the two men loaded the casket onto Uchiyama's truck and drove around aimlessly. Fortunately the truck was equipped with air conditioning. It belonged to Uchiyama; the company he worked for was a franchise, and drivers were required to own their vehicles.

They drove along the Sumiyoshi River, stopping on the way for a night's rest. Little other traffic had come this far to escape the earthquake. Without being asked, Uchiyama volunteered the details of how he and Mitsuru had met.

"That tea smelt really good," he ended by saying.

"So you delivered it to her? I was the one who sent it."

"Really? She gave some to me. I've got it with me, see?" From his breast pocket he produced a pouch of Peony Rosette, carefully wrapped in foil.

In the deep valley where they were parked, the rustle of trees and raindrops on the surface of the river was broken occasionally by the cries of wild monkeys and other forest animals.

"I came here once on a school excursion," murmured Aki, half to himself. "I'd like to make tonight the last night of her wake. But you know something, I'll bet a night like this would have been just to her liking."

Uchiyama nodded, but did not say anything.

Day dawned, the half-dark of early morning lingering on. They set off down the narrow, twisting valley road until they came to a funeral hall. Under a covered gallery, relatives of earthquake victims who had spent the night there were dozing on newspapers and cardboard. Some thirty coffins were lined up, waiting. Aki and Uchiyama cautiously unloaded Mitsuru's coffin and laid it at the end of the queue.

The hall doors opened and the cremations began. Their turn finally came, just before noon, and Aki and Uchiyama carried the coffin in near the ovens. There were six. The wall was lined with little white urns. Mitsuru would go into one of them.

While they waited, they walked along a path lined with rhododendrons. Other people were on the same path, most of them dressed formally in mourning clothes, which looked incongruous. Again and again, they passed the same families: people who walked as if skirting the rim of a crater and spoke in soft, timid voices.

The old woman they'd seen in the hospital corridor the day before was coming towards them, supported by the girl, with whom she now seemed to be getting along. "We just have to be thankful we can have her cremated like this," she was saying. "Poor Sa-chan and the rest – buried alive, and then the fire. Their bodies got burned too... but think of the difference."

"Grandma," said the girl in a low remonstrating voice.

The wind was blowing from east to west. Grey smoke from the crematorium chimney drifted from Mount Aburakobushi towards Mount Maya, crossed a valley, and was borne up on a rising current

JASMINE

of air. Kobe destroyed, Mitsuru gone. Sadness, mingled with relief at having seen his sister properly off, drifted sideways through Aki's heart like smoke.

Five or six undertakers were standing by with signs that read "All your funeral needs attended to." Aki smiled wryly. *Not a bad thing – that business should continue during a time of disaster.* It was the Huxley partner's thinking. The morning news, heard over Uchiyama's truck radio, had reported that in anticipation of a post-earthquake reconstruction boom the Tokyo stock market had recorded its highest rise in seven months.

Mitsuru was now ashes and bone. For Aki, this was unbelievable. And for Uchiyama, too.

Without any of the extra services offered by the undertakers, the two men made their way back to the truck. Holding the urn on his lap, Aki asked Uchiyama if he would mind taking him to the nursing home in Mikage.

With his mother were her sisters and several of the Tachibana relatives, come to see how she was. Some were learning of Mitsuru's death only now. Aki gave a brief account of events, from the discovery of the body to the cremation. The relatives expressed sadness, and appreciation for his efforts. Yasuko remained asleep the whole time.

The family grave was in Jissoin Temple in Suma; from the mass funeral in Ashiya until after the forty-ninth day memorial service, when the remains could be interred, an aunt living nearby would keep the mortuary urn in her home. Mitsuru's cousin, a lawyer in Fukuoka, began to discuss the ownership rights to the condo. Aki couldn't begin to imagine how that issue might be resolved, as the whole apartment block was wrecked. He would leave the matter in his cousin's hands.

According to her helper, Yasuko had shown very little response to the earthquake. "She calls me a murderer," she remarked in passing. Aki lowered his head silently, embarrassed. He started to leave, but the nurse followed him out into the hallway. The week before the earthquake, she said, her voice muffled in tears, Mitsuru had dropped in to see her mother. One by one, she listed the gifts his sister had brought along that day: "*Inari* rice balls, potato salad, stewed figs..."

This woman is really grieving for her, Aki realized, touched.
"...and a music CD."

Curious, Aki stepped back into his mother's room and flipped through the CDs. Among them was the "Haydn Set," performed by the Alban Berg Quartet. He had bought a copy for himself in Tokyo. Somehow this pleased him.

When he returned to the truck, Uchiyama recounted what he'd heard on the radio: boats for Tempozan were now leaving from Harborland at two-hour intervals. If Aki could get to the harbour, he'd be able to return to Tokyo.

"Route 2 and the other trunk roads are closed to ordinary traffic," said Uchiyama, "and the branch roads are almost all blocked off. But I can take you there on my bike."

Aki quickly agreed to the plan, thanking him.

As Uchiyama lifted the motorbike out of the back of his truck, Aki borrowed his cell phone to call Xu Liping. Xu assured him that Li Xing was well. She'd just gone back to Osaka by car, driven by Chen. Not to worry, she'd be fine. She'd get home on schedule.

At the harbour, Aki and Uchiyama shook hands. They had met in life under the most extraordinary, wrenching circumstances, and each expressed gratitude for the generosity of the other. And then they said goodbye.

At Tempozan, Aki transferred to a hydrofoil for the Kansai International Airport, and booked the next available flight to Tokyo. As his DC10 took off northward, it veered to the east. Aki looked down upon the streets of Osaka below. Which was Li Xing's apartment? Wherever it was, she was there. The thought filled him with agitation. Being high in the air, with nothing between him and the ground below, only made it worse. At least he knew where Mitsuru was, small comfort though it was.

Although it was midwinter, floating in the sky over Kobe was a gigantic cumulonimbus cloud.

The next afternoon, a man introducing himself as head of the China Section in the Metropolitan Police Department's Public Security Bureau called at the Huxley office. He wore a dark blue suit with a grey pocket handkerchief and a wide-striped necktie, and his hair gleamed with pomade. An overly fastidious look, one often affected by men of smaller than usual height. Aki had on an ordinary grey wool jacket, no tie.

"My name is Kudo. How do you do," he said. In the pauses as he spoke, the left corner of the man's mouth twitched slightly. He'd phoned Aki several times over the past week, but Aki had not been in.

"Oh, I see. You were in Kobe. Terrible thing, terrible. Who would ever have thought it? Were any of your relatives affected?"

Aki calmly brushed aside the question. "No, not really. So, how can I help you?"

"Very glad to hear that. I must say I was impressed by an article in the Korean paper, the *Chosunilbo*, which said: 'The calm and orderly behaviour of the local inhabitants was impressive, with no looting whatsoever.' You know what happened after the Great Tokyo Earthquake of 1923. Six thousand Koreans were murdered. Now..." He held his palms together as if in prayer, fingers to his lips, then exhaled on his fingertips. "You are acquainted with Zhang Liang at the Chinese consulate in Osaka?"

Aki set down his paper cup of coffee on his desk, and nodded.

"If you don't mind, may I ask how well you know him?"

"Well, that's hard to say... " Aki mumbled, starting to fudge the answer. He then thought better of it. Why not hear the man out? After all, this was about Zhang Liang. "Let's see, we get together once every few months – once every six months is more like it. He gives me a call and we go to a little place inside Tokyo Station and chat..."

Wait. Aki gave his visitor a good look. He'd thought there was something familiar about him. Now he remembered. That same little place inside Tokyo Station... the bar Camellia. Last November, Zhang had met him there, given him a packet of Big Red Robe tea, and shown him Li Xing's photo. Seven or eight seats away from them at the bar had been a middle-aged man, getting rapidly sloshed. There had been something a bit forlorn about him. Seeing the wide stripes of red, blue, and white in his necktie, Aki had had the momentary illusion that he was Ma Zuqi from Shanghai Public Security.

Ah, so the drunkenness had been an act. He turned his attention again to what the man was saying.

"Zhang Liang is with the Ministry of State Security. Although I'm sure you know that." As was only to be expected in someone in the

China Section, Kudo was well versed in mainland affairs. He also knew all about the Chinese Communist Party's espionage activities in postwar Japan. The various agencies he mentioned matched the names of those supposedly sponsored by Zhou Enlai that Aki had heard about from Xu Liping. "He's connected to the Y Agency."

"Do you know about the Shiratori incident?"

No matter what he was asked, Aki decided he would keep his comments vague and noncommittal. Anyway, though Kudo kept putting questions to him, he didn't seem to be fishing for answers. Rather, he gave the impression that he was laying out all he knew and checking Aki's reactions. The purpose of this visit remained to be seen.

"Shiratori incident?" Aki echoed.

In January 1952, on the streets of the northern city of Sapporo, Shiratori Kazuo, head of the Security Division of the Sapporo Police Department, was shot and killed. After determining that the crime was the work of a military organization within the JCP, the police apprehended eight suspects and placed five of them under arrest. The remaining three were thought to have fled to the mainland. The statute of limitations on the murder had already run out, but if the culprits had gone overseas, that law did not apply.

What was Kudo getting at? Aki broke his rule of giving nothing away. "Didn't Zhou Enlai's spy operations in Japan include the Y Agency?"

"That agency's got nothing to do with Zhou Enlai." The corner of Kudo's mouth twitched.

Aki shrugged.

"Not Zhou Enlai. Zhang Liang."

At this, Aki uncrossed his legs and sat up straight.

Kudo explained. Zhang's appointment to Japan dated from mid-August of the year before last, but from around August or September of last year, his intelligence work had increased considerably. Compared with the activities of previous government operatives, he showed unprecedented initiative. Last autumn, he set up a new operation; it was called Y Agency. Why it was called that, no one knew.

This, moreover, was evidently something he undertook single-handedly, without any direction or permission from his superiors.

Unlike previous spy operations in Japan, he focused on contacting and developing relations with conscientious professionals – young politicians, high-tech venture businessmen and Internet bond entrepreneurs, hedge fund managers, and senior members of foreign-owned think tanks.

"People very like yourself, in other words. Also, you're a member of a committee that's influential in determining government policy vis-à-vis China."

Aki forced a smile. "I have many Chinese friends. Zhang Liang is one of them."

"He's using a great deal of money."

"What if he is? What business is that of mine?" There was a bite to the way he said this.

"Yes, but you see – one wonders how he's managed to get hold of such a large amount of money without his superiors knowing."

If they'd gotten this far, Japanese public security officials were no slouches, thought Aki. They may have lacked the enthusiasm or resources to go after new information aggressively, but when it came to counterintelligence they did pretty well.

Just then, Aki's phone rang. He decided to ignore it. Kudo got to his feet.

"You go ahead and take the call. I'll let myself out. Thank you for your time."

Aki stood up, too. The phone stopped ringing. Backing off, Kudo was attacked by a great sneeze that he tried, but failed, to suppress with his breast-pocket handkerchief.

"Excuse me. Ah, too early in the year. Way too soon yet for pollen."

Aki smiled slightly and then, with a gleam in his eye, asked, "Anything else?"

"No, no, nothing else today. I just wanted to fill you in about Zhang Liang, that's all."

"Thank you. Tell me, Mr Kudo, how long have you been in the China Section?"

"Ten years, give or take."

"That makes you an old hand. You've got Zhang under surveillance, but before him was a fellow named Cai Fang. Do you know him?"

"Of course. But even if we ever picked up anything compromising about him, we'd never take any hostile action in his case. Definitely not."

"Right. Right, I see that," nodded Aki.

His hand on the doorknob, Kudo started to let out another massive sneeze – but this time he just managed to whip out his handkerchief before exploding with a sound like a lump of meat going splat in a pan.

"You've always been one of my assignments, you know. Of my predecessors, the third to last was assigned to your father. He died over there, your father, didn't he?"

29

It was nearly a week after the earthquake and the Awaji puppet performance that Aki finally went home. The pile of mail awaiting him contained an airmail letter from Shuichi in Moscow, postmarked 14th January, before he could have known about the Kobe disaster and Mitsuru's death.

Greetings.
 Sorry I haven't written. I swear, I'm forgetting how to write Japanese...
 Still wandering in a forest of paper. There are sixteen different archives in Moscow alone — communist archives affiliated with the former Marx-Lenin Institute, the Foreign Ministry, the KGB and other intelligence agencies; military documents from the Red Army and the Ministry of Internal Affairs; documents from the public prosecutor's office and the police. Not to mention all the related archives in other branches of government.
 I'm focusing my research on six of them. One is the Presidential Archive, which I told you about two years ago. It contains super top-secret documents, which Yeltsin kindly made publicly available. Nothing to do with glasnost; in order to shore up the power he grabbed from the Communist Party of the Soviet Union, he wanted to expose the Party's past sins, that's all. Then when he realized that records of his own past were in there too, he quickly made it off limits again. That's the way it goes around here.
 At the CPSU archives, which I commute to a lot, there are flocks of birds inside. Big ones, like crows. They all take off at once, dozens of them. A swirl of dust and they're gone. We wait twenty or thirty minutes for the dust to settle, and then we dive back into the mounds of paper. There are hundreds of thousands of records relating to Japan and the Japanese Communist Party alone.

The files on Mao Zedong don't interest me – a big yawn. Enough people are already busy poking holes in his mystique, anyway. The BBC interview with his personal physician was a scoop, though. Turns out Mao had an undescended testicle. Who'd have guessed? Takes someone who looked after him for twenty-two years to come up with a gem like that.

Zhou is a hell of a lot more interesting, any day. He came to Moscow off and on, before and after the war. Partly it was for treatment of a heart ailment, but also it was to confer with the Comintern, get instructions.

So there are a lot of documents here on Zhou. Makes perfect sense to me that Stalin and the Comintern's spies had him marked. Sino-Soviet antagonism goes all the way back. Mark my words, all kinds of new information is going to emerge about Zhou's youth, his days as a Shanghai spymaster, his role in the 1936 Xi'an Incident when Chiang Kai-shek was kidnapped, etc., etc.

By the way, I found something else pretty interesting. Actually, that's why I'm writing. In one of the boxes from 1937 I found a note marked like this, in English capitals: "AIDE-MÉMOIRE OF ZHOU-EN-LAI HAN-LAN-GEN (ACTOR, JAPANESE)." Neither of the names was given in Chinese, so I could be wrong, but the first one must be Premier Zhou Enlai, and the second – especially because he's identified as a Japanese actor – could easily be your father, who I think appeared in Huaying productions under that name. Han Langen would be the Pinyin spelling.

I spent a couple of days looking for anything else with the surname Han, but got nowhere. I did come across two more references to an "aide-mémoire," though. One was dated June 1, 1946: "Lock up the aide-mémoire." The other one was marked October 1955: "Destroy the aide-mémoire."

What do you think? Stick an equal sign before the name Han Langen and it could mean that he was Zhou Enlai's... what? Private secretary?

Then I had another thought. Hitchcock's "The 39 Steps," one of his early films from his British period, features a performance by a guy with a little moustache called "Mr Memory." This guy's famous for his ability to remember anything and everything, and he takes random questions from the audience. Things like, who was in the 1921 Derby? Bingo — Mr Memory gives all the names of the horses, in order, and the amount of money they each won.

Turns out he was hired by enemy spies bent on stealing revolutionary new technology from the Royal Air Force. Not one page of the documents was lost, but everything got stolen. He sneaked them out overnight and returned them in the morning. Nowadays you'd just run off a copy on a Xerox machine. Anyway, the whole formula went into Mr Memory's head. Seeing that bit about Zhou Enlai's aide-mémoire reminded me. If you've never seen the flick, go check it out.

If you ask me, there's a good chance your dad's still alive. There's no record he was ever killed — and don't forget, six years ago, that time you went to Shanghai, it was because Xie Han wrote you that he might be alive. If it's true, that's fantastic. I want first rights to an interview.

This has turned into one helluva long letter. Almost feels like I'm talking to you face to face. I'll be here another year. I've found some fascinating material, and there'll be more. With the Cold War over, more and more new facts will be coming out, and new books that'll change how we view history. I'd like to write one myself if I can.

Of course, finding anything in this mountain of information comes down to sheer coincidence. But I'll take my chances. Coincidences are taboo in fiction, they say, but real life contains more of them than you'll find in any book. Coincidence rules.

As I wander through this forest of paper, sometimes out of nowhere I hear Mitsuru's voice. I wish more than ever that I could see both of you. Take care, stay well.

30

Lock up the aide-mémoire. June 1, 1946.

Around that time, traitors' trials were underway in the high courts of Nanjing, Jiangsu, Shanghai, Hebei, Tianjin, Ji'nan, Amoy, and elsewhere in China. In Shanghai High Court, Han Langen answered all the questions put by the prosecution and judge the same way: *Wang le.* I've forgotten. Was this somehow connected with that written order to lock away the aide-mémoire?

Destroy the aide-mémoire. October 1955.

That was the year Waki Tanehiko got a letter from a woman summoning him back to China, and had sailed off to Shanghai. Whether the letter was in fact sent by Zheng Pinru, none could say. The real Zheng was supposed to have been killed in February 1940. In the meantime, Waki had established a thriving trading company in Kobe, married, and fathered a child; for him to leave all that and smuggle himself back into China could only mean he was compelled to do so, either by the contents of the letter or by the identity of its sender. If he found out that Zheng, whom he'd thought was dead, was actually alive and had written to him, his behaviour made sense. But barely two months after leaving Japan, he was arrested in Beijing on the charge of spying.

Did this connect with the instruction of 1955? And whose instruction was it?

Aki recalled what Xie Han had once told him: "*Han Langen may have forgotten everything, but they hadn't forgotten him, and they asked him – lured him – back.*" "*Who are 'they'?*" "*The top level of Mango could have been mixed up in it. I can't be sure, and even if I had some idea, in this country it's impossible to name names…*"

Xu Liping, meanwhile, had come up with the theory that in addition to the various spy rings overseen by Zhou, he'd had another – *a private agency; let's call it Y Agency.* It was one of that agency's spy ships that had taken his father to the mainland. Thus the identity of the top-level figure whose name had also occurred to Xie Han, the figure whose name could not be named "in this country," was pretty clear.

Aki put Shuichi's letter back in the envelope. His friend had to be informed of Mitsuru's death. He'd write to him. But first he was going to try to remember Hitchcock's "The 39 Steps." He'd seen it as a student.

He swivelled in his chair and murmured, "Mr Memory." Little by little, the final scene came back to him. The man was on stage in the middle of a performance when he was shot by an associate. He was carried offstage and laid on the floor, dying.

"*What was the secret formula you were taking out of the country?*"

"*Would it be all right, my telling you, sir? It was a big job to learn, the biggest job I ever tackled. I don't want to throw it all away.*" He then recited the complicated formula for building a new type of engine, ending, "*This design will render the engine completely silent. Am I right, sir?*"

"*Quite right, old chap.*"

Aki remembered Mr Memory's satisfied, shining face.

"*Thank you… thank you. I'm glad it's off my mind. At last.*"

Zhou Enlai's aide-mémoire… Suppose Zhou had had his father arrested in Beijing and locked up as someone who knew too much about his past. Then came the Anti-Rightist Movement, the Sino-Soviet split, the Great Leap Forward and all its attendant damage, and finally the Great Cultural Revolution. A series of purges, each one leading to the deaths of tens of millions. Master politician that he was, Zhou had to be constantly on guard, walking a tightrope where one misstep could mean loss of power, imprisonment, execution. In fact, on 6th January 1967, a five-metre banner was hung up in Tiananmen Square by a group of Red Guards, reading "Imprison Zhou Enlai!" And Mao's wife, Jiang Qing, tried hard to bring about his downfall because he knew everything there was to know about her past in Shanghai.

In 1976, when the Cultural Revolution was nearing its last gasp, Zhou relaxed. Perhaps then he recalled his old "aide-mémoire." Thought fondly again of Han Langen, of Waki Tanehiko. But all too soon he died of cancer.

Aki stared at his own face reflected in the study window. *My father was thirty-seven or -eight when he slipped back into China. I'm older now than he was then.*

Just then a yellow train on the Seibu Line slid into Ichigaya Station, cutting across the reflection of his face.

31

Prudently, Zhang Liang had said that he wouldn't send any papers involving Cai Fang by diplomatic pouch, that he would take them to Beijing personally and not leave them lying about his office in the consulate, either. He carried them around in his black German-made attaché case. Li Xing was fairly certain of this, but she'd spent all day yesterday combing the study while her husband was out, just in case. She found nothing.

But today, towards evening, she went into his study on a whim and found his attaché case sitting under the desk. Had he forgotten it? As he went out the door that morning, she'd been on the phone with the wife of the consul general, who called to invite her on an afternoon shopping trip to Hankyu Department Store – she turned down the offer, but having failed to see her husband off, she noticed that he'd left without his case.

The thing had a combination lock, so it probably wouldn't open. She pushed the button anyway, and with a satisfying *click* the latch sprang open. A document was tucked in the inside pocket on the lid. Fifteen unlined pages, each headed "Official Paper of the Chinese Communist Party" in red ink, were crammed with neat, right-to-left writing.

The author of the report, Zhang's friend, was now an associate professor at Xinjiang University who, as an archaeologist involved in mummy excavation, had been a member of the team that found the famous "Beauty of Loulan" in the Tarim Basin. For one so qualified, digging down a mere thirty or forty years into Cai Fang's past should have been a simple task, and yet clearly he'd had great difficulty – a measure of the chaos created by the Cultural Revolution.

This is what Li Xing learnt:

Cai Fang was a Uyghur. Most likely involved in the underground separatist movement. His birth name was Tamur Damat. He was born in 1954 in Urumqi. His parents, both of them professors at Xinjiang University, were Uyghur Muslims. In 1968, during the Cultural Revolution, he was orphaned by the Red Guards. He was then a boy of fourteen. Later, he was taken in by a man called Cai Youcai, a kindly Han Chinese intellectual forcibly displaced from Beijing. Renamed Cai Fang, he was formally adopted into the Cai family.

In China, one's personal history generally begins to be compiled on graduation from elementary school; it is officially registered when one lands a job, updated periodically, and preserved even after death. The official register listed him only as Cai Fang, of Han ethnicity, born 1958. Even his age was false.

The chaos of the Cultural Revolution meant the wholesale destruction of documents, valuable records, and the country's historical heritage; at the same time, a vast number of papers were forged.

In 1980, at the age of twenty-two – twenty-six, actually – Cai Fang went to Beijing to enrol in Peking University.

The report went on to refer to the cottonseed plant in Tarim, the destination of the missing seven hundred million yen, the connection with the Islamic separatist movement…

The final page was not so much a part of the formal report as a scribbled personal memo to Zhang. Within the structure of the ministry, he was viewed as the brains behind Cai Fang. A thorough and complicated plan was laid out for erasing that perception, so that Zhang would escape any court of inquiry. The names of a dozen or so of his co-workers, bosses, and higher-ups were listed, with a diagram illustrating the connections between them. Ideas were spelt out on the type of contact to be maintained with each of them. The enemy wasn't someone to be trifled with. Zhang had better watch his step, or he could come to grief.

Li Xing set about committing it all to memory. This was easy enough, she'd had practice memorizing lines, but midway through the task she felt a growing sense of futility. She decided, finally, that her only real course of action was to confront Zhang Liang and tell him who she really was.

She sat on in his chair, her mind so absorbed that she didn't hear the phone ringing. By the time she noticed it, she sensed that it had been ringing for some time. What if it were Aki? But he would never call her here.

She rose and slowly crossed the room. She felt languid; somehow her responses were dull. If only the caller would give up…

It was Zhang. Let's eat out tonight, he said.

"Will there be anyone else?"

"No, just us. I made a reservation at Zuien."

She felt a flutter of apprehension. Normally he would decide these things only after consulting her. Today of all days, she had no say in it.

Although she'd already settled on that evening's menu, gone shopping, and laid out the necessary ingredients, she gathered everything up and put it back in the refrigerator. She then ran a comb through her hair, but didn't bother with any makeup. Slipped on a grey flannel skirt and white turtleneck sweater, threw a beige jacket on top. Stepped into grey pumps edged in orange. The restaurant Zuien was in Higobashi, barely a fifteen-minute walk away.

She cut through the tennis courts in Utsubo Park, came out on Yotsubashi Avenue, and walked north. As if he'd planned it, Zhang appeared from a side street, and the two of them walked along in silence till they reached the restaurant. A private room was ready for them.

Zuien, the largest of the long-established Chinese restaurants in Osaka, was owned and operated entirely by Chinese. The main offerings on the menu were Cantonese, but Huchou, Szechuan, and Shandong dishes were also available. The place did some catering for the Chinese consulate and would accommodate special requests.

"I ordered their best set course," said Zhang, eyes restless in anticipation.

The owner stopped by to welcome them, and stayed to chat for five minutes. They didn't talk about the Kobe earthquake. Li Xing had never met him before, but Zhang didn't introduce her – an odd lapse for a diplomat.

A bottle of red Dynasty wine made its appearance, followed by a platter of elaborately arranged appetizers, then stewed abalone, steamed blowfish, Shanghai crab – a parade of delicacies each more expensive than the last. She forced herself to wield her chopsticks.

Zhang's peremptory attempt at red-carpet treatment had about it the rattle of bones.

Unable to manage another bite, she laid her chopsticks down, at which point he said: "You saw the report, didn't you?"

Li Xing's throat flooded with colour to the neckline, the pale skin turning pink.

"Well, what did you think? Were you surprised, or…" Zhang fixed his eyes on her neck, imagined the other, hidden parts of her body, and wondered how far the flush went.

"Yes, I was surprised."

"Will you tell him?"

"No." She drew in her chin and shook her head. The colour faded.

"You can't forget Cai Fang," he said accusingly.

"Did you leave the papers there on purpose?"

He ignored this. "Everything you read is true. I'm not a cardboard villain or bad guy like they have in the movies. I'm a certified Party member and a genuine patriot. Yanyan, have I ever lied to you, even once? Cai Fang has betrayed the Party and his country, both. Did so from the first. He's an anarchist, a Trotskyite, a terrorist. He's misappropriated public funds. You saw where the seven hundred million went. I'm going to go after him, and I'm going to get him. There's nothing you can do. You used to belong to him. Now you're my wife; and by bringing him down I'm going to make you truly mine."

She stiffened. With careful emphasis, she said, "Listen to me. I'm not Li Yan. That's the name Cai gave me to smuggle me out of China."

Her husband's eyes swam.

"My real name is Li Xing."

"Li Xing? Li Xing… I've heard that name somewhere."

"I was never Cai's lover. I was in love with his best friend, Liu Hong."

"Liu Hong?… Wait – the guy on the most-wanted list. You're the Li Xing they said was his girlfriend?"

"Yes."

"But he left the country. Didn't you go with him? What are you doing here?"

Zhang's eyes stopped moving, and he groaned. He loathed people like Liu Hong, a charismatic figure among reform-minded intellectuals. He'd heard rumours that Liu had a girlfriend who was an actress. That woman was here now – his wife!

The early eighties, when Zhang was at Peking University, had been a time of enlightened politics when reformist intellectuals occupied prominent and influential positions in the Party and the government. Men of superior ability who were Westernized, flamboyant, and popular with women: this was Zhang's assessment of them. He himself had been inconspicuous, mediocre as a student, and unimpressive to look at.

Antagonism towards that crowd had led him to enter the School of International Studies after graduation. Cai Fang was teaching a course there on covert intelligence. Zhang's sense of betrayal was thus doubled: first his mentor and current boss had failed him, now his wife.

Yet he could see the bright side of it, even there. Unmasking Cai Fang was a sure-fire path to promotion, and having this actress as his wife was his way of giving Liu Hong a good poke in the eye.

"No matter what you say," he told her through a mouthful of hot shark's fin, "I'm handing those papers you saw to headquarters, and I'm not divorcing you till Cai Fang is nailed." His tone was cocksure and insulting. "Here, eat some of this. It'll get cold."

"I don't like shark's fin." Then she calmly added, "I'm leaving you."

Zhang gave his head a decisive shake. He knew she disliked him. So be it. He would go her one better. She was old enough by now to understand that only men who'd made something of themselves were qualified to make a woman happy.

"Don't be too hasty. What's it matter if our marriage was arranged by Cai Fang? So what if we didn't get together like other couples, all hearts and flowers? Before I caught on to Cai, he was my boss; I couldn't say no to him. Besides, he singled me out for attention. I was more than happy to accept his recommendation and marry the person he suggested. And now… well, frankly I'm stunned. I had no idea you were somebody else. But why leave me? You're not in a relationship with Cai Fang. Liu dumped you and went overseas to save his own skin. Cai's career is over. Mine's just beginning, and my future's bright."

He polished off the plate of shark's fin and, bending over his swallow's-nest soup, added, "But you had your own agenda all along, didn't you?"

"What was that?"

"You tell me. What'd you marry me for?" After this leading question, he spilt some soup on his tie and began dabbing the spot with a damp napkin.

When he'd called earlier with this dinner invitation, Li Xing had sensed that now was the time to lay things on the line. *No more living a lie*, she said to herself. *End it now… He'll go into a wild rage. But his temper won't kill me.*

Zhang's deep-set eyes reddened and he began to talk nonstop. He'd joined the Party out of conviction and had taken a government post to serve his country, and he believed in the supremacy of the People's Republic of China. He poured out his fury at anyone infringing on or "liberating" any part of this sovereign territory. In his mind Cai Fang with his separatist movement had become a sworn enemy, the embodiment of all things anti-Chinese. He was a monster. That alone explained why Cai's weight had ballooned, he went so far as to say.

The second his speech was finished, Li Xing looked straight at him and began to speak in a steady voice.

She was in love with someone else. She described meeting him, running away with him, getting separated and meeting again. Her words were terse, her voice unhesitating. The malice in Zhang's face couldn't stop her.

"Who is it?" he demanded.

"He's Japanese."

When she said the name Waki Akihiko, Zhang made a waving motion in the air as if to fend it off. This arrow had come from a totally unforeseen direction. He sat there stupefied, eyes fixed, gesturing blindly. His neck itched, but he scratched his wrist. He wanted to yell, but sound wouldn't come.

"Liang," she said, "I can't stay with you anymore."

Hearing her say his name revived him, gave him a second wind. Red-faced, he shouted, "That prick! That Japanese prick!"

But the other man's name had cut him to the quick. He couldn't bring himself to say it, had to get it out of his mind. All his hatred and frustration focused again on his boss, Cai Fang.

"Don't be too sure of yourself. I won't let you go that easily. No divorce. And I'll get Cai if it's the last thing I do. Just wait and see what happens to him."

With this, he stood up. He took his left hand out of his pocket and laid a pile of dozens of toothpicks, each broken in two, onto the table.

"Cai Fang's a dirty Uyghur!" he bellowed as he stormed out of the room.

Li Xing went over to the window and opened the curtain. She undid the latch and pushed the double windows open. The view was cut off by the dark concrete of adjacent buildings, but even so, a cold, moist breeze came in. She leant out into the air and cupped her face in her hands. She remained that way barely five or six seconds. By the time she raised her head and gone back to her seat at the table, her face was composed.

Zhang had apparently gone to the men's room; he was refolding a handkerchief when he came back in, and walked deliberately around behind her before taking his seat. She suddenly wondered – has he been crying?

She held a cloth handbag on her knees. Ever since that spell of forced labour in the leather factory, she'd avoided leather bags completely. Inside the handbag were her divorce papers from the Beijing city government, tightly folded like an amulet.

"You can't lock me in."

"Yes, I can... but I won't," he responded coldly, without any expression. Staying angry was an admission of defeat.

"You'll send me back to Beijing?"

His restless eyes were sullen. "I can do that, too... but I won't."

"What do you want to do?" She might have been asking if he was going to take an umbrella, it looked like rain.

"Nothing. Nothing is going to change."

Zhang tried to pack maximum menace into his voice and words, but when she heard him say this, Li Xing knew instinctively he couldn't touch her. Her eyes strayed to the mound of broken toothpicks. It was the most eloquent thing in the room, speaking volumes about the peculiar attachment he felt for her.

Just then the owner of Zuien came in and inquired if the meal had been satisfactory. Hastily, Zhang scooped up the toothpicks and swept them back into his pocket, then rose and replied, "Very good indeed." To Li Xing's amazement, he then introduced her: "This is my wife, Li Yan."

As Zhang turned to look at her, his shoulders sagged a bit. Her eyes caught this. So that's that, she thought. But it wasn't over. What would come next? She had Aki, but Cai Fang was surrounded by enemies. She must talk to Aki, fast.

As the owner stood at the table, Zhang told her that the owner was head of the Osaka Center for Overseas Chinese, someone you could always count on. To the owner, he mentioned casually that his wife was related to Xu Liping in Kobe.

"Well now! Related to Mr Xu!" The old man stared at her with frank curiosity. "He had a daughter who went back to China. Her name was Xu Lan. She graduated from Kobe College – a real beauty. You look just like her."

32

They walked side by side up the long, steep trail. There was scattered frost on the ground and the stones. From somewhere down on the right came the sound of a running stream.

"Okay, let's hear it," said Aki. "What's in this report on Cai Fang?"

"This goes up and up, doesn't it?" said Li Xing, looking up at the path that led through groves of cedar and oak.

"Can you manage it?"

"Absolutely."

"That's right, I forgot. Your legs are stronger than mine. But watch out. You don't want to slip on the frost." He took her by the arm.

"Okay," she said, "here goes. I'll finish by the time we reach the top. Cai Fang's real name is Tamur Dafat, and he was born in 1954 in Urumqi…"

The night before, after the owner left the room, Li Xing had excused herself, saying she was going to the toilet, and slipped out of the restaurant. She called Aki from a phone booth and told him about the document she'd seen. She also briefly described what had occurred in the restaurant.

"We have to hurry," she said finally.

"Okay. Nothing I can do tonight, but I'll be there first thing in the morning. Xingxing, better not go home tonight. You can't just run away; but for the time being, check into a hotel…" He gave her the name and number of a reliable place in Osaka and made a reservation for her there as soon as they hung up.

The next morning, he skipped two meetings and took the first bullet train out of Tokyo. At a time like this, meeting in Kyoto didn't seem like the best idea, but it was the only place that came to mind. Going to Kobe would take too long. Soon enough, they would have to talk things over with Xu Liping, but they could think about that later.

The sun was already high in the sky, but little sunshine filtered through to the path in the wooded valley. They stopped to rest. Looking back, they could just glimpse the city between the slopes of mountains. They were facing in the direction of Shimogamo Shrine and the woods of the Kyoto Prefectural Botanical Garden; beyond lay the Zen temple Daitoku-ji and the Kinugasa district. Off in the distance, the ridgeline of Mount Atago stood out sharp and clear, the snow on the mountainside and in the villages showing signs of melting. They made their way up to the temple called Tanukidani Fudo-in.

"Is this willow-cotton?" she asked, holding out her palm.

"It's snow."

"But the sun's shining!"

"They called it *kazahana*, 'wind flowers.' Snow out of a clear sky." Aki turned his head and looked off to the right. "This mountain connects with Mount Hiei in the north. Must be snowing there. The wind's carrying it down to the city."

Li Xing tried to catch the wind flowers on her hand, but the moment they landed they melted away.

"In Mandarin it's *qinxue.* 'Pure snow.'"

"Nice. Do you suppose willow-cotton is blowing now in Beijing?" In early spring, bits of willow seed drifted in the air like wispy cotton.

"Not quite yet. Not till after the spring festival."

They faced forward again and began climbing the twisting path. Li Xing continued her résumé of the document she'd read. Aki listened closely.

As they went higher, with steep slopes closing in on either side, the steady narrowing of the path induced a sense of commitment. Presumably, a climb like this served to strengthen a pilgrim's resolution. At the window by the temple entrance, Aki wrote on a slip of paper, "In thanks for our reunion," and made a ten-thousand-yen donation before heading into the main hall where they knelt in front of the statue of Fudo Myoo; soon, five or six monks appeared and began offering incense and chanting prayers.

Outside again, they made their way back down steps that were the start of their descent. Aki had been thinking: Apparently neither Zhang nor his archaeologist friend in Xinjiang has a clear idea of where the ODA money went. Although it's clearly missing. Even if they do prove Cai's a Uyghur, so what? I doubt they have enough of a case to arrest him. Still, once it comes out that a high ministry official has got forged identity papers, there'll have to be a court of inquiry. That's what Zhang is betting on. That's when he'll try to pick up the money trail.

"If Cai goes before an official court of inquiry, he's doomed," Li Xing said.

"You know, the profile itself may have been real, but I'm not so sure about the rest of it – the plan for bringing Cai down, the web of connections in the Party and the ministry. That could all be camouflage. Zhang planted the thing there on purpose for you to see, after all. I'll bet somewhere there's a different scheme."

"Maybe so, but all I can do is tell Cai everything I found. Even if you're right and it does turn out to be a plant, he'll see through it. Staying one step ahead of Zhang shouldn't be hard for him. Let's face it, he's the one who taught Zhang his trade."

Aki had reserved a room in the Miyako Hotel, but as he listened to this he began to think they ought to go and consult Xu Liping right away – not just about Cai, but about what Li Xing's own strategy should be.

"So many things are going on," said Aki, once they were down on the street and inside a taxi. "Something rather funny happened yesterday, for instance. A detective came to see me. Asked me all kinds of questions – or rather, got me asking *him* questions – about Zhang Liang. Seems he's gone beyond his usual role as consul, setting up his own spy ring, giving orders to illegal operatives. I have to say I was impressed; Japanese security isn't lying down on the job. Still, it's probably nothing like the old days… Anyway, I thought this detective was spying on Zhang, but it turned out he's spying on *me*. Weird. Not twenty-four hour surveillance, though. It seems every time I write something or make a statement at a council meeting, file a report, take a trip to China or the US, he's there, checking on it. His biggest concern is my contact with Zhang. He doesn't know about my acquittal, or about that last trip to Shanghai, either. You know what's even funnier? He said they used to spy on my father, too. Said one of his predecessors, the third to last, had that assignment."

This made Li Xing laugh a little. "Who knows? Maybe this man's the son of whoever was assigned to your father."

"Right." Aki laughed out loud.

In Suwayama the electricity was working, but not the gas or water. Li Xing ran over to her grandmother and pressed her cheek against her face as she sat in her wheelchair.

"Thanks to Chen, we old folks managed to scrape through. We're grateful," said Xu.

Chen had fitted right into the household. He carried up water for the old couple, fixed their meals, did their laundry, helped Xu bathe his wife. He did more, too, organizing a motorcycle brigade that delivered relief supplies where needed.

Briefly, Li Xing gave her grandfather a two-part report, describing first the contents of the document on Cai Fang, and then the attitude Zhang had assumed towards her. She spoke simply, without emotion, until she came to the final thing he'd said to her. Shakily, she repeated the words: *Nothing. Nothing is going to change.*

They could hear the gentle pop, pop of the percolator as Chen made coffee somewhere in the background.

Xu said simply that Li Xing wasn't to go back to Osaka. "Everything will be all right," he told her confidently. "Leave the details to me, though I fear there's nothing I can do for Cai Fang. He'll have to deal with the situation on his own. But make sure you tell him everything you've committed to memory."

She picked up the phone and called Beijing. Cai was in his office at the ministry.

"Li Xing – are you okay? Where are you calling from?"

"My grandfather's house in Kobe."

"Ah, not from your home phone, then. What happened in Kobe is awful. Are your *laoye* and the rest of the family all right?"

"Yes, we're all fine. Look, I have to tell you about a report Zhang Liang received about you that I—"

"Wait. Give me the number you're calling from. I'll go to another room. Call you back in five minutes."

Precisely five minutes later, Cai called back. He listened to her account, said he understood, said he would take appropriate steps. The news wasn't unexpected. "By the way, how is he?" he added.

"Fine," Li Xing answered in a cheerful tone, quickly understanding that *he* meant Aki.

"That's good. I'd like you to give him a message."

"He's here right now. Shall I put him on?"

"By all means."

She handed Aki the receiver, which he accepted with little enthusiasm. He never liked taking over the phone from someone else, or having another person suddenly come on the line.

"It's certainly been a while since we've spoken, hasn't it?" Cai went on, "I found out about your father. He's alive. I can't go into any details over the phone, so come to Beijing as soon as you can. As you know, I no longer have much time at my disposal. Get your visa in Tokyo. Better to avoid Osaka, for obvious reasons. I'll arrange with the Tokyo embassy to have the visa issued immediately."

"Where is my father?"

"On the Loess Plateau. I'll take you there. Here's how to reach me. The phone number is…"

The large, Western-style room had small, low windows on the east and south, fitted with shutters on the outside and paper screens on the inside. When Li Xing's mother went to China, the Xu family was still living in the old Graciani house in Kobe, and they kept her room there unchanged. After they built the new condominium structure in Suwayama and went to live there, an exact replica of their daughter's room was incorporated into it at the insistence of her mother. The missing girl never did return – but her child, their granddaughter, did. On the night of the earthquake, after walking all the way from Ashiya with Aki leading the way, Li Xing had slept in her mother's room.

She and Aki now climbed into the lone bed in that room.

"At last that report of Zhang's is off my mind."

"Yes, you can let it go."

"Okay, here it goes… *whoosh!* Ah, yes, much better."

"That's the way. Now forget Zhang, too."

"Can forgetting make it seem as if it never happened?"

"Yes."

"But what if *he* doesn't forget? Then it won't work."

"Whether he does or does not makes no difference. It never

happened. Just let it go. Then everything will be *suan le* – over and done with." But his voice was strained.

"*Laoye* said to leave Zhang to him…"

Aki was silent, his mind busy formulating a strategy for dealing with the man by himself. The information supplied by that detective would be useful. Casually let the guy know he had the goods on his illegal spying activities. Remember to tell Xu as well…

His hands reached for her, and one by one he undid the buttons on her pyjama top. "To tell the truth, I'd forgotten about my father. But they remembered for me."

"You'll have to go to Beijing, won't you? I hope Cai Fang will be all right."

She shifted her hips. Aki lifted the blanket high and said,

> *Beloved, you and I are a compass.*
> *Two heads, four legs, one body.*
> *Now we describe a circle around a point,*
> *Head to legs and legs to head,*
> *Each with head between the other's legs.*

"That's no kind of a poem!"

"At least it's accurate."

"People in liberated China don't do this."

"No? But you and I did, from the start."

"Ah," said Li Xing softly, and then she said it again in a different way.

33

Chauffeured by Chen, Xu set off for Mikage. On his way up the hill he stopped at the nursing home to see Yasuko, but it wasn't clear to him whether she understood who he was. It was sad, he thought, gently touching her arm. Since she didn't even know that her daughter was dead, telling her that her husband was alive seemed meaningless. All he could do for her now was to help her son straighten out his life.

His own wife was in little better shape. How well did she grasp the fact that their granddaughter had come to them? Who could say? This, too, was sad, and yet Xu was rather inclined to see it as providential in its way. For the sake of Yasuko – whom he'd once asked to marry him, back in his university days – he would help Aki, her son, to sort things out. That was also the best way to help Li Xing.

After spending barely half an hour with Yasuko, he walked uphill the short distance to the Garden Oriental Soshuen, having told Chen to wait for him in the parking lot.

The large Chinese-style garden, constructed on a swath of wooded hillside, enclosed a building in the classic residential style of the Japanese nobility and a scattering of small pavilions. Originally built by the founder of a major Kansai-based insurance company as a second home, after the Pacific War it had been bought by the Lin family, Chinese residents of Kobe, who turned it into a first-class restaurant specializing in Cantonese food. Thirty years ago, if you were lucky, in the main dining room or bar you might have shaken hands with the writer Mishima Yukio or seen the actress Arima Ineko drift in like a stray peach blossom.

The day after the earthquake, Soshuen already had its lights on, open for business. In part this was because the premises escaped with only minor damage. Beyond that, though, the owners had been inspired by something that once happened in China. When the Qiantang River massively overflowed its banks and poured through the streets of Hangzhou, it seems that the restaurant Louwailou at the foot of Mount Gu had continued service on its third floor, lighting the rooms with every available candle. The specialty of the house was slow-braised pork belly, which the citizens of Hangzhou were not about to deny themselves, come hell or high water; so they got into boats and rowed through the flooded streets to eat their pork.

For similar reasons, the luxury Hotel Okura in Kobe, on the harbourfront by Meriken Park, had put lights in its windows to spell out the message "business as usual."

Xu had chosen Soshuen for a meeting with Zhang Liang. He intended to probe the man's mind and, as soon as he could, come to an on-the-spot agreement.

Zhang, meanwhile, was still recovering from his wife's unexpected confession. If she were allied with him, he'd have been willing to take things slowly, leave them as they were for the time being. But shock had eventually given way to deep-seated anger and offense, confirming his intention to go through with his plans. News that Waki, the Huxley man, had been arrested in Shanghai in July 1989, then acquitted, was certainly interesting. Better than he could have dared hope for. Add to that an adulterous affair with the wife of the present Chinese consul and... *I may not have power of life and death over him, but this still gives me the upper hand. I'll take care of Waki once I finish off Cai Fang.*

Using the need to file a report on the earthquake as a pretext, Zhang had obtained the consul general's permission for a trip to Beijing. However, just after making a plane reservation by phone, he'd received this summons from Xu Liping. Now, of all times. For a second he hesitated, considered the matter from every angle. In the end, he fastened on one consideration: Xu was his wife's grandfather. With all due caution, why not take this opportunity to get closer to his adversary?

When he arrived at the hotel, Xu was waiting for him, seated at a corner table in the dining room – the closest place to the garden. Sounds from outdoors wafted in, so there would be little chance of other customers overhearing their conversation. Not that they needed to worry: it was only days since the earthquake, and the large room held only two other parties, seated at distant tables.

A heavy jar of darkly fragrant Shaoxing wine appeared on the table. Nothing else.

"A fine old wine," said Zhang in Japanese, taking a sip after it had been decanted into a jade cup.

"It's thirty-year-old Hua Tiao from Shaoxing," said Xu, naming a traditional specialty, the oldest brewed wine in China. "Let me start out by saying there will be no food served tonight. This is not the sort of topic to discuss while eating."

Zhang nodded, thinking, *Score one for him*. Arranging the meeting here, then ruling out a meal, showed what a sly old fox he was.

"I believe you said you'd never been here before," continued Xu.

"That's right. It's quite a place all right."

"Do you mind if we go on speaking Japanese? I may be Chinese, but my grasp of the language is fairly tenuous, I'm afraid."

"Certainly, by all means. Although I warn you, my Japanese isn't that good, either."

"On the contrary, it's excellent. Where did you learn it?"

"The School of International Studies."

"Ah. Well, let's get down to it... Cai Fang is not someone I'm acquainted with. What sort of person is he?" This opening gambit would get Zhang to open up.

"He was a lecturer from the Ministry of State Security at the School of International Studies, which I entered after graduating."

"What sort of teacher was he?"

"Strict... also *nenggan*, very capable. At the time, I was delighted to have him as a role model. Now the idea makes my blood boil. He and I were in the program for opposite reasons, you see. He was set on betraying his country! But I'm grateful to him for two things."

Silently, Xu refilled Zhang's cup. As Cantonese custom demanded, Zhang rapped three times on the table with his middle finger before returning the favour.

"First, as an instructor, he was excellent. I think it's because he was already a traitor to his country, in the position of being a double spy, that he was able to do such a good job."

Xu nodded. Zhang Liang, he saw, was no run-of-the-mill, can't-see-beyond-the-end-of-his-nose pragmatist.

"The other thing is my wife. Whatever his motive in arranging the marriage, thanks to him I got to know an amazing woman. And to think she's your granddaughter!"

Without reacting, Xu studied the man's darting eyes. Zhang faltered, dropped his gaze. Xu asked, "What's the word in Mandarin for the husband of one's granddaughter?"

"Well, in this case, since I'm married to your daughter's daughter, that would make me your *waison nyude nyuxue*." He relaxed slightly.

"Consul," said Xu in a low, hoarse voice, as if he'd been waiting for this moment. "I'm a nobody, an insignificant member of the overseas Chinese community. From Beijing's point of view, I probably seem about as unimportant as a leaf in the wind. As, indeed, I am."

What's the old man getting at? wondered Zhang as he lifted his cup.

"But the life of a leaf is surprisingly easy. It can be carried around by the prevailing wind, or it can fall to earth. Even if it rots there, it doesn't smell."

More baffled than ever, Zhang began to feel irritated.

"Look, it's raining," said Xu. "The leaves on the trees love it, getting wet in the rain."

The traditional Japanese building had been extensively remodelled when it was made into a restaurant; a row of arched windows had been put in and a lawn terrace added, with a roof supported by six untrimmed cypress pillars. Falling drops shone distinctly, each separate, in the light of the garden lanterns, and landed neatly on the grass. Only Xu noticed.

He continued, "In the old days, my grandfather and my father served as the comprador for three banks – the Hong Kong and Shanghai Bank, Bangkok Bank, and the Yokohama Specie Bank, which is now the Bank of Tokyo. Are you familiar with the comprador system?"

Zhang shook his head.

"Commercial transactions with China were so complex that native-born agents used to serve as middlemen with European and Japanese banks and trading companies. Foreign exchange, interpreting, brokerage. That's what the compradors were, elite brokers. Having gotten started as commercial intermediaries, after the war my family ran its own trading company, called Central Commerce. At one time it ranked shoulder to shoulder with Mitsui, Mitsubishi, and Sumitomo. It was I who put the company out of business. Sold it off, I should say. Today it's called..." Xu named a major trading and investing corporation.

Zhang nodded. This family pedigree could only work to his advantage, he thought. "Cai Fang helped himself to seven hundred million yen in Japanese ODA," he said pointedly.

Xu beamed genially, the image of a good-natured old man. "That sort of thing does go on all the time on the mainland, doesn't it? And in other countries as well, I suppose. If every single misappropriation were checked out, I daresay the whole ODA system would collapse. Plenty must go on below the surface, but all in all, it does serve a useful purpose."

Below the table, Zhang thrummed his fingers against his leg.

"Anyway, thanks to my connections with the banking world, it often happens that I find out things that are none of my business."

Hello, what's the old geezer getting at now? This thought came with fresh foreboding.

"Your personal account in a certain branch of Seiwa Bank is connected to secret accounts in the Cayman Islands."

"What's this all about, Mr Xu?" Zhang inquired, stunned, his face a blank.

Xu's forebears, as compradors, were well acquainted with the seamier side of financing. Xu Liping had walked away from that world — and yet the channels of information open to his father remained open to him as well. He had availed himself of them to run a check on Zhang Liang, and found out that he possessed two secret accounts, one with a commercial bank, the other with a Hyogo credit association. For a consul of the People's Republic of China to open a secret account was by normal standards unthinkable. Moreover, substantial sums of money were being siphoned from those accounts to an offshore bank in the Cayman Islands, a well-known laundering site for illicit funds. Money flowed back from there, too. Where did it all come from? Broadly speaking, there were two sources. One was corporations owned by Japanese or by overseas Chinese; the other was an unauthorized bank.

Chinese who were illegal residents of Japan and therefore unable to open accounts in a proper bank could use a flourishing unaccredited bank to send money to their relatives on the mainland. From the Kansai region alone, billions of yen were transferred illegally each year. The transfer fee came to roughly one per cent. Xu had determined that Zhang was receiving huge contributions from this source.

Why so much money? The information Aki had supplied from Tokyo provided the answer. It all fitted in with Zhang's setting up a private spy ring. With a private spy ring, Zhang could expand his reach beyond his usual responsibilities, collecting information about individuals and countries. He would become powerful, and feared,

"Your affairs are an open secret. Let's move to the bar, shall we?" said Xu, getting to his feet.

With the sound of falling rain in his ears, Zhang accompanied him down a wood-floored passage, turned a couple of corners, and was shown into a dimly lit room with the blinds pulled. Instead of a bar, there was a low table and comfortable leather armchairs. A huge mahogany shelf held a variety of liquor bottles. They were the only guests. A waiter ambled over to them.

"I'll have an espresso," Xu said.

And his granddaughter can't drink a drop of coffee: the thought popped into a corner of Zhang's mind.

"A brandy for my companion. I believe you have some Hennessy XO in stock – he'll have that." He turned to face Zhang. "Forgive me for ordering for you, but I understand you're partial to brandy."

A glass of brandy was poured, and Zhang drank some of it. "Mr Xu. Allow me to call you *Yue laoye,* as a relative. It's true, I do have secret accounts in a number of banks. But that's to help me acquire more influence in the Party, through activities beneficial to the Party."

It was impossible to tell from Xu's expression whether he was even listening.

Then, holding his espresso demitasse near his nose, Xu spoke. "The Japanese police are watching your every move."

Zhang rose slightly out of his seat.

"When do you leave for Beijing?" asked Xu.

"Day after tomorrow."

"Put it off a week."

If he did that, Zhang reflected, Cai would have ample time to sneak out of the country. Over his dead body.

Xu continued: "This man Cai Fang may indeed be a traitor to the Party and his country. He may well be contributing to a separatist movement. What would be the formal charge against him – high treason? The penalty for that is death. It exists in Japanese law as well – the crime of subverting the state – a law that would probably never be applied, but there it is. Consider this, consul. Although the Japanese police may be watching you, you needn't worry; there's no law here against espionage. What's trickier is the Chinese side. The secret accounts exist, you say, for the sake of the Party – is that how the Party would see it?"

Zhang raised the large brandy glass to his face. It clouded with his breath. *Let's hear his terms. I might not be able to beat him, but I'll hold out for all I can.* "Why so interested in helping Cai Fang? He's got nothing to do with you. You have nothing to gain."

"Never mind. You personally have nothing to lose. Just give him time to choose: punishment or flight. Either way, you're certain to bring him down and then take his place. All the more reason why you should close that Cayman account. How much do you need, by the way?"

Xu's manner was bland, but there was a hardness in his look. When it came down to it, this man could be bought off, of that Zhang was certain. The Cayman account violated Party regulations, as he himself was aware. Knowing when to back off was an important tool for any diplomat.

"Fair enough," said Zhang.

Xu removed his monocle. The look in his eye was milder now. "While you're at it," he said, "why not give Li Xing her freedom?"

Zhang slowly shook his head, lips tight, eyes jumpy.

Xu persisted. "Consul, you're getting what you want. Isn't it asking too much to want my granddaughter as well?"

"The Cai Fang business is in a separate category altogether from what to do about Li Yan," Zhang said with deliberation. He was digging in his heels, using his wife's assumed name to her grandfather's face. He'd be damned if he'd let her go. Turn her over to some Japanese? Hell no.

Well, well, thought Xu in surprise, pulling on a fleshy earlobe. *He's fonder of her than we thought.*

For a brief spell, there was a certain rapport between the two men. Inside, Xu was smiling in a bemused way. His great-grandfather used to call it *smiling on a cloud of opium smoke*. Xu remembered admiring the aptness of the expression.

"Yes, and it's precisely because the two are in different categories that you're being greedy. Settle for one. You'll get the thing that's most important to you."

"The other is important to me, too," Zhang said adamantly.

"I know. But it's not possible… Is there something wrong with your left hand, consul?"

Without realizing it, Zhang had been keeping one hand deep in his pocket. "No, it's just a habit," he said, and laid his hand on his knee.

"And here I thought maybe you were holding a gun." As he said this, Xu's voice, hitherto low and solemn, lightened. "What do you intend to do about your ties to the underground bank?" he said. In a quieter voice, his tone still light, he added, "There's no way you can defend that to the Party, you know. So tell me: how much money do you need to break your ties with that underground bank?" As he probed, there was a distinct menace in his look.

The two men drew their heads together and talked over the sum necessary to deal with the Cayman account and the unofficial bank.

Later, on his way back to Osaka in the chauffeur-driven car that Xu had provided for him, passing through neighbourhoods ravaged by earthquake and fire, Zhang told himself: *That was a compromise, not a defeat. Yes, I'm fond of my wife, but what I really care about is the Party.*

Having seen Zhang off, Xu Liping got into his own car, Chen at the wheel. Just as they turned onto Sanroku Road, the rain changed to snow. Snowflakes danced in the candlelight leaking from tents set up for evacuees. The sight put him in mind of the steppes, galloping horses. Zhang probably wouldn't admit defeat. No matter. Their next encounter would be something to look forward to.

He arrived home just after Li Xing had bathed her grandmother and tucked her in bed. Aki was out on the balcony having a smoke. Seeing that Xu was back, he opened the terrace door to return to the living room, bringing in with him the sound of the river and a swirl of snow, which died when he closed the door.

The three of them gathered around the oval rosewood table.

Xu spoke slowly, looking back and forth from one to the other. "It's all taken care of. Xingxing, you're free."

She breathed a sigh of relief, her cheeks colouring.

"I won't go into detail, but trust me, from now on he won't be able to make a move."

Xu said no more, and reached for the evening edition of the *Kobe Shimbun*. Based in Sannomiya, the newspaper had gone out of production after the earthquake, its main building on the verge of collapse, but today an evening edition had come out.

From across the newspaper came Aki's voice: "Actually, could we have a *little* more detail?"

Xu put the paper down. "He was getting illegal money."

"Illegal, how?"

"Via an unauthorized bank."

"That was unwise. And that's where the money for his Y Agency came from?"

He nodded.

Aki continued, "So you bailed him out of a crisis. That was quite a trade-off. I mean, one could say you've become his sponsor, that you're the power behind him now."

"Correct. An ironic twist of fate."

"That it certainly is."

A brief silence reigned. From far below came the sound of a motorcycle starting up the hill.

Ironic as hell, thought Aki. He swallowed the things he wanted to say, taking advantage of the silence to look out the window and try a slightly different view.

Zhang must be relieved that in exchange for one concession, the business of the Cayman account and the underground bank would be taken care of. Must be feeling elated, triumphant. But what did he think of the fact that Xu now had him by the balls?

As Aki shifted his attention away from the window, his eyes met the old man's, looking at him as if to say, *Now do you understand?*

"When will you be going to Beijing?" asked Xu.

"I talked it over with Cai Fang earlier this evening, and the visa will come through tomorrow, in Tokyo. I'll be in Beijing the day after tomorrow."

"Good. Zhang was planning to leave for Beijing then, too. I persuaded him to put it off for a week. All things being equal, he'll no doubt go far in the Party. I've removed every obstacle to his success. So be it. He'll never be a top leader, but he'll get to play with the big boys. Be in the winners' circle. Whereas we people are perennial losers. That's the fate of the overseas Chinese. Incidentally, do you know the significance of the character *qiao* in *huaqiao* – referring to Chinese who live abroad? The underlying meaning is 'transient.'"

As he spoke, Xu looked at the pair seated in front of him; first one, then the other, then both together. He thought, *So I played Cupid.* He wasn't at all averse to the idea. *But even these two will have to face the problem of living alone together. Because no couple can ever live in isolation from the world.*

"Xingxing," he said, "how was your grandmother today?"

"Fine. She ate well, and even sang a song."

"What song was that?"

"Something Japanese I'd never heard before." She turned to Aki for help.

"It was 'Sado Love Story,' by Hibari Misora. Xingxing sang one for us, too."

"What did she sing?"

"'Song of the Yellow River Boatmen.'"

"I'd like to hear it."

"Not tonight," said Li Xing. "Some other time, okay?"

"All right, then. Some other time."

The motorcycle stopped in front of the building. Shortly afterwards, Chen slipped into the room. After taking Xu home from Soshuen, he'd gone out on relief work with the motorbike brigade, and was back early.

"Welcome home," said Xu. "Come sit down."

Diffidently, he joined them.

"How did it go?"

"There's some nasty people out there," he complained. "They seem to think it's all a science fiction movie or something. They go to houses that have collapsed, with people still alive in them, and just fool around, never offering to help. Junior high and high school kids. I yelled at them, told them to quit doing it, but they just looked the other way. Wouldn't lend a hand. Made me so mad, I grabbed a couple of 'em and tried to shake some sense into 'em."

Everyone was silent.

"*Laoye*," Li Xing said, "I've decided to go help out at the Kobe Chinese School. The principal came by while you were out. The school is serving as an evacuation centre, and it's full of people now, hundreds of them, not just Chinese but Japanese and Vietnamese and all sorts of people, huddled together. Because it's not an official evacuation centre, they don't have enough helpers or food. I asked him to let me do something, and he begged me to come."

"A very good idea. By all means, you should go,"

Aki had been idly mulling over Chen's angry episode, and now he remembered something from what seemed like a lifetime ago. "Chen," he said, "A day or two after you left Shanghai, your father came to see me. We met right in front of my hotel."

Chen couldn't conceal his agitation. For several seconds his eyes swam; then he hung his head.

"Since you've lost your Anli, this will sound a bit rough, but I'll tell you your father's exact words: 'If you ever come across that rascal in Japan, I want you to give him what-for.' He said it with tears in his eyes."

Chen's shoulders shook.

"But I can't do that. And I'm sure your father really hoped and prayed you'd be safe." Aki's own voice choked up. In his mind's eye he could see Chen's father, his back bending lower and lower.

"Oh, I forgot," Xu cleared his throat, as if to clear the air. "I've got something nice for everybody." He disappeared into the hallway. From there he called out to Chen, asking him to boil some water. In no time he reappeared, bearing a small package wrapped in tinfoil. "Yesterday Mr Shi came over."

"Shi Ying, you mean, from Teite?"

"Yes, that's right. The restaurant was destroyed. He's giving up the business. Tor Road is all but wiped out, he said. A great pity."

Aki thought of the time he and his sister had eaten striped mullet there. Teite was gone, as she was. Xu's voice overlapped with his thoughts.

"This is a very special jasmine tea, something he got hold of just recently, he said. Not for sale in Beijing or Fuzhou, either. He wouldn't say how he got it. I tried it. I'll hold off telling you what I thought. Let me just give you some."

Chen brought in a pot of hot water.

"Did you know that the English word 'tea' comes from the dialect spoken around the port of Amoy?" As he spoke, Xu added one pinch of tea leaves, then another, to the rather large, reddish-brown teapot. Already, Aki and Li Xing began to feel their pulses strangely quickening. The size of the leaves, their colour and curl, were all signs of a fine flavour. "In the making of jasmine tea they speak of 'three scentings, one handful,' or 'five scentings, one handful.' The number of scentings is the number of times the scent of the blossom is transferred to the tea leaves."

The air filled with the distinct, unmistakable aroma of Yin Dan's tea.

"'One handful' means that at the very end, a bit of blossom is mixed in with the leaves, but this tea is unusual in that no petals are in it at all. And as far as I can tell, this isn't just three or five scentings, but seven! I've never seen such tea in all my life. It's unheard of."

He poured a cupful for each of them. Li Xing inhaled the fragrance deeply, laid a hand on her heart, and looked at Aki. He nodded. They each read their own thought in the other's eyes: *Yin Dan is alive.*

It's as if he steered us here, thought Aki.

Li Xing, too, was thinking, *It's this tea that led me here.*

They went on looking at each other, almost as if seeing each other for the first time.

34

The snowfall that had begun in Kobe continued at Narita Airport, and kept up all the way to Beijing. Aki set his watch back one hour and alighted at five o'clock in the afternoon at Beijing Airport. He passed through Customs and stepped out into the arrivals lobby, where he was surprised to see Cai Fang standing beyond the gate. Aki had reserved a room at the Beijing Hotel, and was going to contact him as soon as he checked in. It was their first meeting in six years. Just as Li Xing had said, he was twice as big as before. That and the unexpectedness of being met filled Aki with a surge of affection for the man.

After a handshake, Cai said, "Good to see you. Don't stop here; we'll talk as we go. Walls have ears and screens have eyes. It's snowing in Shanxi, too. Twenty-eight below zero. Did you bring warm clothes?"

"Yes."

They got in a taxi. When Cai lumbered in, his weight made the vehicle list to starboard. The driver muttered, would the passenger please move closer to the middle of the seat, and Cai sheepishly complied. "Beijing Station," he directed. In Aki's ear he murmured, "We're taking the night train tonight, okay?" Aki nodded.

Cai Fang had a chauffeur-driven car that was available to him for private errands, but today he'd elected to hail a taxi, both for the trip to the airport and now for the ride to Beijing Station. Aki had come with a sturdy black medium-sized suitcase, but Cai had only a vinyl shoulder bag.

They sped along a straight, poplar-lined road. Snowflakes drifted down in the grey twilight. Whenever he landed at Beijing Airport, Aki took the big neon sign at the Panasonic factory as the start of downtown. Now he barely had time to register its presence on the left before the Beijing sky – a sky he was seeing for the first time in seven years – was overtaken by a darkness filled with swirling snow.

The station crowds were never less than unnerving, but with the holiday rush for the Lunar New Year, confusion was approaching panic level. Fifty or sixty thousand people swarmed in the station plaza, their commotion a loud droning in Aki's ears as Cai's bulky figure plunged through the crowd ahead of him.

In front of the station building they came to a sturdy-looking iron fence: the first checkpoint. Their tickets were examined and they proceeded into the hall, where ahead of them rose a long escalator. Pushed along from behind, they were carried in a sort of tidal bore to the second-floor hall. This central concourse was vast and dimly lit, with waiting rooms on either side divided according to platform.

They located their assigned waiting room, but the benches were full. The air was full of gritty, throat-stinging cigarette smoke, and a resinous smell overlay everything. Aki put his suitcase down by the wall. Cai handed him his ticket.

They were due to take train 2519, bound for Yuncheng, leaving at 21:10. Along the way they would pass through Shijiazhuang, Yangquan, and Taiyuan, heading south down the middle of the vast Loess Plateau and arriving at their destination of Linfen at 10:23 the following morning. Aki checked his watch against the wall clock in the waiting room. Nearly two hours till departure time.

"I brought supper," said Cai, tapping his shoulder bag. "There is a dining car, but the food's inedible. I ordered sandwiches from the restaurant at the Great Wall Hotel. Should be plenty."

"Good. Thanks. Why don't I get some fruit to go with it?"

"No need. Don't worry about a thing. See, I have wine, too." Cai showed him the neck of a bottle poking out of the bag. "Besides us, there'll be two other passengers in the sleeping compartment, so we won't be able to talk very much. It's safer to talk here. Let's say everything that needs saying, and get that out of the way."

"I suppose because of the suitcase, it wouldn't do to walk and talk."

"We'll be okay here." Cai Fang twisted his large frame around to survey the surrounding hubbub. "All right," he began, "here's the story:

"In 1979 Han Langen was released from Qincheng Prison in Beijing and sent to three different jails before ending up in the jail in Linfen City, in Shanxi Province. Then in August 1989, around the time you were taken into custody in Shanghai—"

Here Cai Fang broke off and chuckled mischievously, to which Aki responded with a grin.

"– he was let out and sent to a village on the outskirts of Linfen called Zhaonanhe. The village has no jail. He's not paroled, but he is able to live a fairly normal life there and have a personal registry. It's a form of exile. Sometimes when a prisoner's term is over, instead of setting him free they'll detain him in this way. You can marry, you can have your own home, you can even send for your family to come live with you.

"Still, it's a mystery: why on earth your father was called back, arrested for espionage in Beijing, and kept locked up all this time – I've checked into it as far as I can, but there's no paper trail. To say records were lost in the storms of the Cultural Revolution is the usual excuse; it's also possible that someone deliberately destroyed the papers. Anyway, here's my advice: remind yourself that this is a country with a history of burning books and burying scholars alive, and overlook what may or may not have happened this time."

Aki nodded. The lighting was dim to begin with, the air such a swirl of dust and cigarette smoke that he had trouble seeing Cai's face clearly.

"I'm not particularly set on digging up the truth," he said. "It's just that if there's any chance my father is alive, I can't sit around and do nothing. I may live elsewhere, but so long as he and I both have our feet on this earth, as his son I want to walk up to him and say something."

Cai nodded several times. "I understand. But I'd advise against trying to take him away with you. That would be a problem, and lead to other complications."

"I'm sure it would. I have no intention of doing any such thing. To tell the truth, I'm more worried about you."

"I'll be all right."

"There isn't much time."

"Don't worry. Actually I brought my plans forward one day. I'd originally planned to take the noon train tomorrow – but I wanted to see you again."

"And I wanted to see you. I really wanted to see you and thank you in person. Li Xing sends her regards. She said to tell you how grateful she is for all you did."

"It makes me happy to hear that. She's a wonderful woman. I envy you."

Aki was touched by this. "I'll tell her exactly what you said. Also, Xu Liping sends his warmest regards."

Cai Fang bowed and then, murmuring "this calls for a drink," shoved his way through the waiting-room crowd and disappeared. He was soon back with some not-very-chilled cans of beer. He handed one to Aki. When they popped them open, foam bubbled out. "*Kampai*," they said softly, raising a toast.

"Beijing Station is great," Aki decided, casting his eyes around. "You can feel the excitement in the air, people setting off for distant places. Tokyo Station is dead by comparison. Japanese people were probably like this in the old days, but the bullet train wrecked everything."

"There used to be a bar in Tokyo Station called Camellia. Is it still there?"

"Yes, it is."

"I told Zhang Liang about it."

"I know. I went drinking with him there."

"Is that right? I'm fond of that station, I really am. It's a good one. The first time I came to Beijing was to enrol at the university. Seventy-two hours by train from Urumqi, in blazing midsummer heat, like an insect crawling across the face of the earth."

"How far is that in kilometres?"

Cai pulled a railway timetable out of his bag. With practiced ease, he thumbed quickly to the table of distances. "Beijing to Urumqi… here it is, 3,774 kilometres. That's the longest distance listed. Beijing to Kunming is 3,279 kilometres."

Intrigued, Aki peered at the table, too.

"And the next longest?"

"Pingxiang – 2,785 kilometres."

"Where's that?"

"It's on the border with Vietnam, in the Guangxi Zhuang Autonomous Region."

"What's next?"

"Guiyang, 2,540 kilometres. How far is it from Tokyo to Kagoshima?"

JASMINE

"I don't know, maybe 1,600 kilometres?"

Just then, all twelve or thirteen hundred people in the waiting room stood up en masse, with a noise like the rumbling of an earthquake. The ticket gate was open. A wave of baggage-laden passengers surged forwards from the rear of the room, carrying Aki and Cai Fang along with them.

They crossed a dark overpass and descended to a still darker platform. Snow blew in their faces. At the step leading up into the train was the third checkpoint. For the first time, it struck Aki that in this country the people who examined your ticket were invariably women. Gruff women.

Finally they arrived in their compartment. Two sets of bunks, four beds in all. No ladder for climbing to the upper bunk; you had to put one foot on a small footstool near the door, grab the railing, and hoist yourself up. This meant pulling up your entire weight with your arms, which was clearly beyond Cai's ability, so Aki decided he would sleep on top. Going to the john in the night would be not be fun, better not drink much.

One of the passengers who would be sharing the compartment came in: a middle-aged man carrying a cheap-looking attaché case.

"How far are you going?" asked Cai.

"Pingyao. You two?"

"Linfen."

A young woman rolled a big suitcase into the compartment and greeted them with a cheery "*Ni hao!*"

"*Ni hao.*"

She had healthy, glowing skin. There was a bandage around her left wrist.

"How far are you going?" asked the man with the attaché case.

"Yuncheng."

"Ah, the end of the line."

A bell and a whistle sounded shrilly at the same time, and with a great clanging, the train lurched into motion. On the windowpane, snowflakes melted and ran down in oblique lines, beyond which were the blurred and desolate-looking lights of Beijing.

The train seemed to pant for breath as it moved. Heading west, it climbed a fairly steep slope.

The man with the attaché case was Cao. He worked for a travel company in Beijing and was on his way to a branch office in Pingyao, where the train was due to arrive at around 7:30 a.m. The young woman worked at a foreign-owned hotel in Beijing and was going home for the Lunar New Year.

The numbers on their tickets indicated that the girl had the lower bunk and Cao the upper, but as he was getting off first, they traded places. Declining the young woman's offer of sunflower seeds, Cai and Aki made a late supper of their sandwiches, which they shared with the other two. They uncorked the wine, but Aki restricted himself to a mouthful, and Cai and Cao finished it off between them. The young woman nibbled on sunflower seeds nonstop. She would hold one vertically between her teeth and crack it open, then deftly remove the contents with her tongue and spit out the shell into a plastic bag.

When Cao began nodding off, the group took advantage of his sleepiness to bid one another goodnight. Up in her bunk, the girl continued to nibble on seeds while reading a magazine. Cao began to snore laboriously.

Aki and Cai went out into the corridor for a smoke. Though Cai's bulk left no space for anyone else to get by, he didn't seem to care. Outside the windows all was pitch dark, making it impossible to say for certain what direction the train was moving in. Occasionally the sound of a whistle would approach, and a long succession of container cars would pass, ending with a boxcar and, in its window, the face of a man in the regulation cap. Orange taillights receded into the distance along with the whistle.

"Where in God's name is this?" murmured Aki.

Cai rubbed the steam from the windowpane with his palm and stuck his nose close to the glass, cupping his hands around his face to block out the light in the corridor.

"Let's see – we were in Baoding before."

"What time do you think we'll get to Yangquan?"

"Yangquan? Maybe three in the morning. That's right, Yangquan was Li Xing's second home, wasn't it?"

Her parents and *nainai* were buried there. She would probably never go there again. The least he could do was stay awake as the train passed through.

"Of course. She'll ask if the train went there. You can hardly tell her you were asleep."

"No, I can't. It's a little thing, but there you are."

"Not little at all. Stay up. Yes, you should absolutely stay up. I'll keep you company. You can tell her I was awake, too. Next is Shijiazhuang. It's another four hours till Yangquan."

Once again Cai put his head against the window, his hands framing his face as he looked out.

"See anything?" asked Aki.

"Yes, rails. They're coming closer. We're going to join up. There, they've merged."

The train swayed as the two sets of tracks came together.

"Excuse me," said a passenger, finding the corridor blocked. It was a plump young man with a moustache.

Cai Fang didn't budge. "Now there's a pond," he said. "Swans are swimming in it."

Surprised, Aki pressed his forehead against the window, cupping his face with his hands. The vibration and chill of the glass felt good. The pond passed. It must have been frozen. But how could swans swim on ice?

"There's an elephant in the pond," said Cai.

Incredulous now, Aki narrowed his eyes and stared. For an instant, suspended in the dark void he saw the figure of an elephant, trunk raised high like a periscope. "I'll be damned," he said. "Is this train going through a zoo?"

"Yes. Look over there, a *qilin* is running over the hill."

"Which, a giraffe or a real *qilin*?"

"A *qilin*, naturally."

Aki saw the animal gallop through a clump of grass on the slope. Cai's voice was saying, "Body of a deer, tail of an ox, a single horn on its head. The male is called *qi* and the female, *lin*. It's considered a benign creature as it never tramples on grass, never tramples on animals, never so much as bends any vegetation."

The young man who had asked to get by, and had been standing fidgeting in the aisle all this time, now did as they did, bringing his face up close to the window and peering out.

"Nothing to see out there," he growled.

"He and I can see it," said Cai. Then to Aki he said, "Well, shall we turn in?"

They re-entered the compartment. Cao was fast asleep, snoring softly now.

"I'll wake you when we get to Yangquan," said Cai, tapping his wide chest. Reassured, Aki climbed up to his bunk. In the darkness behind the curtain of the other upper bunk, the muffled sound of sunflower seeds being cracked open went on and on. It was already after one in the morning. Not everyone would be able to sleep soundly, he thought. The bird-feed noises were going to drive him crazy.

There wasn't enough room to change into pyjamas. He removed his jacket, lay face up with the blanket pulled up to his chin and, turning on the bedside lamp, opened an English paperback. It was Paul Theroux's account of his travels through China, which he'd purchased at a kiosk in Narita. The epigraph read:

> *A peasant must stand a long time on*
> *a hillside with his mouth open before a*
> *roast duck flies in.*
> —Chinese proverb

> *The movements which work revolutions in*
> *the world are borne out of the dreams and visions*
> *in a peasant's heart on a hillside.*
> —James Joyce, *Ulysses*

This is good stuff, he mumbled to himself.

In April 1986, Theroux had left London and travelled to China on a succession of eight different trains. Ulan Bator, Harbin, Beijing, Qingdao, Amoy, Xining, Urumqi... It seemed as if he'd ridden every long-distance train possible, but this train to Yuncheng, number 2519, was not among them.

Aki read on until he came to this passage:

> *In most other countries, a landscape feature was a grove of trees, or a meadow, or even a desert; so you immediately associated the maple tree with Canada, the oak with England, the birch with the Soviet Union,*

and desert and jungle with Africa. But no such thing came to mind in China, where the most common and obvious feature of a landscape was a person — or usually many people. Every time I stared at a landscape there was a person in it staring back at me.

This brought on thoughts of his father. A figure standing on a hillside, staring back at him — yes, that was his father.

Ever since the train had lurched out of Beijing Station, his father had receded from Aki's thoughts. This was odd, given that he was drawing closer to him every moment. The sound of Cai Fang's breathing drifted up from the bunk below. The train plunged on into the night, moving westward at eighty kilometres an hour, deeper into the core of the continent. After a while the book slid from his hand. Shijiazhuang and Weizhou went by as he slept.

The train clanked to a stop. With a start, he opened his eyes. The sound of cars being coupled or uncoupled came from the rear of the train. A voice said, "Taiyuan." Damn, he had slept through Yangquan. Cai Fang, who had promised to wake him in time, was sound asleep. The bunk was so narrow that a third of his body hung out over the floor.

Aki pulled the blanket back over his head. When he next awoke, they were at Pingyao, and Cao, the man with the attaché case, was gone.

He climbed down and sat on the empty bed. The darkness grew lighter, as though sprinkled with grey ash. It was impossible to say when yesterday had ended and today had begun, but the bustle of morning was clearly underway: at each station where the train stopped, hawkers' calls flew back and forth on the platform. Inside the train, the corridor was thronged with passengers on their way to the toilet or the dining car, or just roaming around.

The snow had ceased, but snow clouds still filled the sky. The train was in the centre of the Loess Plateau. Dark smoke rose up from coal- and coke-burning fires; trucks, bicycles, and horse-drawn carts moved along roads muddy with melting snow, heading in the opposite direction from the train. Low adobe houses covered the hillsides. In the cliffs beyond a dry riverbed, the doors and windows of *yaodong* were lined up like portholes, while flocks of narrow-chested sheep climbed winding paths in front of them. Rays of sunlight poked feebly through rifts in the clouds.

"*Ni hao*," said their young travelling companion, climbing out of her bunk. After returning from the toilet, she sat down beside him and started to snack again. Where did she put it all, he wondered.

Cai Fang woke up. As he slowly heaved himself up, he looked exactly like a bleary-eyed cow.

"I slept through Yangquan," said Aki.

"Oh, right, I was going to wake you. I forgot I had to wake myself first. Woops."

The two men looked at each other and laughed.

He turned eyes still half asleep towards the window. "Look, a Yili horse!" A bay was plodding along a mucky road beside the tracks, bobbing its head as it pulled a cart piled high with fuel. "See, its got a big body, and the legs are black from the shin down. These horses belong to the Kazakh people, and they're uncommonly fast. I never knew they'd been brought so far east." There was a tinge of sadness in his voice.

"Yili is a valley north of Tianshan. I'm a Uyghur, but my blood is half Kazakh, through my mother. Long ago, to escape Turkish oppression, the Kazakhs came from the west with their livestock and settled in the Yili valley. The original meaning of 'Kazakh' is free spirit or rebel. A good description of me, wouldn't you say?" He then laughed dryly.

"Russian Cossacks," he went on, "are of the same stock as the Kazakhs. 'Cossack' means much the same thing – 'freeman.' In the old days, they were skilled horsemen."

Aki pictured the snowcapped mountains of Tianshan behind a young version of Cai Fang, galloping through the grasslands in the valley.

"Kazakhs are good at singing. They have an instrument called the dombra, like a balalaika, and they dance and sing to it. Uyghur folk dancing, as you probably know – Li Xing is good at it – is called dolan, the circle dance. The dancers whirl and turn. Kazakhs do it like this," he said, demonstrating by shaking his large shoulders quite gracefully back and forth.

"Thirty minutes to Linfen," announced the conductor's voice.

Cai turned towards Aki and said quietly, "I won't be getting off at Linfen."

Aki's eyes widened in surprise.

"You get off alone. A young man named Feng will be at the station to meet you, and he'll take you to your father. Don't worry. You can trust him."

"But what about you?"

"I'll disappear." Cai seemed to shrink into his large shell with contrition. "Forgive me. I'd have liked a little more time, but this will have to do. It's cutting it close. You provided the perfect camouflage. If you hadn't come, the game would have been up. It wasn't only Zhang's report. I'll keep changing trains until I make it to Hong Kong. It's a long haul, but this is the most unobtrusive way of doing it. I sent my wife and daughter on ahead yesterday. But it's also true that I wanted to see you again. This has been a good trip."

Aki took a thick envelope out of his breast pocket.

"Feng doesn't know the first thing about me," Cai went on. "Keep that in mind. As far as he knows, you're the friend of a friend of Professor Meng at Shanxi University, here to call on an acquaintance. Supposedly it's someone who did your father a big favour, and you've come to deliver a thank you in person. That's the story he's been given. He speaks no Japanese. He's a student in one of Professor Meng's seminars, home for the holiday. Here's the professor's name card. This is all you need. Simple lies are the best. Give Feng a hundred yuan – it's a good part-time job for him. No need to treat him to dinner or anything like that."

"I understand," said Aki. "Thank you very much." He reached out to shake Cai's hand and, after doing so, slipped the envelope into his palm. "I meant to give this to you in Linfen, but if I don't do it now, there'll be no chance. It's from Xu Liping and me."

Guessing the contents, Cai tucked it away in his breast pocket and said, "This will help a lot." In the envelope was exactly twice the amount of money Aki had given Liu Hong to aid in his escape. Aki and Xu had each contributed half.

The train pulled into Linfen. Aki shook hands again with Cai and left the compartment. On the platform, Feng was waiting with a boyish grin on his face.

Aki checked into the Linfen Hotel, which looked out on the town's central intersection. In postliberation China, every provincial city of any consequence had its clean but hastily erected hotel for foreigners – blunt structures made of reinforced concrete blocks like tall, thin dominoes.

From his window on the twelfth of fourteen floors, the view was of an expanse of towering smokestacks. A murky haze cut off visibility in the distance. According to a guidebook on the table, Linfen had a population of around 280,000; it was noted for its coal mining and coal chemical industry; and among its chief agricultural products were walnuts and dates.

Gingerly, he turned the shower handle. There was a hollow rumble as if the entire building were experiencing hunger pains, and the bare pipes shook. Just as he was telling himself it was no use, a vigorous jet of hot water spurted out.

After he had freshened up and changed his clothes, his stomach actually did growl with hunger, so he had a bowl of noodles in the second-floor restaurant, then went back to his room to put on some warmer clothing before going down to the lobby. Feng was waiting with a big map of Linfen spread out on a table in front of him, and had already circled Zhaonanhe in red. It was in the mountains about twenty-five kilometres from the city centre. The snow wasn't too deep, apparently, but since the mountain roads weren't paved, they would have to allow a couple of hours for the trip each way. It was not a particularly risky or dangerous route.

On Feng's advice, Aki gave some thought to how and when he was going to return to Beijing. What would be the fastest and safest way to go? It was essential to get this right, since he had to be back in Japan before Zhang reached Beijing. If the authorities came after him this time, a prison term would be unavoidable. In addition to aiding a political offender to flee the country, a charge of espionage could easily be tacked on for good measure – and with Cai gone there'd be no chance of an acquittal.

In the morning, he could take the 7:36 local from Linfen, arriving in Taiyuan at 12:09; from there, if he went straight to the airport and boarded a plane, he'd be back in Beijing before the day was over.

Jasmine

They set off for Zhaonanhe by taxi, a red Charade. Rays of sunlight poked through breaks in the clouds, and since there was little wind, for a change it didn't feel particularly cold. The temperature that morning was twenty-four degrees below freezing, said Feng. With the sun out, it might rise to twenty below by afternoon.

Aki found this hard to believe. Had his body gradually adjusted to the cold on the overnight trip? In Tokyo, his fingers got numb when the temperature dropped to freezing, yet this far greater cold didn't seem to bother him.

Though the road was a frozen mixture of snow and mud, the taxi tires had no chains. The loess continued high into the mountains. There were scarcely any trees. The ground was cultivated in terraced fields all the way to the top of the hillsides. The main crops were wheat, buckwheat, sorghum, and corn, and at this time of year, it was wheat. Even the deepest hollows worn by wind and rain were planted densely with rows of grain. An uneven patchwork of reddish-brown soil, white snow, and the light green of newly sprouted wheat extended in waves as far as the eye could see. Most of the mountainsides behind the wheat fields contained *yaodong*: caves dug into the slopes, with arched entranceways decorated with red brick. Each cave had a large wooden door with a latticed window on either side, many of which were filled in with newspaper. *Why would anyone want to live so far from the road*, wondered Aki, but Feng explained that access to water was what mattered most.

Along the way, they passed many *yaodong* hamlets, each one busy with preparations for the Lunar New Year. At stands beside the muddy road, peddlers from town were selling an array of seasonal items: bananas and tangerines from the far south; canned goods, hams, and sausages; holiday attire, firecrackers, and red decorations for the front door. Farming families made the rounds of all the stalls, teasing the peddlers. The taxi was sometimes forced to a halt, surrounded by the eddying crowd as it moved along at an unhurried pace. The driver would honk his horn ineffectually.

Before long they arrived in Zhaonanhe, a small village at the bottom of a valley well away from the road.

"From here we'd better leave the car and go on foot," said Feng. "We don't want to attract attention."

There was a scattering of caves in the narrow-cut cliffs on either side. Some were abandoned, the loess caving in, doors and lattices askew. Passing by, Aki had the sensation of being stared at by empty eye sockets. Along the road, a line of new, low concrete telephone poles marched past until they disappeared over the ridge of mountains far ahead. The region had finally gotten electricity recently, Feng explained.

In one yard, Aki noticed a tall wooden pole with some kind of antenna on top. He asked what it was and was told "TV" – the word spoken in a tone of disbelief, as if to say, "You don't know what *that* is?" After that, Aki saw that an antenna pole stood in the yard of every dwelling.

Beside the road, three boys were teasing a half-grown pig, patting its soft belly for the fun of it. Sensing the visitors' approach, all three turned their heads at the same time. Aki raised his hand slightly and called out "*Ni hao*," at which their hands jumped away from the pig's belly. They grinned shyly at him.

The two visitors walked on another fifty meters.

"There it is," said Feng, pointing to a grove of spindly poplars with a winding, snowy track leading into it. Aki's heart beat faster. At the same time as his excitement grew, he felt like backing off, beating a retreat.

A good six years had elapsed since word first reached him that his father might be alive. The years had not been spent in a constant search, and yet acknowledging to himself that it had taken all this time to reach this point filled him with deep emotion. Coming to the end of a long novel is sad. In Aki's case, the prospect of meeting his father was intimidating. He would have liked to stretch out the interim as long as possible.

Though he had yet to lay eyes on the man living beyond this grove, he felt a growing conviction that it was, without question, his father. Time that had elapsed separately for father and son was converging, here and now. He had a feeling that there was little to choose anymore between an encounter with a flesh-and-blood person and an encounter with a ghost.

Step by step he advanced, the heels of his trekking boots pressed firmly on the ground. The snow had turned to needles of ice that crackled underfoot. Inside the grove, the track forked. "It's to the right," called Feng from behind; for some reason, he was staying back at the edge of the trees. As instructed, Aki took the right-hand path. Overhead, a bird flew by with a shrill cry.

The path ended at some cliffs, where three caves were arranged in a semicircle. There was a small communal yard with a walnut tree and a TV antenna.

All at once, the way in front of him was blocked by the shadow of a large moving creature. It was a horned red ox, tied to the trunk of a poplar.

Soft sunlight gone astray in the maze of branches was shaken by the breeze and scattered. The ox moved its jaws, munching.

Aki was drawn up short by the sight of two figures in a corner of the yard. Seated in a roughhewn wooden chair was an old man, and bending over him was an old woman with bobbed white hair.

Something gleamed in her right hand. It was a razor. Instead of using soap or cream, she was spitting on the man's face to moisten his whiskers as she shaved him. He had a heavy, padded coat slung around his shoulders, and was sitting with his mouth slightly pursed, face upturned, eyes shut in apparent pleasure.

Aki went closer. The woman saw him first, and the hand holding the razor froze in midair.

"*Shei a?* Who is it?"

Aki stepped yet closer, without replying. The old man opened his eyes, drew in his chin, and looked at him.

"*Shei?*" he said irritably, getting up out of the chair. His back was straight, his physique to all appearances sound. To Aki, who had imagined a shrivelled old man wasted away from years of confinement in a hostile place, this was unexpected.

"Are you Han Langen?" he said in Mandarin.

"Before you ask someone his name, it's customary to give your own name first," the old man barked. His voice was firm and steady.

"I'm sorry. I've come from Japan. My name is Waki. Waki Akihiko. And you are Han Langen?"

The man's face was as expressionless as hardened glue, with no sign of softening.

Aki felt the ground tilt beneath his feet. He groped automatically for a tree or something to lean against, but the poplar and the walnut tree were out of reach.

"I am, but why a Japanese visitor should come to see me, I have no idea."

"It's because you are Japanese."

"Nonsense."

"Your real name is Waki Tanehiko. And I am your son." Aki's voice came out high-pitched and weak.

The woman folded up the razor and slowly crossed the yard without looking back, then disappeared inside the cave.

Left alone, the old man and this intruder half his age stood facing each other three meters apart. Aki could find nothing to say, search as he might. He felt lost and harried. What had happened to all the things he'd stored up over the decades, all the questions he'd meant to ask? Where had they gone in this instant?

"There are some funny people in this world," said the old man peevishly. "Crackpots, who come to bother you in your old age. I was born and raised right here: drawing water, turning over the soil, sowing wheat and picking cotton, raising goats and sheep. Like my father and my grandfather before me." He clamped his mouth shut, turned around, and motioned behind his back for Aki to go away. "Go on, get the hell out of here."

Aki stood there, stunned. This last sentence had been spoken in Japanese!

The old man stiffened and the back of his sunburned neck seemed to flinch. The hand that had made the shooing gesture remained at his waist. A sudden memory of having swung from his father's arm came back to Aki. That arm was right here in front of his eyes – of that there could be no mistake. But now it belonged to an old farmer, a farmer who belonged to this land, who had turned his back on him.

Seen from behind, his father's figure looked wilted, the starch in his bearing gone. Was it the altered perspective?

Abruptly, his father turned around and, with glazed eyes, body swaying, began to yammer in rapid-fire Mandarin. The words were a jumble, incomprehensible, but after a moment Aki was content just to listen to the sound of his voice. The voice steadied and then rang out: "*Wang le.*" Then, with still greater conviction: "*Dou wang le.*" I have forgotten everything.

In his father's eyes Aki saw an emptiness like that of an abandoned cave. His father's past was buried in that emptiness. He knew that it was beyond his power to reach. Nor could his father dredge up anything from it to show to him.

I want him to remain here on this soil, this loess. This thought formed in Aki's mind. That, surely, was what his father wanted, too.

The old man offered a sort of nod, then slowly turned his back on Aki again. Step by careful step, as if testing the firmness of the ground, he walked off in his black cloth shoes.

Aki called out to him, in Japanese: "Zhou Enlai is dead."

The old man took another few steps.

Aki again: "The Emperor Showa is dead."

Bending his head, the old man ducked under the walnut branches.

Aki: "Kobe's been levelled by an earthquake."

For a second this seemed to give the old man pause, but then he continued on his way.

She'll take care of him, she'll be with him when he dies, Aki thought, as he tried to recover something of himself.

I'm going home to Kobe! Where Xingxing is. Like father, like son.

He watched the old man's figure dwindle in size.

His ashes will remain here, in this earth.

Then Aki turned away himself, to find the red ox so close to him that he jumped.

He heard his father call towards the cave: "Zheng! Zheng Pinru!"

With a smile, Aki began to walk slowly away from the man he'd come to see. He hunched his shoulders, feeling suddenly chilled to the bone. It was as if the cold had been holding back till now.